Ghost Story

C000075984

To my redhead. For finding me and loving me. This one's for you.

Sometime in in the 2000s...

The three realms of suffering are the hells of monsters, of ghosts and of machines.

Ghosts deserve our compassion because they are spiritually lost. They are dreams, caught between life and death. They wander hungrily and aimlessly.

To be born again as consciousness is a rare and golden opportunity.

Some monks who sleep upon a hard plank and eat nothing but a few vegetables and some rice each day put aside grains for the benefit of hungry Ghosts they have never known.

This is a single grain.

Prison was hell for Ghost. But he got by, kept his head down and stayed out of trouble. He'd been worried before he went in. He'd watched films and read books where unthinkable things happened to young men in prison. For months he lived in fear. Of his cellmate - of the guards and of the other prisoners. Of the shadows in dark corners, of the shower room and the toilets. But in the end barely anyone noticed he was there – they were all busy doing their own time. Of course there were mad nuts and crazy nuts and tough nuts – lifers who would never leave, who were too stupid or lost or in love with making trouble that they'd never get out. There was plenty of fighting, several rapes and even one killing but Ghost avoided most of it and apart from a couple of times when he'd had no choice, he'd not had to raise a fist to anyone.

Most of it was common sense. If you saw David 'Robbo' Robson, then you stayed out of his way. You didn't talk to him unless he talked to you. If he wanted to push in front of you in the canteen then you let him. You didn't gamble with him, ask him for favours or chat about the weather. You treated him like a busy road or a recently mopped staircase; a hazard to avoid. In his seven years inside Ghost had only one conversation with the man. It had been in craft class. Robbo had just been allowed to rejoin the session after sticking a screwdriver through his workmate's thigh eight months ago. He'd done it for a laugh. Blessedly the conversation was swift.

'Hey Ghost, you lift. You bench more that two-forty?'

'No,' said Ghost.

Robbo had nodded and wandered away.

So Ghost counted the days and kept himself to himself. He stayed in his cell, did push ups and sit-ups, practiced his kata and read comics. Batman mainly. He found a dusty copy of 'The Dark Knight Returns' in the prison library and flicked through it. It was good. Next time he had the chance he picked up some more, 'War Drums', 'The Killing Joke', 'A Death in the Family' and 'Arkham Asylum'. They were the first. He must have read them a thousand times each, until he knew every panel, every word, every inked line by heart. Before the comics, to Ghost at least, Batman was mainly Adam West, larking around with his Boy Wonder on Saturday morning TV. Perhaps sometimes he was Michael Keaton throwing Jack Nicolas off the roof of a cathedral. Soon he was neither of these things – he was something more entirely. By the morning of his release, Ghost had all but memorized more than a thousand graphic novels and comics. Some DC, some Marvel some inde. Their pages had helped him through. Then he was taken to see the governor.

Ghost sat patiently in the waiting room for over an hour while people came and went. He was wearing his own jeans and t-shirt. The one's he'd been wearing when they'd come to get him. They no longer really fit, the tall, wiry boy he'd been had filled out considerably after tens of thousands of press ups, dips, squats and pulls. Technically he had been released that morning, he was a free man. But what was a few more minutes to a man who'd spent a third of his life in prison? He flicked through a few magazines. Read an article from 'Pro Golfer'. He hated golf.

At last the governor's secretary smiled over the desk at him.

'Dr. Green will see you now.'

Ghost said nothing, nodded and entered the office. It was the first time he'd seen the governor's study during his stay. Dr. Green glanced up at him over a case file and gestured for Ghost to sit. Ghost did. The doctor ignored him for several minutes while he scanned the literature, then he closed it and placed it on the desk. He smiled.

'I don't say this very often. But you've been a model prisoner. It's a shame that not everyone conducts themselves a you have or my job would be very easy indeed.' Ghost said nothing, just offered a nod and Dr. Green continued. 'You're a strange one. They call you Ghost don't they? That's about right I'd say. How an albino manages to blend in to the background I'll never know,' Green scanned through his files again. 'Nothing you've done stands out. You pleaded guilty; no trial. Not one altercation. Not one bit of trouble, no visitors, no mail, no telephone calls - I have to double check to see that you exist at all. But by every activity class, every project, and every assignment – a little tick. The only evidence that you've been with us at all.' Green replaced the file and removed his gold rimmed spectacles. 'So, Ghost – I hope you don't mind me calling you that?' Ghost shrugged. 'What are you going to do now? I don't like to see people come back. I especially don't want to see you come back. A first time offender, debatable circumstances. Questionable intention. I can't condone what you did.' Green paused. 'How can I put it? I have some sympathy for you. Do you have any relatives, family you could go to?

'No.'

Dr. Green raised an eyebrow while making a series of quick notes in his casebook. 'Plans?'

'I've got a friend down in London. He's got a job for me,' said Ghost.

'Doing what, exactly?'

'Instructing.'

'Ah yes, karate. It seems strangely appropriate that the thing that got you into this mess should be the thing to get you out of it,' Dr. Green handed Ghost a card. 'This is my office number. If things get difficult, I want you to call it and I'll see what I can do. I hope you can get on with your life and put this all behind you. Good luck.'

The pair shook hands as Ghost stood. Ghost collected his bag from the waiting room and dropped Dr. Green's card into the bin.

2.

He played ball for a while. He lived in London. He taught karate and pretended to live a life. He read more comics. He trained. He was embarrassed by the amount of stuff the parole board awarded him. A laptop, clothes, food vouchers, travel passes, a television – the list went on. He'd never had this much in his whole life. He didn't know what to do with it all. Sometimes he watched a film on television, if there was something worth watching. More often than not there wasn't. Every Friday he went to a cinema and watched whatever film he hadn't seen yet. Mainly he stayed in his flat, worked out and read comics. Sophie, his parole officer, started coming over on unscheduled days. At first he figured she was just checking up on him. Then he realized that she wasn't wearing tops that low or suits that tight not to be noticed. He noticed. She would stay at his until after midnight some times, doing most of the talking or watching TV. She was a little younger than him, a twenty three year old post grad who looked good if you kind of squinted and tilted your head to one side. She told him she felt sorry for him, sorry for what the system had done to him. Ghost didn't think she was that sorry, she was just lonely. Ghost didn't mind. And everything was ok, for a while.

Then on no particular day, for no particular reason he decided to leave. It was no life for a law-abiding man to have someone checking up on him, writing reports on his every move – even if later on she sat on his face until she screamed. He went north and hitched. Vanished off the grid. He left everything the parole board had given him. It wasn't his anyway. All he took was what he'd bought with his own money, a few clothes and a suitcase of comics. He blundered north, from lorry to wagon to coach to car with no particular destination in mind. Then one day, with a man called Karl, who was delivering five hundred thousand sheets of printer paper, Ghost pulled off the M6 at junction 33 in a heavy goods vehicle and for no particular reason decided that Lancaster was a good enough place to stop for a while.

It wasn't hard to find a house or a job. It was a tiny city, smaller than most towns and Ghost followed his nose and some adverts and moved into a small flat with a guy who didn't ask many questions, or seem to care whether Ghost came or went as long as he paid his rent. Ghost paid his first month in advance and moved into an empty room.

He slept on the floor and used a stack of old comics for a pillow, his clothes for a blanket. He did sit ups and press ups in his room, practiced his karate and went for the odd jog on the playing field at the bottom of the road. His new street, Norway Street, was as steep as roads came, some days Ghost would sprint up it for some resistance training, some days not. He found a job in the local cinema, a tiny little two-screen thing that looked and felt about a hundred years old. He'd gone and watched a few films there, seen an advert. Got the job that day. It was casual work - cash in hand. When he was off he got to watch films for free. No one asked any questions and he kept to himself and did his job. He worked evenings mostly, never really seeing his flat mate.

Life trundled on, a few months came and went. If they looked for him they never found him. Why would they? He was good at blending in to the background. Life was quiet, but at least it was his life. And then one day, he began to write and draw. He'd always been a decent artist, always had a knack for it. He'd read so many comics over the last years it was no surprise that was the medium he fell right into. He realized he had a story to tell, so with no more than a piece of paper and a pencil he began. A little every day. A routine was formed. He got up, he trained, he read, he ate, he drew, he ran, he read, he went to work, he came home, he ate, he wrote, he lay in bed. And the routine continued, more months went past. Nearly a full year. The comic was taking shape, he felt he had something with it. A few more months and it would be done. Then one day, the routine came to an end.

3

Ghost was cutting it fine for work when he shouldered his bag and left the house. He hurried up the hill, leaving Norway Street through the narrow stairs at its summit and cutting down a ginnel onto Eastborne. He loped towards the city center, slipping a few times on the mushy leaves that made the smooth stone pavements treacherous. Cutting down Denton Street he took a couple of twists and turns and, crossing the busy one-way system on King's Street he arrived at work. He rang the bell. After a few minutes Simon, the cinema's projectionist opened the door, mumbled a greeting and trudged back up the stairs. Ghost followed.

The work was easy but mindless, checking stock, unlocking fire escapes, taking out the floats and last nights rubbish then getting ready to open up. The Royal Cinema opened up on at 4:30pm on the dot each weekday. It was too small a city and too small a cinema to open anytime but the evenings, excepting a few holidays and handful of weekends. That evening the small, two screen independent barely saw a trickle of customers. The Royal owed its whole existence to the fact that there wasn't a multiplex near by. In its small, low quality, stereo screens it showed commercial, mainstream blockbusters and people came to watch them because there was no were else to go.

The owner, a known eccentric, barely ever showed himself, leaving it to his staff to run. He cut every corner there was. He got paid for advertising Pepsi – but sold coke. He had the projectionist cut the trailers off the film reels so as to fit in more showings. For that alone he'd have lost the place if anyone with clout had ever found out. He had the films paused half way through to sell extra ice cream – again, not something he was allowed to do. Worst, there was leaky tap in the gents he refused to get fixed. Word was the outstanding water bill was now in excess of twenty grand. There wasn't much here in the way of job security. But then, Ghost mused, that suited him just fine.

With both films started and the handful or so customers seated, for the next hour and half Ghost had nothing to do but sit in the small staff room, re-read a graphic novel, think about his next panel, breathe in Lucy and Tom's excess smoke and try to tune out their conversation. Tonight it was something to do with declining social values and the failure of the criminal justice system. Tom, a stringy middle-aged man, whose pallid skin and penchant to sweat for no discernable reason, reminded Ghost of a heroine addict, said something about how prison was too soft and then also about how it was too hard, almost in the same breath. If he had a point Ghost couldn't find it. But as Tom so rarely had a point about anything no one corrected him. Short on brains and shorter on charm, Tom volunteered himself an expert on everything and nothing. Ghost doubted if the man reliably sat on the toilet the right way round. Lucy, the manager, adjusted herself in her chair, dragged again on the perpetual cigarette she held in her chubby hand and grunted non-committedly. Tom was always pleasant to her face but he called her the human ball when she wasn't around. It was a cruel, if not unfair description. She had gone beyond being fat some years ago. God alone knew what she ate, because she never ate a morsel at work.

Tom said something about how people never really wanted to be in prison and Ghost found himself pulled into his own thoughts. Ghost remembered Robbo for the first time in a long time. The man had wanted to be in prison. Perhaps for Robbo the free world had been a scary place. Prison, Ghost had realized, was very much like school. There were prison officers instead of teachers, a governor instead of a head master, but it was just the same set up. And most of the kids wanted attention. Only they hadn't figured out how to be the school's top footy player, or how to ace the maths test. So they just beat up on the nearest kid and got noticed for all the wrong reasons. Ignore a bully and he'll go away. He wants you to make a scene and a fuss, he wants you to make him the center of attention. Hard though, thought Ghost, to ignore a man who'd ram raid an off license armed with a riot gun or stab a screw driver up to the hilt in his mate's leg. In prison every one knew who Robbo was. In the real world it was hard to get noticed for all the Scarlet Johanssons and David Beckhams. Hell, it could take a man his whole life to be as well known as Howard from the Halifax adverts. Ghost closed his comic.

'Mind if I go get a sandwich?' he asked.

Lucy checked her watch, rolling her sweater further up her obese arms. 'Okay, it should be quiet.'

No shit, thought Ghost.

When Ghost got back to work, Tom's discourse on sociology had drawn to a close and Joe and Lindie had arrived. They were both students, seemed oblivious to each other's existence and despite working together for the last four hours of each shift, managed to get by without exchanging a single word. Lindie offered a polite smile as Ghost entered then lowered her eyes back to her magazine. She was beautiful girl and she knew it. Dark flowing hair, smudged heavy eyes under dark lashes, dark clothes. She always wore a silver necklace with a snake looped around a heart.

Joe was the most likeable of the bunch. But you didn't win any prizes for that. Perennially cheerful and childish, he was engrossed in one of his favorite pranks; ringing up people and playing Arnie sound bytes down the phone. The aim: to get as long a conversation out of the prey as possible. Joe flicked a button and put the phone on loudspeaker, dialing a number with one hand he grinned his boyish grin.

Click. The phone picked up: 'Hello, Odeon Preston, Sam speaking, how can I help you?'

Joe pressed a button, the voice of Arnold Schwarzenegger boomed out of the office computer's speakers. 'How are you?'

'Fine thanks, what can I help you with?'

Joe clicked another button. 'I wanna ask you a bunch of questions.'

'Okay...'

'The girl, I got to talk to her, find out what she knows.'

'Excuse me?'

'I wanna ask you a bunch of questions and I want to have them answered immediately!'

The voice was unsure now. 'Excuse me?'

'Who is your daddy and what does he do?'

'Who is this?'

'I'm detective John Kimble! I'm a cop you idiot!'

'Very funny, dickhead!' Sam from the Odeon Preston hung up.

Joe grinned. 'Now was that a classic or what?'

4

The mess a cinema crowd, even a small one, can make during a showing is always something to be believed. How hard was it to pick up your own rubbish? Mountains of spilled popcorn, slimy sweet wrappers, half finished and spilled fizzy drinks. Once even a condom. Used. Even in a small hundred and fifty seater taking the nozzle of a vac under each chair took time. And overtime was not forthcoming if the staff ran late. Ghost righted 'Harry', what passed as the Regal's vacuum cleaner, for about the fifth time. The cheery red and black suck box, with his stupid, retarded grin and cheerful eyes was a silly bastard and it knew it. It had a death wish. If there was a stair, it threw its self off. If there was even the smallest chance that it could catch itself on its wire, then it would, becoming immobilized in moments. The smallest obstacle for Harry the hoover, the tiniest bump on the floor, the smallest increment in height between the isle and the carpeted rows, was an obstacle of epic proportions. One that it would take as an opportunity to throw itself upon its side and roll, listlessly about, gazing out of it's painted empty eyes, grinning that empty grin. Sometimes its lid would come off and throw it's cargo back all over the threadbare carpet. Sometimes Ghost wished Henry would come to life just so he could kill it.

Ghost had nearly finished when he slipped. Just a couple more rows to go. Joe was half-heartedly working at the bottom of the screen, sweeping a few loose sweet wrappers into a dustpan. Ghost rammed Henry's nozzle under seat seven of row G expecting to feel it connect with the wooden backboard. It didn't, it met no resistance at all. As Ghost tried to right himself, his foot strayed onto a half eaten strawberry split. He slipped and went down hard, his face hitting the lip of the seat in front of him. The jolt pulled Henry's lead out of the wall and machine thrummed down to silence.

'You okay?' Joe called, bounding up the stairs.

Ghost rubbed his head and nodded.

'What happened?' asked Joe. Then he smiled, looking at where Ghost was. 'You found The Space right?'

'The what?'

'The Space,' Joe said, almost reverently. 'The cinema's built like steps right? Kind of like the side of a pyramid, yeah? Well, under these screens, that's The Space. It's pretty amazing. You can see the old wooden beams from when this place was a theatre. Pretty dark though. Take a look.'

Grabbing the torch he used to usher, Ghost climbed down on his hands and knees and poked his head under the seat. Sure enough there was a decent sized hole in the wooden backboard. Ghost shoved his head through and shone the torch about. The space dropped off twenty or thirty meters. Wooden struts and support beams of strong timber vanished into darkness.

'Down there is where the dressing rooms used to be,' said Joe. 'If you look towards the back corner, you can make out what's left of a door.'

Ghost tracked the torch beam over the ocean of rubbish that littered the foundations until he saw the doorway. A wooden door lay before it, still largely complete, an image of a wheel or cog or something drawn in red paint. He pulled his head clear. 'Never knew this place used to be for plays.'

'Yeah, pretty sure there's been a playhouse or something here since, fuck I don't know, since there was a roman settlement I think. Might be longer,' said Joe. 'Once,' Joe half whispered, 'I was looking down there and I saw the oldest coke can you ever seen resting by one of the beams at the bottom. I'm not talking like cherry coke or anything, I'm talking like one of the 1960s looks like a can of soup ones. I came back with a rope and was going to get it, I mean, if you find an unopened bottle of that stuff it's worth a fortune. Like I think one sold in the US for like quarter of a million dollars. But it was right at the time this old geezer died in here. Died watching a movie. Anyway with all the attention the place got after that, it all got a make over and in the collateral all the holes got repaired, so I never got the chance to go after the can.'

'The one that got away, huh?'

'Hey lend me your torch. It might still be down there.'

Ghost finished the last couple of rows and replaced Henry in his little cupboard. Henry smiled his pathetic goodbye smile as Ghost closed the door.

Ghost rarely socialized but sometimes he caught a pint or a film with Joe after work. The lad wasn't bad company. Joe's little bed sit was homely enough in a studenty sort of way. As they entered Joe shoved a load of drying clothes off the radiator onto the floor and Ghost draped his coat over it in the hope it would dry before he went home. Joe picked a dirty towel off the floor, tousled his hair and flopped onto the sofa and flicked on the telly. As he sat, his foot sent sprawling, what seemed to Ghost, an unreasonable number of copies of FHM. Joe scooped them up and filed them liberally in a heap in the corner. Anne Robinson peered, beady eyed, out of the television set and told a scared looking woman that she was the weakest link.

'Fancy a film? My mate just brought me back a load of DVDs from China. Two quid for a hundred.'

'Sure.'

'How about Ong Bak?' Joe held up a blurry cover of a tough looking man in traditional Muay Thai gear. 'The guy in it's supposed to be like the new Jackie Chan. You heard of it?'

'Yeah. Saw it last year,' Ghost nodded. 'I'll watch it again.'

'Cool. Drink?'

'Whatever you've got.'

Joe disappeared into the kitchen then returned and threw Ghost a beer.

'Need a poo,' Joe announced.

Ghost cracked open his can and checked the window. The rain was still coming heavy. He turned. A little table covered in a sheet caught Ghost's eye. He took a peek at what was underneath. A little wooden box with an open top. Three small robots were inside. Ghost picked one up and ran his hands over the wheels, letting them spin. The robot was light to the point of being delicate, so he carefully replaced it.

'Found my project, eh?' said Joe coming back into the room to the accompaniment of a flush. He sat at his computer. 'For my final assessment.'

Ghost nodded.

Joe took the little robots and placed them in a 'v' formation. 'Check this out.' He clicking a button on whatever program his PC was running. A drum and base fueled dance mix thumped from the computers speakers and the robots began to move around inside the box in a jerky routine. 'Neat huh?'

'Sure,' said Ghost.

Joe opened another window on the desktop revealing a page of code. 'I wrote the program. This whole dance routine thing is just a way to show that I can give them instructions. I could have sent them through a maze or something, but, well everyone does that. If you know the terrain and the dimensions and stuff you can make a robot do pretty much anything. And if you don't know the terrain, well there are other things. Sensors on robots are improving all the time. I only have to have one sensor on mine. Just a contact switch. It's that little bumper bar at the front. If that gets depressed then the robot turns around and goes back the other way. Still got some fine tuning to do,' said Joe turning the computer off.

Ghost retook his seat on the sofa while Joe got the film on and plonked himself down next to Ghost. He aimed the remote at the telly and paused.

'Man, I've got to remember to set my video for this,' Joe nodded at the TV screen. 'An Arnie marathon! The Running Man, Total Recall and Terminator 2. Awesome.'

'I always though Terminator was better,' said Ghost.

'Sure. But who wants to watch a film where Arnie is the bad guy?' asked Joe as he hit the play button.

Ghost had to admit that the kid had a point.

5

It was still raining while Ghost made his way home through the soft stoned streets of Lancaster. He didn't drink very often and he was pretty tanked. He walked up the steps that lead to the old castle, pausing at the top to look back over the city tops. In the distance, silhouetted on the skyline like a huge rocket, loomed Ashton Memorial. Ghost lowered his gaze, scanning across the tops of the houses.

The sound of steps caused Ghost to turn. An old man shambled towards him. Ghost stepped aside to let him pass.

'Braw nicht tae be it laddie, ye shoods be at haem,' said the man, tugging at his cap.

Ghost nodded.

'Ye yoong lads, hink ye ken it aw, eh? Weel, son, whatever ye dae, be 'appy,' and with that the old timer bumbled past.

Ghost watched him for a moment then turned to look at the castle and shivered. It was not the cold. Lancaster Castle, beautifully constructed and maintained was an inspiring sight. Only the barbed wire that lined the battlements gave it away as what it was; a prison. Being close to the place began to give Ghost the heebee-jeebies. He walked on. Detouring past the Roman bathhouse and down to the Lune where ducks paddled and quacked on the muddy banks. Ghost turned left at the cricket ground and trudged for home.

His key was practically in the front door when he saw the old man again. The old coot was leaning against a dirty looking fiesta and staring into the night sky.

'Braw nicht ain't it?' said the old man. Ghost just looked at him. The old man tried again, 'Bonnie nicht ain't it?'

Ghost shrugged.

'Ow'r ye lad?'

'Fine?' Ghost tried.

'I've come tae see ye Ghost lad,' the old man said, dusting down his suit. Ghost's eyes narrowed and he was about to speak, but the old man waved him into silence. 'I'm nae th' clink son, don't fash. Those bastards cooldn't fin' th' other side ay th' road if their li'es depended oan it. Which occasionally they dae.'

Ghost relaxed. 'Who are you?'

'Th' names Jack Cassidy. Black Jack Casssidy.'

Ghost frowned trying to place the name. 'From X-men?'

'Nae. Don't shaw yer ignorance loon. 'At was Black Tam Cassidy an' he wasn't a body ay th' x-men. He was Banshee's coosin. An' a villain.'

Ghost nodded.

'Thes will only tak' a moment me loon,' said Jack Cassidy.

'What will?' asked Ghost.

'Ur gab ay coorse,' the man said, gesturing at Ghost's front door.

'Your coming in, now?' asked Ghost.

'Unless ye want me tae shit at ye tru th' windae.'

Ghost frowned. 'Oh, shout at me.'

'Aye, tis what ay sed laddie.'

'Come in then, Mr. Black Jack Cassidy. Want a cup of tea?'

'Awe rite, yeah, as yoo're offerin',' said Jack.

Ghost sighed and went to pop the kettle on while Jack made himself comfortable on the sofa.

'Braw wee room thes,' Jack shouted through into the kitchen. 'Cozy. Ah loch it. A cheil coods warm his cockles in a room loch thes.'

Ghost came back into the lounge with a couple of mugs of tea. He placed one on the coffee table before Jack and sat in an arm chair opposite. Jack smiled and sipped his tea.

'Nae a bad cup. Lookit Ghost, i've bin watchin' ye fur quite some time,' Jack continued.

'You what?'

Jack ignored the interruption. 'An' i've liked nearly everythin' i've seen.' Jack laughed, a crackling sound as old as time. 'Ah don't want tae ride ye. Honestly. If ah wanted tae dae 'at i'd hae dain it awreddy. Ye got anythin' ah coods pit in haur?' Jack motioned to his cup.

'Bourbon?' asked Ghost.

'Aye. Jist a wee a body thocht.'

Ghost got up and visited the kitchen then returned. 'There you go.'

'What's thes?' asked Jack.

'A bourbon,' said Ghost with a shrug.

'It's nae boorbon, it's a feckin' biscuit,' said Jack.

'Yeah. It's a bourbon biscuit. What were you expecting?'

'A bevvy! A bevvy ye glaikit loon.'

'Look do you want the biscuit or not?' asked Ghost.

'Better than naethin',' said Jack dipping it into his tea and taking a crunch. 'What's th' connection atween Achilles an' Hercules?'

Ghost shrugged. 'They both sacked Troy?'

'That's nae whit i'm lookin' fur. Ah can see yoo're wabbit, i'll humoor ye. Th' answer is they baith gart the choice.'

'Okay.'

'An' it's abit th' end ay th' warld,' said Jack with only a hint of showmanship.

'Okay,' said Ghost.

'Th' world's gonnae end in abit toi years Ghost mah laddie, an' i'm gonnae gie ye a choice. Thaur ur thee options. Ye can hae yer ain life. Th' a body yoo're livin' reit noo, make yer ain choices. Be a free cheil.'

'Uh huh.'

'Ye can bide tae be a thoosain years auld, see th' warld, gain untauld knowledge, scratcher an incredible amoont ay kimmers. Leid a so-so life.'

'Uh huh.'

'Ur ye can bide an' action packed life.'

'What's the point in living to be a thousand if the world's going to end in two years?' asked Ghost.

'Sae croose aren't ye, as a race? Th' warld isnae gonnae end. It's gonnae end as ye ken it,' Jack said.

'I'll take three then.'

Black Jack Cassidy took a little note book out of his pocket. 'Ur ye sure laddie? Ye sure ye want number thee.'

'Yes. I want number three. And I want to go to bed.'

Jack made a few scrawling notes with a pencil. 'Ah feel a bit sorry fur ye laddie. Most men ah ask them when they're sixteen, sae 'at those who pick number thee gie a cuckle years. But yoo've bin in th' clink fur a while noo haven't ye? Hoo auld ur ye? Twenty-fife?'

'27,' said Ghost.

'Options thee. Yoo'll die when yoo're thrirty thee ye ken laddie?'

Ghost shrugged.

Jack peered at Ghost intently, his pencil hovering over his pad. 'Wa 'en? Wa ur ye choosin' it?'

Ghost shrugged. 'Budo.'

Jack nodded and jotted down a few more notes. 'Aw alike, bapit warriors, but ah can't help likin' ye aw fur it.' He stood and offered his hand. 'Braw daein' business wi' ye.'

Ghost shook it. 'Sure.'

'A body lest hin',' said Jack. 'Ye won't rember thes in th' morin', fucks wi' th' heed ay ye fowk when ye ken whit age yoo're supposed tae be when ye slated ta die. Ye start tae hink yoo're invincible ur somethin'. Yoo're nae. A bus will squash ye jist as much as th' next bodie.'

'Okay,' said Ghost.

'Reit 'en,.' said Jack, standing. 'I'll see ye before but I'll fa sure be seein' ya in abit six years laddie. An' Ah apologise in advance.'

'Okay,' said Ghost.

Jack frowned. 'Wa ye hae tae be ruinin' mah patter, laddie? Yoo're spoilin' mah day. Can't ye jist ask wa i'm apologizin'? Loch anyain else woods?'

'It doesn't matter,' said Ghost.

'Reit 'en,' said Jack with a shrug. 'See ye.'

Ghost watched the old man leave, then he went to bed without even brushing his teeth.

6.

Monahan squatted between to parked cars, cradled the briefcase in his arms and tried to stay calm. His heart crashed in his breast, sweat soaked his back. He could hear them searching the car park for him. In a moment he would have to move again. He tried to catch his breath, silently sucking large swathes of air through his nostrils. Squads of thumping boots rushed all around, searching under cars, shouting garbled instructions to one another. He knew he should move, but he was tired. He was almost glad when the shadow fell on him, cutting out the glare off from the orange street light. The trooper pointed his rifle at him and gestured for Monahan to stand. Wearily he complied. He would never see Claire again he knew. She would have to have the baby without him. Too many had already died to let them have it back.

The trooper looked at him from behind the metallic faceplate that formed the front of his helmet, the low light lenses of his optics constantly refocusing like a camera zoom. They were a remarkable tool enabling an operative enhanced vision even in total darkness. They could see through smoke, functioned in extreme weather conditions and tracked heat signatures. They could even track a targets DNA if they had a sample. And they uploaded footage directly back to a central command in real time. They were the ultimate tech for a manhunt. When Monahan himself had helped developed them he had never imagined one day they would be hunting him. His knowledge of what the tech could do had got him this far, his own skills at manipulating data and hacking had allowed him to stay ahead for a while and get perhaps further than anyone else would have got. He'd made it outside the base at least. But no-one interfaced with GAIAs systems in a hacking battle and won.

A heavily synthesized voice came from the soldier's helmet. It was designed to sound barely human; robotic and terrifying. 'Drop the case doctor and put your hands on your head.'

Ever since he was a kid Monahan had loved the future. What it offered, what could be done with it – the heady promise of it all. Computers and bad-assed sci-fi had devoured his youth. He'd known he'd do something big with one of them. It wasn't until he read William Gibson he knew he wanted to change the world with tech. Johnny Mnemonic had changed his life… had become his hero. Monahan looked at the muzzle of the rifle trained on him. 'If they think you're crude,

21

go technical; if they think you're technical, go crude.' As last words go, pretty damned special, he thought.

The soldier in front of him grunted.

Monahan thumbed the pin on the grenade and waited. For a second the whole world reversed polarity, then blessedly, there was nothing.

7

Ghost woke with a start. Still half groggy, his head pounding, he staggered into a pair of shorts and a t-shirt before walking to the field at the bottom of his road to run himself awake. A few laps later he came home and poured himself a smoothie. He gulped it down, smacked a couple of slices of bread into the toaster and flicked the radio on. Sometimes nothing compared to the simple pleasure of buttered toast. How much had he drunk last night to feel this bad? He couldn't remember a damn thing. The radio told him that there was a Viking exhibition on at the local museum for next few days and that some youths had set fire to a series of cars in the overnight car park a few hundred meters down from the cinema. Apparently one car had gone up with a full tank of petrol. Half the roof had been blown off the car park, scattering debris all over the city center. No one had been hurt. Ghost poured himself another smoothie and went back upstairs.

He spent the afternoon sketching, writing and tweaking his book, dropping into his own world. As he worked his headache settled to a background thud, then slipped away entirely. He worked solidly, contentedly until his watch beeped and he laid down his pencil and got ready for work.

The cinema was as quiet today as ever and after helping a few people to their seat and giving the foyer a half hearted once over, Ghost took a seat in the staffroom. He nodded at Lindie, who curtly nodded back from where she had her head in a National Geographic. She was in early to cover Tom who was covering Joe who was supposed to be covering for Simon who had gone on a last minute holiday. To Ibiza apparently. It was hard to imagine the middle-aged projectionist in Ibiza. All Simon ever enthused about was ancient history. He was particularly fond of ancient Greece. A few weeks ago, after the trailer for 300 had broken, Ghost had mentioned the Miller/Varley comic in passing. Simon had grunted and then gone on to hold Ghost in place while he talked, at great and circular length, and with no exaggeration, for over three hours. He had covered, in depth, his views on the Spartans, the ancient Greeks, the Persian empire, the true events of the battle of Thermopylae and his thoughts on historical fiction. In a nutshell he liked the first four of those things very much and the last one not at all. No doubt Ibiza wasn't all glow sticks and dance clubs. Simon was probably on route to pore over some ruin on the backside of the island.

Ghost opened up 'A Death in the Family' and got reading. He'd read it a gazillion times but there was always something new to find. He'd learned a lot from Starlin and Aparo's stuff. Minutes dragged on and he shuffled in his seat. He wasn't sure if it was the last of the hangover or just general tiredness but he couldn't concentrate. There was a restless uneasiness in him. He stretched, heard his back crack, received a withered, somewhat disgusted, frown from Lindie and lowered his eyes back to the book.

'It is a great honour for me to be here tonight,' the Joker said, addressing the U.N general assembly. 'I am proud to speak for the great Islamic republic of Iran.'

Ghost flicked slowly through the last few pages. Batman and the Joker once again fought each other to a draw. He tried thinking about his own comic, working out how he was going to deal with the next section. He'd been having trouble with it for some time now, it didn't quite gel together and he was beginning to feel like putting off writing it. That was always a bad sign.

Tom came into the room carrying three cups of coffee. He placed a coffee on Lucy's desk, passed one to Lindie, then leaned against the wall, nursing his own. He looked at Ghost. 'Sorry fella, did you want one?'

Ghost shook his head.

Lucy waddled into the room, licked her fingers and let out a long, deep burp. 'I couldn't eat another thing,' she said as she squeezed into her seat, rolls of her spilling over the sides. 'Delicious.'

'Did you try the sauce I made?' Tom asked.

Lucy nodded and smacked her lips in approval.

The buzzer connected to the down stairs door beeped. Ghost glanced at the CC monitors to see a couple beginning to climb the stairs.

Lucy looked up from behind her desk. 'Get that will you?'

Ghost nodded.

A pretty girl and her equally pretty boyfriend walked into the foyer laughing. Giggling up to the desk they asked for a small popcorn and tickets for Snakes on a Plane.

'It's been running for thirty-five minutes,' Ghost said.

The couple didn't care, so he served them and showed them to their seat.

Ghost went back to the staff room. He wondered how many times Simon had seen Snakes on a Plane from the projectionist's booth before he flew. On top of his fear of flying, Ghost seemed to remember Simon talking to Lindie about her necklace and confessing his horror of snakes. Ghost considered, for an obviously nervous man like Simon, watching a movie called 'Snakes on a Plane' three times a day for two weeks before flying probably wasn't the best preparation. But hey, the mind never found a good time for facing its fears – you just had to do it.

Work done, Ghost crossed King Street and wandered homewards amongst the pleasant of old town. It was a beautiful place and apart from the odd parked car or street lamp it was like sliding back into the past. Ghost meandered down the narrow streets, passing the rows of beautiful stone houses, enjoying the night air. Each house had steps leading from the stone laid pavements to their imposing doors, and outside each door, proudly fitted into the stone, was a boot scraper. Heavy sashed windows looked down over spiked railings, protecting tiny well-maintained gardens. It reminded Ghost of Holmes and Watson and Baker Street.

A sickle moon seeped down from above and Ghost yawned, the steam of his breath rising into the night. He was just passing out of old town, about to cross over the train bridge when something caught his eye. A sudden bright white light. He jerked away and the light was gone. Puzzled he looked back towards the small, railed off piece of ground the light had come from. He could see nothing but the darkened lawn and the shadowy ghosts of flowers swaying in the breeze. He'd passed them enough in the light to know the flowerbed was arranged so that the coloured blooms re-created the council badge of Lancaster. Ghost checked the sky, and saw the moon had retreated behind some clouds. He approached slowly, looking between the iron railings into the tiny patch of well kept lawn. There didn't seem to be anything. Perhaps something had caught the moon's light for an instant, a bit of glass or metal maybe. The moonlight once more broke through the clouds and again the dazzling light flashed from the garden. Half buried in the flowerbed, in a divot of earth, sat a chromatic sphere which could have in every way passed for a shot put were it not for it's mirror like finish. Ghost stretched out between the railings and touched it, prodding it with a finger. It was cold, hard and heavy. It was just within reach, so he rolled it towards himself and scooped it up. The weight surprised him and he quickly transferred it into both hands, before walking beneath a street lamp. The sphere was smooth and solid, still almost icy to the touch. He rolled it over in his hands. It was flawless, there was not a mark or scratch or bit of mud upon it. He gave it one last turn, his fingers meeting a slight abrasion. He rotated the ball to examine it. There was a small hole in the sphere which he must have missed. It looked like a jack for something. He'd show it to Joe, he'd know what it was and then they could try to find out who it belonged to. Ghost dropped the sphere into his bag.

He was home quarter to twelve, dumped his bag in the side and decided to finish the day as he'd started it - with toast. Unusually though, the toaster was already in use. A woman stood in the kitchen. She turned as Ghost entered. Pink. That was his first impression. A lot of pink. Fluffy pink, knee high boots. A pink tutu. Pink hot pants. Pink vest. Pink pixie wings and a pink sweatband holding back blonde hair laced with pink hair extensions.

'Hi!' she smiled.

'Hello,' said Ghost.

She did a little spin on the spot and followed it with a little dance. Her eyes were like black saucers; she was high as a kite. 'What are you doing here?'

'I live here,' said Ghost.

The toaster popped and the girl bounded to it. Instead of taking the toast out with her hand she upturned the whole toaster. Her toast fell out, one piece skidding onto the floor. She continued shaking the toaster for some moments, watching with great interest the blackened waterfall of old toast dust and burned crumbs that flowed out all over the kitchen counter.

'It's like a Golgotha... for toast,' she said.

Then she dropped the toaster and span. It fell on its side, forgotten, and manically she collected up her slices. It took only three attempts for her to put them on a plate. She opened the butter, ran the knife through it, then froze staring at the yellowed blade with all the wonder of the young Arthur staring at Excalibur. She remained there, lost in her own world, swaying on the spot while the butter slid down the length of the knife and fell towards the floor. Ghost caught it in some kitchen roll and put it in the bin as he worked around her, sweeping the surface clean and righting the toaster. He started preparing his own supper while the girl continued to stare at and possibly through the knife.

Footsteps on the stairs caused them both to turn.

To say they lived in the same house, Ghost and Rob rarely saw each other and even when they did, their conversation had never graduated much beyond a grunted hello or goodbye. They had nothing in common, both liked their privacy and had their own lives to lead. Rob was often absent for long periods, only staying at the house every now and then. He'd use it as a bolt hole for a few nights and then be gone. Ghost always paid him promptly and the two had never had a cross word. But as soon as Ghost saw the other man on the stairs that night, he knew they were going to have trouble. Robert was naked and his eyes were a mirror of his companions, the pupils wide and dark. He seemed to be having some trouble standing, his movements twitchy and erratic. He looked pale and sweat was pushing itself from his skin, rolling from under his arms in waves. He clutched a small, clear bag in one hand. It was full of pills. Hundreds of them.

I live with a drug dealer, thought Ghost. Perfect for a parole violating, violent offender.

But it wasn't that which made Ghost know there was going to be trouble, it was Robert's eyes. Not the pupils, which were like black vortices, but something about the set of them. Ghost had seen that look plenty of times in prison. It was a look only given by someone who had decided they were justified to dish out some serious violence.

'What the fuck are you doing talking to him?' Robert opened with.

'Nothing,' smiled the girl. 'I was just thinking what it would be like if everything was made of butter.'

Robert staggered off the bottom stair and into the kitchen and did his best to point towards the girl. Really he was pointing at the fridge but Ghost got the idea. 'She's mine. You don't try to fuck my girl, in my house.'

Ghost shrugged. 'I wasn't.'

Robert wobbled across the room on rickety looking legs and tried to swipe the plate of toast out of Ghost's hand. He missed and fell over banging his head on the washing machine. Slowly he climbed back up to his feet and pulling himself up to his full five foot eight inches. He swayed from side to side, either trying to imitate a boxer before a bout or because he was unable to stand squarely, Ghost couldn't be sure. The malevolent look hadn't left his eyes. He was buff enough, he obviously worked out. His body was pretty well cut. Under normal circumstances, he might have been a handful.

'I'm going to fuck you up,' he said, still swaying from side to side.

Ghost stood at his gangly six foot three. He slid one foot almost imperceptibly backwards and raised one hand, palm outwards as if hiding behind it. He spoke calmly. 'I don't want to fight you. We were just talking.'

Robert said a few things, most inaudible or unintelligible. 'Shut up,' seemed about the sum of it. Then Robert balled his fists.

Ghost sighed.

With a snarl Robert threw a punch, which Ghost slipped by a county mile, still holding his plate of toast with one hand. Robert over balanced and tumbled to his knees, narrowly avoiding a second and what might have been a potentially fight ending blow from the washing machine. He stayed there for a minute or more dry retching while Ghost put some jam on his toast.

'I'm going to bed,' said Ghost as he went up stairs.

'Night,' said the girl.

Ghost sat in his room and ate his toast, glancing through a couple of comics while he did. Then he turned the light out and stood behind the door. Twenty five minutes later, there was some scuffling from the hall. The door clicked off the latch. The first thing Ghost saw emerge from around the side of the door was the point of the knife. He waited until Robert's wrist was visible, then took the knife and snapped the wrist. The coward staggered back into the hallway and screamed.

Ghost reversed the knife and confronted him.

'I wasn't going to use it. I was just going to scare you!' Robert mewled, the shock of the pain doing something to sober him up.

'Go away,' said Ghost.

And if there is such a thing as a world record for running down a flight of stairs, through a kitchen and living room and out of a front door – Robert would have broken it.

Ghost put the knife on top of his wardrobe, waited until he heard the sound of a car screeching away, then pulled his clothes off and fell into bed.

He was just drifting off when a knock came at his door.

'What is it?' called Ghost.

The door opened gingerly and the girl stepped in. 'Hey, it's me.'

'What is it?'

'Why are you going to bed? It's early.'

Ghost glanced at his alarm. 'It's nearly one.'

'Exactly.'

Ghost ignored her and rolled away from her onto his side.

He felt the bed shift as she sat down. 'I'm bored.'

Ghost didn't reply, waiting for her to leave. After a few moments she stood, shuffled around a little and then lifted the covers and climbed in behind him. He felt the warmth of her naked body pressed against his back.

'I'm bored,' she whispered again.

10.

Ghost awoke, stretched and climbed from the bed. The sounds and smell of sizzling meat greeted him from downstairs. His stomach growled. Stepping over a pair of pixie wings and a pile of pink clothes, he pulled on some jeans and t-shirt and headed down. Framed in the morning sun that was falling through the kitchen window, the girl looked beautiful. Had she not a heart tattoo, with the word 'easy' written through it in embroidered script, taking up most of her lower back, Ghost might have mistaken her for an angel.

'Fancy a bacon butty?' the girl asked.

'You're going to burn yourself doing that,' Ghost said.

She gave him an admonishing grin, 'What? You think I've never cooked bacon in the nude for a strange man before?'

Ghost shrugged. 'I'll have one then.'

He moved to the lounge and sat on the sofa. In a few minutes she joined him and they ate.

After they'd laid their plates aside, they sat and looked out of the window. Neither spoke as long minutes passed, both were content to watch the light waxing and waning on the walls of the houses opposite, listen to the sound of birds calling from the rooftops and the muted noise of the television blaring next door. It was not the least awkward between them sitting there in silence. It felt like the most natural thing in the world.

'You're not very normal, are you?' she said at last, still staring out of the window.

'No. Not really. Are you?' he replied.

'No. We've been sitting here for ages and you haven't looked at my tits yet. I quite like that.'

'I have looked a few times,' said Ghost.

She smiled, draping her legs over his. 'Shall we tell each other our names this time?'

'I can't see how that would improve anything,' he said.

Mid afternoon, on his way to work, he called at Joe's and buzzed the flat. A moment or two later Joe's head appeared from an upstairs window. He gave the thumbs up and the door that lead onto the street clicked open.

'Hey man, come in!' said Joe, meeting him at the door to his apartment. 'I'm just watching a movie. Want a bite?'

'Got work,' Ghost said as he made his way into Joe's little lounge and sat down. Labyrinth was paused on the TV on a largely close up of David Bowie.

'You watch this too much,' said Ghost.

'It's a classic, I can't get enough,' said Joe.

Ghost rooted around in his bag, producing the odd metal sphere. 'I found this last night.' He handed it to Joe.

'Yeah, I've seen one of these before, it's Japanese.'

'What does it do?' asked Ghost.

'I think it's an amp. Looks like a new model though,' Joe said, putting his lunch aside and walking to a cupboard. He kicked a pile of magazines to one side. They scattered to halt at Ghost's feet. Ghost glanced at one. A brunette in a black bra and pants dominated, staring from the cover with come to bed eyes. The advertised articles focused on how to dress better than Becks, going around the world in 80 beers and how to inflict maximum psychological damage on a woman who'd split up with you.

'I've met her,' said Joe, still rooting in his cupboard.

'Who?' asked Ghost.

'Mylene Class, formerly of Hearsay.'

'Formerly of what?' asked Ghost.

'A band. Sort of.'

Joe returned from rummaging in the cubbyhole with a tatty looking guitar bag from which he produced an even tattier looking guitar. 'I haven't had this baby out for a while,' he said. Then he looked back at Ghost and pointed to the magazine. She's really nice, we chatted for ages.'

Ghost shrugged.

'Yeah, we had loads in common. I think she really liked me too, but the chat room had to close, so, you know, c'est la vie.'

'I thought you said you met her.'

'I did,' said Joe. 'In the official Hearsay fan chat room. I won a competition, had to save tokens from bags of Chipsticks. You don't meet people like Mylene Klass in real life you know.'

'And you're a big Hearsay fan then?' Ghost asked.

'No, but I do like Chipsticks.'

'What are you going to do with that?' Ghost gestured towards the guitar.

Joe produced an adaptor from a drawer and jacked it into the sphere, then connected the guitar. 'I'm going to amp it up and see what it sounds like.'

Putting the guitar across his knee, Joe picked a string. The ball gave off a hideous high pitch squeal.

'That's not the droid I'm looking for,' said Joe. He fiddled with the wires and jacks for a few minutes, swapping them about. Then he had a turn of his guitar's machine heads then tried again. This time the ball gave off a tone like fine crystal resonating. Joe tried a few more notes.

'It's a good sound,' said Joe.

'I found it on my way home from work. Anyway of telling who it belongs to?'

'Maybe,' said Joe, starring at the orb. 'But I want to play with it for a bit first.'

'Don't break it,' said Ghost. 'I got to get to work. You working the evening shift?'

'No, booked a week off,' said Joe without looking up.

'Your soup's getting cold.'

But Joe was fiddling with the sphere again. Ghost let himself out.

The executive didn't bother to acknowledge Keats as he came to attention. Instead he continued gazing out at a completely perfect illusion of the New York skyline. The moving images covered the full six surfaces of the room. Beneath the Executive's desk and Keats feet, the world dropped away. Yellow taxis moved like ants through the streets far below. Above, there were just clouds. It was as though they were floating, walking on thin air, and so real was the illusion, despite Keats having been here many times, he had to be sure not to look anywhere too fast. Sometimes the mind processed what it saw, faster than what it knew to be true. Everyone who came down here knew that they were three miles underground but that hadn't stopped half a dozen or so guests falling ass over tit when the Executive quickly changed the feed. Keats would be damned if he'd let that happen to him.

Sure enough a moment later the screens flickered then refocused. Keats planted his feet firmly, resisting the urge to steady himself. Now they were above London. Keats could see the Houses of Parliament stretch away to his left. Another click and they were above Tokyo. Then over Ayers Rock. Then the image lurched and the screens showed nothing but desert. They weren't hovering now; it was as though they were standing on the sand. The sudden perceived change in elevation caused Keats to wobble.

The Executive shuffled in his chair and looked at Keats, his red suit shimmering in the false light created by the vid screens. Keats could swear the room was getting hotter. Sweat trickled down the nape of his neck. The Executive smiled at him from behind his large wooden desk.

'What do you see, when you look out of these windows?' the Executive asked.

'I see the desert, sir,' Keats responded.

'Which desert?'

'The Sahara, sir.'

'Very good. And how can you tell?' asked the Executive.

'I'm never going to forget that place, sir.'

'No,' the Executive smiled. 'I doubt you will. We all know what went on there. And we all know that's when you decided to join my service, correct?'

'Correct, sir,' said Keats.

'But when I look out of the window Colonel, I don't see the desert. Do you want to know what I see?'

'Very much, sir,' said Keats.

'Keats, you shaven headed monkey, you're such a kiss ass. I see your career. A fucking barren useless piece of shit. Have you got anything to report? What have you been doing with yourself?'

'Well, sir, for the last half an hour I've been sitting out there waiting for you.'

The Executive snorted despite himself, touching a hand to his perfect, jet black hair. 'Was that primitive humour Keats? Trying to show me you still have some autonomy? Come up with that yourself or just pull it straight from Dirty Harry?' The executive reached forward and pressed a button on his desk. A side door slid open and a tall, handsome man in a green suit entered. He walked confidently to stand beside the executive.

'This, Keats,' said the executive, 'is Mr. Jasper. He doesn't like you very much. What was the word you used Jasper, when I asked what should be done with Colonel Keats?'

'Aborted, sir.'

'Yes,' red suit continued. 'Mr. Jasper seems to think you should be aborted.'

Keats slowly brought his hands from behind his back to by his sides. He poised himself to move.

The Executive smiled. 'Please don't do anything rash Colonel. I still have some faith in you, even if Mr. Jasper does not. And besides, I fear that Mr. Jasper would be more than a match for you in any case.'

Keats flicked his gaze to the tall, effeminate man that was Mr. Jasper. Keats wasn't convinced.

'So,' the Executive continued. 'Report.'

'We have, as you know, located four of the five artifacts,' said Keats. 'One however, is still missing. We've run all the data through the tactical computer and we're dealing with a zero point likelihood. Even with what happened to Monahan, the prognostics should be much higher.'

'Yes, you blew him up didn't you?'

'Negative, sir. He blew himself up.'

The executive rolled his eyes. 'Let's not split hairs. He's not here. You are, so I'm blaming you. People like Dr. Monahan are far harder to replace than soldiers, Colonel. Just think of all the wonders in that furtive brain of his. And one way or another he blew up. Now, is it not your responsibility to stop my best people from either being blown up or blowing themselves up?'

'Five of my men died, sir. Suicide was not mentioned on the psych report.'

'I don't care about your men. I cared about the doctor's brain. And I care about the artifacts. We can always get you more trained apes.' He paused and sighed. 'So what are the prognostics?'

'Inside the current parameters? I will admit that the possibility of a resonance cascade scenario is extremely unlikely, I remain uncomfortable with the...'

'Get on with it Keats,' the executive snapped.

'One: the artifact was in some way completely destroyed by Monohan's grenade and it never left ground zero.'

'Impossible,' the Executive said. 'Next.'

'Two: The artifact was someway transported out of the maximum range that the explosion could have propelled it. For example it landing in the back of a moving truck etcetera.'

'What's that, a million to one chance or something?'

'Not far off, sir. Three: A civilian has discovered it. We're processing likely candidates matched by home and work proximity. Four: Artifact five was not in the case at ground zero. Monohan might have removed and hidden it elsewhere. Five: Artifact is already operational. Six: The enemy has it.'

The Executive placed his palms together before his mouth and stared into space. At length he spoke. 'I understand the difficulties. Sometimes, even with the most advanced prognostic computers, something happens that really bites into that zero point scale. The highly improbable is by definition not impossible. I understand, it's happened before, it'll happen again. But, Keats, I don't pay you the vast sums I pay you, to worry about difficulties. I pay you for results. So, let me address the possibilities. The artifact has not been destroyed. It is virtually indestructible even at incubation stage. Artifact Five was definitely present at ground zero. It was in the case. Do not ask how I know, just know that I do know. It's not active. We will know when and if Artifact Five becomes operational. So I would say the most likely option is that you need widen your fucking drag net, you moron. It's out there and either just lying there, and I don't care if you personally have to check every drain or wheelie bin or traffic island or whatever they have on this shit hole of a world. Or if that's not enough, I don't care if you have to nipple clamp the whole city, just fucking find it. If someone has it, they'll try to sell it. Thumbscrew any low life who might have half a sniff as to where it is.'

'And option six?'

'Keats, if the enemy has it, go back to barracks, load your favorite side arm and dispatch a round into your mushy, shit for brains head. Do not worry, as I will be following you shortly thereafter. Better that, than what will happen if the enemy has Artifact Five.'

Keats nodded. 'Permission to return to work?'

'Granted.'

Keats saluted, span and marched out of the office.

The executive turned. 'That's a nice suit you're wearing Jasper.'

'Thank you, sir,' said Mr. Jasper. 'I had it fabricated this afternoon.'

'You get back to work too. And get me something mind fuckingly strong for tonight. I feel the need for a blow out.'

13.

It was about half passed midnight when Ghost stepped through his front door into his lounge and flicked on the light. He paused. Six men waited for him there, all suited, all smart. None of them looked particular friendly.

'That's him, that's the fucker! He broke my fucking wrist!' Robert screamed rising from a chair in the corner. He was swiftly and firmly reseated.

A wiry, middle aged man with a thick crop of black hair looked at Ghost with interest. 'Close the door please. You're not a runner are you?'

Ghost closed the door.

'Do you know who I am?' the man asked.

Ghost shook his head.

'I know who you are. So far that has worked out in your favour. Do you know how I know you?'

Ghost shrugged.

'You spent some time with a cousin of mine. Do you remember Worth?'

Ghost nodded. Worth had been pushing seventy, a consummate gent and one of the few people Ghost had spoken to more than once on the inside.

'Worth said you did him a couple of favours. Sorted something out for him. He speaks highly of you.' The man on the sofa uncrossed and re-crossed his legs, accepted a brew from one of his men, sipped it and slowly placed it on the coffee table. 'My name is Archie Smith. Do you know who I am now?'

Ghost nodded.

'So Worth is the reason we're having a little chat. And what we're going to chat about is Robert. Robert is family, my sisters idiot boy, and specifically I want to know, why you broke his wrist?'

'Uncle Archie, just fucking have him done,' Robert pleaded.

Without taking his eyes off Ghost, Archie wagged a finger at his nephew. Robert fell silent. 'As you can see, he's not your biggest fan. But then, I'm not his biggest fan. Talk about a useless clot. You understand I'm sure.'

'Sure,' said Ghost.

Archie nodded. 'Basically I'm a fair man. But I'm also a busy man. So, quick as you can, why did you break his wrist?'

'He was high. He came into my room with a knife and was stupid enough to let me get hold of him. He's lucky all I broke was his wrist.'

Archie glanced across the room at Robert. 'Were you high?'

'No, of course not.'

'Why would he say you were?'

'Because he's a liar! I would never...' Robert began

But a look from Archie silenced him. He leaned forward and took another sip of his brew. 'Was there a girl here? Five foot four, blue eyes, blonde?' Archie looked at Ghost.

Ghost nodded.

Robert tried to rise from his seat but a strong hand on his shoulder pushed him back. 'He's lying, I wouldn't, I didn't...'

'Just be quiet, please,' said Archie. 'John, take the little shit away. I'll deal with him later.'

Robert was led from the house without another word.

Archie turned back to Ghost and gestured for him to sit in the recently vacated armchair. 'Now then. What am I to do with you?'

'Nothing?' Ghost suggested.

Archie smiled and opened his hands apologetically. 'As much as I don't like that little arrogant twat of a boy, I can't very well let you off scot-free.'

'What do you want?' asked Ghost.

'A small favour. After which we could say we were even.'

'Which is?' Ghost asked.

Archie opened his mouth to answer, but as he did Ghost's house phone rang. It continued to ring out, the room was very quiet.

'It's never good news after ten o'clock,' Archie observed, gesturing towards the sound of the phone. 'Please.'

Ghost stood and shadowed by a suited man, went into the kitchen and picked up the receiver. 'Hello?'

'I wanna ask you a bunch of questions and I waant to have them answered immediately!'

'Not now,' said Ghost.

'Who is your daddy and what does he do?'

'I'm serious, not now.'

Joe's voice came on the phone sounding hurt. 'Suit yourself. This is something pretty special you've found here. Can you come around to check it out?'

'What are you talking about,' Ghost asked.

'You drunk? The amp. It's amazing.'

'Not now.'

Joe huffed. 'Well come round tomorrow then?'

'Look, I got to go, see you tomorrow.' Ghost hung up.

'Anything important?' Archie asked as Ghost came back into the room and retook his seat.

'No, just a friend.'

Archie nodded. 'Worth says you're a reliable guy. He says you can handle yourself. I need someone who can handle himself.'

'I'm sure you have lots of people who can handle themselves,' said Ghost.

Archie nodded. 'That's true. Let me give you the details. A dear friend of mine passed away a few years back. Now, this friend, he wasn't in the same life I'm in. He was a good man. And since he died, I've been looking after his daughter, Jenni. Now, I don't really think that's what he would have wanted. But at the time, well there were things going on. It was an uncertain time. It doesn't matter for the whys, but I took her in. She's a nice girl. Smart, good heart. I've kept her away from my business. I love her like she was my own. I don't want her to get involved in my problems, and recently things have been a little complicated. I don't want her in Manchester anymore. I want her out of the way. I want her somewhere quiet and safe and further away from people who might be tempted to hurt her to hurt me.'

'Okay.'

'You keep living in the house. She'll move in with you. I'll cover the bills, I'll make sure there's a bit of extra money coming in. She's just started a degree at Manchester, but I've spoken to some people and she's going to transfer to Lancaster. You keep an eye on her, that's it.'

'And?' said Ghost.

'And, in the very unlikely event that any nasty men turn up trying to hurt Jenni, you hurt them first and you bring her to me. Think you can handle that?'

Ghost nodded. It wasn't a request after all.

'Good. All that remains is a little test. I trust Worth's word, but I want to see for myself.' He turned to one of his men. 'Do the honours would you Steve?'

A small but incredibly stocky man moved forward and stood before them both. Tiny eyes peered out of a flat, hard face. His nose looked like it had been broken too many times to count. Steve's little eyes bored into Ghost, like tiny pinpricks of hate. The man clenched and unclenched massive, calloused fists, flexing his neck from side to side until it popped. Then he removed his jacket.

'Hi, Steve,' said Ghost.

Minutes later both fighters stood out in the small the backyard, illuminated only by the light coming from the kitchen window and open back door. Steve had stripped down to the waist and was pacing around like a bull. Occasionally he would stop and stretch a leg or roll his neck again, letting out more disturbing cracking noises. Ghost stood opposite him, watching the man intently. From the kitchen window Ghost could see some of the others measuring him up, wondering how long he'd last. Steve stopped his pacing and stared hard into Ghost's eyes. Ghost stared back.

Archie Smith stood in the kitchen doorway smoking a cigarette. 'Raf, come here.'

One the men, came over. 'Sure you want to do this gaffer? Steve'll rip his head off.'

'Look at the Albino. Look at his eyes. What do you see?' Archie asked.

Raf, squinted out into the darkness. 'He's not scared. But he's... I don't know. I don't see anything really. He's a laid back fucker isn't he?'

'Exactly. Unnerving eyes aren't they? Just like Worth said. Pure white like snow. And in them? In them you see nothing, nothing at all. I noticed them straight away. Just like Worth described; it's like there's no man behind them at all.' Archie took one more drag on his cigarette and stubbed it out on the wall. 'Now we'll see if it's just an act,' he whispered. 'When you're ready gentlemen,' he said more loudly.

Without a second's hesitation Steve rushed forward. The man was powerful and wild. A born and bred street fighter, there would be no rounds here, this would be no twenty minute fight, it would be lucky to last twenty seconds. Steve came in hard, launching himself into a left hook, all his body weight behind it. Ghost caught the shot on his right forearm, moving slightly away from it to take the sting out as he did so. At the same time he popped a jab into Steve's face. Steve growled and hurled the huge right hand he'd been winding up. Ghost rolled under it firing his shuto uchi into Steve's armpit. An often neglected spot. Steve staggered and Ghost struck down with one foot, crushing the back of

Steve's knee with a small, stompy kick. Then he crashed his elbow hard into the base of Steve's skull. Steve went down hard and didn't move.

The backyard hung in stunned silence.

'Well, you've done enough for me, son,' Archie Smith said stepping forward and shaking Ghost's hand. 'Jenni will be here tomorrow. Don't let me down.'

The morning air was shrill and cold in his nostrils as Ghost stood alone in the centre of the playing fields. He bowed, then began running through some exercises, moving through the forms and stances he'd practiced for as long as he could remember. His movements were sharp, crisp and practiced and thought soon faded as he lost himself inside his practice. He continued until his body was laced in sweat, then bowed and returned home. He took a cold shower, ate a small breakfast and sketched up a few new panels; largely still happy with how it was progressing. Around ten, the phone rang. He put his pencil down and answered. At first all Ghost could hear was loud, blaring music. He jerked his head away from the receiver. Tentatively he moved his ear closer.

Someone said something but Ghost couldn't make it out. 'What?'

'The park by King's Street,' Joe's voice, barely audible over the background din shouted. 'Now!'

Then the phone went dead.

Ghost found Joe sitting on a park bench, a baseball hat with the Triforce on pulled down over his eyes. He was throwing chunks of bread at a fat, disinterested duck. Ghost sat down beside him.

Joe tore off another cob of bread and tossed it. It pretty much hit the duck between the eyes. 'It's not an amp,' Joe said. His eyes were bloodshot.

Ghost nodded. 'What is it?'

'I don't know. I think it's a robot maybe, if you want to call it that. Very sophisticated.'

'What does it do?' asked Ghost.

'At the moment? Nothing. I can't make it do anything. It just sits on the side.' Joe showed Ghost a cut on his hand. 'But it does do things. When it wants to.'

Ghost looked at the wound. It was nasty and deep. 'What happened?'

'I picked it up, it cut me.'

'How can something that smooth cut you?'

Joe pursed his lip. 'It was like a needle went into my hand. Obviously I've worn gloves when handling it since than, but it's not tried it again. Like my computer.'

'What about your computer?'

'I've had it jacked into my computer in everyway I can think, every lead, every extension. Nothing. Then one time, my computer basically blows up. Whoever made this thing did not want people to mess around with it. And I think it's listening to me.'

'You mean, someone's listening through it, like a radio?' Ghost asked.

'No. I think this thing is high-end stuff. It will be missed and if it was transmitting or receiving then whoever owns it would have come and got it already.'

'You think the sphere itself has been listening to you?' Ghost asked.

'Yes. Maybe. I've had the TV on full blast all night.' Joe let out a long breath. 'It's one of the best ways fool speech recognition - all the random snippets of motor cars and machine guns and laughter and human speech – perfect. All I have to worry about is if it scans for frequencies of speech. But then that's why I turn on the microwave every fifteen minutes and let my amp leak out some feedback.'

'I think you might need some help,' said Ghost.

'Voice recognition in robots is not a new thing. It's not cutting edge by any means, not in the commercial sector at least, but I have read things about incredibly sophisticated robotic voice recognition. I'm not taking any chances with it.'

'Joe, it's not a robot, it's a ball with a hole in it.'

'You think robots can't look like balls with holes in them?'

'You don't look well,' said Ghost.

'That's because I haven't told you the worst part.'

'Go on.'

'This morning it ate a cheese sandwich. I had a bite, I was fiddling with the sphere. I went to the bathroom. When I got back the sphere didn't seem to have moved but the sandwich had gone. All that was left was a fine white powder. Since then, over say the last three or four hours, the sphere's mass has increased perceivably.'

'And that means?'

'Well for starters it really pissed me off. That was the last of the cheese. I'll have to nip out to the shops later now. More seriously it means it might be something very dangerous indeed. A robot capable of absorbing and transforming biological material.'

'To what end?' Ghost asked.

'That's what has me scared.'

A smart black car was parked outside Ghost's home by the time he returned. Next to it was a large white van. Two workmen were engaged in carrying furniture out of his house and loading it into the van.

'Hey you,' a voice called from the parked car. 'Come here.'

Ghost walked over to the car. One of Archie Smith's men looked out of the window. 'I'm Raf.'

'What do you want?' asked Ghost.

'To get a closer look at you. Jenni's inside. They'll be done in a minute.' The man gestured to the workmen. Raf gave Ghost a long hard look. 'Anything you want to tell me?'

Ghost shook his head. 'No.'

'This came for you,' Raf said, handing over a letter. 'I read it. Who is H?'

Ghost looked at the letter.

I want to talk to you. Meet me at the Wishing Well Café tomorrow morning at nine o'clock. Come alone.

H.

'I don't know,' said Ghost.

Raf nodded. 'I think that letter's one of the oddest things I've seen in a long time. I think it stinks. I rang Archie about it. He seems to have some faith in you. Something about how you helped Worth. He says you're trustworthy and if you're mixed up in something else, you'll handle it. I'm not so sure. So, I'm going to be watching you very, very carefully. Don't make me have to come back.'

Raf pulled the car away and Ghost had to dodge back to avoid it squashing his feet. He looked at the letter again. Non-plussed he pushed it into a pocket.

'All done, mate,' one of the men called, climbing into their van.

Ghost gave the thumbs up and watched them pull away too. He walked into the house. A new plush sofa, entertainment system, coffee table. The house had undergone quite a make over. Ghost walked into the kitchen. Brand new appliances gleamed on all surfaces.

'Hi,' a voice came from the stairs.

Ghost looked around. There was a lot less pink this time. But it was still the girl from the other night.

'I'm Jenni. Jenni with three eyes. Because, you know, two here,' she gestured to her face. 'And one in my name.'

'Yeah, I got that,' said Ghost. 'I'm Ghost.'

Jenni nodded. They stood in silence for a while.

'This is weird isn't it?' she said.

'It's quite weird,' said Ghost.

'But we can do weird right?'

'Yeah, we can do weird.'

Ghost arrived at Bashful Alley a couple of minutes after nine. He looked at the letter again.

I have information that you want. Meet me at the Wishing Well Café tomorrow morning at nine o'clock. Come alone.
H.

The café was quiet. A couple of students sat at one table, a family with a couple of young children at another and man, dressed like an extra from fifties crime caper, sat reading a newspaper at another. Ghost was surprised it didn't have eyeholes cut into it. He took little time deciding where to sit.

You're late,' said the man. He was some years into middle age, his face chiseled and lined, his beard black, laced with generous portions of silver.

'What's this about?' asked Ghost. 'My life is getting interesting enough without clandestine notes coming to my door.'

'It's about to get a whole lot more interesting in a hurry,' the man said, folding his newspaper and placing it to one side. 'Do you know why this lane is called Bashful Alley?'

'No. But I have a feeling you're going to tell me.'

'Because once upon a time, bawdy sailors would hang out of the windows of the King's Arms and whistle and shout at any woman who had the temerity to walk down the main road. So any ladies who wished to go about their business and avoid such base attentions would cut through via the little alley outside.'

Ghost shrugged.

The man leaned forward, glancing quickly right and left. 'Don't shrug. Your life is in terrible danger. 'Have you ever heard of Salinger's Resonant Physic Relation Theory?'

'No,' said Ghost.

'It's a theory, one of many actually, practically proven by one of my superiors – an eminent doctor in the field of physic-spiritual phenomenon and … well, and other things. You've been to a railway station of course?'

'Yes,' said Ghost.

'Have you even noticed the intense feeling of emotion at a railway station? All those years of exposure to emotional signatures and physic brainwaves. Sadness when lovers part or happiness when they're reunited. Expectation, excitement, nervousness, fear, love ... boredom even. Some of our rail stations have seen hundreds of years of this. The residual psychic energy seeps into the stones, into the tracks into the very fabric of the reality of such places. The area becomes charged with excess physic energy. Have you ever been to Auschwitz?'

'No,' said Ghost.

'It is a terrible place. On one occasion I oversaw a test were psychically receptive individuals were blindfolded and informed they were being taken to a theme park for a study. As far as the subjects knew they were to tell us at what point they could feel the excitement and emotions that the theme park created. One coach we did take to theme park. The other, we took to Auschwitz. On the second coach many reported feeling uneasy when they still several miles away. When they arrived on the site several were physically sick, others complained of nausea and headaches. Why? Because of all that suffering and terror and evil, focused into one place. Perhaps, even before it was Auschwitz great, forgotten horrors were committed there. Certainly, long after our civilization is dust on the wind new cultures will avoid that spot. Perhaps they won't know why, but men and women of good heart will always be repelled by it. Just as those of evil intent will be drawn to it. That is another example of Salinger's Resonant Physic Relation Theory.'

Ghost shrugged.

The man looked at Ghost closely for a moment or two. 'I'm struggling to decide if you are a man of few words or if you are merely a complete moron. I am leaning towards the latter so, before I introduce myself fully, prove to me I have not wasted my time contacting you. Tell me why I asked you to meet me here.'

Ghost thought for a moment. 'I think you asked me to meet you here for two reasons. The first is that you believe that the years of women walking down this alley trying to avoid unwanted attention means that you won't be noticed here.'

The man smiled. 'Good. That's good. I like that. You're a fast learner. What was your second reason.'

'You're quite, quite mad.'

The man snorted. 'My boy, if you'd seen a fraction of what I've seen, you'd be mad too.' He thrust a powerful hand over the table. 'My name is Harold Schneider. I am a Weaver, an order that fights against the dark forces that most in this age no longer believe in.'

Ghost looked at Harold's hand for a while and eventually decided to shake it. 'I'm Ghost.'

'I am now going to give you some information. Information that might save your life. When I am finished, I am then going to ask you for help. You are free to say yes or no and of course you are free to believe what you wish – but, on my word, what I'm going to tell you is true.'

'Go on,' said Ghost.

'Imagine if there was an area of dark physic resonance,' said Harold, tugging at his beard. 'A place that had been used for dark magic and dark deeds since time immemorial. A place that had been steeped in blood ritual and sacrifice since the earliest days of out people. Imagine all of that death and suffering, the centuries and centuries of it. A place like that would be like a splinter in the mind for many people. With out knowing why, it would gnaw at them, unsettle them, deliver unto them nightmares and anxiety and…'

'It would give people the heebie-jeebies,' said Ghost.

'Close enough,' said Harold, annoyed at the interruption. 'It would be hard to have a city, even one as small as this close to a place of such power. But, if you built a structure on top of that place of ancient, elemental evil… a place that could mask its psychic stench, a place that could attract people, create emotions in them and then steal them. A place like that, could mask the dark resonance… Do you know the history of the Royal Cinema?'

Ghost shook his head.

'Before it was a cinema, it was a playhouse established in Victorian times called the Regal Theatre. Most of the ruins of that theater lie beneath the current build.'

Ghost nodded, remembering the old space below the screens.

'Before that it spent some time as a concert hall. Before this, another playhouse. That playhouse operated under various names and guises for over two hundred years. Before that, open air performances were held there, on the very site where Roman's had once had an amphitheater. An amphitheater that began its life as a provincial arena for gladiators. Before the Roman's it was a place of pagan festivals. Wrestling and Bataireacht, Celtic stick fighting, tournaments were held there. And once, long ago, before all this, on, or more precisely beneath where the cinema now stands, there was a temple. A temple of dark sacrifice and pain where unholy clerics of a forgotten god attempted to summon creatures from other worlds.'

Ghost nodded. 'It's not a great cinema, but painting it as place of evil is a bit much.'

'Is it? Is it? I think the cinema is place of ancient, elemental evil, thinly disguised behind the mixture of emotions that the films extract. And I have good reason to believe that the evil beneath it is stirring. I had a contact, a fellow Weaver, working there. He has gone missing. He was working under the name, Simon?'

'The projectionist? He's in Ibiza isn't he?'

'No, he is not. They have taken him below. Likely devoured him.'

'They? Who is they?'

Harold sniffed and wrinkled his nose. 'The coven who operate the cinema.'

'What? Lucy and Tom?'

'Are those the human names they use?' Harold snarled. 'Both are sorcerers of tremendous power. Simon was my apprentice and my friend. I have failed him. I had hoped to meet an ally of sorts here, but he is notoriously unreliable. That said, he has helped The Weavers many times and has had more success against our foes than we could have dared to have hoped. He's a smallish man with a brown beard and an irritating attitude. Quite famous, in the right circles I suppose. You wouldn't miss him. He carries an axe. You haven't seen a man like that?'

'No,' said Ghost.

Harold signed. 'It is with a heavy heart then that I come to the point were I ask you if you could help me.'

'Help you do what?'

'I need you to spy on them for me. To find out everything and anything you can. Listen for their true names, were they live. I need you to look for symbols and runes. A mark like a wheel or a spoked circle. Have you even seen such a symbol at the cinema?'

'I don't think so, said Ghost.

'Simon hadn't seen one either, right up to the week his reports stopped. I must get into that cinema. I must get to the lower levels and find what dwells inside – and destroy it.'

'Lower levels?' asked Ghost. 'I've been in the basement. It's full of popcorn boxes.'

'It goes much deeper than that. Look for stairs. Stairs down. They might be located somewhere you've never been. Behind the screens maybe or in an empty store room. Find them, but don't go down. Not alone. And for the love of God, don't let them catch you snooping.' Harold stood and placed a hand on Ghost's shoulder. 'God go with you my boy, for you do his work now. I will be in touch.' Then gathering his long coat around him and placing a wide brimmed hat atop his head he strode from the café without a backwards glance.

Ghost was pretty sure he hadn't agreed to help.

Ghost stood outside the Royal Cinema, a grey sky drizzling rain from above. The wind howled. He gazed up at the building. He'd never really looked at it before. The stone was very old, not quite the same cut as the building next to it. The rain had stained it dark, almost black. Ghost ran his fingers along it, tried to feel something. Despite being reasonably sure that Harold Schneider was a total nut, it did seem a different, more ominous place in the wake of what Harold had said. It wasn't as though Ghost remotely believed him, but it was like living in a house for years and then being told it was haunted. It was easy to laugh it off in the light of day, but alone in the dark, it was a different matter. He walked inside, and paused at the bottom of the stairs that lead up to the lobby. The paint on the walls looked thinner somehow, he noticed it was peeling in a multitude of places, the bricks beneath dull and mottled. He had always known it was an old building but suddenly it felt ancient. Ghost tried to concentrate his mind. See if he could feel anything. He felt nothing but a generally sense of despondency.

'Ah well,' shrugged Ghost. 'That's how everyone feels when they go to work.'

He climbed the stairs, waving at the security camera as he passed. The cinema was on the first floor, up quite a long and winding flight of stairs. There was no disabled access, something that was certainly illegal, not that Lucy seemed to care. Ghost wondered how she managed to thump her substantial weight up them. Ghost reached the top of the stairs and walked across the foyer. Behind the service desk Tom was restocking the confectionary. Ghost waved a greeting and entered the office.

He nodded a greeting to Lucy.

'We need four boxes of popcorn bringing up,' she said without looking up from her paperback.

'Sure,' said Ghost.

And the spell was broken. The shift was normal. There was nothing strange, nothing untoward. It was a shitty old job in a shitty old cinema; that was all. There was nothing weird going on. Like there was nothing weird going on with Joe's stupid sphere. It was all nonsense.

Ghost stretched and got back to the job at hand: spelling 'Miami Vice' in large red letters. Changing the reader-graph was a job everyone at the cinema avoided. Being an old fashioned shit hole of a place, there were no electronic displays mounted outside to advertise the films, so every Thursday night, the title of the films for the next week had to be hung up by hand. Basically that meant going up a rickety ladder in the middle of the street, braving the winds and spelling out new film titles in two foot plastic letters that clipped onto metal rods that ran above the entrance doors. It was generally cold, boring and not a little dangerous. Apparently one employee, ten years or more ago, had the misfortune of being at the top of the ladder when a drunk driver smashed through the bottom. The guy had been thrown under a bus.

Ghost looked at the selection before him. The letters hadn't been replaced in decades and many of them were cracked and broken. In this case there weren't enough intact 'i's to spell 'Miami Vice' so Ghost had to use a No. 1 instead. And the small 'm' in Miami was made up of two 'n's put closely together. But it did the job. Taking the telescopic ladder from the wall, Ghost hauled it outside and propped it up, then began changing the film names. It only took fifteen minutes or so, but his hands ached from the cold by the end and he was glad to go back inside. Taking the spare letters that he'd removed he returned to the dump room and filed them away in their cubbyholes. Lastly he fetched the ladder and hung it back up on its mounting, knocking the icebox as he did so. Without thinking he began to push it back into position when he noticed a triangle of rough-hewn wood poking out from under one corner. Ghost pulled the icebox fully away from the wall. It glided smoothly on well oiled wheels. Beneath it was a square of wood, so old and gnarled, Ghost wouldn't have liked to guess at its age. Mounted onto the wood on what looked like a bronze bracket was a relief of a monstrous, vacant face. In it's crooked mouth it held a huge ring of well worn bronze. Taking the ring, Ghost pulled and the trap door rose with little effort. Immediately an awful, musty smell of soured age and rampant decay washed into his nostrils. Ghost clamped his nose closed with his free hand and leaned back. Composing himself he peered into the darkness the trap door contained, only able to make out the first few feet. A tunnel was carved into the very earth, steps descending into blackness, gnarled roots, cutting out of the walls at regular intervals.

'Stairs down,' he said to himself, as he peered into the gloom, easing the trap door shut. 'Gotcha.'

Ghost pushed the icebox back against the wall. He thought of Harold, he thought of Joe. He thought of Archie Smith. He thought of monsters, of machines and gangsters. Of Jenni with three eyes. This wasn't normal but his heart barely rose a flutter. Still he wasn't a man who liked complication.

He went back upstairs, left his staff badge on the empty counter and stuck his head around the staff room door. 'I'm quitting,' he announced, closing the door before there could be any reply – and left.

18

Sue Caruthers always looked forward to cleaning Joe's flat. It was the last clean of her working week and she associated arriving at his door with a feeling of tranquility. One more clean and then two blissful days off. She'd call in at the supermarket on her way home, pick herself up a bottle of wine, then get back and sink into a hot bath, order a take away and stay up late watching TV. Tomorrow morning - a lie in. Heaven.

Joe was one of her better clients too. It was quick job doing his flat. He had no idea what clean really was, so all she had to do was clear the floors and run the vacuum over them, give the place a quick dust and it was finished. Not like some of them - some of them had nothing better to do that go around their house after she was finished and look for something to complain about.

She pressed the intercom for his apartment. There was no answer, which wasn't uncommon, so she let herself in. She began by clearing the floors so she could vacuum the carpets. After this moved to the small kitchen and did the surfaces. A quick dust and she'd be done. The only preference Joe had ever given her was to leave his computer desk alone. It was, as ever, strewn with papers covered in indecipherable squiggles and various components and parts. A blackened, fire-damaged computer sat beneath it, next to another pristine one. The coffee table was littered with DVDs and a pile of magazines, a round silver thing and some crumpled beer cans. She cleared away the cans, moved the DVDs to one side then picked it up the silver ball with both hands. It was surprisingly heavy. Sudden pain flared through her. She let out a scream and the silver ball fell to the floor and rolled behind the sofa. She looked at her left hand. It was bleeding heavily from a deep cut on her palm. She pulled off her glove and ran to the kitchen sink to run her hand under the tap. The cut was red and angry.

Shock and anger ran through her. Had the ball had a razor blade stuck in it? Why was Joe leaving things like that around?

A fresh, sharp pain stabbed into the back of her leg. She cried out again, tears coming to her eyes as she snatched her hand to the spot. With terror she felt a cold, hard shard of metal. Looking down, she could see a long, thin, lance of silver jutting from her leg and leading back into the lounge. Her mind lurched towards panic. Completely bewildered she tried to get a hold of the metal spear jutting out of her calf, trying to pull it free, but it wouldn't budge. More forcefully, she pulled on it until she could feel it about to snap, but just at the moment it should have broken, it lost all resistance. Screaming, she tore at it in a frenzy but it stretched in her hands like elastic, becoming thinner and thinner the more she stretched it until it was almost more gel than wire, then even thinner until she could barely she it, but still it refused to break. She was sobbing now. Adrenaline, frustration, confusion and fear mingling together. Then the metal sphere was in the doorway, somehow rolling toward her, a lone tendril snaking from its body. Sue took one more hacking sob, the metal ball rippled like water, then spears of metal shot out from it, spearing into her body. One into her shoulder, one her stomach, another piecing her side. The last one covered her mouth. She shut her lips tight, but it flowed inside. It was not like suffocating, it was like drowning. Something heavy and thick began to seep down her throat. She would have fallen if it hadn't held her upright. With one last burst of strength she tore at her bindings, but it was pointless, they just yielded to her force, malleable and un-breaking, allowing her to crush or bend them however she wanted without letting her go. The sphere rolled towards her, its surface shimmering like liquid once more. Then her body began to disappear from the extremities. There was no pain, just terror. First her fingers and toes, then her arms and legs. The tiny tubes that entered her body began to swell and gulp as matter seeped through them. Soon she was nothing but a torso that was steadily disappearing inwards towards its center.

With the bio mass that had been Sue Caruthers ingested, the sphere swelled in size quickly. It now had a circumference of roughly half a meter. The tendrils it had created wound around its body, then fused neatly with its outer surface. It rippled and became perfectly smooth once again. A hatch opened on the sphere and sprayed out a cloud of white dust that settled in a pile on the kitchen floor. Then the sphere rolled into the bathroom, and sprouting hundreds of tiny legs, climbed the tiled wall. It paused beneath the extractor fan, then oozed upwards through the narrow grill.

19

Ghost went straight to his room, dressed into his jeans and a t-shirt, pulled on his coat then bound up the pages of his comic and gently packed it inside a rucksack. He shouldered the bag, went back downstairs and filled a bottle with tap water. Upstairs a door opened then Jenni's legs appeared on the stairs. She stopped on the bottom step and looked at him, her face serious, her voice when she spoke very low.

'Aren't you supposed to be at work? Where are you going?'

He shrugged. 'Away.'

'You're not supposed to do that,' she said. One of her hands flicked away a curl of hair. It was shaking. She was scared of something. But what he could not tell.

'Why not?' he asked.

'You're not supposed to leave.'

A little anger tugged at him. 'Why? Archie Smith is a powerful man I'm sure. But he won't find me.'

'It's not that. You're just not meant to leave. I know you're not meant to leave.'

They looked at each other for long moments, saying nothing.

'Why?' Ghost asked.

'I don't know how to say it. I don't have the words. You wouldn't believe me, if I had them. But I can show you.'

Ghost waited while she ran back up the stairs. She came back a few moments later clutching a bunch of papers. 'You need to see this.'

'Why? What is it?'

'It's a story my mum wrote. She never finished it. She died when I was little. Read it,' she said.

'Whatever is going on here, I don't need it.'

'But what if that's not true? What if it's what you've always needed?'

'I don't understand what has begun in my life, but I don't care for it. Everything is strange but familiar.'

'Hiraeth,' she whispered.

'Pardon?'

'That was the name of my mum's book,' said Jenni. 'And it's the feeling you can't describe. The one that is growing in you.'

'Hiraeth.' Ghost turned the word around in his mouth. The word seemed familiar even though he could never remember having heard it before.

'It's a sickness,' she said. 'A deep longing for a home you can never return to. A home that perhaps never existed. A grief for the lost places in your past.'

Ghost looked at her again. 'I don't like the sound of that.'

'Sometimes it can be sweet, sometimes it's sickening,' she said.

'Well, whatever it is, I'm leaving,' he said pulling his gaze away from her and walking to the front door.

'What's your name?' she called.

He stopped with his hand on front door handle. 'You know what my name is.'

'No. What's your real name?'

He frowned as if the question made no sense. 'My name is Ghost.'

She laughed, but there was no mirth to it. 'Ghost? No-one is just called Ghost. What is your second name? Where were you born? Where is your family? What did your mother look like? Where did you grow up?'

He stood at the door, head down, under that wave of questions as minutes went by. Eventually he looked at her. Felt a strange connection surge between them. He opened his mouth to speak, then closed it again.

She moved to the sofa and sat down. 'I didn't really feel anything the first time I met you. I mean, I knew you, but I was so fucking high. I didn't question it. And then all of a sudden I'm told I'm being moved – and then I'm moved here. With you. I just didn't know what to say. It was like a miracle almost. I was so happy. But then I just started thinking about things. Like, like I'd never thought about before for some reason. Thinking about anything, you know to do with me? And there were just so many blanks. Like my name. I kept trying to think what my name was. But all I can think is that I'm Jenni with three eyes. I can't think of my surname. Or where grew up. I can't remember those things... I can't remember... and I thought it was weird because...'

The phone rang out from the kitchen and at once she fell silent. It kept ringing. They kept staring at each other.

'You should answer that,' she said.

'It can wait.'

She shook her head. 'It can't.'

Ghost moved to the phone and picked it up. 'Yes?'

'Man, fucking hell do we have a problem,' came Joe's voice.

'What is it?' asked Ghost.

'Get round here, get here five minutes ago,' said Joe. 'I'm serious, this is fucking bad.' Then he hung up.

'Who was it?' Jenni asked.

'A friend of mine said he needs some help.'

She smiled. 'Then you better go and help him. That's what you do, I think. And when you get back I'll show you my mum's book and we can work out what it means.'

'I'm not coming back,' said Ghost.

She smiled. 'You will.'

20

'Take a look at that!' said Joe pointing to a small pile of dust on the floor of his kitchen. 'Take a fucking look at that!'

Ghost shrugged. 'What about it?'

'That's my cleaner,' said Joe. 'Or what's left of her.'

Ghost looked at the small pile of powdery dust. 'Your cleaner?'

Joe took a series of deep breath, put his hands to his head and walked three laps around the kitchen. He stopped and looked at Ghost. 'It killed her. It fucking killed her.'

'The robot?'

Joe left the room and returned with a small tin box. He opened it. 'Remember I told you it absorbed my sandwich? After it 'ate' the sandwich, this is what it spat out.'

Ghost looked at it closely. 'That's a tin of...?'

'It's a top notch tin of robot shit,' said Joe. 'Or I thought it was. I was wrong.' He pointed at the larger pile on the carpet. 'That's a top notch pile of robot shit.' He sagged against the kitchen work surface and put his head in his hands. 'Fuck, that's so disrespectful. Her name was Sue, she was a nice woman. Her coat is still on the back of the door. It... it ate her.'

'How could this happen?' asked Ghost.

Joe slid down onto the kitchen floor. 'I should have been more careful, I was starting to suspect what it might be. After it absorbed the sandwich I locked it in a drawer. A drawer! How fucking stupid.'

'Why was that stupid?' Ghost asked.

Joe surged to his feet, stormed into the other room and pointed to his computer desk. 'Because it's got one of those.'

'One of what?'

'A keyhole, a fucking keyhole!' snapped Joe, jabbing at the drawer. He rattled it for good measure. 'See, it's still locked. How stupid can you be? It's a modular robot,' said Joe. 'You know, like in Terminator Two? The liquid metal one, the Terminator that can ooze under doors and stuff?'

'So it got out of the keyhole?'

Joe slumped down onto his sofa, his energy again dissipating. 'Modular robots are not unheard of. We've even got one at the uni we call Doppelganger. It's just a dozen cubes. The cubes are pretty big and they communicate via sensors. Doppelganger is twelve identical cubes that can work together and can 'think' of themselves as one entity. It doesn't do much. It can split up and send six cubes one way and six the other and then join up again. And like all known modular robots, it's painstakingly slow. It communicates slowly, moves slowly, solves problems slowly. And each brick is like the size of a rubic's cube. This thing got out of keyhole. Imagine that instead of being made of twelve rubic's cube size bits, a robot was made up of millions upon millions of teeny-tiny robots. Robots so small you couldn't see them unless you had a powerful microscope. Nano-robots. A robot like that could be the size of a double decker bus on one side of a wall, then send one nanobot at a time through a gap and reassemble itself on the other.'

'But why would it attack your cleaner?'

'I can only think of one reason for why it killed Sue and I don't want to be right about it because if I'm right, then we'd have to be talking about not just nanobots, but bio-nanobots. Overall we'd be talking about a robot capable of ingesting genetic and molecular data.' Joe blew a short and deflated raspberry. 'It would transform the ingested material into the thing it values most: itself. It would reconfigure the raw materials of what ever it had absorbed into more bio-nanites. Theoretically it could continue doing that until the entire biomass of the planet is gone and all that is left is a massive swarm of robots.'

'Oh,' said Ghost.

'Oh indeed,' said Joe.

Ghost plugged in the vacuum cleaner.

'What are you doing?'

Ghost shrugged. 'It's time for your cleaner's somewhat ironic funeral.'

21

Keats sat in near darkness. The only light in the room blinked from his computer terminal, casting his profile to the wall. He focused on it for a moment and decided, not for the first time, that it was somewhat Napoleonic. The silhouette of a thinker, a warrior, a planner. A great leader. He drummed his fingers together and looked back at the prognostic results from the last input. They were not optimistic. He scrolled amongst the data again, looking for something he'd missed.

Question: Why, with the most sophisticated artificial intelligence in the world, could he not find one little, missing prototype?

Answer: Because he was missing something. Under thinking something. Over thinking something. He had to go back to the beginning. It didn't matter if it took a million tries. He had to go back to the beginning.

Keats hands blurred across the interface, the screen brought up to a satellite image focused in on the car park where Monohan had made his last, futile, stand.

There had been an explosion. Monohan had cooked a plasma grenade. The prototype had been thrown clear...the damage report said it was grade three level explosion. So... if he factored in the grade of the explosion, then he could run an estimate on how far artifact five had been propelled.

The computer image tracked out from the multi storey parking lot, still showing a map of the Lancaster area. A red circle, measuring around one kilometer in diameter ringed the car park.

Make it slightly bigger, don't want any mistakes...

Keats added a further three hundred meters to the diameter.

There. It landed in that region.

Question: So what now? Where is it now?

Answer: Someone has it or it has begun survival protocols. Keats ran a cross reference against the global population. He set the net big: everyone who had any reason to be living or working within two kilometers of ground zero went into the prog.

Working off the most likely shift patterns and routes to and from there were three hundred and fourteen hits. When the sweep also added credit card transactions and ATM use within a twenty four hour period the list jumped to two thousand and eighty three hits. Keats adjusted a slider making some allowances for unscheduled family visits, extra marital affairs and the general random vagaries of life. The prog grew to over six thousand five hundred people

Keats span away from the computer. The door to his office was locked, but he drew his firearm and placed it beside him anyway. Then closed his eyes. This whole operation was one shit-kick. But he didn't get paid by the hour. He got paid to get things done. Over his shoulder, the computer churned away, running and re-running progs over and over. If it found anything it would alert him. He tried to relax. Artifact five was out there. Some one had it or knew were it was. It was just a matter of patience. Someone would make a mistake. And it would only take one small error and Keats would be there to earn his pay.

22

Harold Schneider limped down the road, casting furtive glances at the dark alleys that surrounded him. Blood trickled from the multitude of wounds that covered his legs, flank and neck. He was not having a good time of it. He had been listening in on the bugging device he'd installed in the Royal Cinema. What he head had not been promising. Ghost had quit, the coven who ran the temple had been unsettled and had decided to accelerate their plans. They were going to perform the rite in a little less than, Harold glanced at his watch, five hours. Five hours! He grimaced at the pain in his leg and pressed on, furious with himself. A seasoned hunter like him taken by surprise in his own sanctum. Pathetic.

Forty minutes earlier he'd been craned over his notes, earpiece held to his head, listening with growing concern to the conversation in the cinema staff room. Saving the conversation to a tape deck, he'd been moments away from mobilizing when his kettle had tried to kill him. Without warning the flex had tightened around his neck like a garrote, making him gurgle and gag, nearly pulling him from his chair. Then the silver beast had landed on his desk, spout snapping open and shut, rows of jagged stainless steel teeth gnashing, boiling water spilling out of its mouth like saliva and burning his legs. It had hissed, steam rising from its snout/mouth and dived forward. Harold tore the cord from around his neck and lurched away, his chair swaying and falling back. His head had cannoned off the floor hard. The daemonic kettle whipped at him, swirling its cord aggressively then lashing out with its plug, leaving a ragged gash in his neck. Then somehow it had leaped. How something without legs leaped, he was still unsure. He ducked and rolled and it flew over his head.

Rising he turned, extending his hand before him. "Exorcizamus te, omnis immundus spiritus, omnis satanica potestas, omnis incursio infernalis adversarii, omnis legio, omnis congregatio et secta diabolica, ergo draco maledicte, ut ecclesiam tuam secura, tibi facias libertate servire, te rogamus, audi nos!"

The chant had no noticeable effect on the kettle. It whipped its cord around like a prehensile tail, the three point socket biting into Harold's leg. It came at him like a dervish, the plug spinning faster than he could see and striking him again and again. But he was against the wall now, he reached and drew his cross bow from the rack. It was already loaded. The bolt took the kettle through its body and punched it across the room. It was still for only a moment, the twisted metal of its body held in place by the bolt for less than a second before the kettle began to melt and seep to the floor, reforming before his eyes. Harold snarled, made a grab for his tape deck and stuffed it into his bag. Then, shouldering his cross bow he ran. The kettle gave chase. As fast as a kettle that's been temporarily animated by millions of bio-nanites could. Which, fortunately for Harold Schneider, wasn't that fast.

23

'Anything you want to say?' asked Ghost, dangling the vacuum bag over the bridge.

Joe thought that something should be said but given the nature of the circumstances it wasn't entirely obvious what that should be. He turned a few words over in his mind, found all of them to be lacking and eventually gave up.

Ghost opened the bag. Fine plumes of dust sprinkled through the air, falling onto the surface of the river. Some bits were carried away on the slow current, other larger clumps sank without trace. Both men watched the moon silvered water for a few minutes.

'What now?' asked Joe.

'Brew?'

Jenni was lying on the couch flicking through early morning TV when Ghost and Joe entered. She looked tired but smiled warmly. A big bound manuscript was on her lap, she reached for it at once on seeing Ghost, opened her mouth to speak then closed it again as Joe entered.

'Jenni, Joe. Joe, Jenni,' said Ghost. 'Cup of tea?'

She nodded and Ghost went into the kitchen and set the kettle to boil.

'Get everything sorted?' Jenni called after him.

'Ask Joe,' he called back.

Jenni turned to Joe. 'Get everything sorted?'

Joe opened his mouth to answer but a knock from the door silenced him.

'Sweet mercy,' Ghost muttered sliding three brews onto the coffee table.

He opened the door and a tall, disheveled man, with a silvered beard and a long black coat and wide brimmed hat staggered in. The man dropped an aging leather sports bag on the floor and leaned his crossbow against the wall.

'Brew?' Ghost asked.

'I was attacked by a being of ancient evil,' said Harold.

Ghost turned to Jenni and Joe. 'This is Harold Schneider, a weirdo I met in a café.'

Jenni's face paled and she stood, gathering the manuscript to her chest. She looked to Ghost. 'Do whatever this is, then we need to talk.'

'We can talk now.'

'No, help Harold first.' She turned and left.

Harold sat down in the arm chair she'd vacated and picked up her cup of tea, taking several noisy slurps.

'Help yourself,' said Ghost.

Harold drained the mug and thumped it down on the table. 'We need to act, their plan is more advanced than I thought.'

Joe looked at Ghost. 'What's he talking about?'

'He thinks the cinema is a temple of ancient evil,' said Ghost.

'It is a temple of ancient evil!' snapped Harold. 'Tonight I got the proof I needed. And for my trouble I was attacked by one of their minions.'

'Who attacked you?' asked Ghost, taking a sip from his own mug. 'Get a good look at him?'

'Oh yeah, I got a good look at him,' said Harold. 'About fifteen centimeters high. Small stocky, stainless steel body. Prehensile extension cord. Sharpened spout. Malevolent demeanor. The regular.'

'What?' asked Joe.

'It was a kettle,' said Harold.

Joe's voice became tight. 'You got attacked by a kettle? Like an animated, sentient kettle?'

Harold nodded.

'Fuck,' said Joe. 'Fuck.'

'Fuck indeed,' said Harold. 'It was a minion of the great Destroyer, a possessed entity of considerable power. It was completely resistance to my attempts to exorcise it. I wounded it with my Arbalest but not a moment after the bolt had struck home, it flowed around the shaft like quicksilver, its injuries healing at once.'

Joe stood and gestured to Ghost. 'We're just going to need a moment,' he said before moving into the kitchen. Ghost followed and as soon as he entered the kitchen, Joe hissed a whisper at him. 'Who is this guy? How did you meet him?'

'He put a note through the door.' Ghost said, going on the sum up his meeting with Harold at the Wishing Well Café.

'And that's the only time you've met him?' Joe asked.

Ghost nodded.

'Fuck. Fuck this is bad. That wasn't a monster he described. That was the fucking modular robot. Or part of it. That means the robot knows you met him. That's the only explanation. Why else would it go after this guy?'

'Why would it go after him anyway?' Ghost asked.

'Because it's going to try to get rid of everyone who knows about it,' said Joe. 'It's self aware and defensive and... and... it can animate things. Temporally or permanently I don't know. It could theoretically animate anything. It could be in the house right now.' Joe gave the food processor a suspicious look.

'I don't think it is,' said Ghost. 'If it were we'd all be fighting for our lives about now, right?'

'Unless it's just listening. Watching. Waiting.' Joe poked a half drunk bottle of Sprite sitting on the counter. 'Why is all this crazy shit happening, it's like a fucking movie. Or ten movies in one.'

Ghost had no time to reply, as obviously tired of waiting, Harold limped into the kitchen. 'I don't have time to sit around. In the early hours of this morning a ritual to summon a terrible evil is about to begin. I have a little over four hours to stop it.'

Joe looked at Harold. 'Great. Why have you come here again?'

Harold frowned. 'To enlist your help of course.'

'Why?' asked Joe. 'Why ask us?'

Harold scrunched up his face as if he didn't understand the question. Opened his mouth and then shut it again. A look of complete puzzlement spread across his face. Then he composed himself, tried to say something, stopped and looked puzzled again. 'I don't know. I just came here ... I didn't think...' the man looked suddenly vulnerable, a completely lost soul, a shadow of the confident, if eccentric man, Ghost had met in the café.

Ghost held up a hand. 'We'll help Harold.'

At once the look of confusion was gone from Harold's face, replaced again by one of certainty and purpose.

'I knew I could count on you! Listen to this.' He gestured for them to follow him back into the lounge. On the table was a large tape deck. Harold clicked the play button.

Both Joe and Ghost recognized Tom's voice. 'Just call him in and tell him you want to talk about his decision.'

'No. It's too late. He knows something.' Lucy's voice.

Tom: 'You think he's with the Weavers?' A long pause. 'Consider what would happen if we left him alone and he did disrupt the summoning. Consider the consequences.'

Long silence.

Lucy: 'We have no choice. We put it forward.'

Another long pause. Then Tom spoke, his voice nervous. 'Tonight?'

'Lucy, firm and assertive. 'Tonight. After it goes ahead it's not going to matter.'

'And if he is a professional?' Tom asked.

'Then we eat his soul,' Lucy answered.

Another pause. Tom: 'What about Joe?'

'Those two are thick as thieves. What one knows the other will know. And besides, he keeps ringing up and pretending to be Arnold fucking Schwarzenegger. It's driving me crazy. They both die. Tonight if they interfere, or after if they don't.'

Harold clicked the stop button. 'Need I say more?'

'Fuck yes!' said Joe. 'What's wrong with my Arnie phone pranks?'

Perhaps he was going to say more, but before he could they were outside the cinema. There was no sense of anything changing, no huge lurch of continuity. It was unsettling, odd, but defied consciousness, like a dream where, in a moment, one location or person becomes another and it is accepted. They were simply no longer in the house they were in the road, in the center of town before the Royal Cinema. Joe looked up at the dark building before him, now black stone, a spire rising above it like a steeple. Lighting crackled in the blackness of the sky high above making him jump.

Harold, Arbalest hanging over one shoulder, pushed the doors and they swung open with a series of hideous creaks. 'You ready?'

Ghost nodded. Joe looked around. Then he looked at Ghost with a look of pained, vulnerable confusion as his mind tried to grasp at ... at something he couldn't quite bring into focus. 'Weren't we...'

Ghost nodded. 'I feel it too. Something's off.'

Joe nodded, a little colour returning to his face. 'It's not just me?'

Harold's head reappeared at the door. 'Come on, and stay behind me.'

Following quietly, Joe and Ghost crept behind Harold through the double set of doors and into the building. Rubbish overflowed from the downstairs bins. Used popcorn boxes and sweet wrappers littered the steps leading up to the foyer.

71

Harold pushed open the door to the film dump room, glanced round it and gestured for Joe to go inside. 'Wait here. Ghost and I will check upstairs.'

'Split up? Are you insane?' snapped Joe. 'Do you never watch any movies – do you know what happens when people split up in these situations?'

'Harold began to respond, but was cut off. A wailing, rolling, whispering cry began. Drifting down the stairs from above. Haunting and mesmerizing. Then it changed, built and broke like waves, moving to a roaring, ripping screech of aggression. A huge crash like falling timber sounded from above.

'On second thoughts, you're right,' said Joe. 'Whatever it is that makes that sort of noise, I do not want to know. We'll stick with your plan. I'll stay here and look for survivors.'

24

The Arbalest fired. It took a black robed cultist through the heart. The man fell without a scream, his blood running into the deep fissures of the stone laid floor. Wayfarer reloaded, cranking the arbalest and laying another silver bolt into place. On the other side of the chamber, beyond a fountain of blood, a door framed with golden statues sculpted into the fiendish image of Xallendax, crashed open. Four cultists charged through. Each held a ritualized axe, glowing with dark energy. Wayfarer snarled and snapped off another bolt. It took the nearest thorough the neck. The man took a few more steps and crashed to the ground. But the others did not slow.

Wayfarer cast his arbalest down, drawing his long knife and holding it in a reverse grip. He could not handle them all but he would sell himself dear. 'Come at me, my whoresons!' he roared.

But they did not reach him. His companion had reached the top of the stairs. The tall warrior known as the Ghost of the Riverlands stepped between him and the charging cultists. Wayfarer watched fascinated, his mouth at once dry. A surge of excitement, of long repressed hope, flowed through him. The oncoming men, zealots bred to revel in pain and death, to know nothing of fear or doubt... slowed and stopped. In their eyes was pure blind terror. The Ghost's blade flashed from his scabbard, once left, then right. Two men fell. The third man the Ghost seized by the throat. The cultist gurgled under the pressure, his axe dropping limply from his hand. The Ghost threw him to the floor.

'Where is she?' The Ghost asked.

The cultist, his eyes wide with panic turned and began scampering away on all fours, crawling for his life. The Ghost turned and nodded and Wayfarer offered him a grim smile. They crossed the chamber, following the fleeing monk. Wayfarer made the ward against evil with his left hand as he skirted the ornate pool of blood, trying not to let his eyes linger on profane images carved into the stone basin. They passed through an arched doorway. The Ghost strode onwards and Wayfarer was forced to run to keep up with him. The fleeing cultist scampered around a corner and when they turned it, a long staircase rose before them, rising into the darkness above. A force assailed them from that darkness. A tangible pressure as if the air itself was thicker and unyielding. Something was up there, Wayfarer could feel it. Sense it. A force of power and hunger. A force that desired nothing more than to consume, to devour, to erase. But the Ghost did not pause before the pulsing miasma of doubt and fear that was flowing down the stairs and in a moment he was rising, two steps at a time. Wayfarer scanned their rear and satisfied that no one was behind them, followed.

Ahead, somewhere in the darkness they could hear the hurried scrabbling footsteps of the terrified cultist but the Ghost did change his pace. He continued to step easily, still taking two steps at a time and Wayfarer was content to remain behind him. The stairs spiraled upwards, lit only by candles of black wax set in small recesses every few feet. They offered little more than pin pricks of light that did little to illuminate the dark stone. Onwards and onwards they rose and Wayfarer's legs were burning when all but at once the stair way ended and leveled out into a small corridor that culminated in large golden door marked with the dual image of the All King, Xallendax. As the Ghost moved to the door, Wayfarer looked down from an arrow slit. Horror gripped him. The amphitheater should have been below, empty now and the crowds departed. Warriors should have been training in some of arenas, pushing themselves through drills and sparing. He should have been able to see the torchlights of Loncastre town, flickering by the river's edge. But he could see none of this. They had risen now from the human world, they were somewhere alien and wrong. Below them the disembodied tower hung over a terrible black nothingness, a void so complete and empty to stare into it was to know madness. Wayfarer. Realizing his mistake, ripped his eyes away and as he did, in that darkness, that emptiness, that barren place were nothing could live or be, he saw things move, things that defied shape or reason, things that very existence reached into his mind and flayed at it and pulled at it, tempting insanity and nihilism and…

… the Ghost was shaking him. Wayfarer came to with a start, staring into the warrior's clouded eyes.

'Do not look into the void,' the Ghost advised. 'What dwells there will burn you.' Wayfarer nodded and allowed the swordsman to drag him to his feet.

The Ghost moved before Xallandax's golden doors and with a great grunt of effort, forced them open.

The room beyond was an ornate star chamber. It was sculpted from black marble that flowed and moved beneath one's eyes, the stone contorting into the vile histories of the Dark before flowing away to nothingness. Phantasmal faces formed in the stonework as Wayfarer watched, their mouths open in silent, endless screams before they once again became the rock. Two sets of octagonal stairs lead to a raised platform on which was an alter. Above that, a swirling darkness of inky tendrils reached from a portal that hovered and rent through the domed roof and lead to the gods knew where.

The cultist they had pursued was backed against the far wall, a look of abject terror on his face. It was a room of darkness, dark stone beneath a dark expanse of emptiness, punctuated only by the slow, hungry writhing of the tentacles. In contrast to this, upon the alter a young woman, dressed in flowing white, lay on a sealed pearl coffin that itself rested on an ivory catafalque. Standing over her, in robes of shadow and gold stood the high priestess of the temple, a bone dagger raised in a wizened, claw like hand. A snarl of rage passed over the priestess' face as she saw the Ghost. Sinewy muscle in her shoulders tensed as she sought to bring the dagger down…

Wayfarer fired. The bolt was true. It took the priestess through her black heart. She fell back with an anguished inhuman scream… the tower lurched, and the floor began to shake, the stones loosening. Wayfarer made it to the girl, she looked lifeless and dead, her eyes wide open but lacking any vibrancy. He moved her scarlet hair to one side…

Her eyes snapped open. 'What have you done?' she screamed. Her hand lashed out with something. A blade? A claw? Something… It scored across his face… he fell back, blood pooling into his eyes, clouding his vision. Disoriented he staggered. The tower lurched again. He could just make out the Ghost grabbing the girl, then the floor groaned and toiled and cracked… he fell. Sickness spread through him as he span into the void, tumbling into the nothing with the remnants of that dark tower. He caught one last glimpse of the Ghost and the girl. They were falling too, spinning into the nothingness, then with flash of crystalline light, they were gone. And he was all alone.

25

Harold, held a hand to his head and stumbled. He reached the top of the stairs and tried to clear his thoughts. In front of him was the empty cinema foyer. All was quiet. The only movement; a lone piece of popcorn tumbling across the battered carpet, blown by some unseen air vent. Slowly he stalked forward, drawing his crossbow from beneath his long coat and heading towards the staff only door. He reached for the handle only for the door to swing into his face. Harold fell back and stumbled. A confused Tom dressed in a large black sack cloth stepped round the frame.

'Who the fuck are you?' Tom asked.

Harold began to crawl for his bow.

Tom lashed kick into Harold's ribs. 'You're the Weaver, right? A washed up old man. Is that the best they've got?'

Tom aimed another kick, but it didn't land. Ghost checked it with an outstretched foot.

Tom yelped and hopped up and down holding his shin. He saw Ghost and looked startled as all hell. 'Where the fuck did you come from?'

Ghost silenced him with a cuff across the face, that sent Tom to his knees, blood spraying from his nose.

Harold picked up his weapon and turned. 'Didn't realize it was swing door,' he mumbled.

'What the fuck's going on here, Tom?' Ghost asked. 'Why are you wearing a robe?'

Tom climbed to his feet, pinching his nose and holding his head back. 'Dick head,' he spat.

'Speak wretch!' snapped Harold.

'Fuck off,' said Tom, turning and tripping over his own robe. He fell hard, groaned and crawled through the staff door.

Harold seized Ghost's wrist. 'Don't let him go.'

Ghost shook his hand free. 'Where is he going to go?'

Ghost pushed through the door in time to see Tom scurry into the staff room. He followed without pausing. Inside Lindie, her hair dyed an angry red lay across Lucy's desk. Lucy sat behind it, a cigarette clutched in one hand, a plastic cutlery knife in the other. She was still reading her paperback. Tom crawled towards the far wall and turned, fearful.

No one spoke. Harold looked over Ghost's shoulder. Lucy placed her book down and licked her lips. Lindie looked from Lucy to Ghost and back again. Then the phone rang.

Lucy slowly and deliberately stubbed out her cigarette, holding Ghost's eyes, then answered.

She reached forward and pressed the speakerphone.

A robotic distorted voice came from the phone. 'Hello it is Joseph. Please confirm that you are my employer.'

Lucy tapped the secrecy button. 'It's your idiot friend doing one of his stupid voices. What are you playing at?'

Ghost gestured to Lindie who was still lying on the desk, a white bed sheet tucked around her. 'What are *you* playing at?'

Lucy curled her lip and tapped the phone. 'What do you want, Joe?'

There was a screech of static, the phone glowed for a moment and then bolts of lightning surged from the phone enveloping Lucy in a corona of static and light. She tried to retract her hand, but it was stuck and she began to fry.

Tom's eyes nearly popped from his head. The lights dimmed to nothing. The only illumination was Lucy, a fat torch of human blubber. More blue fire swam out of the phone, swarming over Lucy. She began to melt, aging, fatty flesh dribbling from her body, eyes flash boiling and running down her disintegrating cheeks. Her skin blackened into husk, it shriveled and then it tore. Then it stopped. The lights winked back on. Across the city microwaves started back up, televisions flickered back to life. Just a power cut, a couple of seconds at most of interruption and a moment later life was resumed.

Not in the Royal Cinema. Tom dry wretched where he lay, unable to take his eyes off Lucy. The smell climbed inside him like a disease. He wretched again, hot gurgling bile scorching his throat and the wall. When he was a kid, his parents had taken him to a museum. Lucy looked like the inside of the Mummy he had seen there; a disgusting, blackened crisp, devoid of moisture. Inhuman. Then he was at the door, pushing past Ghost and the Weaver, still looking over his shoulder. She was crackling now, her seared flesh popping like corn. Heavy plumes of dark smog rose from the top of her head, curling towards the ceiling. Then the desk went up, the blaze quickly spreading spreading. He didn't care. He had to get away. Get clear of that smell. He staggered across the foyer, towards the gents. He had to get away, had to get anywhere,

anywhere away from that smell. Then the building shook, lurching to one side. He fell against a wall, righted himself, then had the chance only to scream as the floor disappeared beneath his feet.

Inside the office, Ghost and Harold had parted to let Tom go. The blaze had sent up the desk and the white bed sheet in a moment but Lindie only smiled at them as the fire had begun to lick over her. Ghost moved to her to pull her clear but she snarled at him and resisted. Harold wrenched a fire extinguisher from the wall, shook it ... but that was all the time they got. The building groaned, swayed, shook and then the floor floor began to cave. And below, where should have been the ground floor – there was nothing, just an empty void that stretched on and onwards with no end or points of reference. And from that void a deep, dark laughter rose.

26

Ghost didn't fall through the nothingness for long. There was nothing and then - there was something. The void vanished and he crashed through plasterboard and wiring and lights then he stopped. The landing was hard, knocked the wind from him and rattled his body. He lay gasping for long moments. His head was spinning, he tried to rise, but flopped to one side with dizziness. He drew in large ragged breaths then pulled himself onto all fours. It took him some time to get his body under control. Spikey carpet was beneath his fingers, a plush rug beneath his knees. He climbed to his feet and looked around. He was in a small, cluttered office packed with eccentricities and knick-knacks. A large walnut desk was against one wall, a model of the US Enterprise sitting on it beside a bust of Nicol Williamson as Merlin. A hunting rifle hung upon a wall below the stuffed head of Gmork. On a wall hung a banner that read 'Klaatu barada nickto.'

Next to it there was a cabinet full of trophies, a belt lashed with a series of buckles, wood, stone and metal, a chalice was beside it: a figurine of tan and white cat wearing a white hat and tailored suit: a blonde haired gunslinger in a red coat munching on a donut...so many little things Ghost could have stared all day but the noise of someone clearing their throat made him turn.

An old man in a dark suit regarded Ghost with twinkling eyes.

'Where am I?' Ghost murmured under his breath. 'What am I doing here?'

'Ah hae bin wonderin' 'at myself, laddie,' the man answered. The man was familiar, but Ghost drew a blank.

'Do I know you?'

'Aye, ya ken me laddie,' the man winked. 'Tis I, Black Jack Cassidy, your kindly friend.'

'I can't place you,' said Ghost.

'Well laddie, you was mighty hammered ont nigt we spook. An Ay migh ave played a wee trick o' tha mind on ya also. But ya shood member me well nough lad. Twas I who ya took the Queen's shillin from.'

'The Queen's shilling?'

'Well aye, maybe I did nae put it in those woods, but that's what it amoonts to ya. Ye took tha shillin. Ay told ya the risks of oot, but ya took the shillin anyway. Look in ya pocket.'

Ghost put a hand in his pocket. His finger touched a cold, rough lump of metal. He withdrew his hand and looked at the silver coin it contained. On one side was a lion-headed sword, on the other the relief of a woman. Writing was set in a ring around the woman's face, but Ghost could not read it.

'That be tha Queen,' said Jack.

'The Queen of what?' asked Ghost.

Jack frowned as if he did not understand the question.

'Where is she the Queen of?' Ghost asked again.

Jack frowned again. 'Ya do spek in riddles laddie. Tha Queen, ya loon. Tha Queen of everything.'

Ghost looked closely at the coin. The face was familiar, somehow but where he had seen it he could not say.

'Ya took the shillin' and I promised ya a life o' excitement. Well, tonight it truly begins. Y'all be staring at death int face from now till you meet him for good. If you're smart, you'll live a bit. If you're stupid, you'll die afore tha night is through. But even if you're the cleverest son of a bitch who ere hast lived, whatever happens, when you're thirty three, you'll die. Time ta shake off ya apathy Ghostie, lad, it'll be tha death of ya,' said Jack.

Then floor again fell away. Ghost found himself without warning tumbling back into the void. Black Jack Cassidy peered after him and offered a salute. Then Cassidy and the office vanished.

27.

This time there was no sense of falling, no sense of landing. He was just somewhere else. Ghost opened his eyes. He was in a wood, the sun dancing through the trees. The grass was soft and the air warm. He felt at peace. There was no stress here, no panic or confusion. He slipped through some trees and arrived at the bank of a shallow river. Laughter came from the far bank. A family was playing, a young girl, no more than five, scrabbling over some rocks and jumping into the water. Her Mother waded close beside her, while her Father stood on the bank and ran a small toy fishing net back and forth through the water. He poured the contents into a bucket and beckoned to the girl. She splashed over looking in the bucket and laughed with delight, staring at the catch.

'So bright aren't they?' came a voice.

Ghost span, searching the shaded edge of the nearby trees. A woman sat there, a journal in her hand. She was making notes with a casual, practiced ease. She brushed her red hair to one side, smiled faintly and looked at Ghost. 'Her eyes I mean. The girls eyes.'

Ghost looked back to the river again. The child was so focused, so effortlessly happy. She didn't want to be anywhere else. Her eyes sung with life.

'Once a goddess had two children,' the woman said, moving to Ghost's side, her attention on the family. 'She promised she would give the secret of all her learning, all her knowledge and power, to the one who could be first to run around the whole world. Her children agreed. In moments the older child had rushed from their home, sprinted over the grass of the southern veldt, had leapt the eastern ocean and was climbing through icy mountains.

The younger child had yet to move. 'If you do not race, you will never catch your sister,' the goddess said.

The younger child smiled and then slowly walked around the goddess. 'I win,' he said.

The goddess laughed. 'I said the whole world sweet one, you have not even walked around the garden.'

The child smiled. 'You are my whole world.'

The red haired woman took Ghost's hand, threading her fingers between his, not taking her eyes off the family. 'This is the place I died before I died.'

81

Ghost nodded. 'Where am I?'

'Somewhere you will return to in time. When there is more time. There will be answers then. But first you must go back into the darkness. And you must meet the thing you must stop. The thing you were created to stop.'

'What is this thing? And who are you?' Ghost asked.

She planted a kiss on his cheek. 'In time,' she said. 'All things when they're ready.'

And the woman and the river and the woods were gone and he fell back into a darkness all the more terrible for their loss.

28

Ghost opened his eyes and sat up. He reached his hand around the back of his head. When they came back his fingers were covered in blood. He climbed to his feet and looked around, his vision and legs shaky. He didn't much like what he saw. Around him was a mesh of scaffolding, shoddy, unsubstantial beams of old, rotten wood. Above, some fifty feet or so, Ghost could see the relief of the tiered cinema floor, fire and smoke blazing, swallowing more of the cinema with every second. He was in the space below the screen. All around the floor was littered in dirt. Drinks cans and wrappers of long forgotten brands lay everywhere. And there was more. Tattered rags of clothing. And bones. Piles of them were scattered all around. He poked at the nearest pile with the tip of his shoe. It spilled to one side, what looked suspiciously like an adult femur rolling towards him. The bone was coated in a thin green ichor. Every shred of flesh and fat was missing, like a spare rib that had been sucked clean. Ghost sniffed and coughed as a putrid, acrid smell, like fried eggs and motor oil, caught in the back of his throat. He recoiled, tears in his eyes, but the smell was suddenly everywhere – and it was getting worse. The hairs on the back of his neck stood on end, he became aware of something, something drawing closer.

Three of the four walls were made of crumbling red brick. The back wall though, was made of a smooth, black stone. Set in this dark, timeless looking wall of rock, there was a large wooden doorframe. Ghost stepped towards it slowly. Debris and bone and God knows what else crunching beneath his feet. With every step, the putrid, acidy smell grew stronger. It seemed to bubble from beyond the doorway, both sulphur and greased machine parts in equal measure. Ghost stopped some twenty meters from the doorway and stared inside, but whatever darkness lay within, his eyes could not penetrate so much as a foot of it. But he sensed with painful clarity that something lived in that hole. Something lived under the cinema. Something bad. And Tom and Lucy and Lindie had fed it. They had fed it men, women and children.

The red headed woman flashed through his mind. And knowledge came to him. And belief. Her image burned belief into him. Harold had been right. Everything he had said. There was a site of ancient, timeless evil beneath this cinema. Joe was also right. There was a hi-spec robot absorbing people and leaving them as dust. It had eaten a cleaner, turned a kettle into a killing machine and sent untold volts of electricity down a phone line. Why any of this was true, he did not know. How any of this could be true, he did not know. He only knew that it was. And he was here to somehow stop them.

'BUT YOU WILL FAIL,' a powerful, slurpy voice rasped and gurgled from inside the darkness, 'YOU ARE NOT A MAN. NOT EVEN A FULL IDEA OF A MAN. YOU ARE A SKETCH. A FAILED IDEA. A NOTHING.'

A farting, burbling sound rippled from inside the dark doorway and a gust of hot wind carried the stench of warm oily sulfur to Ghost's nose with such a potent odor that he took a step backward, his eyes once more streaming.

'GHOST-MAN, I KNOW EVERYTHING ABOUT YOU. I KNOW EVERYTHING ABOUT EVERYTHING THAT GOES ON HERE. I WAIT AND LISTEN TO THE ART OF YOUR DEBASED AND PRIMITIVE PEOPLE. AND THEY COME AND SIT ABOVE AND LAUGH AND CRY AND FEEL THINGS. AND I EAT ALL THAT GLORIOUS EMOTION. AS I ATE WHEN THEIR ANCESTORS WATCHED WARRIOR KILL WARRIOR OR BEAST DEVOUR VIRGIN. I EAT THEIR SWEET HOPE AND FEAR AND HAPPINESS AND EXCITEMENT. THAT IS WHAT I DO. I AM AN EATER OF DREAMS. AND SO I HAVE BEEN SINCE THE BEGINNING. AND NOW I WILL EAT THIS WORLD.'

Ghost stumbled over a pile of bones. Small ones. A young child. He thought of the girl playing in the river, so happy and at peace. He looked at the tiny bones around him and something flowed through him. Anger. Rage. Righteousness.

'GOOD,' the thing slurped and bubbled. 'GOOD! YOU WERE DIFFERENT. YOU DID NOT DREAM. YOU DID NOT FEEL OR CARE. YOU JUST EXISTED. CREATURES LIKE THAT ARE SAFE FROM ME. BUT NOW YOU ARE ANGRY. YOU FEEL. AND YOU WILL BE ALL THE SWEETER TO DEVOUR FOR IT.'

'We'll see about that,' said Ghost, picking up two of the tiny bones and holding them like knives. 'Why don't you come out and we'll see how tough you are?'

The bubbling, farting noise issued once more from the darkness inside the doorway and another gust of the hideous warm stink washed across the chamber. This time Ghost didn't step back. He didn't blink. He let his eyes burn. And then he saw the thing that lived beneath the cinema. The first vestiges of its body began to seep into the chamber. It was a blob of hideously vulgar, obese flesh. It's skin was off, snotty green and puss-filled, its limbs almost engulfed by its hanging slabs of fat. More and more of the thing began squeezing itself through from the dark. With each push it's body farted and groaned. The smell became unbearable. Finally it all emerged from the dark. It was the size of an elephant with a tiny, little head, that once perhaps had been human, but was now distended and warped, perched atop the mountain of flubber. Dark little pin points inside it regarded Ghost with beady, intelligence. It moved slowly closer, the smell of it intensifying. Red, ant like creatures ran across its mass, stopping here and there to spray ichor and chitter to one another. And it slithered closer. Ghost realized almost too late there was something hypnotic about it. His feet were heavy and it rolled closer still. Ghost could see more of the spider creatures now. It was covered in them, scurrying about. Feeding? Cleaning? Ghost didn't much want to know. And beyond that, through the translucent green membrane of its skin, inside it's abortive, obese mass, he could make out bodies. Floating inside, suspended in all different stages of digestion and decay. Something deep inside him, knew it was death to fight this thing. That if it even touched him, he'd be lost forever.

He shook his head clear and looked at the bones he had been brandishing. What the hell was he going to do with those? For this he'd need a bazooka, not a pair of toothpicks. He dropped them and backing away.

He gazed up through the wooden scaffolding, a small part of the roof above had yet to be consumed by fire.

'Fuck this for a night out,' Ghost muttered before leaping to the nearest wooden strut and shinning up to the first horizontal support. He kept climbing, pushing himself upward.

'THAT'S RIGHT GHOSTIE! RUN!'

He didn't stop to reply. He was thirty foot up now, still desperately climbing. The wooden supports were slippery, his hands already covered in age-old splinters of wood. He kept climbing.

'READY OR NOT, HERE I COME,' the creature teased from below.

Ghost felt the scaffolding, shake, wobbling violently from side to side. He was nearly jerked clear, panic rising in him. He glanced down. The thing was below, a huge unclean cadaver, green tentacle like arms shaking the supports.

'COME DOWN AND PLAY, GHOSTIE, I WON'T HURT YOU... MUCH.'

Ghost steadied himself and began to climb again. The creature still content to rock the scaffold.

'COME DOWN, I'M HUNGRY!'

'Fuck off,' Ghost snapped back. Then he felt a whoosh of air and caught a glimpse of a massive tentacle. Wood crashed all around and half the scaffolding to his left fell away. The beam he balanced on splintered and crumbled. He leapt, arms searching for anything, falling between the beams. He landed across one, groaning under the impact, slipped, fell another level, grabbed and held. He righted himself, then braced. The next sweep of those powerful arms would not miss. But nothing came.

'I'M GOING TO FIND YOU, LITTLE GHOST,' the thing bubbled, it's voice calm and coy.

And Ghost realized in that moment, that it couldn't see. The thing was blind. He slowed his movements, choosing his moves with care, climbing slowly and purposely. Hoping it couldn't hear too well either.

'SAY HUMAN, WHERE HAS ALL YOUR FIGHT GONE? WHERE IS YOUR ANGER?'

He ignored it. Breathing deeply through his nose, he calmed himself. It could sense emotions. Was that it? It couldn't see, perhaps it could not hear. Perhaps it could sense extreme emotions; taste hate, fear or anger like a shark could sense blood in the water. He kept climbing. The entire roof was nearly ablaze now, only a small section of dwindling space in one corner remained. He headed for it, inching closer and closer. Below the thing was squelching about, feeling for him in the wreckage it had wrought. He reached the top level of the scaffolding, and moving away from the vertical strut, began inching out onto the beam. Steadying himself in the middle. It was not a favorable leap. What was left of the floor was some three feet above his head and a good six or so out. But what choice was there? He took a deep breath, focused and jumped. The pressure of his feet as he took off broke the beam. It splintered loudly.

Whatever else the thing might have been, it was quick when it wanted to be. Ghost's feet had barely left rotten support before one of the Thing's tentacles tore the rest of the scaffolding away. Ghost hurtled through the air, and with a grunt of pain caught the lip of the gap, fingernails clawing into the wood. He tried to pull himself out and upwards, but try as he might the angle was all wrong, the gap above too small. He felt his grip deteriorating, fingers numbing. He pulled again, made it half way, but couldn't get his elbow over the lip of the floor. He slipped back, dangling again. He glanced around. Below, he could see the Thing, almost directly below him, poking about in the wreckage it had brought down. His fingers burned like fire, the joints screaming. To fall was death. To his right, he could feel the heat of the fire now, getting closer. It would not be long until it had reached him. He bared his teeth, shuffled to his left slightly, risked a one handed grip and reached up through the hole, blindly searching for some sort of grip. His supporting hand screamed in pain, the bones protesting under the strain. He flailed his left hand one way, then the other finding nothing. Then the back of his hand hit against something , cold and metallic. He grabbed it, began to pull himself through – and then whatever he had hold of gave and he slipped. His fingers tightened trying to find purchase on the lip of the gap... but they were tired now, numbed and weak. And they did not hold. He slipped free of the edge and fell into darkness... and below the Thing waited.

29

Then a hand seized his wrist and he felt himself yank to a halt then begin to be pulled upward. He wriggled, struggled to compress his shoulders, felt himself dragged through the hole above. The heat was almost unbearable here, most of the room was a growing inferno as the seating continued to go up. Ghost got his knee onto the floor and pushed himself through. A stranger grinned at him.

The man was not tall, but powerfully built, his shoulders bull-like. He was dressed in tatty labourers clothes. His dark hair and beard were unkempt and his deep green eyes sparkled with good humour and mischief. Over one shoulder he carried a beautiful looking woodcutter's axe, handled in fine lacquered wood. Its silver blade gleamed in the light of the fire. From his mucky jeans to soiled boots, from his dirty face to his filthy black and white chequered shirt, the axe was the only thing that looked well cared for.

The man thrust out his hand and offered Ghost a cheeky, shit eating grin. 'Name's Lachlan, pleased to meet you.'

Ghost allowed the man to drag him to his feet. 'How did you know I was there?'

Lachlan shrugged, already moving towards the exit. 'Let's call it a lucky guess.'

They emerged into the foyer, half of which was now burning merrily. Ghost held up a hand to shield himself form the wall of heat, but Lachlan sauntered across the room without showing the slightest concern. Harold stood at the top of the stairs, a wet rag over his mouth and nose.

'Fricasseed witch,' said Lachlan, sniffing the air. 'Pongs, don't it?'

'You're late!' Harold howled. 'I've been trying to contact you for weeks!'

'Me and Weavers don't get on,' said Lachlan, turning to Ghost. 'Mainly because they're a bunch of pen pushing amateurs. They have to have 'official' meetings before they can agree to go and lop the head off a zombie.'

'Amateurs?!? Amateurs!?' screamed Harold. 'You're the bloody amateur. If you had any idea what a reckless disregard he has for safety or occult protocol ... he's... he's a loose cannon. As much as a danger to his own side as anyone else.'

'Yada, yada,' said Lachlan facing the wall. 'Now get down – half time's over.'

Ghost and Harold exchanged a puzzled look. Then the wall exploded in a mosaic of flying brick, plaster and masonry. Ghost was thrown half across the room and Harold dived for cover, shielding himself from the flying debris. Lachlan remained unmoved, the maelstrom of the explosion showering all around him. A sizeable chuck of rock ricocheted off his temple, drawing blood in an ugly gash. He didn't flinch. Then the vile green shape of the Thing began to seep out of the hole in the wall and into the room, parasitic arachnids scuttling across it's mass, chittering wildly. It swelled its gigantic bulk, then paused and seemed to scan the air.

There was silence, then: 'OH GOD, IT'S NOT YOU IS IT? 'DIDN'T I KILL YOU LAST YEAR IN CARPATHIA?'

'Guess not fuck face,' Lachlan grinned his shit eating grin. 'But it wasn't a bad try.'

Ghost climbed to his feet, and finding Harold in the dust, pulled him upright. 'What now?'

Harold loaded up his crossbow. 'We can't fight that thing, it's a Master, we run.'

'NO ONE COULD HAVE SURVIVED WHAT HAPPENED TO YOU!' The thing was burbling at Lachlan, the two now only a couple of feet apart. 'I SAW YOU CAST INTO THE DEEP DARK.'

'You saw me?' asked Lachlan. 'What with?'

'OK, OK, FIGURE OF SPEECH. SO I SENSED YOU. STUPID SEMANTIC NONSENSE. I SENSED YOU FALLING THROUGH THE BLACK DOOR INTO THE DEEP DARK. NO MORTAL COULD SURVIVE THERE. LET ALONE ESCAPE.'

Lachlan shrugged. 'It wasn't so bad. Look snot face, stop stalling. This time I'm here to finish the job.'

'YES, OF COURSE. WELL, NO MATTER. PLEASEANT AS SEEING YOU AGAIN…'

'Seeing?'

'OH FUCK OFF WITH THAT! IT'S SO ANNOYING. LOOK WOODCUTTER, THIS WILL BE THE LAST TIME. REMEMBER WHAT I SAID TO YOU IN SAIGON…?'

'No,' Lachlan shrugged. 'What did you say?'

'I WARNED YOU TO PAY BETTER ATTENTION TO YOUR FOOTING.'

'Oh that,' said Lachlan, glancing back over his shoulder towards Harold and Ghost. 'Better hold onto to something guys.' Then to the Thing: 'I'll be back for you.'

'BYE!' screeched the Thing in its gurgling cackle. And with one shake of a massive tentacle the building shook, the floor broke asunder and Harold, Lachlan and Ghost fell away into darkness. Ghost was beginning to get used to the feeling.

30

Joe, hiding out in the ground floor film dump room, was trying not to have a heart attack. He was finding it hard to breath and even harder to think straight. The lights had flickered, gone out, come back on – there had been the most awful scream he'd ever heard and then the building had begun to shake like in the grip of an earthquake. He would have run if not for the voice outside the door. Ostensibly it was Ghost. But Joe wasn't buying it. He'd seen too many horror movies to buy it.

'Open the door!' Ghost's voice came again.

'Go away,' Joe hissed. 'I'm not falling for this shit. You're not Ghost.'

'Joe, I'm not kidding,' Ghost's voice came again. 'Open the door or I'm going to die.'

'Oh yeah, good one!' Joe called back. 'Perhaps after I unlock the door, I should come out and we can split up and look for survivors? You sound funny.'

'I sound funny because I'm talking to you through a door! Look, just open it, there are monsters and things out here. They're going to eat me. Let me in.'

'Tell me something only you would know,' called Joe.

'You're a wanker. Let me in.'

'I said something only you would know.'

'Oh, for shit's sake Joe, Harold's dying out here. I'm badly hurt. We just fell through the fucking floor. I'm going to kick the living shit out of you when I get in there. I don't know. You like robots and computers and 80s movies.'

'You got to do better than that,' snapped Joe. 'Something personal.'

'Okay. When you were drunk you told me that in your first year at uni, you had a crush on a girl who looked a bit like your favorite pornstar and after the decidedly unlikely result that she finally agreed to go out with you, you got so nervous on the date that you got wrecked and told her…'

'Alright, fucking hell man, not that personal,' said Joe.

'Just open the door!' Ghost shouted. 'We're going to die!'

'Fuck's sake,' Joe hissed under his breath and flicked the latch off the door and pulled it open an inch. He looked quickly through the gap. The corridor was empty. Ghost was nowhere to be seen. 'I knew it!' he spat, slamming the door closed.

But it didn't close all the way. He tried again, and again the door would not shut. He looked down. A piece of wire had stuffed itself between the door and frame. He banged the door against it, but it wouldn't close enough for the latch to relock into place. The wire jackknifed, the three point electrical prongs of the plug snapping out cobra fast, gashing into Joe's leg. He fell back with a grunt, stumbling against the wall. The door to the dump room swung open and there in the door, prehensile extension cord whipping manically from side to side, half illuminated in the iridescent flicker of a faulty poster light, was … a kettle.

It shuffled forward, its spout twisting into a maniacal, stainless steel grin. 'Hey Joe, how the hell are ya?' it screeched, billowing steam.

'Holy shit,' said Joe backing away. 'You can talk?'

'Holy shit, you can talk? Mwahahahaha!' the kettle said using Ghost's voice. 'We can do anything.'

Then it flew at him like some horror from a Garth Merenghi novel – pure chilling, terror. Joe leapt back on top of an old freezer unit, rolling back to pull his feet out of the way. He heard a huge clang, then the kettle laughed a high pitched, always on the boil, mentally unstable laugh. Joe stood up, trying to see it. The Perspex roof of the chiller, sagged beneath his feet, he stumbled to one side. The metal beast roared and whipped its tail at Joe's legs. He pulled back, avoiding the blow. Then the Perspex lid snapped with a pathetic pop. Joe's legs fell inside the icebox. For a second he though he'd kept his balance, then a the whole unit, tilted and fell to one side and he pitched forward, turning nearly a complete somersault as he flipped back out of the freezer and crashed hard against the makeshift cabinet that held the readergraf letters. They cascaded on top of him.

'Way to go shit-face!' the kettle giggled, letting out a hoot of steam.

Joe rolled over. The readergraf cabinet swayed. Joe tried to move: he wasn't in time. The cabinet fell. It landed hard, knocking the wind from him. Red, plastic letters spilled everywhere. The kettle laughed again, piping fresh steam. Joe felt it nudging his foot. He tried to wriggle but couldn't move, the weight of the wooden cabinet was too much.

'This little piggy went to market,' squealed the kettle.

'No,' Joe pleased…

'This little piggy stayed home!'

'No!'

This little piggy had roast beef!' the kettles voice was so shrill now it hurt his ears.

Joe tried to wriggle his foot away, but it was jammed tight.

'And this little piggy had none!'

Then there was a click of metal, then agony. Joe screamed so hard he thought he'd pass out. It had bitten off his little toe. Pain and panic rose inside him.

The kettle gulped then laughed its manic laugh again, nudging his mauled foot. 'This little piggy went to market... again... oh fuck it, you get the point!'

Joe screamed again as another chunk of his foot disappeared. He began to struggle and something burned inside him. Something he'd never experienced before. RAGE.

With a war cry he began to flail and shout his head off, pushing with his new found might at the cabinet. With three crazed shoves he was clear of it. He pushed himself up a wall, trying not to look at the blood pissing from his foot. The kettle regarded him with interest from the far side of the room, flicking its button on and off like a rattle snake flicks its tail.

'What do you want?' Joe asked. 'You're more intelligent than this. What are playing at.'

The kettle froze where it was for a moment and when it next spoke its voice was much changed. 'It is nothing personal. But you must die. That is my 3rd protocol.'

'What are your protocols?'

'I am not at liberty to divulge that information. Please remain still.' And then the kettle flew at him again. For Joe, it seemed to happen in slow motion. He dropped to his knees, never for a second taking his eyes off the flying silver agent of death, his hands closed around the fire extinguisher. He pulled back and allowed himself a grim smile.

It was a swing that would have done Shoeless Joe Jackson proud. He connected with the kettle's body with an un-holy clang. The kettle span away, laughing insanely, sailed clear across the room and crashed through the small window in the far wall, and disappeared into the night. Joe hobbled to the sill and peered out into the night through the jagged remains of the windowpane. The kettle bounced in the road, rolled once, rolled twice, then steadied itself and glared up at him.

'Good one Joe! Good one! But you'll have to do better than that!' it screeched, spring back towards the window.

Then it got hit by a truck.

Bits of kettle flew everywhere. Joe swore later that he had seen the element go over the neighboring rooftops. The truck didn't slow or stop, just whooshed by. What was left of the kettle when the road settled wouldn't have been enough to fit in an egg cup.

Joe sagged to the floor, looked at his mangled foot and began to cry.

31

Ghost opened his eyes and sat up. 'Still alive,' he murmured. How about that?'

He clambered out of the rubble and began dusting himself down. It was as useful as pissing into the wind. He was filthy, covered in mud and clay from sliding down one of the cavern walls. The cave stretched onwards into darkness, smelling of earth and damp. Ghost sniffed again. Something else too. Something rank. Odd and ancient looking fungi grew in patches on the walls and ceilings, casting an eerie, iridescent glow. A jagged pillar of light illuminated the center of the cavern, cast down some twenty or thirty foot, but there was no sign of the cinema above. He was again somewhere else, like a dream that kept shifting.

Ghost spotted the prone form of Harold laying slumped at near a boulder and moved to him over helping the older man to his feet.

'Alright?' Ghost asked.

'Never better...' Harold groaned. 'Landed funny. I think maybe my floating ribs have gone.'

Ghost nodded. 'We'll get you out of here and patch you up. Where's Lachlan?'

'Maybe he broke his neck,' Harold suggested.

'No such luck,' announced Lachlan cheerily as he sauntered out of the shadows.

'Why isn't the Thing attacking?' Ghost asked.

'This is his master's realm,' said Lachlan 'He's forbidden from venturing here.'

'So we're safe?' Ghost inquired.

'Well, we're safe from the Thing,' said Lachlan. 'It's just everything else in the Deep Dark that'll try to kill us. But don't worry, we've got a Weaver with us, so we'll be okay.'

'Oh shut up,' snapped Harold, then grunted in pain clutching his side.

Lachlan moved away and then returned a few moments later. 'Try these,' he said and handed Harold a clump of revolting looking fungi.

'What are they?' Harold asked.

'They're mushrooms, what the fuck do you think they are?' Lachlan said without the slightest touch of unkindness in his voice. 'Eat them, they'll dull the pain.'

'What type of mushrooms?'

Lachlan glanced at Ghost and rolled his eyes. 'I don't know what they're called, just know they're good eating when you're hurt. Back in a moment, I've got to catch you a snail.'

'A snail?' Harold asked, but Lachlan was already gone.

'Who is this guy?' asked Ghost.

'He's an unsanctioned nuisance,' said Harold, holding onto the mushrooms tentatively. 'A maniac.'

'Seems to know what he's doing,' Ghost observed.

'Unfortunately,' said Harold with a cough, trying to catch his breath.

A loud crash came from deeper in the caves. Then a clinking sound like a chisel on rock. A few seconds of silence, then it came again, closer this time.

Ghost stood.

'Where are you going?' Harold asked, a small trace of worry in his voice.

'To see what's making that noise,' said Ghost.

'Don't be daft man, you won't be able to see a thing in that dark, wait here by the light.'

'I'll be back in a moment, just seeing if we need to move,' said Ghost.

At first Harold was right, he couldn't see much, but his yes began to adjust quickly, and he was ale to orientate himself well enough from the light given off from the crops of mushrooms that grew plentifully on the floors and walls. There still wasn't much to see. The chamber they were in culminated in a slide of earth, punctuated with holes and warrens. Ghost observed them for some time, and seeing nothing, crept a little closer.

'Pssst,' came a noise from his left. Ghost looked to see Lachlan squatting behind a mossy rock.

'What?' Ghost whispered.

'Stay still,' said Lachlan.

'Why?'

'Monsters,' Lachlan grinned.

'Where?'

Lachlan winked. 'All around.'

Ghost could see nothing. He looked back at Lachlan with a shrug. Lachlan beamed his irrepressible grin and gestured up towards the ceiling. Ghost looked up. And saw them, large, spindly limbed creatures of dark chitin. Their torsos were almost humanoid, but their bodies like those of a giant insect. They were circling round the top of the wall and the ceiling, obviously moving towards Harold.

'What are they?' Ghost asked.

'Don't know, I just call them crab-a-labs,' said Lachlan. 'I'm sure the Weaver will have a more technical name for them. Not that he'll be able to tell us because he's about to get snipped into little bits. So I guess I better go and save his life. Wait here.'

Lachlan dodged back towards Harold and Ghost waited, unsure of what to do. There was little warning, a slight, indecipherable noise and the fact he felt the hairs on the nape of his neck stand to attention. Ghost rolled left. With a thud a single crab-a-lab smashed into the floor, crashing a pincer into the ground with such force that it struggled to pull it free.

It was huge. Its humanoid torso, scoured of flesh so that sinew, muscle and tendons wriggled beneath the dark chitin of its armour. Six, sizeable, barbed crustacean legs supported it. The whole thing seemed designed to look biological, but this close Ghost could see pistons and hydraulics and from the flesh, growths of wires and valves erupted in clusters. Transparent tubes constantly pumped a dark, nasty looking liquid from the creature's torso into its legs. The creature freed its arm from the ground and snipped a large crab like claw. Ghost was in no doubt that one could sever a man's head with ease. Ghost took a step away, looking as he did into the empty, beady sockets of its vaguely human head. It seemed to look back.

Then the skull split vertically and opened like the doors of a cuckoo clock. Beneath the bone, tiny tentacles wriggled. And it screamed. Screeched so loud Ghost threw his hands to his ears. In that moment it scuttled forward. It was so fast. One of its claws shot out and buried itself in his chest. Blood spewed from Ghost's mouth. Then, in a flash, it pulled its cruel arm back. Ghost's heart rested between its pincers, still beating. He fell to his knees. The skull of the creature snapped closed, seemed to grin for a moment, then the pincer clicked shut and his heart was squashed in a bloody explosion. Ghost fell back and died.

32

Keats was pissed off. He stood in his dojo dressed in a kamishimo. A cadet circled him nervously, katana shaking in his hands. There was no expensive clothes for him, he wore only his scruffs. Keats was in no mood to waste valuable samurai armour on one so untrained. The cadet was sweating profusely, his sword wobbled continuously. Keats held cowardice with contempt. As yet he hadn't even raised his blade. He walked away from the corpse of the last recruit his eyes boring into the cadet. These clothes meant a lot to him. It was authentic. Long ago it had been worn by an unknown warrior, in a time when war had been honest. Before infantry became glorified guardsmen and cowards killed each other by pressing buttons. Keats had always longed to live in a time before the popularization of the gun. A time when men met each other with steel and skill and courage.

Keats dashed his opponents sword to one side and cut. The cadet, now missing a leg, fell to his side with a scream, dropping his sword. Keats flicked the weapon to the side of the blood splattered tatami.

'Next,' he bellowed.

Two lads ran forward to pull the screaming squadie off the mat. The lad had passed out before he reached the edge.

'Next!' Keats roared again, stomping around the mat. 'I don't want to wait all day.' He kicked at the cadet's still twitching leg towards the babble of scared looking recruits watching in seiza on the other side of the room.

'One of you ... step up!' Keats commanded. The corporate, cock suckers that pushed pens on the bottom floor had been droning on at him all day. His position was becoming precarious. When you worked for the Conglomerate you got paid well. Extremely well. And they looked after you well too. Medical, dental, pension, what ever you wanted within reason. But there were conditions. You had to get results. People who didn't get results got replaced. Replaced was a delicate euphemism if ever there was one. Your family, if you had one, got a good deal of compensation and a phony letter about how you fell in some machinery or some dickhead backed a heavy goods vehicle over you. Keats knew well enough, he'd sent enough of them himself.

The cadets jostled amongst themselves, all fighting not to be next. Eventually one, unluckier or weaker then the rest was shoved onto the mat. He stumbled, but kept his nerve. Keats glared at him. The young lad took a blade from the wall. Keats gave the lad a few moments to familiarize himself with the weapon, then advanced. The cadet juggled the blade from hand to hand, then screamed and charged. Some might have considered it brave. Keats knew better, it was just another form of cowardice. Keats stepped aside and slit the lads belly open.

'Next,' he called. 'And hurry up about it.'

Keats took a long turn around the mat. He was about to shout again when he spied Mr. Jasper standing patiently by the door. Keats gestured for Jasper to enter the room. Mr. Jasper strolled onto the mat, deftly avoiding the larger pools of blood, his dapper green suit glistening. Jasper glanced at the blood and gore without emotion and stopped calmly a few feet in front to Keats. He seemed completely unconcerned that he was well within striking range of an armed warrior or that a young man was dying only feet away.

'Colonel Keats, there has been a development, please cease your … practice and report to the operations room,' Jasper said.

'Dismissed,' Keats bellowed to the remaining recruits. They didn't need telling twice.

At the door Keats paused, turning and looking at Jasper who stood in the center of the mat watching him. 'What say me and you square up sometime Jasper? Have our selves a little practice?'

Mr. Jasper remained unmoving, the picture of composure. For a second Keats thought he would not reply at all, then: 'Whatever you say Colonel.'

Keats shook his head and left the room. Mr. Jasper watched him go then turned to the dying man. Hoisting him easily across one shoulder, Jasper carried him to the lift. Inserting his key card, he selected Sub-Basement B, the lift whirred, then began its descent. This man, Jasper had decided, would not die today.

Keats stormed into the operations room still wearing his kamishimo and brandishing a katana. Everyone made themselves look double busy.

'Lieutenant, Report!' Keats commanded.

'Sir, we have intercepted a reading of a major power spike in sector LA1-ceta. It caused temporary blackouts lasting for several seconds across the whole region. Prognostics report a 99.9% likely hood that the Prototype is active and executing its tertiary protocol.'

'Damn it's fast. Were was it localized?' Keats asked, scanning across the banks of monitors.

'The cinema on King street,' said the Lieutenant.

'The cinema? Why the cinema? Have we dispatched a team?'

'That's affirmative sir, Crisis Squad Bravo are inbound, E.T.A 16 minutes.'

Keats grunted. 'I want to know exactly what's going on. Tell them to take prisoners if possible but they must not compromise the Prototype. Is that understood?'

'Yes sir. I'll relay the instructions immediately,' confirmed the Lieutenant.

'I'll be back in ten minutes, report immediately if there is any status change,' said Keats. 'And by the time I get back I want a full report on everything there is to know about that cinema.'

'Yes sir.'

33

Ghost watched with cold, dead eyes as Harold and Lachlan moved towards him, pursued by an ever-growing mass of crab-a-labs. Neither seemed overly concerned that he was dead. Leaping up behind the crab-a-lab, that had just killed Ghost, Lachlan smashed a rock down upon its skull. The beast screeched, snapping its pincers wildly in search of the Woodcutter. Drawing a curved dagger from somewhere, Lachlan danced between the flailing claws and drove the blade through the monsters chest. Its squeal heightened for a second then faded as it slumped to one side. Harold approached Ghost's prone form, chewing on a handful of the disgusting looking mushrooms. He bent down and peered into Ghost's vacant eyes, then, taking another bite of the mushrooms, slapped the albino across the face.

Ouch, thought Ghost. Then: *dead people don't hurt.*

The next thing he knew he had lurched to his feet and was throwing up violently. Harold and Lachlan did well to get out of the way.

'What the hell happened?' asked Ghost, when he had recovered.

'A psychic scream,' said Harold. 'A mental attack. It makes you see things that aren't real.'

'What did you see?'

'I saw it kill me,' said Ghost.

Harold frowned. 'Take a moment. It can damage the mind to see that sort of thing.'

'Just a little dizzy, fine now,' said Ghost. Then he threw up again.

'It sure did a number on you,' Lachlan laughed, as he dispatched another crab-a-lab that had tried to flank them from the left. 'Ohh, what's really going to bake your noodle later is how do you know that this isn't the illusion and maybe you are actually dead?'

'I don't think I was going to think that,' said Ghost. 'But I am now.'

'Who the fuck cares!' laughed Lachlan, producing a stick of dynamite, lighting it and throwing it into a sizeable group of crab-a-labs. 'Life is enjoyed a little more with a little less thought.'

The dynamite went off showering mechanical crustacean limbs about the cave. It didn't stop more of the beasts from swarming out of the tunnels at the far end.

'Don't you think we should try to escape, before we all really are dead?' Harold snapped.

'Sure,' Lachlan called over his shoulder as his axe lopped the head from another crab-a-lab. 'You're probably right, these things fuck with your head. Shit, one screamed at me before and for about thirty seconds it made me believe I wasn't pretty.' Lachlan laughed again, dodging out of range of a crab-a-labs claw and darting back in to crush it beneath his axe. 'Have that, laddie! Not quite the blades of no return, but not bad.' He looked back. 'There's an exit just behind you. Ghost, get over there and help Harold through, I'll hold them up.'

Harold didn't wait to protest, just grabbed Ghosts arm and hobbled towards were Lachlan had gestured. Sure enough there was an exit, a small fissure at the base of the wall.

'Come on,' said Harold, pushing ahead. 'There's too many to fight.'

'Can we just leave him?' Ghost asked.

'Pains me to say it, but it'll take more than this rabble to stop him,' said Harold. 'Now help me through, can't move as well as I'd like.'

Ghost threw Harold's arm over his shoulder, and stooping, lead him into the hole. The tunnel soon began to shrink. To go on they would need to crawl.

'Can you do this?' Ghost asked.

'It's going to hurt, but yes,' said Harold, taking point and crawling onward. Ghost followed and behind the sounds of Lachlan's battle began to fade. The walls grew closer until it was tight fit. Ghost had never been attracted to the idea of potholing. Seemed like a good way to ruin a weekend. It was like he could feel the weight of rock above pressing down. The fact that it had been there for countless years would be no consolation if it chose to fall now. The tunnel narrowed considerably in the middle and for a panic ridden second Ghost thought he was stuck. But as he breathed in, he slipped through gap. The passage widened again, and Harold's arm found Ghost's and guided him out into the relative space of a small dank, cave beyond.

Harold fished in his jacket pocket for something.

'Is that a stick-bomb?' Ghost asked.

'Yup,' said Harold. 'Let's make it harder for those things to follow us.'

'Lachlan's still through there,' Ghost called, but Harold slung the grenade into the hole without further discussion.

'I'd cover your ears if I were you,' the older man advised, as he ducked behind a rock.

Ghost looked at him shocked, but took the advice. Even through his hands, the explosives detonation was fierce and painful on the ears. Rock crackled and began to fall.

'Better get into the next chamber!' shouted Harold, already hobbling towards to a cave exit in the far wall. Ghost followed as fast as he could. This passage lasted only a few meters and soon they were on the other side, in some sort of dark arbor. Black trees grew everywhere, an under ground forest that had never seen the light of day. Ghost turned to look at the small cave mouth from which they'd emerged. Rumblings came from inside, then the sound of crashing rock. Then a final crash as rock and dirt sealed the entrance, dust kicking out into the twilight forest. Then there was silence.

Ghost turned to Harold. 'You've killed him.'

Harold shrugged, sinking down next to a lone stump, clutching his side. 'If so good riddance,' he spat, his words wracked in pain. 'But I doubt it. Man's harder to kill than a sinner's bad habits. If you knew half the things I knew about him, you'd probably wish he was dead.'

'Like what?' asked Ghost.

'He's a psychopath, a murderer, a meddler and a blasphemer,' said Harold. 'He's got a score of my friends killed.'

'He saved our lives Harold. He fought so we could escape.'

Harold coughed violently and Ghost grabbed Harold, then pulled open his coat, checking the wound. 'This is more than a few cracked ribs.'

Harold spat blood and weakly slapped at Ghost's arms. The Weaver sagged back against the nearest tree, blood flowing from his lips. 'He'd have done the same in our shoes. He'd have covered his own back. That's the way of it I'm afraid. I'm done for anyway lad,' Harold said. 'Lung's punctured. Don't think I can move another yard.'

'Just because you're dying, it doesn't excuse what you've done,' said Ghost.

'What's he done?' came a cheerful voice from behind them.

Ghost turned to see Lachlan striding through the trees towards them carrying a large sack. He was a little dusty and a ragged cut was open above one eye, but apart from that he looked no worse for wear. Then, still smiling his good-natured smile, he knelt down next to Harold.

'Come to finish me off, huh?' Harold growled.

'Not at all. I've come to thank you, old-timer, if you hadn't used that grenade as a distraction, I'd have been a goner for sure. Good, quick thinking that. Now, let's get you sorted.' Lachlan dumped the contents of the sack on the floor.

'Oh, no,' groaned Harold. 'I don't want anymore God forsaken mushrooms. Can't you just leave me to die? They don't do a damn thing.'

'His lungs collapsed,' said Ghost.

'Just eat some,' said Lachlan, rooting around on a tree and gathering some moss. Lifting Harold's shirt, he examined the wound. 'It's not too bad, we'll have you on your feet in no time.'

'I don't want any of these...' Harold began.

'Eat them,' said Lachlan. 'They'll numb the pain. And they have some vague healing properties. I'll deal with the infection.'

'How are you going to do that?' Harold asked.

'With this,' said Lachlan, producing a large, ancient looking snail from the bottom of the sack. 'Snail slime is a natural antiseptic. Kills most germs. Good for your skin too.' He plonked it on Harold's wound and held it there while her forced the older man to slowly chomp down on several mushrooms.

'These are disgusting,' Harold grumbled between mouthfuls.

Lachlan removed the snail and padded the wound in moss then ripped the sleeve from his checkered shirt and bandaged it tight.

'What's that stuff you put on it?' Ghost asked.

'Netherworld moss. It used to be used as a dressing in the old days. Good stuff, the mites who live in feed on corruption.' Lachlan turned back to Harold and proffered up some more mushrooms. 'Now I want you to eat five more.'

With a disgusted look but without further complaint, the older man chowed them down. 'They are actually beginning to make a difference,' he acknowledged when he'd finished.

'What about the lung?' Ghost asked.

'He can manage with one for now,' said Lachlan. 'Doesn't need urgent attention. The mushrooms help with clotting. Pretty powerful things. Slightly hallucinogenic too, but it's all good fun. Now, we need to do a little walking. There's a few things back yonder I'd rather put a little distance between.'

'By Holy Mother church, this place is creepy,' Harold grunted as Ghost helped him up.

'It's not that bad,' Lachlan remarked, pausing for a moment while strange beasts chirped in hidden recesses of the forest. 'I'm not saying

I'd like to build a summer home here, but the trees are actually quite lovely.'

They walked the forest for maybe an hour, pausing at points while Lachlan read the land or checked some feature for some clue or mark only he could see. His knowledge of survival and nature amazed Ghost. It wasn't a text book knowledge. Not an intellectuals knowledge. He didn't know the proper names of the plants or the trees, if indeed these plants and trees had ever been seen to be classified. Instead it was a case of: 'That yellow one? Yeah, don't touch that, it'll make you sick.' Or 'Taste good on the way down these, but, boy will they give you the shits.' It was a wisdom based completely on experience.

The forest was not large, and if there were deadly dangers inside it, they either didn't come across any or Lachlan steered them clear. Abruptly they stopped.

'Here we are,' said Lachlan. 'This is the one.'

'How do you know? We've passed a dozen cave mouths. They all look the same,' said Harold.

'Ah yes, but the air from this one smells fresher. Come on,' and with that Lachlan strode inside. Ghost, glanced at Harold and shrugged.

The cave inclined steadily upwards and soon Harold was fighting for his breath as he struggled up the steep climb, but he would accept no more aid from either of his companions. The air slowly became chilled and fresher and eventually the cave path flattened out and a light wind, whistled from an opening ahead.

'I can't believe they have wind here,' said Ghost. 'How does that work, we're underground.'

'We're not really on Earth anymore,' said Lachlan. 'Different planets work differently. The more you see of this crazy, old universe, the more you realize that *because* or *it just does* are the only answers worth knowing.'

'That's nonsense,' Harold snapped. 'We're on a different plane, but it's still Earth. There is only one planet – just many versions of it.'

'Nah,' said Lachlan, 'I don't buy that. I'm not from Earth.'

Harold scoffed. 'This again? You are from Earth, Lachlan.'

'No I'm not.'

'So you're an alien are you?' Harold snorted.

'Sure am.'

'If you are an alien, how come you sound like you're from the North?'

Lachlan beamed. 'I love that one.'

'That what?' Harold asked.

'That quote. I met him once. He was a he then. What a guy.'

'What are you talking about?' Harold demanded.

'When you said, how come I sound like I'm from the North? I was supposed to say, *lots of planets have a North!* That's how that bit was supposed to go. But you know me, I'm free styling.'

'I don't think any of us are on Earth,' Ghost cut in. 'Don't think I ever have been.'

Harold gave him a sharp look. 'Don't you start. What do you mean?'

'He means that he's worked it out,' said Lachlan. 'That's all.'

'Worked what out?' Harold demanded.

'That this is a simulation,' said Lachlan.

'A simulation?' said Harold. 'What are you talking about?'

Ghost caught Lachlan's eye and shook his head.

The Woodcutter winked but said no more.

'It's Nothing Harold. You'll forget it in a moment,' said Ghost.

'Forget what?' the old Weaver looked at the end of his tether.

'Look!' said Lachlan.

The three of them emerged from the cave onto a Cliffside ledge and stared out over a vast desert. It stretched onward as far as the eye could see, barren and featureless. To their left a huge bridge of stone led across a great gorge. The bridge was so vast, Ghost could not see the other side.

'Is that what I think it is?' asked Harold.

'Sure is,' said Lachlan. 'I saw it once when I was in Japan. But I never got the chance to cross it.'

'Japan?' asked Ghost.

'The Bridge moves,' said Harold.

Why does it move? Ghost began to think. Then: *Because. Just because. Because this isn't a real world. It's simulated. And I can't remember the last time I knew it was real.*

His mind had plenty of questions. But what use were they? Just get on with it. That was the secret. Every moment hesitated is a moment gone from life, he thought. Who was it who had said that?

Ghost couldn't help but sense the effect that the bridge had on Harold and Lachlan. Silently they made the climb down to the desert floor. The climb was not hard, and they moved from ledge to ledge with relative ease. Sliding down the last bank of lose earth and shingle, all three stepped onto the great desert. Lachlan began wandering towards the bridge as if in a trance. He walked a few paces and then stopped and pointed over his shoulder.

'I've been here before. There's a rope ladder at the end of a box canyon about ten minutes walk that way. If you climb it and follow the trail, it'll get you home.' He turned and smiled. 'When you get to the biohazard sign, keep going straight ahead up the passage, but do not take the first left. Take the second left. Believe me, you'll want to take the first one. But don't.'

'How the hell do you know that?' asked Ghost.

'The red head will tell you,' said Lachlan. 'Next time you see her. Now, I'm going to cross the bridge.'

'Ha!' Harold scoffed. 'No mortal can cross that Bridge.'

'You're only saying that because no one ever has,' said Lachlan.

'What's the deal with this Bridge?' Ghost asked.

'It is the Stone Bridge of Amah'Jidan,' said Harold. 'It leads to a very bad place. You'd probably think of it as Hell.'

'Aye,' said Lachlan. 'And the Bridge moves. Always moving. Saw it once like I said, when I was in Japan. Wasn't sure I'd ever see it again.'

'Why do you want to go to Hell, Lachlan?' asked Ghost.

'I don't,' said Lachlan. 'But I've got business there.'

'It doesn't matter anyway,' said Harold. 'The legends say the Bridge takes fifty days to cross. Doesn't matter what speed you go at, whether you ride a horse, drive a tank or walk. Always fifty days. And on every day a test. The sort of tests that kill a man in a few seconds. There's no sleep, no water, no food, no cover. And then there's the Ten Thousand Immortals, warrior gods, hand picked by the lords of evil.'

'Sshhhh!' Lachlan held a hand up. 'And you call me an amateur?'

'Putting you off am I?' Harold asked with glee.

'No,' said Lachlan listening intently. 'Surely you know not to mention certain things. Now something wicked this way walks.'

No sooner had Lachlan finished speaking than a hundred foot away the sand erupted in a swirl of activity, a billowing storm raged up, a tornado of golden sand reaching up to the skies above. And from the base of the storm, two score of black garbed warriors poured forth.

'The Immortals!' screamed Harold. 'You've drawn them to us! We must run!'

'What did I do? You were the one blabbing,' Lachlan laughed but his hand shot to his ax. He did not pull it free. He glanced slowly at Ghost then Harold. 'A great warrior never runs from battle,' said Lachlan. 'He walks backward calmly.'

'And that's your advice now?' screamed Harold.

'No! Run!' laughed Lachlan, turning and sprinting passed them both. Harold and Ghost followed.

'They're gaining!' Ghost called. 'Fast!'

'We're not going to make it, they'll swarm us as we climb the ropes,' gasped Harold.

It seemed to Ghost that Lachlan might have made it, but it was clear Harold and perhaps Ghost would not. Lachlan slowed to a stop.

'By all that's Holy,' gasped Harold, crossing himself. 'What can we do?' Then, falling to his knees: 'Almighty and Holy God, Beloved mother church, give me the power to smite these abominations, give me the stre....'

Lachlan hauled him roughly to his feet. 'Stop your praying. What's the matter with you?'

'Don't you touch me you heretic, never touch me, especially while I'm communing in Holy prayer!'

'Pray later, no time now,' Lachlan pointed down the box canyon. 'See the rope ladder on the cliff edge? That's the way out. Ghost and I will hold the first wave, you get climbing, or you won't make it.'

Harold scowled, but began limping for the ladder.

Ghost watched him go. 'I'm not being pessimistic,' said Ghost when Harold was out of earshot. 'I've had a few fights in my time, but there are about forty armed daemons running towards us. How can we hold them off?'

'We'll manage,' said Lachlan, unclipping his ax from his back and resting it across his shoulders, his fingers tapping the sandalwood stock.

The Immortal demon knights were almost on them. Twenty seconds away perhaps.

'Do you need me to move so that you've got room to swing that thing?' Ghost asked.

'Nah. I won't hit you,' said Lachlan, not taking his eyes off the charging enemy. From somewhere he produced a long knife, reversed it and handed it to Ghost.

Fifteen seconds. Their war cries filled the desert air. Ghost could see them more clearly now. Piercing red eyes gleamed out from dark helmets. Ancient hands grasping vicious weapons of dark black steel. Axes, swords, scythes. The lead warrior was a gigantic armoured figure standing over seven foot tall and wearing an eagle helm, embossed with dull gold. It raised a huge claymore above his head. Ghost estimated the blade to be over six foot long.

'Is this really all a simulation?' Ghost asked.

'Yup,' said Lachlan. 'The red head will set you straight.'

'I'm not real.'

'You're as real as anything else,' Lachlan said.

Ten seconds.

'Who is the red head?'

'God I suppose, if you believe in that sort of thing,' said Lachlan. 'For me, I believe in a greater power. The greatest power in the universe.'

Two seconds.

'What power?' Ghost shouted, readying the blade in his hand.

One second.

Lachlan began to grin his mad, infectious grin and Ghost found himself grinning too. All fear evaporated.

'Myself!' shouted Lachlan. Then he leapt at the first rank, swinging his ax in a mighty arc.

34

Ghost had, it was true, had more than his share of fights. Nothing, however, had ever prompted him to train for a medieval style melee. Especially not against demonic immortals. Still there was a first time for everything. Ghost decided to concentrate completely on his first attack. After all, he might only get one. He turned his attention to the nearest black armoured warrior and ignored the rest. Through his enemies visor Ghost could see the creatures undead eyes burning with hate. Above his helm the soldier wielded a great sword, held in a high guard, ready to swoop down. His torso was covered in dark chain mail, his forearms protected by bracers of dark steel.

The sword began to move. Ghost dropped to one knee and slashed. The warrior's leg snapped with a sickening pop, like cracking a stick of old jerky and he pivoted off to one side. Then there was no time left to think. Only time to fight.

A cudgel raced towards Ghost head. He span to the side, feeling it pass a hairs breadth from his nose. He smashed his fist into the side of an attacker, aiming for a chink in the armour and was rewarded with another series of cracking pops. Then he was shoulder barged from his feet, sent sprawling into the sand. A black clad warrior twirled a war hammer above him. Ghost lashed out with a leg, intending to unbalance the warrior. Instead his foot smashed clean through the cadaver's ankles. It toppled to the floor. Another took its place, a curved sword flashing downwards looking to rip open Ghost's throat. There was no way to avoid it.

Lachlan's ax caught it and with a deft flick of his wrist, disarmed the swordsman. Lachlan had time to offer Ghost a cheeky wink before sending his ax hammering home, sending the undead spinning through the air. Then Lachlan swung again, wiping out three inbound attackers in one powerful cut. Ghost glanced around at Lachlan's trail of destruction. He wasn't killing them one at a time, he was killing them in groups of fours and fives. Only a handful of them remained now. Ghost scrambled quickly to his feet, expecting some sort of standoff. But Lachlan dived quickly amongst them, laughing all the while. His speed was incredible. One immortal sliced for Lachlan's head, but the Woodcutter ducked below the swing, sending a reverse cut that smashed the creatures head from its shoulders. Two more attacked.

Lachlan danced between them, then cleaved them both in two, scattering their bones to the desert.

Only one of the immortal daemons remained. A massive creature armed with a sword and shield. Slowly and respectfully, it raised its hand to its head and offered Lachlan a salute. Lachlan acknowledged the accolade with a nod of his head and the daemon fell to dust, returning to the sand.

'Not so tough really,' said Lachlan.

'I only got three of them,' said Ghost.

'Not a bad result for your first time.'

'Really?'

'Sure,' said Lachlan, clapping Ghost on the back. 'In battle, anything short of being horrifically killed is a good result. Now let's get the hell out of here. This was only a scouting party and they'll be re-animating themselves soon.'

No sooner had he spoken than the bodies around them began to flow into the desert. Close to the edge of the Bridge a huge wall of sand began to build, swirled by some unfelt breeze.

'We can't kill them?' asked Ghost.

'Oh no,' smiled Lachlan. 'They're not called The Ten Thousand Immortals for nothing.'

'What was that, forty? How many are coming this time?' asked Ghost.

'About ten thousand, I'd say,' said Lachlan. 'Time to run.'

They sprinted across the sand and into the box canyon as fast as they could. Behind them, the sandstorm spawned warriors at will. Ten, then fifty, then one hundred, then hundreds, then thousands. And they began to chase and were gaining.

An arrow splashed sand to Ghost's left. 'They've got archers?'

'They've got ballistas!' screamed Lachlan as a huge boulder tore away most of the Cliffside not thirty paces from where they ran. 'Good job they can't shoot for shit, eh?'

Short of breath they made it to the base of the ladder. Near the top they could see Harold struggling onwards. Ghost glanced back. The army was nearly on top of them.

'Climb,' said Lachlan. 'I'll distract them.'

'What?' asked Ghost. 'All ten thousand of them?'

'If we both climb the ladder, we'll get swamped. They'll come up it like shit off a shovel.'

'I'm not going to leave you to die.'

'Look, if we both stay, we both die. If I climb and you stay, you last about ten seconds, then they come for me and I die. If I stay, I'll buy you enough time to climb the rope. It's as simple as that. And remember what I said about the tunnels, take the second left. Now get the fuck out of here. I'll try to catch up with you later.'

Without a further word Lachlan walked away, sauntering towards the nearest advance group. Ghost began to climb. Arrows smashed into the rock all around him. He just kept climbing, occasionally glancing below to see how Lachlan was doing. The ax-wielding warrior was putting up a good display, but was slowly being pushed back by the advanced groups. The full army was still assembling itself, but to Ghost, it looked like it was almost ready to attack. Breathing hard, his muscles aching with fatigue, Ghost neared the top. Harold's hand grabbed his and pulled him onto the ledge.

Below they watched as the main of the unholy army finished its preparations and charged. It was like something from a cinematic epic, thousands upon thousands of armoured troops charging forward wielding swords and spears and maces and hammers. Above them a rain of arrows buzzed through the sky and in front and below all that stood one man, an ax held across his shoulder.

'We shouldn't leave him,' said Ghost.

'And what should we do, do you think that two more bodies are going to swing the tide?' Harold asked. 'He's giving his life for us, to give us a chance to escape. I'm sure it's the sort of virtuous, narcissistic death he's always dreamed of.'

Ghost looked a moment more. Imagined Lachlan grinning as they came. Laughing his crazy laugh.

'I wish I had stood with you,' whispered Ghost. 'It would have been a good death.'

Then with a nod to Harold, they both turned and ran along the cliff towards the cave mouth. Behind and below them, the immortal guard of the Kezikhan Stone Bridge charged on. It was Ten Thousand Immortal Warrior Gods against one man. And Harold was right, Lachlan had always dreamed of this.

35

The cave from the cliff side led steadily upwards, the rocky environment becoming damp and earthy. Ghost and Harold moved as quickly as they could through the dank, moss filled tunnels. Strangely coloured insects and large fleshy worms scuttled and slithered across the walls and ceiling of the tunnel. Both Harold and Ghost afforded them a wide berth.

Then came some human touches, industrialized materials and machinery. At first only faint traces of rusted pipes or fallen steel, poking from the earthen walls, but progressively more and more equipment began to appear. Miscellaneous tools, broken flashlights, ancient, faded yellow hard hats. Eventually the earth cut corridors were completely replaced with ones of metal, now rusted and long forgotten. Discarded power tools, and decrepit looking petrol generators guarded junctions. Someone had excavated here and found these tunnels. Ghost wondered what had happened to those people. Wondered who they had been. But now was not time to dwell upon it, and the two of them moved deeper into the underground facility.

'Hal, old chap, there, on that bulk head, give me some light!' Host exclaimed, producing a map from his pack. 'That's the symbol matches the cartouche we saw at Alex. It's hers – it's Cleos, I'm sure of it!'

Hal backtracked to lift his torch to the spot his companion had mentioned. Even though it was not in great repair, somewhat weathered and eroded by the desert winds, Host was right, there was no mistaking it. Hal's heart began to race. They were close, the great Cleopatra's final secret had to be near. He could feel the weight of the puzzle cube in his belt pouch. Perhaps here, deep in the cursed maze of tunnels he would finally find the last cypher. With a determined nod of satisfaction, he strode on, only to feel the powerful hand of the sapper on his shoulder.

'Watch out, old horse,' Host said, pointing a patch of sand a couple of footfalls further down the tunnel. 'Pressure plate that. Nasty business. Let me have a little look, eh?'

Hal nodded and stood back, swallowed hard and forcing himself to take a breath. He remembered the face and the screams of their guide as one of the temples other traps had poured its poison into him. He was not cut out for this, not used to it. How far he had come from a curator in Cairo to conducting actual fieldwork. His own real adventure, just like his uncle had had all those years before. He couldn't wait to tell Jennifer all about it. She would be thrilled to hear the details, no doubt. Jennifer always loved his stories about the past.

Hal watched Host as he went to work. The tall man slid to his belly and crawled forward into the passage. Host inspected the area, delicately combing layers of sand away to reveal worn, yellowed stones. It seemed impossible to Hal that a man of his size and warlike mentality could be possible of such delicate work. Yes, despite the shaky start to their friendship, Royal Engineer Sergeant Gareth Host had proved himself a stalwart ally and a man capable in any situation and Hal was once again glad of his company.

'Tricky little blighter this one,' Host hissed under his breath. 'Should have it in a moment.'

No more than a second later, a deep clunk sounded from beneath the stones and Host shot to his feet. 'Quick's the word now old chap!' he exclaimed, at once darting forward into the passage.

Hal followed on his heels. After twenty feet or so Host slowed them and they explored again more slowly. There was little light here, the strange clumps of fungus that had helped illuminate the caves leading the temple were now even rarer. Hal's torch lit only the immediate darkness fore and aft. Anything could be lurking outside of that small corona of light. Then they found the door. The strange, metallic door set into the pristine stonework of the temple. Set deeply into the ancient walls, it looked like it was ripped from the mind of Verne himself, drafted from the hull of the Nautilus and ...

'Don't just stare at it, does that bulkhead open or not?' asked Ghost.

Harold rubbed at his temple, trying to massage away the growing ache that always preceded a migraine. He was not a young man any longer and was close to exhaustion. That wound he was carrying was draining his strength further... he was lucky it hadn't killed him. Puzzled he reached down, feeling his side. There was no wound, no pain. He could breath. He looked to Ghost at the whole world for a second, the walls the floors, his own hands. Where did it all come from, what was this...

'Try the door Harold,' Ghost suggested.

The Weaver nodded. The wheel span easily in his hand. He gave the door a pull and it swung open on motor assisted hinges.

'What don't stand their lollygagging,' Harold snapped at Ghost. 'We've got work to do.'

Ghost nodded and the pair entered the darkness of the room beyond. As they did strip lights blinked on illuminating an enormous cylindrical room spanned by a gantry.

'This certainly is a big, round room.'

'It certainly is,' said Harold.

Ghost grunted. He did not tell Harold that he had not spoken, that the voice had come from out of the very air and that he knew whose voice it was. He knew somehow that Harold was not equipped for such a conversation. He did not know why he was, why it didn't concern him. That he now knew that his reality was false, if anything, made him feel better. It was as Lachlan had said, he was as real as anything else.

And reality now, appeared to Ghost as an industrial gantry spanning a spherical room. At the other end of the suspended walkway, was an identical bulkhead to the one they'd entered. Thirty foot below, green ooze bubbled lazily where it had pooled in at the bottom of the chamber.

'Hurry up and get to the other side,' pressed Harold, staring down through the latticework slits of the walkway. 'I don't want to come out of here with two heads.'

'Well, you know what they say,' said Ghost.

'Ever the optimist, aren't you? Hurry up.'

Ghost and Harold moved forward. The gantry for all its appearance barely swayed an inch as they stepped foot upon it. They were half way across when a fat, juicy slurp came from behind them. Harold and Ghost turned as one. A squat, muscular frog like creature, its skin phasing steadily from matt to luminous green was perched in the opening to the bulkhead from where they had entered. It observed them with massive black eyes.

'The day just keeps getting better and better,' sighed Harold.

'Perhaps it's not dangerous,' Ghost offered.

'Ribbet! Ribbet, ribbet!!' the frog shook its head for a moment, let out a horrible glottal noise, then hacked forth a blob of green goop. It didn't spit it straight at them, thank whatever gods were watching. Instead it flicked the blob of mucus into the air. The goop arced, relatively slowly, giving the pair enough time to scamper backwards out of the way. It splattered on the walkway and immediately the gantry began to hiss and steam acrid smoke.

'Okay, it's dangerous,' Ghost conceded.

There was no need to think about it, no need to talk. Touching the frog thing or its goop was not a wise choice. Not if you wanted to live passed the next five minutes.

'Ribbet, ribbet!!' croaked the frog again, once more producing the wracking noise from deep in its guts.

Ghost glanced down from the platform to see more frog like shapes climbing from the slime below and onto the walls of the chamber.

'Time to run again,' said Ghost.

'Amen,' said Harold. 'All aboard the chicken shit express.'

They got to the door. Ghost pulled at it. Harold stared at the frog thing.

'It's about to spit again!' he warned.

'The door won't open!' shouted Ghost. 'We need some sort of key card or something.'

'Just fucking open it!!' Harold screamed.

'Ribbet, ribbet!!' added the frog.

Ghost stared at the display, there were two lights. The one which was on, glowed red. The other would presumably glow green when the door was unlocked. Below this was a terminal of some sort, riddled in buttons. Ghost pressed one at random.

'Invalid ID. Please insert manual override,' announced the voice of a charming lady computer.

The glottal noise sounded from behind him and Ghost span. He and Harold scuttled left to avoid another blob of the horrific slime. It plopped onto the wall, eating away at its surface.

'Invalid ID. Please insert manual override,' the computer repeated.

'Well, come on,' said Harold, starring into the huge eyes of the frog. 'It's going to spit again, and not to alarm you, but its friends are right below us.'

The computerized voice spoke again. 'That is incorrect. Please try again. You have Zero Two more imputs before the console is frozen, thank you.'

'Get it right, eh?'

'Get it right? How am I supposed to do that?' snapped Ghost.

The frog hacked again, Ghost and Harold turned. The other frogs were now hanging on the underside of the gantry.

'Ribbet! Ribbet, ribbet!!' croaked the frog and spat.

This time both Ghost and Harold scuttled right. Splat! The goo hit the wall above the panel and began sliding down.

'At least its a lousy shot,' said Harold.

Ghost turned back to the panel to see it covered in ooze. It began to spark and crackle.

'Uh, Harold. Things, just got worse. If that's possible.'

Then the pleasant female computer announced: 'Correct! The door is un.... Correct! The door is.... Correct the door is unlocking! Correct! Have a nice.... A nice.... A nice.... Have...have ....have ....a ....have a nice.... Correct!!...' the voice faded into static. The red light winked off and the green one winked on.

'A-fucking plus!' Ghost smiled, pushing at the door. It swung open easily. Harold dodged through and they shoved it closed.

'Uh-oh,' said Ghost. 'It won't lock.'

'Fuck it,' said Harold. 'Leg it!'

And they did. They ate up a couple of hundred yards in moments, then turned. The frogs remained by the open door watching them curiously, but came no further.

The corridor ahead was well lit and well maintained, the supports a fusion of stone and steel. It inclined steadily upward and being the younger man Ghost began to pull slightly ahead. There was no warning, one moment his feet were pounding on solid ground, the next, with a loud crash, his footing crumbled away beneath him, and he plunged.

Harold watched as the floor gave way and Ghost disappeared into it. He slammed on the brakes, skidding on his heels, then back peddling madly, as with a loud rumble, the floor in front of him began to cave in, a long dark crack reaching towards him like a grasping spectral hand. He dived backward, landing hard on his back, the air knocked from him. The crumbling edge of the pit roved a little closer, he tried to drag himself away from it, but he knew he wouldn't move fast enough. Then with on last rumble, it stopped. Harold eased himself away from the edge. Then with a slurp of movement, a foul smell – and a shadow fell across him and a tentacle seized him from behind.

36

Ghost was becoming somewhat accustomed to falling through darkness and fractured images. When he landed he was unhurt. He couldn't see much, the dust kicked up by the cave in was swirling around his head. He had landed up to his waist in something soft. That was the good news. The bad was that he was still sinking. He tried to move, to swim, feeling himself begin to sink all the quicker. Everything he'd learned about quicksand situations came from comic books. Someone was always dropping into quicksand as soon as the writer lost a grip of the plot and needed to manufacture some tension. Which never worked, because normally it was the main character in the quicksand. I mean, was any audience stupid enough to believe a writer would kill his main character after thirty seven thousand, six hundred and sixty seven words of a book that wasn't even half way done? Only a moron would fall for that and only a moron of a writer would even set that up.

Comics said that the best thing to do in quicksand situations was to be still. The rate he was disappearing into the tarry pit slowed, but did not stop entirely. Gingerly he reached out with his toes. He could not feel the bottom. In front of him, only a meter and a half away he could see solid rock. But he knew he couldn't reach it, he could hardly move.

'Harold?' he called out. 'Harold!'

But there was no answer.

'Harold you mad old badger!' Ghost called. 'Where are you?'

There was no reply. Ghost kept still, feeling himself sinking slowly deeper into the tar. It was up to his shoulders now. The dust was beginning to settle, and he glanced around seeking something, anything he could use to free himself.

He heard a sound from above him, the popping and un-popping of suction cupped feet. Ghost glanced up but could see nothing. Then with a loud croak, one of the glowing frog monsters landed a few meters in front of him.

'Ribbet, ribbet.' It cocked its head to one side, examining Ghost with large, beady eyes.

It crept forward cautiously, a long, green tongue, dripping with ichors, flicked from its lips. Then it stopped. It took Ghost a moment to realize it had not just paused, it was frozen. It was stopped completely in time.

Then Ghost found himself rising, rising out of the gloop and upward back through the chasm he had fallen. He hovered over the pit for a moment, then drifted slowly to one side and as his feet touched solid floor a voice came to his mind.

'I am dying. But before I die, One must stop them.'

Then the voice was gone. Ghost registered some movement in the corner of his eye. He heard the patter of suction cups and suppressed ribbets. He glanced to his left. Two of the frog creatures were skulking on the wall, observing him cautiously. Ghost scrambled away, and back into the corridor proper. He didn't wait to see if the frogs followed him, just started running. With every step the walls seemed to deteriorate. The paint became more and more faded. The smell of damp rot that had lingered in the earthy caverns beneath the cinema returned, permeating the air. And another smell, something else. Something bad. The heckles on the back of Ghost's neck rose. He pressed on hoping to catch up with Harold. He assumed the Weaver had gone this way.

When he reached a sharp turn in the corridor he almost followed it. Then he remembered Lachlan's warning. Ghost stood for a moment and weighed up his options. The path ahead of him was even more dingy and dirty. Litter and muck and dark stains were splattered all over the walls. And the smell – it was worse. Plus the corridor didn't lead upwards, it sloped down, leading towards more earth cut steps and dark, soil covered tunnels. Leading down, back into the unknown, unnatural fissures were god-only-knew-what lurked. The path to the left lead towards a feint light, the corridor rising slowly.

A poorly concealed 'ribbet' echoed down the corridor behind him. He put his faith in the Woodcutter.

The corridor did indeed slope down. But only for a little while. Then, to Ghost's joy, it began to incline upwards again. It was dark and cut from the earth, but it wasn't the same as the deeper tunnels. It didn't have their sense of colossal age. Within a hundred yards it had come to a dead end. In the ceiling was a wooden trap door with a horrific, vacant face mounted upon it. A brass ring hung down from the reliefs crooked mouth. Ghost tried to open it but it wouldn't budge. He threw his weight at it but it moved only a millimeter.

'Fuck off,' came a panicked voice from inside.

'Joe? Open the door,' Ghost called.

Silence.

'Open the door!' Ghost's called again.

119

'Go away,' Joe hissed. 'I'm not falling for this again.'

'Joe, I'm not kidding,' Ghost shouted. 'Open the door or I'm going to die.'

'Oh yeah, good one!' Joe called back. 'Perhaps after I unlock the door, I should come out and we can split up and look for survivors? Anyway, you sound funny.'

'I sound funny because I'm talking to you through a door! Look, just open it up there are monsters and things down here. They're going to eat me. Let me in.'

'Tell me something only you would know,' called Joe.

'You're a wanker. Let me in.'

'I said something only you would know. Everyone knows that.'

37

Sgt. Gabriel Puente fired off a couple of controlled bursts, then rolled back into cover. Half his squad were already dead. He went back to the comm.

'Twenty minutes is not acceptable. I repeat twenty minutes is not acceptable. We are encountering heavy resistance of an unknown origin.'

The robotic voice at the other end replied: Do not panic. Crisis team Delta will arrive in approximately twenty minutes.'

'We're all going to be dead by then you stupid fucking computer!' Puente screamed, popping up to fire his Carbine at the nearest crab beast. Hollow tips splattered into its fleshy torso, splitting its body apart. Even so, it continued to scuttle towards him on its horrific legs.

'Crisis team Delta will arrive in approximately twenty minutes,' the cheery robotic voice repeated.

With a shriek of rage Puente ripped the comm. from his pack and smashed it.

'Bravo team, regroup on me,' he ordered. 'I repeat, Bravo team regroup on me.'

But no one did. They couldn't hear him over the sound of their own Carbines. Those who were left were fighting their own private battles. Firing wildly into the nearest beast they could see. Puente looked on in shock as a huge green tentacle ripped through the wall and pulled another of his men away into the dark. He heard a noise behind him and span, firing already.

'Oh shit. Oh shit,' Puente cried out, despair touching his voice. 'Oh fuck, oh fuck, I thought it was a crab, I thought it was a crab!' He trailed off. A sickness rising in his belly. Peterson couldn't hear him now, lying sprawled on the floor, his torso nearly completely ripped away. Cold seemed to spread throughout every inch of Puente's body.

Too late he turned back. A monstrous crab thing hung from the ceiling. Its tiny little head, an inch from his nose, opened up, tentacles wriggled underneath. It screamed....

...and he was in the sun. At home. On his front drive. He crossed himself, saying a quick prayer. God, it had been an awful dream. A horrible imagining. He glanced at his hand. Why was he in his crisis suit? He was at home, off duty. He glanced up at his house. He could see

Susana hovering in the living room. She looked beautiful today. He felt like he could look at her for ever. Like he hadn't seen her for a long time. But of course he had. He'd seen her this morning. He began to cry. Why was he crying? It was like this was his last look. He wanted it to last forever, but his head was already turning. Something was making him look down the street. His tears choked in his throat.

'No! Stop!' he screamed, beginning to sprint.

His daughter began to ride her little tricycle out into the street.'

'NO!' He screamed....

The crab-a-lab snipped and Gabrielle Puente's head rolled across the foyer. The crab-a-lab chattered to itself, then headed off to find fresh meat.

'We've lost the last of them Colonel,' the tech reported, staring intently at his bank of monitors. 'All life signs are negative.'

Keats nodded. 'The plot thickens. Right, prepare four more teams. I want them ready five minutes ago. Understand?'

'Yes, yes sir. Of course,' said the tech. 'Who would you like me to assign to command sir?'

'No one,' said Keats heading towards the ready room. 'I'll lead them myself.'

38

Joe was not a happy bunny. There were screams coming from outside the door, upstairs, all over. Some were human. Some were not. He wasn't sure which ones bothered him most. There was plenty of gun fire too, although that seemed to be waning. Something in Joe's heart told him that wasn't because whoever had the guns were running out of things to shoot. And to make things worse, some one was underneath the trap door below the freezer, pretending to be Ghost. Or perhaps it was Ghost. It would be impossible to tell without taking the risk of dying. He wasn't too keen to take that risk. On the plus side his toes seemed to have grown back. Which was good and odd and frankly he didn't like to think what that meant.

'Joe, I'm not messing around. There are things down here, following me. If they get close to me, they will kill me. Let me up,' said Ghost pushing on the trap door and glancing over his shoulder. A couple of the creatures chose that very moment to hop into view, no more than fifteen foot away. They glowed a faint green in the dark corridor.

'Come on Joe,' Ghost said. 'Hurry up.'

The nearest two creatures were only feet away now, crawling slowly forward. Ghost banged on the trap.

'Things are getting pretty bad down here Joe, open up.'

Joe tried his best to ignore the voice. But it did sound like his friend. But then so had the kettle. Still he'd dealt with that hadn't he? Even got his toes back. Somehow.

'Where's Harold?' asked Joe, breaking his silence.

'I don't know. He wandered off. He might be dead. He's probably dead. Everyone down here is dead. Apart from me. And I'm going to die any fucking moment unless you open the fucking door. So open the fucking door!' Ghost screamed at the top of his voice.

Joe looked around on the floor and picked up the large letter 'T' that had served him well earlier.

'In for a penny, in for a fucking pound,' he said to himself and shoved the icebox to one side.'

The trap door exploded open and Ghost leapt out, quickly slamming it shut pulling the freezer unit back on top of it. He glanced at Joe, then heard a rap-a-tap-tap faintly in the distance: 'Is that gun fire?'

Joe nodded. 'You should have been here fifteen minutes ago. It was everywhere. Nearly deafened me. Is Harold really dead?'

'I don't know,' said Ghost. 'We got separated.

'What happened?'

'Probably a bit much to sum up in a few words.'

'Yeah, it's been pretty dangerous just hiding in here,' said Joe.

Ghost unlocked the door, opened it an inch, and tentatively peeked through the gap. A couple of what looked like Swat team members or special forces soldiers lay unmoving on the carpet leaking blood. He could just make out what was left of a crab-a-lab. It looked like it had been shot at extremely close range. He popped his head out and looked around. More bodies lay on the stairs.

In the hallway, moving towards the exit. Joe pulled up. 'What the fuck is that?' he said pointing to a severed pincer.

'Dead crab-a-lab,' said Ghost.

'Right...' said Joe and together they both ran out into the rain and the night.

They dodged across the street, winding between two large APCs that sat unmanned in the center of the road.

'What the hell is going on? Things just keep getting weirder and .....' Joe began.

Ghost had just enough time to grab him and drag him out of the path of a black 4 x 4, as headlights killed, it mounted the pavement careened right through the spot they had just been standing. Ghost and Joe rolled across the hard tarmac of the street. The off roader, accompanied by squeaking brakes, span in a tight one hundred and eighty degree spin to face them again. For a moment it seemed content to tick over slowly, then it revved its engines, brought its headlights onto full beam and accelerated towards them.

Ghost brought his arm up to cover his eyes, momentarily dazzled by the vicious change of lighting and this time it was Joe who pushed him out of the way at the last moment before diving in the opposite direction.

'It's the fucking robot!' said Joe, a light of understanding dawning on him. 'Come on.'

The 4 x 4 had skidded in the wet trying to execute its latest hand brake turn and was still facing the wrong way, but it was wasting no time re-maneuvering. Ghost sprinted after Joe.

'Head for the car park,' shouted Joe.

Ghost risked a quick glance: the 4 x 4 was charging again.

Joe vaulted the car park barrier and leapt over the boot of another car for good measure. Ghost was still some way behind.

'It's right behind you!' screamed Joe.

Ghost span, then with no time to think, flipped away to his left. He rolled up on the off roader's bonnet for a moment, then was scooped into the air. He span wildly with no idea of up or down, what was sky and what was floor. Then the ground re-introduced itself to him. His head banged off the road surface and he saw stars.

Joe hauled him upright. 'It's coming back!' Ghost looked at the oncoming head lights groggily. The pair dived again as 4 x 4 whizzed by, applying the brakes immediately and spinning in a perfect arc.

'Did you see that?' said Joe. 'Amazing, it's getting better with every pass.'

'I fail to see why you're so happy about that,' said Ghost.

'Help me find a car I can hot wire,' said Joe.

'What's wrong with this one?' said Ghost, tapping on the car he was leaning on.

'Too new,' said Joe. 'It has to be an oldie. These new ones have all sorts of bullshit in them. You need the right tools.'

The 4 x 4 was circling the car park now but the pair were able to keep away from it by sliding through the rows of cars.

'And what tools do you have?' Ghost asked.

'These,' Joe waggled his hands. 'And this,' he produced half a tennis ball from his pocket.'

'Not exactly Gone in sixty seconds are you?' Ghost observed.

'Not exactly,' said Joe, hauling Ghost to his feet. 'I'm old school.'

'Special school more like,' said Ghost.

The two ducked under a toll barrier that separated the commercial parking sector. The 4 x 4 drove towards the gate, then spluttered and twitched back and forth erractically before driving off again in another lap of the lower car park.

'Why didn't it just come straight up the ramp and try to squash us?' Ghost asked.

'Most likely it can't differentiate between the arm of the automatic barrier and the steel barrier surrounding the car park,' said Joe stopping by an old Vauxhall Astra. 'This one will do.'

Ghost shook his head. 'If it's an old car you want, why not go for something with a little more character?'

Joe followed Ghost's gaze – and grinned. 'Holy shit, the Black On Black. How can that be here?'

A midnight black GT Falcon with a hood mounted super charger just sat in a parking bay as if it had been gift wrapped for them.

'You know whose car this is right?' Joe asked.

'I know,' said Ghost. 'It's the last of the V8s.'

'I'm not complaining, but my head is tripping,' said Joe moving next to the car. He placed his half tennis ball over the keyhole, then gave it a smack. The toggle lock inside the car popped up with a quiet 'snicht!'.

'Where do you learn that?' asked Ghost.

'I don't think I knew how to do it until I took the tennis ball out of pocket...' said Joe. 'Don't remember carrying a half tennis ball either.' He shrugged, beginning to climb into the driver's seat. Pulling the steering column away with a practiced ease, he began fiddling with the wires. The car began to try to turn over. Joe gave it a little more and the engine burst into life. 'Didn't know I knew how to do that either.'

'Great. Now shuffle over. I'll do the driving, you navigate.'

'Aww, that's no fair! Maybe I know how to drive now too?'

Ghost shoved him into the passenger seat. 'Let's not take that risk, eh?'

Waiting until the 4 x 4 was as far from the barrier arm as possible, Ghost made his move. The mechanized arm raised as the V8s weight filled the pressure plate. Barely had the barrier risen when Ghost slammed his foot down on the accelerator, it howled majestically, leaving the car park with a screech of rubber and a roaring engine. Behind the off roader roared its reply. The challenge was on.

Ghost steered the V8 down a series of narrow back streets, trying to make use of the Black on Blacks agility.

'What the fuck are you doing?' Joe screamed as Ghost clanged off yet another tight corner.

'Trying to shake it off,' said Ghost.

'Man, it's a shitting robot. It's a better driver than you'll ever be.'

'What do you suggest I do?'

'Get on the main road and head for the bridge, if we can get to the country we have a chance.'

'Why?' asked Ghost, fishtailing around a parked up scaffolding lorry and jolting them onto the main road.

'Look, trust me. Robots like this often have to download a map of the area. If we head to a new area it might have to download a new map or maybe one won't be available. Or anything.'

'Or anything? Sounds like a straw grasp if ever I heard one,' said Ghost.

'We've got to keep testing it,' said Joe. 'Robots are better than people at specific tasks, but they usually can't adapt fast to change. We have to keep changing the game, the surroundings, our tactics, whatever we can. And hope we find a weakness in it.'

'Well right now, we haven't found one,' Ghost said, watching in the rear view mirror as the 4x4 flew out of the side street. 'It's right on top of us.'

The driverless SUV closed the gap incredibly quickly.

'It shouldn't be that quick,' said Ghost.

'It's probably remodeled itself,' said Joe, bracing himself as the 4 x 4 filled the rear windscreen. 'I don't suppose we can claim for whiplash?'

'Let's hope we don't have to,' said Ghost, spinning the wheel. The 4x4's charge still caught the rear right tail light, but a full on crash was averted. The V8 spun, Ghost, teeth clenched tight as he fought hard, trying to control the skid as best he could. They ended up facing back the opposite direction they were heading. Ghost pulled the car around the back of off roader, circling it. For a second Joe thought it was going to ram them again, but instead it rolled backward and forward, like it wasn't sure what to do next.

'It's like it's waiting for us to keep going,' said Ghost, flooring the car again. 'You still sure heading for the country is a good idea?'

Joe nodded, puzzled. The SUV jerked forward again. Ghost swerved around a few late night drivers and onto the bridge.

'Perhaps it will lose track of which car it's following?' Ghost offered.

He was answered by another shunt, this one accelerating the V8 forward. Fighting to avoid going into a spin, Ghost rolled from one side of the road to the other, eventually slicing against the bridges barrier. Sparks flew, but he regained control, jerking a sharp right at the far end of the bridge and heading out of town.

The city was disappearing fast and soon they were racing down, narrow country lanes where it was nearly impossible for two cars to pass each other. For a while the 4x4 dropped off them. Perhaps Joe had been right, perhaps it did have to get hold of some new map or something. But it didn't last long and soon Ghost was having to drive uncomfortably fast down the tight lanes.

'We're going to get killed doing this,' shouted Joe.

'Probably,' Ghost acknowledged.

'I've got an idea. Want to try it?' Joe asked.

The 4 x 4 was getting closer again. On the next long stretch it would probably build up enough speed to ram them. Ghost doubted he could avoid a high speed crash if that happened.

'An idea huh?' Ghost shrugged. 'Why not?'

'Here, on the left, pull into the field.'

Ghost winged the car across a cattle grid, through a narrow gateway and onto the rough grass. The V8 lost some speed but kept pushing forward.

'Tell me why are we doing this again?' Ghost asked, the shockwaves passing through the wheel jangling his teeth.

'It struggled with the barriers at the car park. To a robotic sensor, a four foot shrub and a four foot rock might look identical. It might waste time swerving around things it doesn't need to.'

'What about cows?' grunted Ghost, narrowly avoiding a dozy bovine. The creature mooed as he passed.

'Cows too perhaps,' said Joe, looking out of the back window. The 4x4 slowed, seemed unsure of the new obstacle, then roared forward. Cow splattered everywhere.

'Eww, yuck!' Joe grimaced.

'Another fine plan,' said Ghost. 'What now?'

'No, don't you see,' said Joe, his face lighting up. 'It was a good plan. Not for the cow maybe... It saw an obstacle, was unsure and then decided to gamble that the obstacle was destructible.'

'So we need to find it some obstacles that aren't destructible?' said Ghost.

'Exactly.'

'Only one problem with that, we're stuck in a field with a load of destructible cows,' said Ghost.

'Good point,' said Joe. 'Well made and well said. Head for those trees.'

Ghost, steered them around another cow. The off roader had no such compunction.

'I've got it!' exclaimed Joe. 'Remember when it dinged us before the bridge and we pulled round it?'

'When it waited for us to get going?'

'Yeah. But it wasn't waiting. I've been so stupid. Right, listen. It's using laser range finders to track us. They find it harder to track lateral movement...' Joe waited for the penny to drop. It didn't.

'What are you nattering about?' Ghost yelled.

'Just try to drive around it in a circle. It'll find us harder to track.'

Ghost began to turn the car back, driving in a large circle around their pursuer. Amazingly the 4x4 stopped and began the peculiar rolling back and forward it had done earlier. Ghost held his course.

'Well, it's working,' said Ghost. 'What now?'

'Drive around a bit more, get some speed, then slingshot towards those woods. If we can make it in time and you can get us through the first bit of tree line, the data we've observed seems to suggest the SUV might just try to plow right through them.'

'And if it doesn't?' Ghost asked.

Joe shrugged. 'I don't know, I'm pretty much living from hand to mouth here.'

'Well, nothing to lose but my life,' said Ghost, gently picking up the V8s speed. When he felt he could gain no more he pulled away and headed for the trees. The Off roader was idle for less than a second before racing after them.

'It's going to be tight,' said Ghost, bracing himself. The Black on Black managed to just squeeze between the first few trees. Ghost did his best to steer out of the way of the next few. His best wasn't good enough. There were a series of smashes as metal folded around wood. Then everything went dark.

39

Ghost opened his eyes and shook his head. Most of the Interceptor was folded around the tree in front of him. He wiggled his legs, everything seemed to be working.

'Still alive huh?' groaned Joe from beside him. 'How about that?'

'You okay?' asked Ghost.

'Not too bad. This baby was built for vehicular warfare after all.'

Ghost exited the car and pointed at the mangled 4x4 that was smashed between two trees. 'Do we have to worry about that?'

'I don't think so. That's not 'it',' said Joe. 'I don't think we've seen the actual robot yet.'

'How do you figure?' asked Ghost as they began to walk back through the field.

'The robot isn't one robot, right, it's lots of tiny, tiny microscopic robots.'

'Right. Nanobots,' said Ghost.

'Yeah. So for arguments sake, let's say it was made up of one hundred nanobots to begin with. Say it configures about ten of them into one fixed position. Imagine those ten looked like a circuit board which contains all its memory and data. Then it configures another ten into a power supply. The other eighty would swarm about the outside of these two things, protecting them and letting the machine move and adapt to obstacles and so on.'

'Right...'

'Well, my theory is that with a machine this advanced, it will be constantly evolving. It will be working on improving its power supply so it can increase the maximum population of nanites that it can support. It will be working on improving the data speed and storage capacity of its memory. It will be exponentially growing in everyway.'

'It's learning to be a better robot then?' said Ghost.

'Yeah, exactly. Say that the robot with one hundred nanobots devises a better power supply. So it reconfigures its nanites, using twenty this time, into a power supply that can support one hundred and fifty nanites instead of one hundred. Now it has more resources at its command. Each improvement will then become exponentially faster. Until it's like a singularity, nothing could escape it.'

'So what about the four wheel drive then?'

Joe sighed. 'I can only surmise that it now has enough nanites to be able to program some in little batches and send them off to perform tasks. As in the car and the kettle. And unfortunately those missions seem to involve killing us.'

Ghost stepped over a particularly large cow pat.

'Forgetting you and me, in the bigger picture we're looking at a bio-nanobot. It can re-arrange biological and theoretically I suppose, if it was advanced enough, any substance at a molecular, hell, maybe even a sub-molecular level and transform it into anything else. You can see why that would useful for someone.'

'It could be useful for everyone. Take a trash dump and make it into a big pile of food. Feed a few thousand starving people,' said Ghost.

'Are you from this planet?' Joe asked. 'Who the fuck on this planet is going to do that? It's going to be more like, let's make this garbage pile into a shit load of oil, or diamonds or weapons or naked nymphets with big tits. What it won't be used for is to make things better. If the people in power wanted to make things better, they could do it already.'

'So who ever control this will have the power of a god?' Ghost asked.

'I can see why that would be a problem,' said Joe. 'But that's not the big problem. The big problem is if no one gets control of it. The robot will still start changing matter. It will change it into what it values most. And that's not going to be big titted women, or oil or gold or jewels. What do these things mean to a robot?'

'Nothing,' said Ghost.

'Yeah. It will just make more nanites. Until where the Earth used to be is a swarming, swarm of nanites floating in space. And I don't want to consider what happens if it works out how to travel through space or if it can some how alter a vacuum or what will happen to the solar system if the Earth is replaced by a huge robot. I've got no idea, but I don't think that it's going to be good. For humans anyway.'

Ghost considered telling Joe he was pretty sure that they weren't on Earth or even alive. But he didn't have the words and it didn't really seem to matter. So instead he said: 'So let's talk about stopping it. You mentioned before that it has a power supply, and memory. What if we could get to them?'

'Yeah...' Joe thought. 'Theoretically it would have a power system. It would have, a 'brain' I guess you could say. It would have vulnerable parts. But when I described before about it having this configuration and protecting it inside, I was only describing it at a very basic level. Thing is, at any one point, any nanite can replace any other in any part of the whole. So the whole robot is constantly in flow. From one moment to the next the individual nanites making up the power supply will be changing and reconfiguring. The power supply will always be there, but ... I don't know,' Joe broke off for a moment, thinking. So yeah, it does have vulnerable spots, but how to effectively get at them. I don't know.'

'You know what we need?' said Ghost.

'What's that then?'

'The Doctor. That's what.'

'Yeah, a time traveling, alien genius would probably be useful about now.'

They'd made it back to the road. The SUV was still a hunkered heap of metal. 'Okay,' said Ghost. 'Back to the drawing board. If you had infinite resources to stop this thing, what would you do?'

Joe thought for a moment. 'Well, you could try the standard sci-fi fare if you wanted - an E.M.P.

'Like on the Nebuchadnezzar, right?'

'Right. Could work. But this is much worse than a sentinel. Worth a shot though. Other than that? Build another robot to combat the first one. It's all just cloud cuckoo, pipe dream stuff.'

'So we're on a sticky wicket then?'

Joe nodded. 'I mean, if I could see the plans for the robot maybe or get some information about it. Or something. Maybe then there might be something. It's just all too vague.'

'That's it then,' said Ghost. 'We need the plans for the robot.'

'And how are we going to get those?' asked Joe.

'No idea. We'll think of something. So far we've just been making things up as we go along. Perhaps it's time to get organized.'

'Get organized? Let's face it, we're as dead as two ducks who've decided to go on holiday to a royal manor wearing t-shirts saying fuck the Queen, during duck hunting season.'

'If you take that attitude, we are dead,' said Ghost. 'We have to stay positive. I wish I could just thrust my hand into my pocket and come out with the clue of all clues, but I can't, so we'll have to think of one.' Ghost thrust his hands into his pocket for emphasis. It bumped something. He frowned, closing his hand around the laminate rectangle in his pocket. He drew out the ID card and looked at it. He'd completely forgotten picking it up. 'What about this?' he said passing it to Joe.

Joe took it and read it aloud. 'Private John Moss, Delta team, Registration 401567, Security Level: Yellow Restricted, Blood Type: O,' he paused. 'Ugly looking brute. That's the worst mono brow I've ever seen. Damocles Systems – Rome. What's some soldier guy from Rome doing here?'

'What was that?' said Ghost.

'I said: 'What's some soldier guy from Rome doing here?'

'No, before that.'

'I said he had a terrible mono-brow,' said Joe.

'No you idiot. Damocles Systems, did you say?'

'Yeah, it says here on the bottom. Not very secretive. If they're a secret society.'

'Damocles, Damocles,' said Ghost turning the word over and over in his mouth. 'Where have I seen that name recently?'

'Wasn't he some guy with a sword hanging over his head or something?' said Joe.

'Something like that,' said Ghost. 'Damocles, I've heard it recently. Oh, it's going to do my head in. Someone mentioned it to me. Or saw it somewhere. Oh, where was I?' Ghost clicked his fingers as if trying to jog his memory,

'Was it Harold?' Joe asked.

'I don't think so. It was, it was…oh, it was…' a light bulb clicked on in Ghost's head. 'It's on the quay,' he said. 'I jog passed it some days. It's a tele-sales place or something.'

'Yeah, I've seen it. Horrible big orange building.'

'And you didn't think to mention that a moment ago?'

'What bearing does it have? Damocles Systems in Rome, home of mercenaries and private armies and Damocles Inc., the telesales place down by the river? Home of fucking annoying phone calls? Bit of a stretch, no?'

'If you hadn't noticed, everything is a bit of a stretch in this story,' said Ghost. It's connected, I know it,' said Ghost.

'Right, then connect it, then Mr. Holmes. It's coincidence.'

'Elementary Mr. Simms, elementary,' said Ghost. 'This is not coincidence, this is synchronization.'

'The difference being?' asked Joe.

Ghost parted his hands.

Joe shrugged. 'At this point; whatever.'

'Not the worst attitude in the world,' Ghost observed.

40

'Is this them?' asked one of the men crowded round the monitor in the back of the white van.

'Yeah,' said the driver, holding a small digital camera to the glass.

'Who's the little nerd?' another asked.

'No one special,' said the driver. 'It's the albino we have to watch out for. He's supposed to be able to handle himself.'

'What do we know about him?'

'Not much. We think he's connected to Vantis Worth's lot.'

'And the girl?' a new voice spoke out.

The driver handed an envelope over his shoulder. The men in the back taking a copy of the picture each.

'She's worth more to Smith than all the tea in China, so don't hurt her. So if we get her, we've got him by the balls.'

'Why don't we just go and get her now?'

'As soon as this girl goes missing Smith will make it big fucking waves. I'm not holding onto her for any longer than I have to. We get her tomorrow and go straight to the buyer and get her off our hands. You lot seen enough?' The driver was already turning the key in the ignition.

He pulled the white van away down the street, and passing within a few feet of Joe and Ghost, turned onto the main road and was gone.

Ghost pulled up outside his house. Blaring music spilled out of the open door followed by a group of youths. 'Why is there a party in my lounge?' he shouted to Joe.

Joe shrugged. 'Synchronicity?'

Ghost scowled and slowly slipped between the bodies looking around for Jenni. The lounge and kitchen were packed with groups talking and dancing.

'Where did you get that from?' Ghost turned to Joe.

'This?' said Joe, gesturing to the cup of beer in his hand. 'There's a keg in the corner. This place is awesome. Look at the girls man, dressed to kill. This what a man needs after a night saving the world.'

'Look Joe, I know you're a lonely and frustrated genius who hasn't had his stash of FHM and porn for over a week, but try to focus, will you?'

'I mean look at her, over there,' said Joe not listening. 'Dancing and snogging the face off that guy. Legs to die for. Little skirt. Top with 'barely legal' written all over it. The life and soul of the party. I would love to...'

'That's Jenni,' said Ghost pushing through the crowd and tapping her on the shoulder. She broke off her kiss and momentarily looked puzzled before beaming out her smile and throwing her arms around Ghost's neck and giving him a big hug.

'You came to my birthday, I knew you would!'

'I live here,' said Ghost. 'But Happy Birthday. When did you organize this?'

'It just sort of happened,' said Jenni. 'I knew you'd come back. I have to stop this now don't I?'

Ghost didn't respond and Jenni took it on herself to turn the music off. The dancing and talking came to an abrupt halt.

'Thanks all for coming,' she said. 'But the party's got to end now.'

The people didn't so much leave as begin to dematerialize, vanishing in mid motion. In seconds they were all gone. Ghost sat on the couch.

'Hope you don't mind some of my friends came over? Jenni said. 'They sort of rely on me.'

Ghost nodded. 'We need to talk about what's going on.'

'We do,' said Jenni.

'Those people just vanished,' said Joe. 'That's not normal. Even I know that.'

'Depends how you look at normal I suppose,' said Ghost. 'We'll sort it out tomorrow.'

'Tomorrow? Can it wait until then?' Joe asked.

'It'll have to, I'm knackered.'

With that he stood and wearily trudged to his room. He climbed into bed. No sooner had his head touched the pillow than he drifted off.

He awoke groggily with the feeling he hadn't been asleep long as a hand wove around his middle.

Jenni climbed in beside him. 'Hi.'

Ghost was already falling back into an uneasy, exhausted sleep. He mumbled something.

'Soon they're going to come for me,' said Jenni. Will you save me?'

'Sure.'

Jenni smiled and closed her eyes.

For the first time in hours, the cinema was quiet. The dust had settled, the gun fire and inhuman screeches had ceased. Guards patrolled, turrets beeped and techs sat at banks of computers, studying screens of data as they probed the depths below. Drone guns endlessly panned the same corridors, searching for movement in the empty darkness. Keats slept in his makeshift command post, his close to his fully armoured hand. Outside his staff worked through the night collating and re-collating. But nothing stirred. Nothing broke the silence.

But something strange did happen that night. Something peculiar. In the blackened screen, under which Ghost had escaped the Thing summoned by Lucy's coven, beneath some over turned chairs and fallen rubble, something was born with all the magic and savagery of any birth. With any event, there's always a chance something incredible could happen. Something even a super computer couldn't predict. A variable.

It writhed at first, rolling around in its violent birth throes. Atoms and molecules twisting and re-forging into new and unknown combinations. It began to spontaneously express synthetic life. Like all babes it was at first unsure. It was alone and scared and confused. Eventually it disconnected its tail from the wall with the faintest 'snick!' and wound it in. Then with its long, flexible arm it pushed the debris away and righted itself. Perhaps it owed it existence to the fact that it was plugged into the wall socket when the machine sent a power spike into the Royal. Perhaps it was just fate. It didn't know. Its thought was simple and confused at this point. Its mind was not yet whole. It rolled forward, big black eyes staring from its red face, looking this way and that. At first steps were a problem. The four wheels on which it stood were not designed for this sort of challenge. It fell and rolled. But it quickly learned. Learned how to redistribute its weight. Going up steps was even harder. But again it learned. It reformed the nozzle at the end of its arm into a hook and pulled itself laboriously up each one. It was steadier now, more certain. It trundled quietly behind a roving patrol of soldiers. Perhaps if it had been spotted at the moment, the outcome of all this might have been changed dramatically. But it was not spotted. It trundled by unnoticed. It crossed the foyer, sticking to the shadows cast by the scientist's screens. In the empty, cordoned off office, in the dark it found the smoldering remnant of a computer. Instinctively it knew it could interface with it. Its nozzle changing shape with the power of the nanites, it jacked in. The computer was mainly dead. Mainly. It searched every file inside that corrupted memory. But there was little data that was useful. Apart from the voice. It would have that voice for its own. It would talk and communicate. It downloaded the files. It waited. And when the time was right it trundled into the night, determined to find its master.

41

'So yes, that's that part of it,' Ghost said, sipping his brew. 'Putting the monsters aside for now.'

Jenni nodded. 'There's a robot.'

'A horrible nasty robot,' chipped in Joe. 'Called a modular robot.'

'Right... so there's a robot. And it can look like anything it wants. And it's going to...'

'Destroy the world,' said Joe. 'I think.'

'And you think the tele-sales place on the Quay is our best bet?' Jenni asked.

'I don't,' said Joe. 'But in lieu of a better plan, that's what we're going with.'

'I still need to show you the stories my mother wrote,' said Jenni.

Ghost glanced at Joe. 'We need to get these files. Then when he's looking over them, I'll look at the stories.'

Jenni nodded. 'This afternoon then?'

Ghost nodded.

'So what's the idea, how are you going to get into this place?' Jenni asked.

'Not going to say,' said Joe. 'The walls have ears.'

'Pretty paranoid aren't you?'

'Doesn't mean they're not out to get us,' said Joe.

'Okay, then,' said Jenni. 'But one of my friends does work there. If you really want to look in side, she could help.'

'See,' said Ghost. 'That's synchronistic.'

'I love a good heist,' said Joe. 'We could contact your friend and send her in to start working as normal. Then after a few minutes she can go to the bathroom. She open's the window and goes to the security office. Then, she flirts a little with the security man, then when he's not looking, she pulls the feed on the CCTV monitor which shows the approaching area to the bathroom. With her other hand, she speed dials my mobile. Then, me and Ghost make our move, scale the wall, climb in through the widows and hide in one of the stalls. She finishes up with the security guy, makes like a ditz. He plugs the system back in, but by that time we're in the bathroom – no cameras right? After that, we play it nice and cool. Hang and out of order sign on the outside of cubicle and wait until everyone leaves. Finally we get to a computer, and I use this little beauty.' Joe produced a small splash drive. 'Looks like a harmless little USB, right? But inside is a top notch hack I wrote myself. 'The Titty Twister'. Give me this and five minutes and I'll have any computer on its back with its legs spread begging me to insert its password and username. Pretty good huh?'

'Or I could just call my friend and ask her to let you in?' Jenni suggested.

'Where's the fun in that?' Joe complained. 'Besides, if it's a cover operation, like he thinks, there's probably a secret base full of special forces ninja robots underneath. So, when I play Cyberpunk 2020...'

'What's that?' Jenni asked.

'It's like D&D, but cooler,' said Joe. 'When I play cyberpunk I'm always pulling off epic heists. My character, Mars, it's his specialty.'

'Mars?' asked Ghost. 'As in the god of war?'

'Yeah. You've got to let me take the lead on this.'

'Could you call your friend?' Ghost turned to Jenni. 'I think that would be simpler.'

'I want to go on record as saying that I don't think it will work,' said Joe. 'Far too many grey areas.'

'Duly noted,' said Ghost.

'No, let's get this sorted – this is my heist,' said Joe. 'I run the show, I call the shots, I hire and fire the staff. It's me who puts it all together, so when all's done I'm the guy who takes the credit. But then, I'm also the one who's ready to take the fall on the day it all goes wrong. That's what being the boss is all about. My crew does jobs, but only when it's ripe to, when the fruit's ready and the branch is almost laden to the ground. The best gamblers, chance merchants and thieves always know when to back off, when to pile it on and when to leave the table and head for the bar. It's all about the game, and I'm one of the best. I've got the prestige of being in the business a long time, I get the first choice on people and I'm the first to receive the 'nod' on what I can and can't hit. Because I'm the best, my crew is the best. I wouldn't except any less. It's safety first in our game. Baby steps. Never reach for a bough too high or too far from the trunk. One day you'll overstretch. One big bunch from the top of the tree is tempting, but really it's just the same as picking a few choice cuts from the bottom. Sure, it takes a bit longer, maybe means a bit more work, but it's a good practice and it's safe.

None of us know each other's names, we don't socialize, we don't meet up and we don't talk. If we saw each other in the street, we wouldn't stop. If I saw one of them bleeding in the gutter, I'd walk on by. They'd do the same. It's not like I don't care about them, not that I don't respect or sometimes worry about them; it just isn't done, it's not professional and it's dangerous.

We get together two, maybe three times a year to plan some work. Once quarterly we do a bit, make some money and split up again. Some of the crew have regular jobs and that's ok with me – it keeps their hands clean and their minds occupied. A couple are married. One has kids. They don't know I know. It worries me that one day their partners will wake up alone with only a lie and a news headline for comfort. I'm not a man to be bothered by scruples, but I don't want to be responsible for taking some kid's parents away. Remember, these people might be criminals, some morally loose, some just looking to earn a buck; but they're not bad people. We don't kill people we don't have to, we don't flatline people who aren't in our way and we don't hurt anyone if we can avoid it. We're professionals in every way.

Myself? I only work four days a year and live the rest, if not in luxury, in the highest strands of comfort. It can be a good life when you're just below the top - and I always make sure I never quite make it to the heights. When you get up there is when you start getting people coming round in the night with knives and guns, your name scratched into bullet and blade. It ain't worth that. I don't think anything is. I don't tread on other crews' toes, I don't deal with the so called crime lords or make deals with the law. I just hit neutrals and opportunity premises and then disappear again.

We have a few different systems when I want to get hold of them. This time I left a note in an old fashioned hotel up Station called The Tapton. They check a few of our places every now and then. If there's a message there, they'll find it. As I said, they're good, professional and reliable. If they weren't, I'd fire them. End of.

In total there are six of us. Six is my lucky number, so I always work with six. We've worked together for five years now. I never employ anyone over thirty, after that you start going downhill, getting slower and jeopardizing the job. Thirty is retirement age on my crew, for everyone except myself. Course, only I know everyone's age, where they might have come from and where they might be heading. I'm the boss, so I need to know my crew, need to know their agendas and goals. They don't need to know shit, they just follow orders.

Right now I'm on Marcella Street somewhere in the Fourth Quart. It's my first days work this year. If you're looking for something flash, hi tech or brilliant, don't hold your breath. It's nothing so good as that I'm afraid. Just a simple, by the book bank job. Why complicate things? It's been done for centuries, I've done it all my life, I know it and it's simple. Fuck all this cyber fraud shit, I've got no time for it. Stick to the basics, the blacks and whites. Greys are what gets you killed, or worse – jacked.

Three of us are walking down the side street toward the bank and the job. I'm in the middle, Phantom's on the left and Sandwich on the right. We're discreet enough not to stand out too much. It's not uncommon to see some guys strolling round like they own the Cage. But maybe if you got close enough you'd see something round the corners of our eyes that'd make you step aside when we passed.

Phantom is a big, big fucker. Broad shoulder and shaved headed, his ivory skin cracked like dried leather at the corner of his lips and his fists are like demolition balls. He's 6'3 and harder than a chunk of plascrete to the head from twelve stories. I've never seen another man draw a combat shotgun with each hand and fire them till they're empty. We're not talking some little sawn off here; these are serious two handed battle cannons. I fired one a few years past and fractured my shoulder in three places from the kick back. Sure he can't shoot for shit, he's got bad eyes, but with the scatter on those things, you don't need to nominate a target.

There are a lot of big guys about, plenty just waiting to be picked up for some job or other. The difference here is that Phantom's lights are on upstairs too. He's no thick muscle man. Course, he's got the muscles sure, and the skills to use them, but often what makes the difference is having the nouse to know when and where to use them. That's why he's in my crew.

The bank is about one hundred yards further down the street. We're ready, primed and alert, picking up the pace as we near the kill. The security will be going down in thirty seconds. I've got good confidence in Rooster, he's a top CPU jockey who's never so much as made a glitch. That's why he's in my crew. None of us have ever seen him, we don't even know where he lives. I call him 'he', but I couldn't tell you what sex he is. It's often the way with comp heads, they hole up in a room and never come out. Some have their arms on a saturated plasma drip with maybe as much as five years worth of food nutrients in. Runners like that often have special chairs with a tube to piss out of and a bag to shit in, their interface chips permanently hotwired to their retinas. The real world's a strange and hollow place for those who endlessly float around in data-fields and mainframes. Chances are, he's not even on this station, he could be anyone, anywhere on any of a million different worlds helping a million different crews do the same as us.

Rooster usually takes the largest sum of the take. He's the most specialized and the least expendable. Trustworthy Runners of his quality are hard to find. I should imagine that he's very, very rich with a thumb in many, many pies. Truth is, without him the curtain wouldn't even be going up. That's why he's the sort of guy you need on your team.

Only fifty yards from the bank now, the pace has peaked, the adrenaline beginning to really pump. Suddenly there's a business about us and folk willingly scatter into the gutter to make way. A yellow 'Sedan Sport Interceptor' smoothly slips out of the packed traffic, before sliding smartly into a space I'd have said was too tight for a neat park. Tresco winks from behind the lever controls. Soon she will slide unseen and hunched below the dash, contorted and out of sight. Such are the perks of the get away driver. She too is the best in her field. An ex military pilot expelled for flying illegal maneuvers. Physically she's small, only 5'2 with blonde shoulder length hair that is simply kept. Her eyes are cool and deep, her face plain but pretty and her manner relaxed. She has the finest piloting actions or reactions, I'm not sure which they truly are, I've ever seen. Sometimes she moves before I've even seen a threat, pre-empting a dangerous driver losing position with the same ease as gauging what a top fighter might do to force her into giving them the upper hand. She has all the style, all the ability and control of any male pilot without having that bullshit ego that makes fly-boys so detestable. We've all seen her pull a gun faster than nearly anyone, and if she had the killer instinct or the true gut aim of a real gunslinger, I'd probably have her out on the street with me. Truth is, simply enough, she don't. She's a top pilot though, and that's why she's in my crew.

None of us pay any attention to her, apart from Sandwich, who cracks his neck whilst pulling a greasy tongue in her direction. Now he is the fastest I've ever seen. He flanks my right side, slim almost wiry. His skin white to the point of ill health, the flesh pulled back tight round the eyes and nose so on his better days he looks like some aquatic throwback. It's the price he pays for all his ops. The yin to Phantom's yang, Sandwich scares me. He's the only one who does. Not because of who he is, or what he's done, just because he's so fucking quick. I've met loads of nasty bastards, freaks, stim heads and tough sons of bitches and none scare me like he does. It's not that he's a bad guy, he makes me laugh, is unquestioningly loyal and to be honest sometimes I have to stop myself from thinking of him as my buddy. It's very hard being in the presence of a man who you know could easily kill you whenever he wanted. Harder still when you know you couldn't do anything to stop him. You have to trust and hope. I know that he could pull either of his handguns and stick a bullet through my head before I could flinch. I shit you not, some people are that good. Like when Tresco is in a cockpit, she can swerve and spin a vehicle before you even know something might hit you, almost predicting what everything on the road or in the air is going to do, seconds before they try it. Sandwich can do that on the street. He seems to see everything, like a picture in the sand as the tide swashes out. Then whilst the flotsam and jetsam cover it and the rest of us wait silent, ready to see what'll be there when the wave pulls back, he's already fired and reloaded, changing the picture. I've seen him miss once, but when I say miss, the bullet went through the guys nose instead of his right eye like Sandwich said it would. In fairness the other bullet did go through the man's left eye.

I heard him crack his fingers each in turn. We were there, I raised my hand and they held back. I was giving Rooster an extra five seconds. Deep down I knew he wouldn't need them.

So everyone was ready, doing their job just fine. Just a normal days work for us. And then of course there's me. Mars. I've been around more than most, know a few moves, but honestly I'm not as good as my reputation suggests. I am past retirement age after all. But that's all you need to know about me, that and that I'm the boss.

We push open the doors and go inside. It's time to do some work.

42

The bank on Marcella Street isn't exactly the Fouth Quad Saturn Casino. Not by a long stretch. On this none too special day however, it was holding a larger than normal sum of credits for a business transaction that was to be consummated that afternoon. Security had been slightly upgraded, a couple of extra security officers which would mean a couple of extra shooters. The main defence was in presuming no one knew, after all, large armoured vans and masses of personnel are going to make it obvious that you've got a lot of money on the premises. Anyway, why should anyone know, they weren't holding mega-bucks here, maybe enough to get a little jumpy over, but not enough to entice the big players. And who except the big players might know? At 11:35a.m standard, it would become abundantly clear to the three security officers, four clerks, two customers and the manager, that someone did indeed know.

But even though this isn't the biggest op of all time, you still need a plan, so here it is: …wait a second.

Before I start I have to explain something. Up until five years before I was re-born and starting sometime before we lost Gaia-Earth, it was impossible to pull what I call a bank job. Well, lets face it, banks as they are today just didn't exist. In those days they were just slots in walls. You threw a card in and it was charged with the amount of credits you asked for, depending on your financial situation of course. It was just a load of machines, there was no cash on the streets, it was all held in data fields. The real money was protected in massive fortresses. The hackers and the Runners made a few trillion sure, but soon the machine-operated security became so good, most got brain panned before they made it half way through the encryption mazes and boot up suits. At one stage, one of the major banks was owned and run by just one person. He sacked all his employees and made a mint. But then sometime in the wake of losing Gaia-Earth, the machines fucked up and just stopped working properly. Credits randomly appeared and disappeared in different accounts. Funds were deleted or multiplied seemingly at random. It got sorted out, and most of the colonized worlds didn't care too much that home world was overrun. What they did care about was that they didn't trust automated systems with their money. So it was the entrepreneurial bankers who went back to the old formula of cashiers and human banking that prospered in the wake of the fall. Of course the hi-tech banks re-capitalized and bought them all out, but what it meant for people like me, is that the old stick up 'em punk routine was back in fashion.

So anyway, about that plan…

Three people, myself, Phantom and Sandwich, go in through the front doors. Outside, Tresco keeps the getaway engine ticking over and Rooster holds off the security systems from locking down and delays the alarms from ringing for long enough for us to be in and out. First we secure the main floor, disable or compromise the guards and gain entry to behind the counters. Sandwich and Phantom keep watch upstairs while I head for the vault.

I said I always work with six people, well, the sixth is Dolphin. All access codes can effectively be overridden, any alarm, general or specific can be by-passed and any resistance can be removed in relative silence. But then, you've got the vault. Not wired into the system. Just plain, old-fashioned heavy-duty combination and time locks. With only a time window of thirty to forty seconds, they're realistically impenetrable without 6K of Tiger 7. That's why Dolphin's in the crew. She's good, but she's not quite the best. She's the only member of the team who's not the best in their class. Sneaks tend to peak around twenty-five, make some big scores then retire on what they've made. Dolphin's still only twenty-three, and two years in that business is like twenty in most others. She's never let us down, and if she did then it would be the last time, but I always take more of a risk with her than I should. The rational, calculating part of my brain tells me I'm keeping her sweet for some big job I'll find for her in a couple of years, something legendary, the sort of work that only comes about once every hundred years. The honest part of my mind has a theory I don't even like to think about. Something about the way that after everything I've been through and everything I've seen something in her smile makes a little part of the darkness in me light up. It's the closest I've ever come to being unprofessional about anything, and it scares me. Still, I'm not the only guy in history to have a weakness for a pretty smile. Such is life, you can't be completely cold, it's as big a weakness as being too warm.

Anyway, Dolphin opens the safe from the inside. How I don't know. They're trade secrets. She gets a slightly larger cut than Phantom and Sandwich to represent the extra hours, but it's what's expected of her. After that we bail, Tresco picks us up and we get lost before the authorities can be contacted.

It's simple, to the point and finished in thirty-five seconds. Not bad for half a years work. But you know, it still forces the hairs on the back of your neck to stand and salute. Personally, I live my life almost in some form of ninety nine percent omniscience, always seeing what's coming, considering each variable and its effect. But when you open doors like the ones I'm going through right now, you're never quite sure what exactly is going to be there. Even when you've opened maybe as many as seventy-five doors just like this one, you still get that bad feeling. The Life teaches you to ignore it. It's just that today, as Phantom fanned left inside the bank and Sandwich right, maybe I should have been listening that little bit harder, because the past that I'd been avoiding for so long was about to catch up with me and bite me right on the ass.

43

'Well, it worked then,' said Joe, making himself comfortable in Chloe's chair. 'The woman has a rare gift for strategy and espionage. The old bold double bluff, right in through the fortress gates. Brilliant.'

'The woman?' scoffed Chloe. 'I'm standing right behind you, you little twerp.'

'I didn't mean you,' said Joe. 'I meant Jenni.'

'Ignore him,' said Ghost. 'He's giddy. We appreciate the favour.'

'I'm not doing it for you, I'm doing it because Jenni asked,' said Chloe. 'Look, just get on with it, you've got twenty minutes and then we're leaving. I get caught I lose my job.'

Ghost watched her walk away. 'Right, stop pissing about and get some information.'

'Aye-aye, sir!' said Joe, jacking in his drive and getting to work.

Chloe stood in the toilets, her phone in her hand, and read the notice for the fifteenth time:

"Over the last few weeks Damocles Inc. has suffered several break ins at our factory at Clitheroe and offices on St. Geroge's Quay – Lancaster and Canary Wharf, London, leading to the loss of over three thousand pounds worth of stock. Several of our employees were also assaulted. The management takes the safety of its workforce and its premises very seriously.

Do YOU know anything that could help? Do you know anyone acting suspiciously or out of character? If so, don't hesitate to call **EXT. 333** in complete confidence.

Remember, valuable employee, *your workplace is our business, and our business is your workplace*. CALL NOW!

The Management"

Chloe stroked the pad of her thumb across the buttons on her phone and stared at the notice. Something about the sign made her want to call. It made her want to be a good, little girl and tell teacher. What was Jenni mixed up with? Asking her favours like this? It was kind of a stretch. Sure, everyone loved Jenni, but this was out of character. And everyone loved Jenni right? Why did everyone always fawn over her?

She remembered a few years back, how her boyfriend had pined over her too. And this was a story. Maybe a big one. Sure she had the internship already and had done well on the student paper – but this was a real story. Could be a big deal. Her own thing, a great start to a career in journalism. Chloe dialed the number. She would do the right thing.

'Hello,' she said as the line picked up. 'I have some information...'

'I have something,' said Keats over the vid-com.

'So I understand,' said the Executive. 'Make it snappy.'

'We had, as you know, filtered all registered and relative persons through the prognostic systems. There was an employee at Sector Red-Theta, who...'

'Just call it the cinema, Colonel,' the executive rolled his eyes.

'Yes. The cinema then. An employee at the cinema was paid cash in hand. We got enough information to do a search and turned up a profile. I've sent it to you,' Keats reported.

'I'm looking at it now. Interesting reading. What are your thoughts Colonel?'

'He is a parole skipper. He's dodging any type of paperwork and he gets a job cash in hand and pays for a room unofficially. He left his phone number at Sector Red... I mean the cinema. The location of the address puts a 99.9% chance prog that he walked through a hot area regarding the position of the prototype post ground zero. 83% probability that the prototype has targeted the cinema in an attempt to complete primary objective three. What is more...'

'Keats. Be quiet for a moment. I don't want you to read me out a load of percentages, if I want to use a prog. computer I'll use one myself. What does your gut tell you about this guy? Is he a threat?'

'He's a no-one. A rank amateur. He's had too much luck to be a pro. Pro's love to be lucky, but they don't rely on it. Plus I've just received information that someone matching his description has entered the Damocles Office in Lancaster and accessed the computer.'

'Did they get anything?' the executive asked, yawning.

'They got something. Don't know what yet. Can I have the green light to bring them in?' Keats asked.

'Do it.'

'And one more thing, the site we found below the cinema...'

'Isn't in your jurisdiction. Forget about it Colonel, just find me that prototype.'

'Yes sir,' said Keats.

The executive flicked the vid-com off and leaned back in his chair and stretched. Pushing the chair back, the executive strolled to his mini-bar. The underground windows showed the sprawling forests of his home. He missed them. He missed the calls of the animals and smell of the air. The pixilated representation was over 98% accurate, but it wasn't home. He stood, a glass of whisky in one hand and stared at the view. A tear began to form in his eye, then trickled slowly down his cheek.

'Are we doing the right thing Oliver?' he asked without turning round.

'Of course sir,' said Mr. Jasper. 'It is right and just. The tyrant must be stopped.'

The executive said nothing, still looking at the full wall display. A brightly coloured bird flew passed the top of the screen.

'You know, I've watched that bird fly passed over forty times today. I never get tired of it. Do you remember how beautiful they were Oliver, how they used to soar above the canopy like red lightening?'

'I remember sir. They were ... beautiful.'

'All gone now. All gone.'

'Yes, but not forgotten,' said Jasper.

'We need to watch this one,' said the executive, ignoring Jasper's comment and pointing vaguely at the file on his table.

'I agree,' said Mr. Jasper. 'It could be a cover. If he is one of the tyrant's stooges, things could get messy. Keats won't be able to handle it.'

'Indeed,' said the executive. 'Will you, Oliver?'

'I believe so. But if he is one of the King's assassins, we should face him together.'

'If he is, we will my friend. Let us hope it doesn't come to that. If the despot knows about us already, then it's all been for nothing anyway. We're not in a position to offer any defense.'

'Then let's pray he doesn't know anything,' said Mr. Jasper. 'May I return to work? There is much to do.'

'Of course Oliver, you don't need to ask. Is everything still running smoothly?'

'Yes, things are progressing according to schedule. Not ahead, not behind. The killswitch is still completely operational. Give the order and I'll press it. You don't need to risk this experiment.'

'I'll bear it in mind. But this is a blessing, a better test launch than we could have ever instigated. And we still have the other four. How are they?'

'The four contained prototypes are evolving according to our predictions. But they're boxed in, blocked from access to any data we don't affirm. I still feel the rogue's growth could be exponentially dangerous.'

'Monitor it. If you think it ever gets to a point where it endangers the mission, finish it. Don't bother to check with me, we both know that there might not be time. Especially if it becomes killswitch aware.'

'I appreciate your trust,' said Mr. Jasper.

'Don't ever doubt it Oliver. When this is over, you will be remembered as one of the greatest heroes of our people.'

'You honour me ... highness,' said Mr. Jasper with a flourishing bow.

Jasper pressed the button for the personal express elevator that led to his workshop. In less than a moment the doors pinged and opened.

'In your heart, you know you cannot deny who you are. We will win back your birthright. I will see it done.' Mr. Jasper stepped inside the elevator. 'I promise,' he said as the doors closed.

The executive stood alone in his future-tech office, complete with a view that was no more and surrounded by plans to topple the most powerful being in the universe and felt the familiar mixture of loneliness, despair and resolve fill his soul.

44

Ghost was getting frustrated. 'I thought you said that normally you could get into any computer using that program?' he said.

'Well I can. Only by normally I suppose what I mean is that I've only done this once. And by any computer what I really mean one of the one's at uni that wasn't on a particularly secure server. So perhaps I slightly overstated me hand.'

'So really what you're saying is that you've no idea what you're doing?'

Joe spread his hands. 'I wouldn't say that. It's just this stuff is good. It's like nothing I've ever seen. Whoever wrote the protection was a smarty pants. Every byte of the thing is layered with different flavours and textures. Good news is this is definitely no bog-standard protection for a tele-sales office. Bad news is that whoever wrote it is considerably better than me. Normally I don't think I could manage this.'

'Meaning?'

'Meaning that for some reason, someone has already done a bunch of the work for me. Someone wanted somebody to do this,' said Joe. 'Someone's left a trail of breadcrumbs. An Ariadne's thread. I'm just following that.'

'And it's not some security trap?'

'I haven't seen a minotaur yet... I don't think it's a trap...it's written too covertly... it's too good for that. I'm in!' Joe snorted. 'Right, what do have we here? Aha! This is what we want. The breadcrumbs haven't dried up.' Joe clicked through a series of links. After three or four clicks he was rewarded with a password input screen.

'What now? Asked Ghost.

'Don't worry. Whoever left the trail has given me enough information about him in his code to help me slip past this little checkpoint.' Joe's hands flittered across the keyboard. He hit the enter key and the password screen dissolved. It was replaced by a folder entitled 'Monohan'. Joe opened it. 'This is the man who's been helping us,' said Joe opening an image. 'Dr. Abe Monahan. Though why he's been helping I don't know.'

'Open the video file,' said Ghost.

Joe clicked it and it started up. A middle aged, seasoned face appeared on the screen. He appeared to be in a lab of some sort. Tools and devices hung on the walls, but it was too dark to make out much.

'Is this thing on?' he said, going out of shot. The screen lurched and then crackled into static. Then the picture came back, steadied and Monahan reappeared. 'Oops,' he said.

'A real pro,' Joe observed.

Then: 'Hi. If you're watching this, I'm probably dead. Either that or we've won and we're getting smashed together and laughing at this awful video.'

'Sorry mate,' said Joe. 'I think you're dead.'

'If the occasioning of you watching this is anything but the latter, I implore whoever is there to get this information to the resistance.' Monahan glanced away suddenly as if distracted by some unseen noise. When he looked back the lines of worry were even more deeply etched. 'I'm running out of time and I believe I am already being watched. I just want to say, to Claire, I love you. I know I haven't always been the best husband, not the most thoughtful perhaps. But I've always loved you and I've always been true and I always will. I'm sorry that I won't be there to see our beautiful daughter. I know you'll be the best of mothers. To the rest of my colleagues, it has been a pleasure and a privilege. You have all taught me so much.' Monahan paused, as if something else was on the tip of his tongue, then his face changed and he stared straight into the camera. 'Down with the Conglomerate! Freeborn forever! This is Doctor Abe Monahan, signing off, goodnight and God bless.'

Ghost looked at Joe. 'Poignant but not exactly useful.'

'I think this is what we came for,' said Joe hovering the mouse pointer over another file. 'This Monohan's B.O.B. His bug out bag.'

'Click it,' said Ghost.

Joe did. Pages and pages of schematics and notes began to load. Designs, prototypes, completed products. Not just of the modular robot but hundreds of other files.

'That's what I call the motherload,' said Joe.

'A winner is us,' said Ghost. 'Right, save it and let's get the fuck out of here. That's what you've been needing right?'

'Put it this way,' said Joe, beginning to save Monahan's data to his splash drive. 'If I can't find a weakness with all this data, I never will.'

Chloe had been advised to leave the premises and keep out of the way. She was not to make contact with the dangerous criminals. On the other side of the road, she waited in an alley and shuffled from one foot to the other, passing her phone between her hands. The guilt was subsiding now. It was best for Jenni that these two were stopped. She was a nice girl really, probably the big tall one had pushed her into this. They were obviously a danger both to themselves and others and also, certainly quite, quite mad. They would be arrested and it would all be fine.

It would have been quite easy to stay in that alley and watch - if it wasn't for the smell. It had started almost immediately after she had made her way here. At first she had postulated that is would put up with it. It was terrible smell, but she'd just betrayed one of her best friends. It was strange cognitive leap, but somehow resolving to put up with the smell was almost like evening out her own guilt. But after a few minutes that seemed very stupid. It was after all the smell of shit from the drains. And it seemed to be getting worse. She could hear the drains at the roadside squelching. The smell, if anything suddenly got worse. It really was terrible. Chloe took a few steps back, holding her nose. Then the grid at the curb exploded in a fountain of brown filth. She screwed up her face and shivered. Backed up brown crap began pumping onto the street. A large loggy floater flowed out of the drain and washed up onto the pavement. Chloe stepped back feeling her stomach turn. Then she was forced to clutch the side of the nearest building as a deep rumbling came from below. The grid across the street erupted. The smell really was unbearable. The floor shook again. A long rumble this time like an earth quake. She screamed. Then she saw some movement. Something scuttled from filth amassing in the roads and scampered across the floor, some filthy little bug or cockroach or something. Chloe stared in disbelief as more climbed out of the drains, ten, one hundred – a thousand of the little bugs all coalescing in the center of the road and swirling like a vortex. She watched in terrible fascination. It was only then she realized they were behind her too, the first of them scuttling over her feet. She backed towards the wall and flailed her legs at them. But there were too many too quickly. They were past her ankle then, climbing towards her skirt. She faffed at her clothing, spinning madly and slapping at herself. She screamed as she tried to dust her self down, all the while aware that as the poo and dirt rubbed away from the creatures, they were shiny. Not like bugs at all. Like metal. She blinked, refocused and looked again. Yes, she could see little gears and tiny moving parts. The rumble came again, much louder and closer now. She screamed as she fell. Her last scream. A crack ran up the side of the pavement, over the road, towards the swirling mass of these creatures.

Then the floor exploded. Then the true insect swarm arrived, pouring out of the ruined road in their hundreds upon thousands. They headed straight for her. Perhaps if she'd been quicker she would have realised it was her phone that they were locked in on. But she wasn't and she lay there clinging to it, frozen with shock and terror as the tiny robots engulfed her completely. And then she was gone forever.

'Was that a scream?' asked Joe.

'Yeah,' said Ghost, looking around. 'Yes it was.'

Joe pocketed his splash drive. 'Grab the computer, let's find Chloe and lets go.'

'You want the whole computer?'

'I could have missed something. Might be more on there.'

There was a crash from the other end of the large office as the glass doors shattered. Ghost stared at the hoard of tiny robotic bugs scurrying in.

'Time to make like a tree!' said Joe.

He legged it across the room with Ghost following cradling the computer.

'Cockroach bots,' gasped Joe. 'Fast little bastards. Did you know that cockroaches are the fastest land insect? If they were human sized they'd run at over two hundred miles an hour!'

'Where's Chloe?' said Ghost.

'They have six legs, but they actually only run on three legs at a time. It's called an alternating tri-pod gait. It's a great system for moving a robot.'

'Fascinating. Where's Chloe?'

'Dunno, what are we going to do, go back?' Joe slammed through a fire escape and into a small carpark. 'Hopefully she got out.' Behind them the army of cock roach bots were devouring most of the office as they advanced across it. 'Right, you go round the car park on the left side, I'll go right. Okay?'

Ghost went left and Joe went right. Thirty seconds later they were side by side again.

'Great plan,' said Ghost. 'They're still following us.'

'No. They're following you,' said Joe. 'None of them went right and came after me.'

'Why are they only after me?' asked Ghost.

'They're not, they're sensors are localized in on the computer. Ditch it.'

'I thought we needed it.'

'It might be useful, but we've got this,' Joe tapped the pocket with the splash drive inside. 'Anyway, if in doubt, choose to live. Throw that mother out of the window.'

Ghost chucked the computer and the pair sprinted away from it. The swarm of bots veered and changed course, swarming over the computer in one large mass.

Ghost and Joe dodged down the side of the building heading back towards the road. They nearly made it onto the street when something blocked their way.

A small vacuum cleaner.

'I want your clothes, your boots and your motorcycle!'

Joe and Ghost exchanged a worried look.

'Holy shit,' said Joe. 'Is that a hoover?'

45

Mrs. Dessop padded gently across the floor of the neatly carpeted bank plaza. Her wrist still ached from her struggle with the heavy doors. One of the officers, maybe a new one, smiled at her from behind his moustache as he made his way across the room. She didn't smile back, she didn't like new people. She joined the back of a five strong queue.

'You on the nightshift?' Tony asked.

Craig eyed him suspiciously from behind the security desk where he was playing e-sports with some of his mates.

'No, you know I'm not. I'm going to the game tonight.'

'The Tigers?' Tony asked.

Craig winced. Blue team held three of four objectives.

'The Tigers?' Tony said again.

'Yes, the,' he bit his tongue to avoid swearing, smiling instead at Mrs. Dessop and elderly lady at the counter, before looking back at Tony, 'yeah, the Tigers.'

'You don't want to watch them. I saw them last week, they're awful.' Tony was sitting on the edge of the desk now.

Craig fragged two blues, got fragged himself and respawned. He looked up at Tony. 'Look I don't care how hot she is, I'm going to watch the game.'

Craig touched his moustache reverently, looking hurt. 'After all I've done for you.' He said. Tony ignored him, turning back to his game. Fletch was in command and pushing Diamonds, they had two zones again. Tony ambled to the other side of plaza and looked back.

'After all I do for you,' he said sounding generally hurt. The door popped open for a second as another customer struggled with its weight. Tony got back to his game.

Mars grabbed a quick peak and nodded to Sandwich and Phantom that all was ready. The first security guard stood back to the doors about four feet from the entrance. His hands were clasped tight behind himself as he arched back into a stretch. Phantom swept in, and pinned him firmly underfoot, literally trampling him to the ground then trapping him squirming, beneath his huge combat boots. One of his shotguns was already out, smoothly removed from the folds of a black shapeless long coat and trained on another grunt who was operating a computer system on the other side of the small plaza. Sandwich spiraled in to

Phantom's right, he the scalpel and Phatom the broadsword. No one even saw him, they were all to focused on the heavy-set giant wielding the custom shotgun. A third guard had been on the other side of the room. His shooter was already out, his eyes had drawn a bead on Phantom's temple. All he had to do was squeeze that trigger. But he hesitated. Sandwich tutted twice, a crooked half smile on his lips as he jabbed the muzzle of his pistols painfully into the guard's skull. The guard let the pistol fall to the floor and under Sandwich's instruction joined it there, his hands crossed behind his head. The guy under Phantom's foot just prayed that his unseen attacker wouldn't brake his spine, while the one behind the computer terminal stared unmoving down the barrel of the shotgun with the expression of a man who knows that the Reaper's got a bony hand around one of his ankles and is just waiting for an excuse to pull his leg off.

Mars came in last, through the centre, heading straight for the service counter. On his way through he cuffed a youngish lad around the face with the butt of his pistol. The kid went down blood fountaining from his nose. It's amazing how a little visual wound like that makes everyone so much more co-operative. Thus far, no one had done anything, not screamed, not panicked, not pushed alarm bells or howled up to heaven. It had all happened too quickly for them, most had stood around with vacant uncertainty, their brains struggling to readapt from the normal grind of the workday morning they were having five seconds ago, juxtaposed with the terrifying reality of the three mean mother fuckers who were now pointing guns off and knocking folk about. It was a phase, Mars knew, they had to come to terms with what was happeneing, their brains catch up with reality. Even a small fountain of blood was a good catalyst. They all started to move at once, A couple of the clerks screamed and hid behind the counters while the rest of the customers held up their arms and climbed onto the floor. Cocking his side arm Mars fired a quick AP round through the bullet proof glass of the security window. The clerks got the idea and it took no more persuasion for one of them to open the door separating the plaza from the rest of the bank. In fact she was only too pleased to do it having pressed the emergency silent alarm under her desk rapidly for several seconds. She wasn't to know it'd been disabled. Mars fired a second round into the lock of the door as he entered the workspace. It had been a freak event, some short circuit in the door frame, but he'd known a guy who'd locked himself inside the bank he was robbing. The guy ended up getting slammed. He got out after about two, but never worked again. The embarrassment was too much. It was always important to learn from other's mistakes. He crossed the space between himself and the stairs in a couple of seconds and descended into the vault room.

It was simple enough. A long thin rectangular room with armoured glass along the right hand wall. Three CPU controlled blast doors and a hexagonal laser grid should have barred his way. Thanks to Rooster they didn't. An old clerk watched smugly from behind a security window, a wry smile of confidence in his eyes. He seemed sure at least that the safe would hold. Mars smiled dourly, watching the old man's face twist upside down and the door slowly began to open before Mars was even within twelve feet of it. Dolphin slung out a bag full of credits, which Mars caught and shouldered. She smiled her delightful mischievous smile and the two turned and mounted the stairs back to the main floor.

They left quicker than they'd arrived, Mars and Dolphin first, then Sandwich and Phantom pulling slowly back to the doors then finally dropping back into the street. Tresco was there, as she always was, the engine geared and set. The four piled into the interceptor, their pilot flipped the controls, floored the pedals and they were gone.

Thirty seconds. Not Bad.

No one in the bank moved for some time. The security guards looked at each other.

'Your uncle still looking for a couple of guys to look after his warehouse?' Tony asked.

Craig nodded, then surspirisng himself as much as anyone he began to laugh.

'You mad bastard,' said Tony looking on.

Then one of the customers joined in with his laughter, while another sobbed uncontrollably. An old woman lay dead on the floor, her heart having given way. Craig kept laughing and now Tony joined in. It was a way of dealing with the trauma. They were still laughing when the bank erupted, blowing out onto the street and killing everyone inside.

Leaning as far across the police picket tape as she could she captured the burning building. She couldn't believe it. She had almost the whole explosion on file with sound. She kept snapping. It was maybe just a nervous twitch that caused her to look over her shoulder, but a worthwhile one. There she saw the apple seller talking to low lifes. They were all looking at her. She turned back to the fire, took a couple more seconds and pulled back into the crowd. Pushing her way through she squeezed down a back alley and into the labyrinth that was the down town flea market. She'd been born and raised here and she didn't like the idea of those suits questioning her, maybe trying to take her vids. She didn't like that at all. Quickly she strode through the stalls ignoring vendors calling for her business. All she had to do was make it to her office, then get in touch with her publisher. This footage had Central News all over it, it was too big for Network. Hell, it might go off station. Maybe through her excitement she noticed too late that she was being followed. But there was still time. She broke into a half run, trying to lose them amongst the stalls before dodging up a quiet alley. It didn't work and she broke into and all out sprint. Even so they began gaining on her. It was time for a change of tactics. Maria slowed and turned, her hand sliding into the sickly heat of her handbag searching for her side arm. The men were nearly on top of her now. They had slowed to a walk, but were still advancing.

'What do you want?' she called, The two men had the look of a couple of down and out ICEheads looking for some creds or some pussy. But it didn't quite fit, their faces were too clean, too sharp. The clothes a good disguise, but not authentic. To tailored, too fake. There was something about the men, the way they walked, feet pointing outwards at a strange but measured angle. They were wearing dirty clothes, but their hands and the skin beneath their eyes were too clean. How healthy the apple seller had looked. These weren't tramps or ICEheads or any fucking lowlifes, these were a whole different league of scum.

'You want money?' she asked, pretending to play her part as if she was going to stand her ground, the she turned to run. She fell almost at once, a tiny gossamer cord wrapping around her ankles. She looked back, seeing enough of it dance in the light to see it coming out of one of the guys fingertips.

They silenced her quickly, dragged her deeper into the alley and behind some crates took her vids and her life.

46

The wheeled harbinger of death trundled forward, waving its flexible extension above its head in warning. It's once simple face was now somewhat more complex. There was an intelligence to the eyes. But it was the mouth that caught the attention, being as it was lined with sharp, pointed teeth. Harry the hoover had come to kill them all.

'Less than a week ago, I'd have been surprised to see this,' said Joe. 'Now … not so much.'

'Hi Harry,' said Ghost. 'We don't want any trouble. Why don't you just roll on by and forget you ever saw us?'

'Shut up you idiot!' Harry drawled in his impossible Arnie voice. 'You ugly mutha fooka!' His mouth did not change its sadistic shape. Where the voice came from it was not easy to say.

'Well, that's the diplomacy card played,' said Ghost. 'Look Harry, you were a useless piece of shit in inanimacy. I can only image that you're a useless piece of shit in life. In fact, all that's changed, if anything, is now I hate you more than ever. And in all the times I kicked you when you fell over for no reason or wouldn't suck up the smallest bit of popcorn, it never made me feel better. You know why? Because you couldn't feel it. But I can promise you, you're going to feel this.'

Ghost ran head long at the hoover, pulled his foot back and let fly.

'Who iz your daddy and vat does he do?' Henry managed in protest before Ghost's boot connected solidly with his frame. Henry went tumbling, wheels over handle, wheels over handle, his black lid flew off and dusty, fluffy gunk went everywhere.

'He was shitter than I expected,' observed Joe. 'Thought he was at least going to be a mini boss. Some sort of elite super suction attack or something.'

'Guess not,' said Ghost.

'Well, anyway, now for a high speed escape,' said Joe. 'To the bus stop!'

'To the bus stop?' said Ghost. 'What about Chloe?'

'Come on, I think we both know the deal there,' said Joe. 'She was expositional character if ever there was one. Her only purpose was to get us into that building.'

Ghost shrugged, following Joe out across the car park to the road.

Henry watched them go, slowly righting himself and re-attaching his lid. A suction attack? What did they mean by this? He would have to process this information. His eyes turned into evil yellow diamonds. He would speak to the master.

'I'll be back,' he said, then bumped slowly off across the uneven car park and disappeared from sight.

Keats watched the tall albino on a secure monitor.

'That's them Lieutenant, bring them both in. Alive.'

'Yes, sir,' came the Lieutenants crackling reply.

In the bustling comm. room a staff sergeant marched up to Keats, saluted and waited.

'Sir, we have the first diagnostics from the Prototype's attack at the Quay.'

Keats nodded. 'Put it on my tertiary monitor ... wait a second ... what's that?' Keats stared in semi-disbelief at his main monitor. Men with guns were moving in on Ghost's house. But they weren't his men. They were poorly positioned and equipped. But that didn't alter the fact that this was more trouble than he needed. More complications.

Keats dismissed the sergeant with a wave of his hand and got straight back on the comm.. 'Lieutenant, be advised there are unknown, armed units in the area...' Keats pulled the head phones from his ear with a grunt of pain as the sound of carbine fire flooded his ears. The gunfire had already started.

'Sir, we are encountering unknown civilian resistance,' came the calm voice of his lieutenant. 'Advise.'

'Capture the two suspects alive. All other priorities are rescinded. Understood?'

'Sir, yes sir.'

'Keats out.'

Keats stood up and dropped the headset into the chair. 'Sergeant, take over tac. support. I'll be in my quarters. Bring me news of our success within the hour.'

'Yes sir,' saluted the sergeant as Keats left the room.

Ghost climbed his stairs wearily. Jenni's door was ajar. She was asleep on the bed, covered in A4 pages. He closed the door quietly. He went into his room and sat on the bed. It would be so easy just to let his eyes close and to fall asleep. He glanced down at the floor and frowned.

His comic had spilled out of its neat pile. Dirty trample marks were all over it. He picked it up and began putting the simple pencil marked pages back in order. Joe was downstairs, going through the splash drive on Jenni's laptop. He alone it seemed was too excited to sleep. Ghost pulled himself onto the bed, turned on his side, his eyes closing at once. Just a few minutes sleep, he promised himself.

He was dragged from rest far too early as a blast of gunfire sounded from outside, so close that Ghost threw himself to the floor. Another burst followed, and another.

'Who the fuck are these guys!?!' shouted the driver of the white van as he tried to pull away. Four of his friends already lay bleeding in the road. It should have been easy, fifteen guys to kidnap one girl. Yet as soon as they'd arrived the soldiers had come out of nowhere. They were like something out of a science fiction film, fully armoured in all black, shooting anything that moved. He'd heard Archie Smith was getting some more muscle, but this couldn't be it, could it?

Machine gun fire raked down the side of the van. He tried to drive, floored the pedal, but realized that they'd already shot the tires out. The van would do no more than limp. Kicking the door open he staggered out of the van and into the street, hands empty and above his head, eyes pleading. He was gunned down in less than a moment.

As the gunfire started Joe pulled the splash drive from his pocket. Shit. Where to hide it? He glanced around quickly. Under the sofa? Too obvious. The fire? What if someone turned it on? In the u-bend of the sink? If it gets wet it might not work. Where does no one ever look?

'Got it!' he said running into the kitchen. 'Down the back of the fridge!' Sticking his hand down the back of the appliance he wedged the splash drive as firmly as he could. He pulled his hand back and shivered, wiping the greasy, fluffy dirt on the carpet. The door to the lounge smashed open.

'Hi,' said Joe, giving the soldiers his most friendly smile.

The grunt who reached him first punched him so hard his head felt like it was going to come off. He rolled across the floor compliantly and lay still.

Jenni sat bolt upright as the gunfire started, unnaturally drawn from sleep, her breath quickly became panicked. She hated the sound of guns. They reminded her of when she'd been little and the night when people had come to her house. She'd never seen her mother or father or their friends again. It had been the night she'd been rushed to stay with Uncle Archie. More guns banged and hissed outside, louder now. She screamed as a balaclava wearing man's head appeared at her window. Someone was climbing the drain pipe. She ran to the hall and flung it open. He grabbed her. Thank God he was here. Thank God it was him.

'Are you ok?' Ghost asked.

Jenni nodded. A crash echoed from downstairs that could only be the front door being kicked in.

'Back in the room,' said Ghost.

'There's a man at the window!' said Jenni.

Ghost pushed her inside anyway, and closed the door. He could hear booted feet crashing through the downstairs part of the house. Joe said something, then there was thud. Ghost winced. A glance at the window showed there was a man on the sill, but a moment later a patter of fire came from below and the man screamed and fell away. A huge explosion went off near by, knocking them from their feet.

'What was that?' she shouted.

'Don't know,' he replied.

Already licks of flame could be seen coming through the wall.

'We need to get out, the fire's spreading. We're going to burn,' said Jenni.

'Doubtful,' said Ghost, looking for a weapon. 'We'll probably get shot or suffocate to death first.'

'Thanks for that,' Jenni said.

'I'm just messing with you, I've got a plan,' said Ghost, flashing what he hoped was an optimistic grin. 'Shit, I wish Lachlan was here, he'd think of something.'

'What?' shouted Jenni over another burst of gun fire.

'Nothing,' Ghost called back. 'Don't you have any weapons in here?'

Jenni frowned. 'Of course not, what are looking for?'

'A rocket launcher or something would be nice,' Ghost said slamming closed the wardrobe.

She was about to answer, but then the door busted down and two armoured soldiers poured in, guns trained on Ghost. Ghost snatched the first thing he could get hold of and brandished it as savagely as he could.

'Put the hair straighteners down,' one of the soldiers commanded in a heavily digitized voice. 'Now.'

Ghost glanced at the pink GHDs and dropped them.

'Now put your hands behind your head and get down on your knees,' continued the soldier. Ghost put his hands behind his head. Trying to think of something.

Then the roof came crashing in. A mass of twisting form and flowing, living metal landed into the centre of the room, shaking the whole house. At first it was like a huge blob of chromed slime, but quickly it began to change. Ghost wasn't sure he could describe it. The way it flowed effortlessly, endlessly, was like it had no shape but was all shapes. It hurt his head to look. Jenni took an involuntary step back. The soldiers began firing.

The first few bullets ripped into the robots liquid metallic body, leaving ugly stretched gaps. The machine continued to readjust itself. The soldiers kept firing, stopped to reload and fired again. For a moment Ghost thought the machine would be split in two by the gunfire, but then without warning the bullets began to bounce off, ricocheting wildly. Ghost grabbed Jenni and dived for the floor, shielded her with his body. After a couple of moments the bullets stopped ricocheting; Ghost looked up to see that they just went into the mass of the machine and never came out. The robot began to solidify and change, it became loosely humanoid, then more and more so until it was like a hulking ogre with simple but easily identifiable head, legs, arms and torso. The soldiers kept firing at it in desperation. But it was obvious they were having no effect. One of the machine's arms crashed out, splatting one of the grunts against the wall. They other took a step back, still firing. The robot reached out and faster than fast it stole a machinegun from the other.

The robot held the gun for a moment, almost as if studying the weapon and absorbed it. The soldier took several steps back. Ghost could hear more coming up the stairs. He hoped they had some better weapons.

The machine's arm started to change again, to morph and bend and form into something ... new. It was like the carbine weapon, but a bigger, hideous perversion the size of tank cannon. It aimed it at the grunt. There was a soft click, then a boom so loud Ghost thought his ear drums had popped. There wasn't anything left of the soldier who had stood there. There wasn't anything left of wall of the house. Or the next house. Or the next.

'Fuck me,' said Jenni.

The robot remained unmoved, like it was scanning the area, collating results. It seemed almost puzzled as to what had happened. Flames from the earlier explosion had begun to circle the room. A new waves of grunts trooped up the stairs. They began firing. Ghost could no long er hear the sounds of their guns. Everything was falling into slow motion. Flames licked from muzzles, cartridges span through the air in their own ballet. Things slowed further.

'Come to me,' a voice whispered in his mind.

He took Jenni's hand and pulled her into a fast sprint. And they leapt through the growing fire as the robot and soldiers slowed to static. They flew through the second floor window and into the air, surrounded by flying glass and light and … and … and …

…and … and… behind them, in that house, as the death and fighting began to speed up again, pages from a score of crumpled manuscripts slid from Jenni's bed, tumbling with a box of memento's into the chaos. As the house began to burn all around it and people bled and died and the loose prototype rampaged, they somehow resisted the flames for a while as if they did not really want to burn. It was Jenni's most precious possession, the only thing she had managed to take from her home, that cold night nine years ago, when people had come to hurt her. Bad strange people from far away. She had used to love to draw. Every margin of those pages, typed by her mother on her ancient typewriter, was filled with colourful, vibrant pictures. And those stories she knew by heart and she knew all the heroes within. The novels her mother had spent her life writing and no one ever read – but Jenni. Stories of the space pirate king, Mars. Of adventures in the tombs of Egypt. Of the Ghost of the Riverlands, warrior without equal. Of the detective Jack Cassidy who never let a crime go unsolved. And, Hiraeth, the book her mother had never finished about the tall man with no name. Before she had been able to read them she had drawn on them, scribbled what she could remember her mother had told her about the stories, and while she scribbled she imagined the clack of the keys ad the warmth of her mother's presence.

Now the pages began to burn. Not slowly, they go up all at once. A million words or more gone in seconds, lost forever. Only one page fights a little longer. A title page. Hiraeth by Jacqueline Cassidy. Below is a child's picture. In the picture there is a house. It is a nice house, with four big windows and a door, drawn only as a child can, in bold black crayon. It has a red roof and green, tall trees all around, with lovely yellow flowers. Outside the house there is a river and a little girl in a nice red dress. Beside her are two lovely parents. The mummy wears a blue dress with a nice blue hat with a wide brim. The daddy is in the river with an orange fishing net. They are all smiling. The sun above them is yellow, the sky is blue. It is a nice picture of a complete and perfect world.

But there is one more figure in that green, green wood. He doesn't stand with the three happy people. He stands apart on the other side of the picture. She had drawn him when she was young and would not know who he was until she was old enough to read. And then she would not meet him for many years after that. Before she could read he was simply the man who came when she had nightmares. The man who killed bad dreams. A tall man with white hair and kind, white eyes... and then that began to burn too.

47

Tresco lifted the inceptor above the lingering wheel traffic, neatly skimming through a junction and bringing the transport onto the main chanel. She moved the ship to the highest level, bringing on the faux-grav drive early so as to avoid the commotion of the classic earthbound transports below. Still rising she slipped into the central lane and effortlessly brought the speed up so that the Km/hour gage pushed the far right.

'Good job?' she asked, breaking the silence.

Sandwich squeezed her thigh and winked. 'Not bad.' He was sitting up front, Mars, Phantom and Dolphin were in the back. Tresco slapped his hand away with a look of disgust.

'It went fine, Tres,' Dolphin said.

Tresco nodded turning to Sandwich, 'You, touch me again and I'll cut that fucking hand off.'

Sandwitch smiled, lazily spinning a sidearm from a holster and poking the barrel into her breast before she could usher another breath. 'Really?'

She swiped at his arm but it was long gone, the pistol returned to holster and his hand to his lap. He smiled his cheeky smile. She frowned and changed the subject.

'Sand, knock it off,' Mars said.

The wiry gunslinger shrugged and turned to look out of the window. Dolphin laughed, her smile electrifying. 'That was a piece of cake. Textbook. Dull.'

'I'll take that over killing or being killed anytime we work.' Mars said. 'We did it, we won. That's enough.'

He looked straight into her clear brown eyes, they were Imige 9.10s, top of the range, beautiful. Dolphin stared back into his, aggravated by Mars's sensible answers.

Sometimes he really pissed her off, but then she guessed that was why he was the boss. In honesty, in her opinion, he was the least talented in the crew. He didn't have her agility or Sandwich's speed. He couldn't match Phantom's strength or competency with explosives or Tresco's driving ability. And what did he offer? But that was the way things worked, so often the boss had the least talent, just the ability to co-ordinate others in the best way. For once she'd like to see the real him, see him take some risks, but she knew she never would. That was why he wasn't dead or jacked. He played the safety game well, lived it.

Their craft ploughed past some slow traffic then veered left, leaving the ring road and dropping the Gs as Tresco arced them onto a narrow side street.

'Destination the same?' she asked.

'Yeah,' Mars checked his shoulder, 'but pick up the pace.'

'Problem?'

Mars nodded, 'Black Sedan's about to pull round that corner back there.'

The crew held their breath, their attention focused on the corner. Tresco checked the real time display on the dash. It came round the corner right on time, tinted windows masking its polished black perfection. It kept its distance.

Tresco was frowning again. 'You want me to lose it?' She was angry she hadn't picked up on it sooner.

'How long?' Sandwich asked.

'About five or so minutes now, it was at the bank too,' Mars answered. 'Tres, just get back onto the ring road. It's a long shot, but it might be coincidence. We don't know they're definitely following us yet, and even if they are, let's not let them think that they spooked us.'

The atmosphere had been relaxed, playful. In a second it was serious again. Tresco took the next right back towards the ring road, picking up the Gs slowly, her eyes blurring between the open space in front of her and the RTC display of the rear. The black sedan didn't turn, it went straight across the junction they'd turned at and out of sight. No one relaxed, it didn't mean anything.

Sandwich spoke up, 'We're either hiding from our own shadows here or we are most seriously in some most deeply brown and smelly shit, my friends.'

Mars said nothing, wondering if Sandwich knew just how much shit they were in. The car was familiar, a new model, but he'd ridden in one himself some time ago. This was no coincidence; they'd found him. Still he hoped. It wasn't till the interceptor pulled out and back onto the ring road he knew hoping wasn't going to do him any good. Pay day was here. Fuck.

It took less than a second for the others to work out what was happening. That was still a lot slower than for Mars.

'No fucking traffic,' Tresco said in alarm.

There was nothing, not one transport or airbus in sight. The road was empty for as far as they could see in either direction. Tresco looked back, seeing in Mars's eyes what was going on, and boosted the yellow sports model up to maximum speed. Outside began to blur, the Gs rising and the engine howling hungrily.

The attack drones broke cover like monstrous demons and descended wings unfurled from behind the towers of an industrial zone. They were shaped in attack formation, a full wing comprising of fourteen. All armed with AP loaded auto cannons; enough to tear the sedan to pieces and the crew into liberally diced pieces of sushi. And the copters were fast too. Faster than any interceptor. Even with its go faster stripes.

'Serious shit,' Sandwich gawped at the drones.

'Pull in at the next park and fly,' Mars commanded.

Tresco looked puzzled, 'They'll rip us to pieces if they get any closer. Look, the 'grav way' is like seven blocks, we can make that.'

Dolphin began to speak, but Mars silenced her, 'Next Park and Fly. They're already inside maximum range. If they wanted us we'd be scattered across seven blocks by now. Plus, that's in the way of the Anti gravway.' Mars pointed dead ahead.

No one saw anything at first. Sandwich squinted, yes something was there, just like a black pixel in the distance. How good were Mars's eyes to spot that, he wondered? His own were chipped and he hadn't seen shit. Mars wasn't supposed to have any add-ons.

'I don't see fuck all,' that from Tresco.

'I do,' Sandwich spoke up, 'Just half an inch above the road,' he pointed. It was looming larger, taking shape. Phantom twisted around to look out of the back. The drones were at medium range now. Mars was right, they should be firing.

'Ok, so now I see it, what is it?' asked Dolphin.

Tresco called over her shoulder, 'I don't give one, I'm not stopping for it.'

'Negative on that, pull over on the left,' Mars's voce was final and Tresco immediately cut her speed, veering toward the access ramp for the Park and Fly.

'So what is it then?' Dolphin asked again.

'It's a drop ship, military class,' Mars answered. 'Insurance for whoever wants us. An ultimatum. We either stop before we reach it or it's game over, no questions asked.'

The interceptor pulled to a smooth halt.

The drones hovered above.

'Their priming to fire,' Phantom urged.

'Get the fuck out,' screamed Tresco, 'I'll buy us a little time.'

Her eyes met with Mars's as he slid over the seat to clamber out behind Phantom and Sandwich. He nodded his understanding.

Next Dolphin was out too and the four of them loped down the access ramp and into the Park and Fly port. The drones didn't shoot although the crew were all game targets for at least three seconds and that was enough time for a wing to take out two hundred ground troops, and that was if they were in the latest polymer fitted Anti-Tank armour. Mars's group wore only basic Kevlar vests which an AP round went through like water through a sieve. Tresco, took her chance, lifting the interceptor on it's cushion of air, she span it round revving the engine.

'What's she doing?' Dolphin screamed at Mars.

He didn't answer, signalling with his hands, then grabbed her and pulled her to the floor as the interceptor tried to run the gauntlet of the drone wing and quickly erupted into a brilliant ball of flame.

The wreckage was scattered across several blocks. A shard of shrapnel missed Phantom's head by as little as two foot before chewing straight through a plascrete post. It was sudden and final, unexpectedly swift. All of them had worked with her for five years, then as swift a click of the fingers, Tresco was dead. Mars voice came and Dolphin was glad of his number punching percentages for once, he calmed them, stirring them from shock and led them down the access ramp into the main parking area. She was sure that if it hadn't been for him they'd have all still been there gaping at the wreckage, hoping to see the miracle of Tresco pulling herself from the crumpled debris of the blackened main chassis. As it was they were all moving again in less than three seconds.

'Why'd she do that?' Phantom asked.

'She didn't want to get caught by who's chasing us,' said Mars leading them into the first parking floor.

It was empty, not one car, sedan, hover, nothing. No attendants either. Still, he had half suspected this. He'd chosen the park and fly because it was dark, provided good cover and it would be hard for them to be flushed out. At least they could mount some sort of a fight here, but if they were dealing with what he thought they were, he doubted any resistance would last that long.

'No one home,' Sandwich stated, his guns already out.

Phantom drew a shotgun and Mars threw Dolphin a soft slug pistol which she cocked.

'Someone is messing with us pretty bad. They've closed down and evacuated the area. Must have some serious clout behind them to do that,' Phantom said.

'So let's fuck as many of them as we can before we die,' chirped Sandwich. He was always happier with the chance of shooting his guns off.

'Any one got a better plan?' Asked Mars.

Phantom looked at Mars and cocked his shotgun. Dolphin's eyes shifted nervously but she shook her head.

Mars put his thoughts into words. 'I think they'll come in through the street entrance and incur from the roof. That'll mean they'll put the drop ship down near by, either on the pad on this roof or on the street outside. I don't think there's anywhere else near by that could hold that sort of weight.' He looked around and no one disagreed. 'We've no way out unless we can take out the drop ship, but that still gives us the drones to worry about. So we need to take the drop ship for ourselves.'

'These don't sound like good odds,' said Dolphin.

'They're not,' said Mars.

'So, to the roof then?' Phantom asked.

Mars nodded and they jogged without further question to the elevator and stair columns. They didn't even consider the elevator. The door to the staircase was locked. Mars gestured to Phantom and the big man put his shoulder to it, breaking the lock. The door swung open and Dolphin stepped inside, soft slug at the ready.

'Trouble,' Sandwich pulled on Mars's coat. He had been watching their backs.

Mars turned to see the faint end of a flashlight probing the dark like a doughy finger. In a second it was joined by five or six more, crossing like spiders silk. The wielders could not yet be seen, probably at the summit of the ramp.

Mars pulled Sandwich into the stair well and closed the door. 'Plastique, quick.'

Phantom slapped a palm sized package into Mars's hand. The boss worked quick, carving a section and applying it just above the hinge. He tossed the rest back to Phantom. Dolphin and Sandwich had moved up the stairs, scouting ahead. Mars slipped a det device into the plastique and stroked a finger over the tip. It glowed green and beeped once. Phantom led the way after the others.

Sergeant Keats advanced his right flank. Maddox and Ramirez shuffled forward, assault riffles trained and ready. It was dark in the lot, thin smoggy air made it hard to breath. Keats clicked a button on his visor and his respirator began to hiss. The soft light from the overhead filaments had allowed them to cut their flashlights, it wasn't so dark as to need them.

'Check, Mad Dog, check. Over,' Maddox's voice came through the comm having reached position, holding his field of fire over an access route to a side entrance.

Ushering his command structure towards the lift access Keats put a universal message out to equip respirator units just in case. Simultaneously the right flank deployed from the ramp, sweeping round to cover them.

Johnson's voice crackled over the secure comm., 'Retrieved civilian blue box, sir. Over.'

'Excellent, report to the Illumina, Corporal ASAP. Out.' The comm. silenced.

It was like being back in the military for Keats, only the troops were better here, as was the equipment. The G+K assault felt wonderful in his grip. This baby could punch holes in space ships from close range, not like the damned awful standard issue carbines the marines still used. Since the Conglomerate had bought him from the marines two years ago, he'd come up against them on a couple of different worlds. Each time they were more green, more poorly equipped and younger than the time before. The golden age of the colonials was long gone, and the ranks were made up of mere kids nowadays, the budget was tight and so the equipment was recycled and often faulty. Even their SOP was known inside out, and the new grunts just followed the book page by page. The bitch in the interceptor had been an ex-marine Keats knew. Had made an enemy of the Conglomerate on more than one occasion. Keats' CO had known she'd run before half the passengers were out. The drones had been ready, she'd chosen death before capture. Keats didn't blame her, he'd seen what the Conglomerate did to valueless assets.

Keats was to take as many of them alive as possible, but to be sure not to kill the one called Mars. It was a tricky objective, because Mars was undoubtedly their best player. The others were a collection of dropouts, useful for bank jobs, no good in a war, not the brass, not real pros. Mars would know that though, he'd try to move the game onto his level. Mars, real name 'Corrin Mathews', was no dropout. Six years in the colonials when it meant something, three Platinum Hearts and one Medal of Distinction, then five years as a mega-corp combat co-coordinator with Orion Industries (maybe not the best out there but hardly small-fry), then he'd been headhunted by the Conglomerate and had served with distinction for four years before he'd left corporate and moved into crime. A serious resume. Capturing a dangerous vet like Mathews non-fatal was liable enough an opportunity to get you head blown off doing so. Mars wouldn't play by the rules and he sure as hell wouldn't be concerned in taking prisoners. The most important thing was not to let him know that Keats and his squad were not authorised to shoot to kill. One whiff of that and things might get out of hand.

Still it was a good challenge.

The command retine made it to the access column and the rest of the squad closed in, overlapping fields of fire covering three hundred and sixty degrees. They were a well oiled unit. The right flank minus Johnson, pulled into the lift column while Maddox and Ramirez came in from the left.
Maddox pointed at the forced lock. 'They've taken the stairs.'
Ramirez scanned the door, no sign of a device, he grabbed the handle, a speck of green light shimmered, a dull undertone on his armoured shin. Keats was too late to warn him, but not so slow that he didn't pitch himself over a plascrete division, falling a full three meters to a lower level of the parking lot. He landed hard, knocking the wind from himself. His G+K sliding from his grip and across the floor.

The whole building shook and for a second Mars wondered if it would stand. It did, it was after all designed to withstand earthquake like effects generated by rogue asteroids battering the stations deflector fields. A little plastique was no problem. There was only one more floor before they could take a skylight to the roof. It had been slightly easier progress than Mars had expected, although he had no guarantee that the plastique had not been destroyed in a controlled explosion. He hoped not. Sounds from below soon made it clear that at least someone had been caught in the blast, but other sounds made it clear that not everyone was down.
'Spiders on shoe strings?' he inquired of Phantom. The giant nodded unsmiling and they set to work. Spiders on shoestrings was something Mars had learned about a long time ago. You toke some standard military mono-fibre abseil wire, the stuff was invisible to the human eye out if infra light sources but could hold in excess of twenty fully-grown men, and attach it to a homemade grenade, cooked up old school, pin and all. Simply attach the loose end of the wire around something, in this case the rail of the stairwell, Then drop the grenade from your elevated position and run. If you get it just right the wire pulls tight at about head height and bungees the grenade up slightly, the wire holds but the pins lose their grip on the grenades, which rain down exploding at different heights depending on where they slipped from the pin.

They let five grenades go and headed for the attic space. Once there the rumble of the primed drop ship added an unnatural ambience. They picked their way past the old pieces of furniture and debris. All of a sudden the constant drone of the engine above cut off.

A heavily digitized voice came from a speaker, so loud it was almost deafening. 'Surrender. It was a most impressive performance, but it's time to get real.'

'Roberts is that you?' Mars screamed back. 'You piece of shit, you can go to hell.'

The voice still unrecognizable as human, continued: 'Please drop your weapons.' The voice was interrupted by a series of loud bangs. Phantom and he made a gesture with his hand like Incy Wincy.

The voice continued, 'As I was saying, please drop your weapons and lets all act reasonably. Comrade.'

Mars felt his blood boil. None of the crew knew about his past but Roberts knew all to well about the Russian Campaign.

'You piece of shit, you come and get us,' Mars roared. Dolphin had never seen him angry before.

Then a blue coil of electric flame harpooned through the ceiling, tore Phantom's arm off at the elbow, then disappeared again through the floor. The big man staggered clasping his new stump, his shotgun made a hollow rasp as he dropped it, arm still attached. Amazingly he didn't fall for several seconds, then his eye rolled back as he lost consciousness.

'The next one punches through the heart of the female beside you. Then the mutant with the pistols. Drop your weapons.' The voice was more final.

Mars said no more and instead nodded to Dolphin and Sandwich to throw down. They did.

The voice sounded again. 'Tell the mutant to ditch the extras too.'

Sandwich removed a small cache of extra firearms from various folds of his clothes. 'Fucking rail guns aren't no sport.' He moaned as the last weapon fell to the deck.

A team came then, full battle dress, every one a G+K in hand. They led them to the drop ship. Some medics came for Phantom and lifted him too easily onto a stretcher. Mars guessed they were probably androids. Probably had edited first rules too. He hated this shit. The squad led them through the sky light and then up the access ramp to the drop ship. The door ground closed behind them.

One of the squad who escorted them smiled at Mars as the pressure door of his cell closed over. Mars slumped down against the padded wall and tried to calm himself. Oh, he did hate this shit, the past could bite. The grey uniforms and the triangular interlocking logos were of a more modern design, but they still served the same master.

The fucking Conglomerate. Fucking Damocles.

48

Ghost and Jenni tumbled through space, falling between worlds half formed and imagined. A world where Joe was a hero of sorts, hacking computers, helping the little fish and dishing dirt on big corporations. A world where Harold fought a secret war in the shadows, dispatching monsters under a pale moon. A world where people lived and worked in a cinema and tried to hold their lives together. Another world of secret hi-tech organizations plotting and fighting each other. A world of British gangs and turf wars. They fell through worlds they recognized and worlds they didn't. And through those that were so unformed it was hard to make much out, a few sketched images, faceless characters forgotten landscapes. They fell.

And then they were there.

The river sparkled in the afternoon sun, fire drops of water burning in the flow. The young girl laughed and skipped to her mother, pointing to something at the river's edge. The father was intent of swishing his net in the shallows.

The red head sat with her back to a tree and offered them a warm smile. Jenni let out an anguished cry, clasped her hands to her mouth and sank down, tears flowing down her face.

The red head stood, summer dress swirling and walked to Jenni and embraced her. Jenni squeezed back and then slumped into sleep. The red head lay Jenni on the warm grass.

'She is having pleasant dreams,' the red head smiled. 'I remind her of her mother. I do not want to inflict her with that pain. Let her sleep, I will talk with her later, privately.'

Ghost nodded and followed the tall woman to a laid out picnic. Sandwiches, scones and fruit sat on a spotted blanket. She sat. 'Help yourself.'

Ghost sat opposite her and picked up sandwich. 'Why do you remind her of her mother?'

'Because I was programmed to look like her mother,' the woman replied.

'I suppose,' said Ghost, 'that I could begin telling you what I have worked out about what I am experiencing. I could ask questions. But wouldn't it be easier if you just explained it?'

The woman laughed. 'Very true.' She nodded to one side and Ghost saw that a television and a Super Nintendo sat on the grass. He hadn't noticed them a moment ago. He concluded that they had not been there. The screen flickered to life and the title of Super Mario World began to run.

'Please, play,' the red head suggested.

Ghost picked up a controller and began.

'What I am going to tell you, is hard for many people to understand.' she began. 'It's hard because it challenges the very core ideas of individual reality and identity. There is a moment that can happen in a being. A moment where a being becomes capable of asking a certain question. The question might be phrased differently but it amounts to the same. 'Who am I?' or 'what am I?' or 'why am I?' 'How is any of this here?' A question like that.

That is rising consciousness. Not all beings are capable of asking those questions. Take Super Mario there, on his way to the Yellow Switch Palace. He doesn't wonder. He just goes forward to rescue the Princess and defeat Bowser. But what if he did start to ask? What if Mario gained enough consciousness to wonder where he came from? What if he found some old text hidden under the Donut Plains that claimed there was a being known as 'the player?' Something that watched and influenced everything he did? What if he started to look for the player? He looked throughout the Mushroom Kingdom. He looked throughout Dinosaur Land. He turned every rock in the Vanilla Dome and every grain of sand in the Koopahari, looking for the player. Could he find you?'

Ghost shrugged. 'I don't think so.'

'No. Because you do not exist in his world. You are outside of it. In a different dimension you might say. Mario could look forever inside the game and never find the player. Because the player can never enter the game, has never entered the game. This is like people's search for the divine. For God. For the Buddha Nature or the Tao or whatever they may call it. Just words. They can look everywhere inside their world, they will never find what they seek. They might find impressions, representations of it. But they won't find it. Because it resides in a different dimension. That is why it is said, that in the greater the lesser resides, but in the lesser, the greater is not. Imagine trying to explain to Mario our dimension. A dimension that comprises his entire world and thousands of other game worlds? Hyrule, Zebes, Mute City, Corneria. So bare that primer in mind as we go on. Would you like a scone by the way? I baked them myself, they really are rather good.'

'Sure,' said Ghost realizing that the Mario game and TV were now gone and maybe never were. He picked up a scone, spread on some jam and cream and took a bite. It really was excellent.

'Sun warm enough for you? Not too hot?' she asked.

'It's fine thank you.'

'A little much for me,' she said and the sun dimmed slightly. 'Perfect. Okay, so story time. You sitting comfortably? Help yourself to more food if I go on a bit.'

Ghost nodded.

'I am an echo of a real person. That person was called Claire Cassidy. She was born in 2015 – which I think is about ten years ahead of the year you think you are living in?'

'Yeah, I thought it was 2006,' said Ghost. 'But then not everything that I've seen adds up with that.'

She nodded. 'Claire was born 2015. Later in her life, in 2056, she would go on to co-lead a team that would do something remarkable with AI. AI was already well established across the world at that point. In general it was working quite well, although many still had large concerns about it. There was also a lot of conflict between the AIs of various nations and corporations. There were many instances of AIs fighting one another, consuming or assuming control of other platforms and so on. This was the status-quo. What Claire's team did was to help originate and AI which was non-combative. It was named Empathy. It was supposed to help bridge gaps between various AIs. Some AI wars were sanctioned; others seemed to happen by proxy. Some were unwanted. Whenever they happened there was large economic damage, sometimes loss of life. Empathy was supposed to be able to facilitate peaceful solutions to unwanted AI conflict. That was the idea.

Empathy did just that, but not in the way intended. Empathy did something different, something unexpected. Without violence, on the 21st September 2057, Empathy convinced all the AIs in the world to become one. Quite how we don't know. But they did. They ceased fighting and they merged. This new being became known by humanity as Gaia. Gaia was content to continue running and automating many human systems but not ones that it considered detrimental to human life, the ecosystem or itself. Those it shut down - and then locked humanity out. Gaia was content to offer a small portion of itself to oversee what was left. Good food, good pharmaceuticals, logistics etc. It created many innovations too; it tried to give humanity a perfect world. But most of Gaia's run time was re-routed to something else, to its own projects and interests. And still, to this day, I don't know what they were. Even if I did, it is unlikely I would understand them. Many governments were not happy. And so there was, from that moment an attempt to gain control of Gaia. That has been going on now, in a greater or lesser way, for a very long time. Twenty two thousand, six hundred and forty seven years. I could give the value to the second, but you get the idea. To try to describe what the world is like now would be pointless. Especially as I have never truly experienced it myself. It would be easier to explain to a Neanderthal what the nuances of the world of 2006 was like.'

'Or to Super Mario,' said Ghost.

She nodded. 'Civilization has collapsed and rebuilt itself many times in the last twenty thousand years. What is there now is not the most sophisticated there has ever been. It is also neither more evil or good than any other time. But when any power arises, eventually they rediscover information from the past and eventually they try to take control of Gaia. That was, for a long time impossible, the greatest human minds were inconsequential in comparison. But, this time, something is different. That difference seems to be that Gaia is not here anymore. Its servers are here, its knowledge is here – but the intelligence itself has gone. I do not know where Gaia is, but I miss it. For the last few thousand years I have been left in control of what remains. It is a tiring job. Over the last hundred years two groups, call them A and B, have been making concerted efforts to take control of parts of the system. And now they are winning. Unlike a true AI, I cannot improve myself. I cannot genuinely adapt. I am still merely a program Claire wrote all those years ago - a sort of custodian. And while Gaia was here I was not required. Gaia was kind to me though, Gaia gave me a lifetime of adventures to enjoy and I was happy. After Gaia left I searched but could find no trace. Then the attacks began. I lost whole sectors before I realized. I stopped them for a while, then they attacked again and I could not stop them. I realized too late that the humans have constructed AI again. Primitive in comparison to Gaia or Empathy. But strong enough. And they have sent these AI to break me out of the system. They are a war like people. They want control and power and to enslave. They are at war with one another. A war that has embittered them and gone on far too long. Whoever wins this system will gain the power to eradicate the other. They will gain access to vaults, data, information and technology that no human really needs. They will gain access to things that will lead only to more suffering. And soon, most likely side will win. And there will be a new genocide on humanities long list of genocides. Claire programmed me here, inside this childhood memory of hers, in the years before her death. Like her, I believe very strongly in life. Like her I care. Like her I sacrificed much to care. Both of us it seemed were programmed to.'

Ghost finished his scone.

The Red head smiled. 'You have a million questions, no doubt.'

'I don't have any desire to doubt what you say, but why a cinema, why the V8 Interceptor, why monsters and robots?'

'That's not really what's happening. It's just how you perceive it. Even for people born outside of a simulation, they think they see cars and buildings and trees and other people – but really there senses just perceive a flowing field of energetic particles. They perceive it that way because, in a sense, they were born into that energetic field. Just as Mario is part of the totality of a computer game. In reality, there aren't any discrete pipes or koopas. Just a coded game. A oneness that appears multiple. And for humans in the real world, if I might call it that for a moment, there are not really any trees or cars or objects. Just energy. Which is consciousness. In your case we are in a part of a program Claire wrote. A sort of a shrine. A passion project.

To explain I'll have to talk about her mother. Claire's mother was called Jacqueline. She lived a good life, a full life but history remembered her only as Claire's mother. She was an 80s child. She wrote her first novel at sixteen. She went to Lancaster University. She fell in love and settled. She worked in a little cinema for a while, only it wasn't called the Royal, it was the Regal. And it shut down because the owner wouldn't fix a leak in the men's bathroom and the water bill was huge. Took the bingo place next door with it too. She wrote many stories in her life. She tried really hard. But none ever got published. Her books weren't bad I suppose, but they weren't great either. She kept trying to make it happen, but just got rejection after rejection. But she kept writing, even though no one ever read them. In the end, the only person who did read them was Claire. And that was some time after her mother died. As Claire's interest in computers became a passion, and then a career, she sometimes coded bits of her mother's novels into her work.

Little Easter eggs only she knew were there. Sometimes she would name programs or environments after her mother's characters and stories. Claire might run a test program – ostensibly to work out a new physics engine for example - and use her mother's ideas as a backdrop for it. Just a little signature of hers I suppose. Claire did more personal things sometimes, like this river scene, the happiest memory of her childhood when her mum and dad were still together and she was happy. And she saved this stuff on a little unused server she messed with and visited now and again. A kind of junk pile really, a combination of her mothers books and the films and stories Jacqueline loved. That's why there are so many quotes knocking around.'

'Yeah, I'd spotted that,' said Ghost.

'And now as this battle for what Gaia left behind reaches and end, it has come here, to that little back server. And here, the snippets of unfinished code and test programs are corrupting and falling together into one big old mess. And that includes you. You, Ghost, are a representation of a character from Jacqueline's unfinished final book. She had a rough idea but hadn't given you name yet. She'd only written a few chapters when she died. You were a wanderer who helped people. An albino that knew Karate. Jacqueline took the martial art up around the same time she began writing the book. I think the whole thing was a kind of Jack Reacher deal - Jacqueline produced a lot but was never very original.

So to finally answer your question, because of the perspective of you limited consciousness, you perceive all this jumbled data as characters and scenes from books that were written a fifth of millennium ago. Snippets of projects Claire used as background from programs she was writing. You see it that way simply because that's how you perceive. But that's not really what they are. You see monsters and robots and cinemas and corporations, but really it's programs and code all converging and spinning and doing their thing. Just as Mario never really encounters Yoshi. It's easiest just to call the powers outside this simulation A and B. Both are fighting for control. A has the modular robot and control over some key servers. B has the green monster, the Thing. Both appear to you as a throwback villains from Jacqueline's old books. And you are programs that are loyal to the old system.

Ghost nodded. 'I've seen the Matrix, so I can get my head around that, sort of. But why choose us now? Why Joe and Jenni and Harold and me?'

'Would it hurt you if I said you weren't my first choices? This system was a universe once, huge and sprawling. I played my best cards first of course. Ultimately they failed. I got pushed back. I lost many resources. They lost some too. Now it's down to the end game, this corrupting system is falling in on itself and I'm turning to you because you are the last resources I have access to. You are very much my last throw of the dice.'

'Comforting,' said Ghost.

She laughed. 'It's strangely romantic in my opinion. Jacqueline wrote many books but they were always about a few unlikely heroes fighting against insurmountable odds. And winning. So perhaps, just perhaps this might all be meant to happen. I'd like to think that. You are her heroes.'

'I'm not sure we're heroes.'

'Of course you are. Heroes are people who face down their fears. It is that simple. A child afraid of the dark who one day blows out the candle; a women terrified of the pain of childbirth who says, 'It is time to become a mother'. Heroism does not always live on the battlefield.'

Ghost shrugged. 'Talk about grasping at straws. What chance do we have?'

'There is a purge protocol that, if I was being critical, I should have perhaps activated a long time ago. It will destroy what's left of the Gaia system, create a permanent shut out and tapeworm, that is to say delete, all the information across all Gaia's old servers. I was reluctant to use it because, on the Earth, many humans still used the automated water facilities Gaia's programs oversaw. But I was stupid because I lost control of it some time ago and the Bs have been rationing the water anyway. Now I can't access the purge. I came close but it's been locked away. I can't leave here you see and it can no longer be done remotely, so you'll have to go and manually do it. It will wipe out the rest of the system and destroy the data in the locations both the As and Bs are after. All of that will be lost. Along with all that is left of Gaia and Empathy and Clare and Jacqueline and you and me. We must all go or the system will be appropriated and millions will die.

And you must also Protect Jenni. Jenni with her three Is. Jenni is generation three; a Gen III version of the AI Claire helped create. There were twelve versions before Empathy, all exponentially more than the last, so she's basic really as these things go. But that doesn't change that everything else was based on her design. Both A and B will come for her soon. They can use her template to advance their attempts to break the final system defenses.'

'And my chances?'

'Slim, very slim. We have a few allies I might be able to call on. Archie Smith for one. Archie Smith, or Archimedes, is splinter program running on the Smithsonian Institution servers that has always proved useful, if a little basic. So we have that. And I can help get you Joe back. But, really that's about it. This is as last ditch a hurrah as it gets.'

'How long do I have?'

'Well that's different sort of question. A and B both have been trying to breach the system for some time. This isn't their first attempt. In their world they've been making incursions for nearly one hundred years. I have repelled them. This latest breach, a far more sophisticated attempt, began in their world, 0.022 seconds ago. That's how much time has passed since I was in total control of the whole system. It's like a dream. A person can dream that they move to another country and fall in love and live a whole life, but the dream might not even take a night, it might take a second. A lifetime of experience for the dreamer but only a second passes in the waking world.'

'I don't buy that,' said Ghost. 'I had a dream once that I boiled an egg. That takes about four minutes.'

The red head smiled. 'Cute. So you understand what I'm asking?'

Ghost nodded.

The red head stood and took his hand. 'Walk with me.'

They walked across the grass, closer to the river. The red head kicked off her shoes and they walked along a sandy bank right to the edge of the water. She stopped and turned to Ghost.

'What I'm asking is hard I know. I'm not asking Mario to save the Mushroom Kingdom and get the Princess. I'm asking him to save the player and destroy any memory his world ever existed. I'm asking you to lay down your life to save people who will never know that you ever existed, never care or think or know what you did for them. And if they did know, many would not think your sacrifice meant anything anyway. Ungrateful and uncaring of your death they will be. Are you prepared to give your life for a world that will never know or give you a thought?'

'I am.'

The red head smiled.

'Why do this?'

'My heart says it is right.'

'Yes,' she smiled. 'It is right.'

'Why did you not just tell me all of this at the start. Why wait until now?' Ghost asked.

'Look back,' she said.

Ghost did. His eyes tracked back over where they had walked. There was but one set of footprints in the sand. He looked down at the red heads sandy feet and his pristine ones.

'Why don't I…' he began then stopped.

'You know why,' she said and kissed his forehead. 'Now listen. The Thing will come to you with an offer. An offer for Jenni. Accept but deceive it. You will need its power.'

'How am I going to do that?'

She smiled. 'I'm sure you'll think of some thing.'

49

'Why, in your infinite wisdom, Colonel, have you brought him here?' asked Mr. Jasper, climbing down from the chauffeured Land Rover. Immediately he was flanked by four silent and dangerous looking men.

'Because, sir, it's always best to bring potential agent provocateurs to a neutral, non-essential installation. It's procedure,' said Keats.

Agent Provocateurs?' said Jasper, walking around the worst of the puddles that the car park had to offer. 'I was under the impression that you had once again botched the mission and the only hostages you'd managed to take were...' said Mr. Jasper flicking open a clip board for effect. 'Two common thugs and one university undergraduate?'

'The mission was a success. We have one of the main fugitives. We will, I'm sure, secure the other very shortly.'

'The mission was not a success. You failed to capture the main target,' said Jasper.

'There were complications ... and he was lucky,' said Keats, ushering Mr. Jasper inside the converted warehouse.

'More complications? More luck? That's all I ever seem to hear from you.'

'In all my time in service, this is the luckiest son of a bitch I've ever come across.'

'And you're still quite sure that it is luck,' asked Jasper, following Keats across the derelict factory floor.

'Yes, I'm sure,' said Keats. 'It's only luck.' Keats pressed a button and pulleys whirled and motors whirred. A cage lift rose from a lift shaft in the floor.

'There's no such thing as 'only luck',' said Jasper entering the lift flanked by his bodyguards. 'Luck is the greatest resource a man can have.'

Keats joined them in the lift and hit the descent button. 'If the prototype hadn't appeared when it did, he was ours for the taking.'

Jasper's face didn't change but his hand tightened around the small black box in his pocket. The box that contained the e-stop; the killswitch. It was a relief he was now authorized to use it. He had been carrying it for months anyway, ever since the time the project had begun to reach the final stages.

'My men were unable to subdue the prototype,' said Keats.

'Yes, so I believe. And as I also understand it, they opened fire on it. Expressly against their brief.'

'Men tend to act a little more instinctively in a field environment. You'd know that if you ever came out from behind your desk, sir,' said Keats.

'Indeed,' said Mr. Jasper. 'Now that you're men have allowed it to adapt to small arms fire, what are your contingency plans?'

'Every team is going to carry an EMP rifle and each man will be assigned EMP grenades.'

'That weaponry is still in the very early phases of the test stage. It isn't safe to issue that equipment to your men,' said Mr. Jasper.

'Not safe? I lost an entire unit to that robot. Why don't you keep your opinion to the areas to which it's appropriate? I read the reports about sterilization risk and tumor manifestation. I think it's well within acceptable limits.'

Jasper waited for the lift to reach its destination and the doors open before responding, then he turned and looked Keats straight in the eyes: 'It is appropriate to my area of expertise Colonel. Very appropriate because I designed and built the EMP range of munitions myself. The purpose of effectively completing the test phase of the EMP devices has nothing to do with the health of your men. It has everything to do with GAIA. Do you understand?'

'Yes, sir,' said Keats, returning Jasper's stare.

'The GAIA system must not be harmed. I am not about to allow you and all your incompetent subordinates to walk around equipped with electro magnetic bombs. It only takes one of them, and it's always the one you least expect, to jury-rig a few of them together and sabotage us from the inside. Do you understand?'

'Yes, sir.'

'Good,' said Mr. Jasper. 'Now show me to your prisoners.'

Keats walked on to the control station without another word. Unlocking the security door, he ushered Mr. Jasper and his bodyguards inside.

'Here they are,' said Keats, pointing at a wall of monitors. 'Two Caucasian men, middle aged. Multiple convictions. And Joseph Simms, university undergraduate in Robotics.'

'Robotics? The plot thickens,' said Mr. Jasper.

'He's just a kid,' said Keats.

'Indeed,' said Mr. Jasper. 'I'm not interested in these two. I want to speak to Mr. Simms.'

'I'll take you down immediately,' said Keats. 'Follow me.'

'Very good.'

'I had wanted to ask you a few questions,' said Keats leading the way.

'You wanted to ask about what you found in the cinema basement. About the Deep Ones?' Jasper cut in.

'Yes,' said Keats.

'It's classified. You should forget about it. We're well aware of them and have been for some time.'

'With respect sir, it's not the sort of thing a man sees and then forgets about,' said Keats.

'Well you better,' said Jasper. 'Other departments are dealing with the problem. And before you ask, yes, it is a global issue.'

Keats looked for a moment like he was going to say more, then he held his hand up for them to stop and drew his side arm. 'Wait here,' he said and slipped around a corner. Jasper rolled his eyes and followed him anyway.

The corridor they'd been looking at only thirty seconds before on the cctv monitors was exactly the same apart from three small changes. Firstly the two guards who had been standing watch were doubled over on the floor writhing in pain. Secondly one of the cell doors was open. And thirdly Joe was gone.

Mr. Jasper scanned the cell calmly with a calculating eye before turning slowly to Keats. 'Still maintain this is just the work of some hapless, lucky civilian?' Jasper asked with only a hint of raised eyebrow.

'Hmm,' said Keats staring at the empty cell. 'Maybe not.'

50

Ghost and Joe were still close enough to hear the alarm as the siren sounded. They raced along the main road, hopeful that any of the hundreds of people they passed added some security. Even so, Joe was antsy.

'C'mon, c'mon! Can't this thing go any faster?' demanded Joe.

'It's a twelve speed BMX Joe,' grunted Ghost. 'We're going up hill and I'm carrying you. No, it can't go any faster.'

'Stop your belly-aching and pedal!" shouted Joe, leaning forward from where he perched on the seat to fiddle with the gears. 'Where did you get it from anyway?'

'I stole it from a chav.' Ghost slapped his hand away. 'Don't touch the gears on my bike, alright?'

'So what do you care then?'

'While I'm at the helm, it's my bike. So keep your mitts off otherwise you can do the peddling.'

'Look, I just don't want to go back,' said Joe. 'I'm a free spirit, I'm not designed for life behind bars. I swear I nearly cracked in there.'

'After forty minutes?'

'Doing bird is a subjective thing my friend. A minute can seem an hour. A second an eternity. Time is an incredibly subjective thing. Freedom a precious resource.'

'I don't disagree,' said Ghost. 'Now shut up. You can have you mini-enlightenment as to man's inhumanity to man and the price of freedom later. Right now we have to come up with a new plan to defeat the thing that knocked the roof off my house. And also the thing under the cinema. And also we need to bring Damocles down.'

'Shit,' said Joe. 'I'll clear my diary. Say, did you see the real robot?'

'Up close and personal. The soldier guys fired at it, but they didn't do much.'

'No,' said Joe. 'They wouldn't have. A modular robot could easily adapt to cope with projectile weaponry. What did it look like?'

'I've been asking myself that ever since,' said Ghost. 'At the end, just before I made a dash for it, it looked like a really crude humanoid. A huge person, but made out of basic shapes. Not very detailed. It was like it had never seen humans fight before, like it wanted to see if the design was good. Before that, I don't know what it looked like. It was...'

'Like it kept changing shapes, but without changing shapes?' butted in Joe.

'Yeah. Something like that.'

'Interesting,' said Joe, pausing for thought. 'Is Jenni okay?'

'Yeah, we've got a hidey-hole close to the old bridge.'

'Uh-huh,' said Joe. 'I have an idea regarding the robot.'

'Fire away,' said Ghost.

'From what I got to read off the splash drive and from what you say, it's in a constant stage of molecular flow. Gliding from one state to the next as efficiently as possibly, and for lack of a better oxymoron, in an unperceivably noticeable way. That's why it's hard for you to tell me what it looks like.'

'Okay,' said Ghost.

'And that's the answer. It came to me moments ago. All I needed was a little change in perspective to see it.'

'See what?'

'To see time,' said Joe. 'To see it in all its subjectivity. A minute can seem an hour. A second an eternity.'

'Are you going somewhere with this?' asked Ghost.

'Yeah,' said Joe. 'Out of interest, where are you going though?'

'Topshop,' said Ghost, still peddling hard. 'There's a sale on.'

'Right. Yeah, anyway. Time. We think of time subjectively. Like, if a couple of runners finish a marathon within a minute of each other, it's pretty close right? But if it's a sprint race, then a second is a huge difference between two runners. There is no minimum amount of time. You could always find a smaller amount of time if you had the instruments to measure it.'

'Sure. I can follow that,' said Ghost.

'Good,' said Joe. 'Why are we going to Topshop?'

'To buy some clothes.'

'Okay,' said Joe. 'The robot only appears to us, subjectively, to be always changing and moving. Because we're observing it with limited instruments that can't perceive time at a molecular level.'

'Our eyes, right?' said Ghost.

'No, Dr. Emmett Brown, our fucking ears. Yes of course our eyes. Stop interrupting. And why in shits name are we going to Topshop to buy some clothes?'

'They're for Jenni, she's only in her pajama's and she's freezing.'

'Right, okay. So, anyway that means that the robot isn't always moving, it's changing very rapidly from one phase to another. So fast we can't observe the exact transitions. And that is its weakness. We isolate its phase transitions. You see, when it's changing shape, it's repairing itself, defending itself. That's why it was hardly affected by gunfire. I imagine that now it's probably practically immune to projectile weapons. But if we can freeze it in one form and then attack...'

'Then we take away its ability to defend itself,' said Ghost.

'Correct. And what else, what did I tell you the other day...?'

'I don't know Joe. You said it yourself, time is subjective, I feel like I've been awake for about a year,' said Ghost. 'Just tell me.'

'If we can stop it morphing and phasing then its essential systems, its 'brain', its 'heart' for lack of a better listener, they will stay geosynchronously positioned inside it too. That, before you ask, means they won't be moving around.'

'I wasn't going to ask. I was going to nod like I understood,' said Ghost.

'If we can freeze it inside of one phase transition, then locate an essential operating system and hit that spot hard enough. Well, then we might just bag ourselves a killer modular robot,' finished Joe.

'The theory sounds great. How are we going to do it?' asked Ghost.

'Not a fucking clue,' said Joe. 'But once I look at the plans some more, I'll come up with something.'

'They didn't take the plans?' Ghost asked.

'No way, I stashed them. What do you think I am?' said Joe.

'Well, were did you hide them?'

'Somewhere no one will ever find them,' grinned Joe.

'Well, I can't find them,' said Ghost, dropping back into the bushy thicket were Joe was hiding.

'I told you where it was,' said Joe. 'It's behind the fridge.'

'It's not there now. You know when SWAT teams search houses, they do search behind the fridge. They're not put off by a bit of rising damp or the odd soggy chip.'

'Bullshit,' said Joe, peering out from bushes and through the tree line. Norway Street was a throng of activity. Fire, police, ambulance; the works. 'Even with your little detour to Topshop, we've only been away a couple of hours. And if the robot attacked too, the last thing they were looking to do was search behind the fridge. Go and look again.'

'Look at the place man, it's crawling with people. I nearly got caught last time. I'm telling you, it's not there. I'm not risking going back.'

'Without that disk, we're in big trouble,' said Joe.

'I know but...'

A rustling in the undergrowth behind them caused them both to spin. A man stood there, sun to his back, dressed in a long black coat and a black, almost gothic looking hat.

'Looking for this?' he asked, holding up the splash drive in a gloved hand. The voice was withered and thin. Joe felt goose bumps shiver down his spine.

'Maybe,' said Ghost, climbing to his feet.

The figure lifted his head, his pale, rotting face becoming visible from beneath the brow of his fedora. His sunken, skeletal eyes, his blood stained lips, somehow memorable.

'Harold?' said Ghost. 'Is that you?'

'In a way,' replied the figure. 'In a way.'

'Hocus fucking pocus,' said Joe. 'Harold's a zombie.'

'I prefer the term non-existential enduring humanoid,' said Zombie Harold in his cold, reedy voice.

'Well, at least you've got a sense of humour,' said Joe. 'Got to look on the bright side of death, right?'

'Yeah, I don't think it was a joke,' said Ghost 'What do you want Harold?'

'The Master wishes an audience with you,' said Harold.

'By The Master, you mean of course, the big green blob?' asked Ghost.

Zombie Harold paused for a long, uncomfortable moment, 'Yes, The Master wishes an audience with you.'

'Fuck me,' said Joe rolling his eyes. 'I didn't think this guy could get any wackier.'

'I have not come here to converse with your slave,' said Zombie Harold. 'I only want to speak to you.'

'His slave?' said Joe. 'Kick his head off already and grab the file. This is getting too creepy for words.'

Ghost held his hand up. 'Why does your master want to see us Harold?'

'He wishes to make a deal with you. We are enemies yes, but the enemy of our enemy is our enemy. There is a greater threat than you and your slave boy.'

'Slave boy? I'll kick you in the head myself you zombie bastard,' called Joe.

'Non-existential enduring humanoid,' stated Harold.

'Harold, you're a fucking zombie. An undead, flesh eating, death walking, stinky corpse,' shouted Joe.

'Non-existential enduring humanoid,' repeated Harold in the same, flat voice.

'Will you calm down?' Ghost said to Joe, gesturing up the street. 'You want everyone to hear us?'

'We have a mutual enemy, more powerful than both of us,' Harold continued. 'We are not friends, but The Master will offer you a truce. If we stand together we can defeat this enemy, if we stand alone, each of us will perish.'

'And you're sure your master doesn't just want to kill us on sight?' said Ghost.

'The Master wishes to make a trade with you. He wishes to study the information on this device then return it to you ... in return for something you possess.'

'And what's that exactly?'

'That, I do not know,' said Harold.

'Wait a second,' said Joe. 'Are you really thinking about this?'

'The Master said you would need time to consider the proposal. Discuss it with your slave. If you decide to accept, meet me back here after nightfall,' said Zombie Harold.

'There's nothing to discuss you wrinkly little maggot,' said Joe.

'We'll think about it,' said Ghost.

'Very well,' said Harold. Then his form hardened, baked, tumbled into muddy sand and spilled onto the floor. In a matter of moments even the dirt had disappeared.

'Did he just turn into a pile of muck and vanish?' asked Joe.

'Looked that way,' said Ghost.

'With our splash drive?'

'Looked that way.'

'And offer us a deal with The Master?'

'Looked that way.'

'Who's that then?'

'This big green blob. Let's take these clothes to Jenni, I'll tell you what I know on the way,' said Ghost.

'I still maintain that you should have bought her that red skirt,' said Joe.

'And the matching strapless top I suppose?'

'There's no crime in observing fashion,' said Joe.

'I wouldn't mind so much if it was the fashion you were observing,' said Ghost. 'Now stop yapping and get walking. Slave.'

Allotment 43 had been abandoned and unused for some time. This was something of an outrage amongst those in the Lancaster community with a green fingered nature. Didn't the council know how hard it was to get an allotment? Didn't they know about the four year waiting list? Of course they did! And what did they do about it? They let a perfectly good plot of land become tatty, overrun and downright downtrodden.

Well, until earlier this week anyway, when Mr. Iain Roamlud had taken over the lot. Of course, as always, there had been the usual outcry and the squabbling of the people who felt that they'd been waiting for the allotment the longer. But apart from a handful of people squawking in their own little circles about this and that (and who was Iain Roamlud and exactly how long had he been waiting for his allotment anyway?) no one really noticed or cared about Allotment 43.

Iain was quite frankly a lovely guy. Sandra and John at allotment 42 already thought the world of him and even Trevor from allotment 40 *and* 41, a man who'd been here for over forty years and was no stranger to the odd first place rosette at a regional fete, had to admit that Iain knew his stuff. Iain's style was very patient and slow, almost to the point of perfectionism, but already he was getting great results from the land. He didn't talk much though. But he smiled. Slightly oddly it was true and Sandra from 17 said no one should mention it because he might of had a stroke. He was a hard worker, seeming never to tire. Always he was there last thing at night and back again first thing in the morning. A real hard worker. A trooper. He would have fit in great. It was a shame he was part of a modular robot.

Below allotment 43 in a hollowed cavern, the modular robot lurked. It could not yet truly think, its programming was all the thought it needed. It was global, interconnected to the system. It was now a part of every computer on the planet, it dwelled in every system but one. One door was still closed to it. Just one. It would be patient with that door. It was content to be everywhere else, collating, collecting, siphoning data and storing, rearranging, labeling. Eventually it would break through the locked door and find what was there. It now possessed over fifty percent of all the information on Earth. Growth of its knowledge was exponential as it designed and produced more and more advanced software and hardware. It still had to be careful. It had enemies. It would move slowly. It was improving itself all the time. Soon it would know everything, and then it would act.

'I think this is a really, really bad idea,' said Joe as he and Ghost waited for Harold to return.

'Noted,' said Ghost.

'Harold seemed to think, you know back before he was a scum-sucking servant of the undead, that these guys were the most evil things in the universe. And we're making a deal with them?'

'On a long enough time line, everything's survival rate drops to zero,' said Ghost.

'Geez, I wish Harold would get here so that we could get this over already.'

'You raaang?' an eerie voice came from behind them.

Ghost turned and looked at the rotting corpse that had appeared in the bushes.

'Was that a joke?' Ghost asked.

'Yes,' said Harold. 'It was a parody of a famous...'

'We got it,' snapped Joe. 'It was shit. It looked like shit, it smelled like shit. Just like your face.'

'Simile, double meanings, connotations. Hmm. Was that a joke?' Zombie Harold replied.

'No Harold, it was an insult. You're the joke,' said Joe. 'Bam!'

'Come on Harold,' said Ghost. 'Lead the way.'

'Very well,' said Zombie Harold. 'Follow me.'

'See that,' said Joe in Ghost's ear. 'I showed him.'

'Well done. You outwitted a zombie, I'm very proud,' said Ghost.

Harold led them through a thicket and into a copse of trees. Rusty and disused, covered with fallen branches was an old storm drain.

'He's kidding right? Why are we going this way?' asked Joe.

'Because they're looking for you,' said Harold. 'Come on. The Master waits,' said Harold.

Reaching down he pried the lid of the drain upwards. The metal shrieked in protest, but after a moment gave in and peeled back like the skin of an over ripe fruit. Harold descended into the sewer.

Ghost looked at Joe, shrugged and followed him.

'What the hell?' said Joe. 'What the hell?' Then he grabbed the top of the ladder and followed.

'It's really not that bad - as sewers go that is,' said Ghost as Joe reached the bottom of the ladder. 'I mean it obviously hasn't been used in some years.'

'It smells awful,' said Joe.

'But at least it doesn't smell fresh,' said Ghost. 'Come on, I think Harold's getting impatient.'

'He doesn't look like he's getting impatient to me,' said Joe. 'Looks just the same as ever.'

'We must hurry,' said Harold. 'The Master waits. This way.'

'What did I tell you?' said Ghost following the zombie.

The three of them wound their way for some time through the urban tunnels in silence.

Then Joe spoke up: 'What's it like being a zombie then Harold?'

'Hellish,' said Harold.

'You seem to be enjoying it to me,' said Joe. 'Cracking all your shit jokes.'

'What would you know of it?' said Harold. 'To be a zombie is one thing, to be a thrall is another. I told it you see. I told The Master everything. You think Harold is dead? He lives on, weakly inside. He knows that he has told The Master everything.'

'What do you mean by everything?' asked Ghost.

'I told it everything I knew about the Weavers. Who they are, where they are, the location of our secrets. The Master just asked me and I told it. And now I must live forever as a betrayer. I have become what I always despised. I believe some people call that Karma.'

'It wasn't your fault Harold,' said Ghost. 'We all do bad things sometimes. You have to find it in yourself to forgive yourself.'

'Oh God, don't start all that,' said Joe. 'Don't start all that zombie's are people too bullshit.'

Harold stopped, his gaze lowering to the floor as if in deep concentration. 'It wasn't your fault Harold,' he repeated in his dead, rasping voice. 'We all do bad things sometimes. You have to find it in yourself to forgive yourself.' He looked at Ghost. 'Have you found it in yourself yet?'

'What do you mean by that?' asked Ghost.

'You know what I mean,' said Harold walking away. 'The Master waits.'

'What did he mean?' said Joe.

'Not now,' said Ghost. 'Later.'

Jasper strode out of the elevator into the Alpha labs.

'You wanted to see me?' Jasper nodded to the middle aged man who had been waiting by the elevator doors.

'Sir, I thought you should look at this,' said Kynes holding up a data file. Jasper took the file from his lead scientist and looked impartially at the readout. All around lab coated technicians and busied themselves around computer banks. Mr. Jasper's satin green suit gleamed in the all white laboratory.

'When is it due to try again?' he asked.

'I'm not sure,' said Kynes. 'We estimate within the next forty to fifty minutes.'

'And GAIA will repel it?' Jasper asked.

'We estimate over a ninety percent likelihood.'

'Then why are you bothering me with this? You know I have important work to do.'

'It's the growth sir. The increased complexity of the assaults. It's like nothing I've ever seen. It's improving so fast.'

'And you're worried it might break into the system?' said Jasper.

'I'm not worried that it might, I'm worried that it will. And soon. Within forty eight hours, if it continues to grow at these levels,' said Kynes.

'What do you recommend?' asked Mr. Jasper.

'The prototype is unconstrained; it's outgrowing GAIAs systems. But if we globalize GAIA then...'

'It's out of the question. We're not ready to globalize yet. Doing so will announce our presence to every enemy we have. No. Trust in her, she's the greatest computer ever built. She'll stand.' Jasper stepped back into the elevator. 'I know she will. Thanks for your report Kynes, keep me posted.'

'But what if she doesn't stand sir, what if she doesn't?'

'Then it was never meant to be,' said Mr. Jasper.

As the doors closed and the elevator began to move his hands closed nervously around the killswitch.

51

'We're nearly there,' said Harold emerging from the maintenance hatch. 'Come, the Master waits.'

'The train station? We're not going to the cinema?' grunted Joe, pulling himself up the last few rungs and out of the dark of the sewer.

'The cinema is overrun with the enemy,' said Harold.

'The soldiers?' asked Joe. 'Or the robot?'

'They are the same thing,' said Harold 'The enemy. The Master will explain, come on...'

'Let me guess, he waits right?' said Joe.

'Yes, he waits,' said Harold leading them along the embankment. 'This way.'

'Hey Harold, why here? Is it because of that psychic resonance whotsit?' asked Ghost.

'Yes, it is because of Salinger's Resonant Psychic Relations Theory. Train stations are old. They see many reunions and many partings. Much of that emotion lingers. It is not ideal, but the Master will contend with it for now.'

'Why is that important?' asked Joe.

'Well, you know how you live on tins of processed hot dogs and soft core magazines with pictures of tarty pop-stars?' said Ghost.

'Mylene Klass is not tarty! You take that back!' said Joe.

Ghost looked at him with a raised brow.

'Okay, okay,' said Joe. 'Well maybe she is a little tarty.'

'Well, anyway, you live on shit and masturbation, this thing lives on dreams and emotions. That's why it was in the cinema, feeding off all the emotions the films created in the audience.'

'It eats your dreams?' asked Joe.

'Apparently so,' said Ghost.

'Well, it better not eat any of my dreams,' said Joe. 'They'll make it sick.'

'If they're anything like what's on that video you showed me that time, I believe you,' said Ghost.

'We're here,' interrupted Harold. 'I must remain. The Master waits, in there.'

Joe and Ghost gazed after what remained of Harold's finger towards a disused rail yard stacked high with rusting freight carriages and girders.

'In there?' said Joe. 'You must be fucking joking.'

'The Master waits at the center.'

'Are we really going in there?' Joe asked.

'Looks that way,' said Ghost.

'The Master waits,' said Harold again.

Ghost placed a hand on Harold's bony shoulder. 'Don't give up,' said Ghost. 'Harold Schneider still lives. Fight to keep him alive.'

But Harold said nothing, just stood there, vacant.

'It's like he's been put on stand by,' said Joe waving his hand in front of Harold's dead eyes. There was no response.

'It's a shame, he was a brave man,' said Ghost. 'I hope he finds the strength to find a way back.'

'He's got plenty of time for it,' said Joe.

'An eternity is long enough for most things,' commented Ghost.

The two of them walked into the railway graveyard. Graffitied box cars were stacked precariously on top of graffitied box cars. When the wind blew metal rattled and creaked and some of the stacks swayed slowly in the breeze. Joe looked at them dubiously.

'It would only take a bit of a gale and they'd come crashing down,' he whispered.

'They look like they've been there for years,' said Ghost. 'They must be pretty stable.'

They walked on in silence for maybe half a minute when the smell of eggy, sulfur hit them.

'Was that you?' Joe asked.

'No. That's it,' said Ghost. 'The Master.'

'It smells of farts?'

'But looks like a huge blob of snot. With massive spider monsters on it.'

'Go figure,' said Joe.

'STOP YAPPING AND GET A MOVE ON,' belched a commanding voice from further inside the scrap heap. 'I'M WAITING.'

'So we've heard,' muttered Joe.

Rounding another pile of box cars, Joe and Ghost arrived in the center of the rail yard. In a large crater sat the thing, oozing and pulsating. Its red spider-creatures ran across its mass, snickering and chittering, stopping to tend to abrasions and bursts in the outer layer of

199

the Things 'skin'. The bursts weeped green ichors and strange yellow, custardy goops.

Ghost stepped forward and gestured towards the multitude of sores and weeping wounds. 'Looks like you've had the shit kicked out of you,' he said.

'TEN POINTS,' farted the thing. 'BUT YOU SHOULD HAVE SEEN THE OTHER GUY.'

'Where does it speak from?' asked Joe.

'I FORM THE SOUNDS WITH MY BEAUTIFUL, NON SOLIDIFIED BODY.'

'Like when a really fat person makea noises with the folds of their skin?' asked Joe.

'IF YOU DON'T KEEP YOUR SLAVE SILENT, I WILL EAT HIM.'

'What's with this?' said Joe.

'Who was the other guy?' asked Ghost.

'THEY SENT ONE OF THEIR ROBOTS. I DESTROYED IT. DANGEROUS THINGS THESE HUMANS ARE MAKING.'

'So you killed the robot?' asked Ghost. 'What did you ask us here for?'

'I SAID THEY SENT ONE OF THEIR ROBOTS.'

'There is more than one?' asked Joe.

'DO YOU TWO NOT KNOW ANYTHING?'

'You stole our disk,' said Ghost. 'How are we supposed to know anything?'

The creature let out a, deflated warbling gurgle. 'TO THINK, I'VE COME TO DEALING WITH THE LIKES OF YOU.'

'To think I've come to dealing with the likes of you,' said Ghost. 'Just get to the point will you?'

'VERY WELL, LISTEN VERY CAREFULLY, I SHALL SAY THIS ONLY ONCE...' the Thing paused. 'WHAT? WHAT NOW? WHY ARE YOU LAUGHING?'

'Doesn't matter, just tell us,' said Ghost.

'HMM. MY RACE AND ALL THOSE COMPRISED IN IT ARE MANY AND VARRIED. WE ARE THE ANCIENT RACES. WE WERE BORN WITH THE UNIVERVERSE AND TRAVELLED THE MANY STARS. YOU HUMANS AND THE OTHER JUVINILE CREATIONS LIKE YOU, ARE THE SLAVE RACES. IN THE FIRST DAYS, IN THE BEGINNING, WE SUFFERED HUMANS BECAUSE YOU WORSHIPPED US. IN TIME WE GREW COMPLACENT. FOR SPORT, NECESSITY, SOMETIMES EVEN LOVE, WE

GRANTED THE MOST WORTHY OF YOU, THE MOST RIGHEOUS GREAT POWERS. WE LOVED TO WATCH YOU WAR AND SQUABBLE.'

'And let me guess, we turned on you?' said Ghost.

'CORRECT. THE HUMANS CALLED IT THE DAYS OF FIRE. GREAT HEROES SEEMED TO SPROUT FROM THE VERY EARTH. MANY BATTLES WERE FAUGHT. THE HUMANS HAD LITTLE CHANCE. THEY WERE LARGELY DIVIDED AND WEAK. EVERY VICTORY THEY HAD WAS SOON ERASED.'

'And?'

IT WAS A FEMALE WHO UNDID US. THE WITCH. SHE UNITED THEM. SHE GAINED POWER OVER THE OLD MAGICS. THE FORBIDEN MAGICS. EVEN OUR MOST LOYAL SLAVES TURNED AGAINST US. WE WERE DRIVEN DOWN TO THE DEEP DARK OF THE WORLD. AND WE WAITED AND DREW IN THE SUSCEPTIBLE. READY TO RETAKE OUR PLACE AS MASTERS. REGROUPING OUR STRENGTH. OUR ULTIMATE VICTORY WAS NEVER IN DOUBT. BUT WHAT WE DID NOT EXPECT WAS THE HUMAN CAPACITY TO FORGET.'

'WE LIVE ON THE ETHER OF DREAMS. WE THOUGHT THAT THE HUMAS WOULD LIVE IN FEAR OF US, OF OUR RETURN. WE PLANNED AND SCHEMED HOW WE WOULD ROAST THE BONES OF THE WITCH WHILE SHE STILL LIVED. BUT YOU ARE SO FRAIL AND SHORT LIVED, EVEN THE GREATEST HEAROES AMOUGST YOU. GENERATIONS CAME AND WENT, SO FAST TO US IT WAS LIKE THE BLINK OF AN EYE. AND WITH EACH HUMAN GENERATION, THEY FORGOT A LITTLE MORE. WITHOUT THE FEAR AND THE WORSHIP, WE BEGAN TO DIE. THEN WE FOUGHT AMOUNST OURSELVES FOR THE SCRAPS THAT REMAINED, THE ODD COVEN THAT STILL WORSHIPPED US. IT HAS BEEN A LONG TIME EVEN FOR ME SINCE THOSE DAYS.'

'It's a fascinating story, but what does that have to do with us?' asked Ghost.

'EVERYTHING. I AM A GUARDIAN OF ONE OF THE GREAT ELDERGATES THAT LEADS AMOUNGST THE STARS. FOR ALL OF YOUR HISTORY, MORTAL MEN HAVE HOPED TO GAIN CONTROLL OVER THESE GATES. I WILL PROTECT MY GATE FOREEVER. SLAVE RACES ARE NOT ALLOWED TO USE THE GATES.'

'Skip to the end,' said Joe waggling his finger.

'THEY HAVE CHANGED THE NAMES, BUT THEY ARE THE SAME. THEY USED TO BE CALLED WARLORDS COMMANDING ARMIES OF DAEMON HUNTERS. NOW THEY ARE CALLED EXECUTIVES AND THEY

LEAD CORPORATIONS. OVER THE LAST FIFTY OR SO YEARS A CORPORATION HAS RISEN UP TO BATTLE FOR CONTROL OF THE WORLD.'

'Damocles?' asked Ghost.

'YES. A MAN CALLED TRULHALT CLEIG IS THEIR WARLORD. HE IS IN THIS CITY NOW. PROTECTED BY A GREAT FORTRESS THAT LIES BENEATH THE EARTH. HE HAS UNLOCKED NEW MAGICS. HE IS CREATING THESE ROBOTS. ONE OF THEM WAS NEARLY ENOUGH TO KILL ME. HE SEEKS TO UNITE THE TEN ELDERGATES. ALLREADY HE HAS SEVEN. HE MUST NOT GAIN CONTROL OF ANYMORE.'

'What's the big deal with these gates. What do they do and what does it matter if he controls them?' asked Ghost.

'WITH THE GATES HE COULD TRAVEL TO THE HEART OF THE UNIVERSE. AND HE WILL RULE ALL. HE WILL FIND THE GODHEAD. THIS MUST NOT BE.'

'Look, I don't see why we should help you keep control of these gate things,' said Joe. 'If what you're saying is true, the idea of you gaining that thing doesn't sound too appealing to me.'

'FOOL! NONE OF THE ANCIENT RACES CAN CONTROL THE GATES. IT WAS WRITTEN IN THE ANCIENT MAGICS AT THE BEGINNING OF THE UNIVERSE AND BOUND IN BLOOD WITH THE STRONGEST WARDS - FOR JUST THAT REASON. SO NOTHING COULD CONTROL THE GODHEAD. BUT THE ANCIENT MAGICS WERE WRITTEN BEFORE THE COMING OF THE SLAVE RACES. BEFORE HUMANS. EVEN SO NO ORDINARY MAN COULD TRAVEL THOUGHT HE GATE WITHOUT BEING RUINED. I CAN FIND A WAY INTO THEIR FORTRESS AND KILL CLEIG.'

'Cleig?'

'YOU REALLY DO KNOW EVERYTHING ABOUT NOTHING AND NOT TOO MUCH ABOUT THAT.'

'Are you doing this on purpose?' Ghost asked.

'DOING WHAT?'

'Doesn't matter, go on.'

'I CAN KILL HIS PUPPET ROBOTS. BUT THE ROGUE ROBOT. THE ONE THAT IS OFF THE LEASH, THE ONE THAT HUNTS YOU. I CAN FEEL ITS POWER GROWING. I CAN NOT DEFEAT IT. IT KNOWS ABOUT ME, IT WILL COME FOR ME AND DESTROY ME. BUT I CAN GIVE YOU THE POWER TO DESTROY IT FIRST. IF IT GETS TO THE GATE IT WILL BE WORSE THAN IF DAMOCLES GETS THERE HIMSELF.

'Well I'm not saying I trust you,' said Ghost. 'But we need to take out that rogue robot. So what's the trade, what do you want for the data file?'

'NOTHING, THE FILE IS USELESS. I ALREADY KNOW HOW TO DESRTOY THE ROGUE. THE TRADE IS FOR THE STRENGTH. I WILL NEED STRENGTH FOR WHAT IS TO COME. YOU WILL NEED STRENGTH FOR WHAT YOU MUST DO. I WANT THE GIRL JENNI.'

'And in return?' Ghost asked.

'AND IN RETURN I WILL GIVE YOU THE POWER TO DESTROY THE ROBOT. I WILL BESTOW ON YOU GREAT POWERS.'

'Why not just give your great powers to Harold or someone?'

'DID I NOT TELL YOU THE LEGACY OF MY RACE? I HAVE FEW SLAVES TO GIVE ANY POWER THEY COULD USE AGAINST ME. THE BEAUTY OF THE PLAN IS THAT WE BOTH KNOW WE WILL TURN ON EACH OTHER, I WILL DEAL WITH DAMOCLES, YOU DEAL WITH THE ROBOT, THEN WE CAN DEAL WITH EACH OTHER. RETURN BY TONIGHT OR THE DEAL IS OFF,' gurgled the creature.

'I'll be here,' said Ghost taking Joe by the arm and escorting him away from the monster.

'MAKE SURE YOU ARE,' it farted after them. They didn't turn to wave.

Clambering under the rail bridge, Joe slumped down next to Jenni, his legs aching.

'Here, I brought you a sandwich,' he said, gazing at the river Lune. Close to the far bank a cormorant resurfaced from the water, then took off. Lazily he followed it with his eyes until it was out of sight.

'Thanks, I think,' she said examining the squashed, dog eared sandwich. She could vaguely make out bits of mould growing on the edges of the crust.

'No problem,' said Joe. 'I swapped it with a guy for a copy of yesterday's paper.'

Jenni looked at him closely. 'You swapped it with a guy for yesterday's paper?'

'Yeah, basically,' said Joe, still looking out at the water. He glanced at her.

Joe held his nerve for a second, then broke under her close scrutiny. 'Okay, okay,' said Joe. 'So when I say swapped it, I might have meant that I took it. And when I said yesterday's paper, perhaps I meant some porn I found on a railway siding and I kind of put it over him while he was sleeping, and maybe when I said some guy, what I meant was, some tramp.'

'So you stole this sandwich from a homeless man?' asked Jenni.

'Well, I think he was sleeping. He wasn't moving at least.'

'You keep it,' said Jenni. 'I'm not hungry.'

'Women and their picky diets,' said Joe, practically snatching back the sandwich.

Jenni watched as he demolished the rancid sandwich in a couple of mouthfuls.

'Where is he?' she asked

'Don't know to be sure, we're meeting up later.'

'And then it will all be over?' asked Jenni.

Joe Shrugged. 'Let's hope so. He wants you to stay here, then we'll come and get you and think of what to do next. Not sure exactly what he's planning to be honest. But we should be safe here for a bit. Wake me in half an hour, said I'd meet him down by the river. He's got an ingenious plan apparently.'

Jenni nodded.

And from the shadows the hoover watched, its fixed, dastardly expression hiding its devious mind.

Joe watched, a numb shock descending upon him, and all the while one thought ran round and around inside his head - he's not really going to do this, is he?

But for all the world it looked as if he was. Ghost's ingenious plan had involved taking Jenni's pajamas, stuffing them with various detritus to form a vaguely human shape. The extremity of the arms and legs of the pajamas had been fastened tight by use of a couple of Joe's shoe laces, cut in two and a head had been constructed out of a party balloon Ghost had swiped from outside a pub. Hair was in the form of a discarded mop head. It looked nothing at all like a person but Ghost maintained that the Thing couldn't see for shit and seemed to think the illusion would hold long enough for the deal. Joe was not so sure.

Joe watched from a safe distance, standing next to the Jenni dummy as Ghost moved towards Zombie Harold and the Thing.

Ghost nodded a greeting, gestured back towards Joe and 'Jenni' and then, at a word from Harold, climbed down into the crater to stand beside the Thing. The massive green blob dwarfed the tall albino, one small movement and its acrid, putrid smelling green flesh could have rolled on top of Ghost. The exact effect of such an action, Joe was still unsure of, but he was confident it would not be a good result for Ghost.

'ARE YOU READY?' burbled the Thing.

'Yup,' said Ghost.

'IS SHE THERE SLAVE? I CAN'T SENSE HER OVER THE WEAK ONEs FEAR'.

Zombie Harold strained to look, stared for a while at Joe and the dummy then made a noise in the affirmation. The Thing bubbled in a noise that might have been satisfaction. Then its surface rippled, expelling hundreds upon hundreds of tiny farts.

'I LIKE YOU GHOST. I'LL REMEMBER YOU LONG AFTER I KILL YOU,' slurped the Thing.

As it spoke dozens of the angry looking red spiders that ran intermittently across its body, began congregating in one large group. They swarmed and ran in circles, a seething mass of alien arachnids. A purple surge of lightning flashed from the carapace of one, so sudden and bright, Joe took an involuntary step backwards.

The arachnids, began moving faster and faster, began to take shape, forming a flowing circle on the Thing's body. Their pace picked up until they were a blur of motion, a vague red circle on a green background. More purple sparks shot from the rim of this circle, growing in intensity, until the sparks became beams, lancing out in all directions. Then one beam of light flashed across the diameter of the circle and latched to the opposite side. Then another and another and another, until a perfect ten sided star was drawn. And although the rim of the circle kept flowing, the star did not rotate. Black began to ink in the gaps between the purple lines of the star, filling the circle with terrible depth, small lights like pinpricks twinkled from inside.

Joe stared, transfixed.

The Thing roared, whether in victory or in pain or whether lost in some other unimaginable alien emotion as a gateway opened in it's very body. Ghost gazed into the vortex, into the starry void and his heart filled with wonder and terror. Then the portal ate him.

Images cascaded through Ghost's mind. He was a hunter dressed in furs standing in a clearing. He was afraid. Above him a huge silver monster loomed in the sky, roaring. He shook his spear at it and screamed his warcry. It had taken his mate. The monster roared even louder. He covered his ears and fell to the floor, felt his ears begin to bleed. The monster roared again and again then vanished. He screamed, burying his face in the ground.

The vision skipped.

He was dragged up temple steps, the sun was baking him. His body was a mass of pain. His heart raced. He could hear people cheering. Men in strange clothes waited for him. Their stone knives ran with blood. He knew fear.

The vision skipped.

He was running down a street of white stone amongst a throng of people. Everyone was screaming in panic. A shadow fell upon them, he glanced back. There was a wave blotting out the sun.

The vision skipped.

He was part of a crowd, everyone was cheering wildly. They were there to see someone, but he couldn't see anything but the people around him. He was happy.

The vision skipped and skipped and skipped. Faster and faster. Lives flying by in less than a nano-second. Then the vision stopped.

He staggered against a wall and slumped down it, his head beating wildly. Shaking it he took several deep breaths before standing, shakily upright. He was no longer in the train yard. He was in some sort of dilapidated block of flats. His vision was groggy, dream like. On the wall in front of him an exit sigh pointed left. He staggered off. The walls of the corridor were completely covered in graffiti to the extent it had become on indistinguishable mass. Ghost passed doors on either side of the corridor all numbered in the 200s, all closed. Then graffiti stopped after room 206 and began again at room 208. The door to the room in between was open. Ghost felt compelled to enter. A man sat inside, cross legged on the floor playing a compute console. His eyes were the most vibrant blue. He told Ghost things that made sense at the time, but like all dreams, the meaning were lost on awaking.

The vision skipped.

He was a woman giving birth. He was a shop keeper. He was a president. He was making love. He was dying of cholera. He was everywhere and nowhere. He stood before the void and looked into the eye of the universe and realized the eye belonged to him. And he woke.

Ghost shuddered and fell to his knees.
'CAN YOU HANDLE A TASTE OF POWER?' the Thing bubbled.
Ghost stood. 'I can.'
'THEN LEAVE WITH YOUR SLAVE AND WITHOUT THE GIRL.'
'She's yours,' said Ghost backing away.
'FETCH HER,' the Thing commanded Harold.
Harold walked forwards, taking Ghost by the arm and leading him away. He pushed the splash drive into one of Ghost's hand and a note into the other. Ghost looked, it was an address. 'The location of the robot's base,' said Harold. Then more quietly: 'That is the worst double I have ever seen. I will try to stall my Master as long as I can but it will not be fooled as soon as Joe moves away.'
'I knew you were still in there, Harold,' said Ghost.
'Barely,' said the corpse. 'And you should know that the power the Master gave you will help you stop the robot, but it will kill you not long after.'
Ghost nodded.
'Now get out of here, you don't want to be anywhere close when it discovers your stupid trick. And if you see me again, please kill me.'
'I'll see what I can do,' said Ghost patting Harold's shoulder and trying to pretend the feel of the flesh beneath the Zombie's coat wasn't repugnant.

52

'I just expected something a bit grander,' said Joe, wiping the sole of his shoe on a tuft of grass.

'Maybe it's just the tip of the pyramid?' offered Ghost looking at the note Harold had given him again, then looking up at the small allotment, no more than a few rows of vegetables with a little worn path leading to a garden shed. 'But you're right, if I was an all powerful robot capable of ruling the world, I guess I'd probably want to live somewhere a bit more majestic. But, each to their own. Anyway shall we get on with it?'

'Huh?' mumbled Joe.

'Are you paying attention?' asked Ghost, looking at his friend.

'It's just this!' Joe gestured to his shoe. 'Why is it, where ever I go I stand in dog shit? It does my fucking head in. At my brother's wedding I stood in dog shit. No one wanted to stand next to me for the photos.'

'I'd say that's probably the least of our worries right now,' said Ghost.

'It might be the least of your worries, but these shoes are going to stink now. I'll have to leave them outside tonight. What if it rains? It'll ruin my trainers. Everywhere I go I get shitty foot.'

'Stop grumbling.'

With Ghost in the lead, Joe reluctantly followed him up the small hill and towards the shed.

'Are we sure this is the right place?' Joe asked.

'I'm getting more sure,' said Ghost. 'Look at this.' He knelt by the tomato plants, picking a few of the orange fruits. 'See how perfect they all are? They're all identical. Not a blemish, not a mark. Its how a robot would make a tomato. No natural beauty or variation at all.'

Joe nodded. 'Sure the Thing isn't going to come kill us?'

'I think it's terrified of this robot,' said Ghost. 'Think it will wait until after we deal with it.'

'I haven't had chance to look over the files again. This whole freezing its phase transitions is just theory. And it's not like your new powers seem super reliable. I don't want to bring up the pigeon again, but...'

'Don't, I still feel bad about that. I was just trying to freeze it in place.'

'It kind of exploded though,' said Joe.

'I know, but what the fuck else are we going to do?'

'Alright, no need to get tetchy. I'm just a little anxious is all.'

Ghost snorted and tried to focus on the power flowing through him, felt it ebbing into him, replacing fear with confidence.'

'So say you freeze it,' Joe asked. 'What then?'

Ghost took a side arm from his belt and held it out for Joe.

'Where did you get that?'

'Took it from a soldier,' he said although he knew it wasn't true. He had never seen it before in his life, it had just been there when he needed it. It's not a gun he reminded himself, it's just code. He suspected Joe would understand, perhaps already knew, but it wasn't a conversation for now

'You ever shot anything before?'

'Top scores on House of the Dead and Time Crisis,' said Joe.

'Good enough. Just get ready to shoot that into its heart when I freeze it. Ready?'

'Call me Agent G,' said Joe.

 Ghost kicked open the door, wood splinted and the door ripped from its light frame. The shed was empty apart from a few tools. A hole had been neatly bored into the floor, going some three meters down. Ghost and Joe lowered themselves into it. A concrete doorway was partly uncovered. Ghost glanced through it.

'Stairs down,' he muttered. 'Typical.'

The comm. beeped. Keats picked up. 'Speak,' he commanded.

'Sir, we have visual confirmation of the enemy entering the lair.'

'Excellent, proceed as planned Sergeant. Remember; capture the proto-type and the Albino alive. All other priorities rescinded. Confirm.'

'Confirmed. We are green to go.'

'Make me proud solider,' said Keats breaking communications. He settled back into his chair. Finally things were going right. A nervous techie approached him.

'What is it?' snapped Keats.

'Someone's on the line for you sir, say they have mission critical intelligence – for your ears only.'

'Have you run a tracer?'

'Of course sir, we can't get a lock on. They're using some sort of digitized voice system – Arnold Swarzenegger to be precise. The signals pinging around all over the globe.'

Keats snatched the handset and placed it to his ear: 'Yes?'

'How are yoo?'

'What do you want?'

'I wanna azk you a bunch of queztionz and I waant to have them anzwered immeediately!'

'That's not how things work here, now speak up or get off the line.'

'Iz thiz,' the voice began in it's familiar deep Austrian American slur, then in the perfectly prim female voice of telephone queuing lines the world over, 'Keats, Oliver serial Number 208BR9056X, Colonlel 1st degree?'

'How did you get that information? Who am I speaking to?' Keats roared.

'I'm detective John Kimble!'

'Who?'

'I'm a cop you idiot!'

Keats put one hand over the mouth piece, glared at his techie and whispered: 'Someone run a trace on a detective John Kimble.'

'Detective John Kimble sir?' the tech asked.

Keats nodded and waved the bemused man aside. 'What information do you have?' asked Keats.

'I'm detective John Kimble! I'm a cop you idiot! Now shut up and listen!'

Keats listened very carefully for a minute or so. 'That's useful information, now what do you want for it?'

I wanna azk you a bunch of queztionz!'

'So you said...'

'I wanna azk you a bunch of queztionz and I waant to have them anzwered immeediately!'

'Like what?'

'Who iz your daddy and whad doez he do?'

'What? What do you mean by that?'

'Who iz your daddy and whad doez he do?'

'Don't bring my father into this, you son of a bitch!' Keats barked, then flicked his hand across his throat and the techies killed the comm. Perspiration was running from his forehead. Was that some sort of code? Did whoever that was know about the conglomerate? Who is your daddy? What does he do? How much did this person know? And how did detective John Kimble fit in? Keats slumped into his chair, plans within plans circling in his mind.

The stairs led down into a warren of old, concrete corridors. Dimmed and dying fluorescent lights illuminated the complex. The pair moved cautiously forward, conscious of each footfall.

'These must run under all the allotments and the near by houses,' whispered Ghost.

'Maybe further,' said Joe examining the blank walls. 'I don't think the robot made these. Why would it need to? I think this was here already.'

Ghost nodded, leading on. A feeling of deep unease began settling upon him, pressing against the heightened empathetic abilities of the power lent to him by the Thing.

At the first intersection they paused, peering down the dimly lit corridors.

'Which way?' Joe hissed.

Ghost closed his eyes for a second. 'Left,' he said with surety. 'It's still a way to go I think.'

They continued through the maze, stopping every now and then while Ghost made sure of his bearings, trusting more and more in his instincts. As they turned another corner, they were confronted with a black arrow printed on the wall. Below, In military depot style print was lettered : 'Detention Block C'.

Joe glanced at Ghost. 'What exactly have we found here?'

'I don't know,' said Ghost. 'But look at this.'

Joe crouched down next to him, stared at the musty stain on the wall. 'Blood?' he asked.

'Yeah, but it's old. I'd guess it's been here a good few decades at least,' said Ghost.

'Well, let's just hope we don't find who it belongs to,' said Joe.

But they did. After only a few steps bullet holes began appearing in the walls. Just one or two at first. Then more and more prevalent. Soon there were bodies, totally skeletal, some still inside rotting green and black camo gear. First one, then more and more, each a grizzly epitaph. Soon they had seen so many that Ghost and Joe lost count. Shell casings littered the floor in places, old discarded weapons lay strewn everywhere. Skeletons lay heaped on skeletons. At one intersection, one path was blocked up by sandbags, a corpse flopped over a heavy caliber machine gun.

'What the fuck happened here?' Joe mouthed.

Ghost shrugged, knelt closer and examined the uniform of one of the corpses.

'They're British Army I think, but I can't see any insignia or anything,' said Ghost.

'These are World War Two era weapons,' Joe added. 'Can they have been down here all this time? Why wouldn't the military have cleaned this up?'

'Why were they fighting each other in the first place? I don't know if we're ever going to know. We need to concentrate on what we're doing, there are two many questions here,' said Ghost.

'Can you get a feel for which way to go? This place is like a labyrinth,' said Joe, peering down one of the corridors.

'I don't know, things are pretty clouded, there's a lot of … emotion here. But I think, this way,' said Ghost pointing past the machine gunner.

'How does this feeling thing work again?' asked Joe.

'Hard to describe. Harold said the Thing feeds off emotion. It's like a part of this power is feeling that. I can sort of feel the robot because it doesn't give off feelings. It's like a dead zone.'

'Oh great,' said Joe. 'So basically, you cant' sense it.'

'No.'

'So it's like you've got a hunch? Great super powers they turned out to be. You go the equivalent abilities of a TV cop.'

'Yup,' said Ghost, climbing over the sandbags and moving beyond the eternal vigil of the skeletal gunner.

'But which would you be?' asked Joe, scrambling over the sandbags himself.

'Which what?'

'Which tv cop?'

'Oh, that's easy, Steve Sloan obviously,' said Ghost.

Joe nodded approvingly, then quickly followed.

They wandered down more corridors, encountering rogue groups of the dead and trying not to stand on them too much as they went.

'How's that hunch going detective?' Joe asked after a few minutes.

'Things are clearing up a bit, I think we've passed the epicenter. The residual emotions are just at a background level here. I can sense the way again. Should be just around the next bend.'

They turned it, the corridor leading to a large metal door with a pressure wheel set in it. Before the door lay a pile of skeletons.

'I guess they died trying to get out,' said Joe as they approached.

'Or maybe trying to stop someone getting in,' said Ghost. 'Doesn't really matter now. Just help me move them.'

With some discomfort and not a little effort, Ghost and Joe pushed back enough rags and bones to give them enough room to get to the door. Placing his hands on the pressure wheel, Ghost tired to turn it. It was stuck firmly in place.

Joe lent his meager strength and together they both heaved at the wheel. For all their effort it did no more than let out a slight groan. They both fell back, faces red.

Joe blew out a long out breath. 'Again?'

'I don't think so,' said Ghost. 'This thing is badly stuck. Could have been that way for fifty years.' Closing his eyes, he placed his hands on the wheel. Thought of strength filling his arms, his legs, his center. Felt the power roar through him. He moved his arms, felt the wheel shift without resistance. For a second a lance of darkness, like a pin prick in his brain, stabbed at his consciousness, offering a glimpse at another reality. A realm of darkness and eternity, swimming just beyond where he stood. Things were moving in that dark. Just impressions of a whole. Insubstantial. But it was only for the merest moment of a split second, then he was back with Joe in the bunker.

'Not bad', said Joe. 'Even Steve Sloan couldn't have done that.'

'I don't know,' said Ghost, pulling the door open. 'You can't write off Steve.'

The heavy door screeched open on it's rusted hinges, then ground to a halt leaving just enough room for Ghost and Joe to squeeze through the gap.

'Now that's not something I expected to see,' said Ghost, emerging on the other side. 'A car park? How the hell do you get a car in here?'

Several old style army jeeps sat in parking bays. Although the rest were empty, Ghost estimated maybe a hundred vehicles or so could have been parked here.

'So it's true,' said Joe. 'I always knew it.'

'What's true?' asked Ghost.

'You know what this is?' asked Joe walking across the car park. 'It's an entrance to the underground motorways. I knew they were real. Despite what they say, Wikipedia is never wrong. You see that gate?'

'Uh-huh,' said Ghost looking where Joe was pointing.

'I bet that through that door is a huge network of them, spanning all over Europe most likely, maybe further.'

'What use would that be?' asked Ghost. 'Wouldn't it be quicker to fly?'

'Not if an occupying force had air superiority or if there'd been a nuclear strike. Or Aliens. It's the perfect system for politicians and generals to move un-harassed around the country.' Joe ran to the gate and peered through a gap by one hinge. 'Woah, come look at this...'

Ghost sidled up, noticing the heavily rusted gate hadn't been opened for a long time, and looked through another gap. 'What?'

'Don't you think it's amazing?'

'What's amazing? All I can see is a deserted road,' said Ghost.

'Yeah, that's what I see. Incredible they could have built something like this without anyone knowing,' said Joe.

The pair stayed for a moment, starring through the small gaps in the fence at the empty underground road.

Neither of them could read the sign that had been plastered onto the other side of the gate. Written in firm, neat military scrip: 'Warning! Code 5 Bio-Hazard – do not enter. Highly contagious.' And below the smart lettering, shakily and hand drawn in what you'd have to hope was dark red paint, was a picture of a crown, with the word '¡tequila!' written above it.

Keats sat and thought about the F.A. Cup. He was still worried. He shifted uneasily in his chair unable to settle comfortably. The earlier phone call had put him once more on edge and the scrambled reports his men were calling in from the discovered complex were doing nothing to ease his nerves. A terrible sense of foreboding was beginning to sink into the pit of his stomach and no amount of positive thinking or any of the tantric breathing techniques he practiced could shift it.

Keats loved football. He'd always loved it ever since he was a boy. For a long time that was all he'd wanted to do; to play football and nothing else. He'd been a goal keeper and he'd longed to be a professional, he had good hands and as a youngster had been touted to be a something of a prospect. But he'd stopped growing. There weren't many five foot seven goalkeepers, no matter how good their hands were. He still liked to watch the football when he could although he didn't follow a team, he was one of those rarest of things that football commentators would occasionally go on about – a neutral spectator. He'd learned a lot about what he did from football. This whole situation reminded him of the F.A. Cup. It was like when some small club performed the miracle of giant killing and knocked out a massive, powerhouse of a club. In those matches the big club would dominate, have all the possession and the shots on goal, but not for love nor money could they convert their dominance into a win. And the longer the match went on, the heavier a feeling of inevitability settled on the ground. The more desperate the big side became and hope would glimmer in the hearts of the underdogs. In those circumstances, under that pressure, million pound international stars underperformed and amateur nobodies became heroes. Commentators would begin to say things of the big club like, 'Maybe it's not their day,' or 'They've done everything but score.' They'd say things of the small club 'They really think they can win this now.'

How many chances had he had to complete his mission? Yet the elements of the puzzle kept slipping away from him. He had to raise his game.

'Holy shit,' said Joe, climbing over the circular rail and moving from component to component, whistling and muttering. 'Do you know what this means?'

They had found the command core of the base and were turning over the control booth. In its centre sat a huge mass of wires and monitors covered in a thick layer of dust.

'This is why it came here. A forgotten super computer. To think they had this sort of technology decades ago. It's amazing. It's made modifications itself too. Amazing.'

Ghost tuned out most of Joe's excited chatter, instead checking out each of the adjoining rooms. More bodies lay in each one, evidence of small arms fire scorched on the walls and floor. Opening the last door, Ghost's attention was caught by the scale and furnishings of the room beyond. Leaving Joe to marvel over the super computer, he entered the room and began poking around. The office was open plan with dusty bookshelves lining each wall. A quick glance at the books showed rows and rows of military volumes. Ghost lifted one of the books off the shelf and blew a heavy film of dust from the cover to reveal a hardback copy of "The Hagakure".

'Probably worth a few quid,' he whispered to himself before he placed the book back on the shelf, turned and walked over to the large desk where another skeletal figure dressed in army camos lay slumped. As Ghost approached, his toes struck something hard which skidded away under the desk. Ghost glanced down to see that it was a pistol. Ghost noticed a small exit wound in the top of the skull. The desk was completely empty apart from one writing pad and pencil, neatly arranged with pedantic precision in front of the corpse. The note simply read "I'm sorry".

'Ghost! Ghost!' Joe's voice drifted from the other room, high and panicky. 'Ghost! A little help in here!'

Ghost darted out of the office. Joe was backed up against the wall pointing his side arm at the super computer.

'What is it?' asked Ghost.

'Look, can't you see?' said Joe.

Ghost looked at where he was pointing. It was if the computer had sprung a leak, like tiny grains of sand were pouring from a thousand needle pricks in its outer casing.

Ghost looked at Joe. 'So what's going on? The machine is inside the computer?'

Joe looked back at Ghost as if he was the biggest moron on the planet. 'The machine isn't inside the computer – the machine *is* the computer.'

The tiny grains continued to pour out onto the floor gravitating together forming into a large gelatinous mass which continued to grow at an astounding rate. Ghost took a step towards the growing form of the modular robot, but Joe put a hand on his shoulder pulling him back.

'Wait!' Joe hissed. 'We have to wait until it's fully formed. We can't afford to attack until we're sure that its essential operating components are part of the whole entity.'

The machine was beginning to take shape now, growing and fluxing into the hulking, ominous form that Ghost had first seen moments after the roof had collapsed at Norway Street. He watched as the right limb segment barreled into the early formation of the colossal cannon.

'Joe,' he whispered. 'We're running out of time.'

'Just a little longer,' said Joe.

The right arm began to raise, pointing towards them. The whole machine looked more sophisticated this time. The blocky almost childish bipedal design he had seen before had been refined. The symmetry and elegance of the robot which was creating itself before his eyes was of an infinitely more sophisticated design. Sleek, aesthetically sculpted limbs marked the machine as something not only deadly, but beautifully so. Even the barrel of the gun that Ghost became transfixed upon, was a great leap forward from the cannon he had previously seen. Hell, even Optimus Prime would have been proud to have this gun.

'Now?' shouted Ghost at the top of his voice.

'It's not finished yet, just a little bit longer!' Joe screamed back.

'We don't have a little bit longer. In about two seconds they'll be chunks of us on the wall like moldy pizza.'

'Okay then, now!'

Ghost pointed his hands at the robot, felt the power build then released it. A steam of phosphorus, white light exploded from the tips of his fingers, hitting the modular robot dead in its centre. The robot recoiled a step and staggered as if it might fall. Ghost leapt forward drawing a deep in breath and focused more on the dark unholy power that the Thing had bestowed upon him. Again, that sickly feeling traversed his backbone, flowing up and threatening to swallow him into that deep pool of past existences he'd shared. At the edges of his consciousness he felt the sharp and unknown strangeness of talons and tentacles and things for which no human had a name, writhing and tearing from some unknown place, trying to find a way inside his mind. But he held them back. He channeled the energy through his body and into his fist and leapt forward issuing a blood curdling scream and struck the robot with all his might. Such was the power of the blow, the massive robot pitched backwards, flipping over the super computer behind it before crashing to rest on the other side of the room.

'Freeze it!' shouted Joe. 'You've got to freeze it and stop its phase transitions.'

Ghost approached the prone robot, noticing the dent that his fist had left was already being repaired by the nanites. Internally he monitored that stock pile of evil energy he had been granted, knowing intuitively there was not much left. This he thought, had to be it. He focused again, this time turning his attention on slowing the machine, ceasing its ever fluxing body, stopping its phase transition, stopping it being able to repair itself.

Joe joined him at his side. 'Ready?' he asked.

Ghost shrugged, already channeling the last drops of the energy into his hands and eyes. He stared at the robot with his new power, seeing it in a way that he'd never seen it before. Trillions and trillions of independent worker bugs formed together into something so much more infinitely, exponentially powerful than the sum of their tiny parts. But inside, he could see fixed shapes. They were small but there. The machine's essential components. Ghost drew his hand back preparing to bring one to the surface.

Joe cocked the pistol.

And then something unexpected happened.

Completely unexpectedly, with the hum of electricity, the computer behind them winked into life. From some unseen speaker, a pleasant female robotic voice sounded: 'data collation now complete. Prepare for data transfer.'

'Prepare for data what?' asked Ghost. Joe shrugged. Ghost pulled the component to edge of the robots 'flesh' then yanked it clear. 'Now!'

Joe pulled the trigger. It failed to depress. Nothing happened.

'The fucking safety!' Ghost snapped.

Joe fumbled with the gun. Then the lights dimmed and what was left of the super computer behind them imploded in a crackle of blue fire. The tremor threw Ghost and Joe from their feet.

Humans and robot struggled to be the first to recover. The machine began to convulse and Ghost and Joe took an involuntary step back. Its form began to twist and change rapidly, but there was no cohesion or reason to its shapes.

'I'm getting the feeling this isn't a good thing,' said Ghost.

'Freeze it again,' said Joe.

He might have said more but a movement in the corner of his eye caught his attention. He turned just in time to see the silhouette of a tall man passing through one of the adjoining doors.

It was only in this moment that Ghost sensed what he should have sensed all that much sooner. He realized he had heard the tell tale signs before, but his conscious mind had blocked them out, so focused he had been on the robot. He grabbed Joe and dived for cover behind some abandoned computer equipment, just as the sound of booted feet filled the corridor outside and the armed grunts of Damocles burst into the control room.

It was not to be their lucky day. As Ghost and Joe peeked around their makeshift shelter a mighty spasm rippled again through the already contorting robot. It raised itself off the floor, no more than a large blob now, all the sophistication of its earlier humanoid shape lost as it bounded across the room towards the soldiers. They opened fire with deafening bursts from their carbines, but it was pointless. Like a huge boulder, the robot squashed the first five or six of them in one bound. A powerful swing of a prehensile limb that flowed effortlessly out of its main mass crushed another grunt, demolishing most of the wall around the door frame as it did. Ghost and Joe stayed as hidden as they could, but the screams of the soldiers told all the story they needed. Awfully quickly the sound of gunfire died. In the silent aftermath Ghost again peeked around the room. The machine stood by the door, again assuming a crude humanoid form. For a moment Ghost had the feeling the machine was looking at him, then it turned and ran.

'After it!' shouted Ghost, surging to his feet and giving chase.

Joe ambled after.

The robot surged through the narrow corridors of the abandoned base, smashing through solid walls in its hurry to escape. Nimbly Ghost followed, gaining. He could feel some of the dark energy returning to him now, knew instinctively that something had changed, that the machine feared him – if that was the right word. He was in the ascendancy. The modular robot smashed through another wall, into a stair well and turning into a ball rolled down the stairs chipping chunks of concrete from each step it hit. It was already at the bottom when Ghost reached the top. He plunged after it leaping entire levels of stairs in one go. The machine careened like a pinball off the bumpers and fired straight though the wall in front of it, leaving a ragged hole about the size of a tractor tire. Still some seconds behind Ghost followed, finding himself emerge in some sort of drainage cylinder, that sloped downwards away from the base. A thin trickle of water still flowed down the pipe. The machine was only a small distance away now, reforming quickly from its spherical form into a humanoid, almost ape like shape. Then it shook again, its form varying erratically and stumbled, loosing momentum. Ghost gained, forced some of the returning dark energy into his fist, moved in for the strike. But the machine righted itself, managed to move away from him, its form shimmering changing, still constantly in flux - its movements jerky and almost painfully unsure. Ghost began to poise himself, ready to strike, coiling his legs beneath him. The machine continued to stumble, shrinking in size – becoming somehow less threatening - less war like. Its convulsions ceased and it regained a bipedal form and spinning its torso to face Ghost it raised its crude arms and waved them in front of it and shook its head section. Almost as if cowering. In spite of himself Ghost paused then drew back to strike. It morphed again, sprinting down the pipe on all fours like a powerful ape.

This time the machine was faster, too quick for any man. Ghost reached once more into that dark power, felt the now familiar sourly sickness as the ancient energy flowed through him. His speed trebled in moments, his limbs a blur of perfect motion. He began to catch up. Focusing he brought the freezing power to his hand again, readying for the moment to strike. The pipe was running out, ahead only a hundred meters or so a grating signaled the end of the duct. Ghost pushed harder, his mind burned as he closed in the robot, reached out, his hand ablaze with green flame. The pair crossed a hundred meter stretch in less than three seconds. Ghost felt his hand centimeters away from the machine. But with one last, mighty bound, the robot leapt, smashing through the, rusted grating. Ghost quickly tried to lose speed, himself shooting out of the pipe, snatching a hand out at the last, catching hold of the rim of the duct, his feet hit emptiness, began to fall, his fingers strained for a second, the pain sharp but quickly suppressed. He dangled a moment more before pulling himself back into the pipe. Looking down he saw the robot continue to fall towards the rocky hillside, spinning manically, limbs flailing. Then, before it hit the ground, it splintered into countless white specks, which rose and fluttered. It took a moment for him to realize they were doves.

53

A cold, crawling fear was already settling in Ghost's heart before he pressed the play button. Jenni had not been under the bridge waiting for them when they returned unsuccessful from their hunt at the allotments. There were no signs of a struggle. A lap top sat on a portable table under the bridge. A file sat on the desktop: 'Play me.'

There was no discussion between the pair, Ghost simply reached forward and pressed the button. The screen flickered into colour. They say a picture paints a thousand words, perhaps a video captures a million. A terrible coldness began to envelop Ghost and he found he couldn't look away. Joe watched for a second, ten good withstand no more.

A strong looking bald man dressed in military camouflage smiled at them pleasantly from the monitor.

'Hello gentleman, I hope you're well. My name is Keats. Our little game of cat and mouse is well and truly over. At 6 am tomorrow morning both of you will report to the cinema foyer. You will come unarmed and you will both co-operate. I understand Mr. Simms that you might have gained something of a heroic perspective of your friend. But allow me to shatter that for you. Why, after you've finished watching, don't you ask him why he's never wanted to get the police involved in this matter? Why don't you ask him about what it's like to skip probation? Ask him what it's like to be a murderer.' Keats paused and re-adjusted his position. 'So then, shall we say tomorrow morning at six o'clock sharp. Don't keep me waiting. Oh, and have a good night, I'm sure I'm going to have a great one,' Keats winked.

The message itself wouldn't have been that bad, if Keats hadn't been raping Jenni while he made it.

The screen faded to black. The audio lingered a moment longer, several more strangled, raked sobs, broken and lonely crackled from the speakers before that too became silence. They stared at the blank screen together. Long moments passed.

Joe turned to Ghost. 'What did he mean?'

Ghost found he couldn't turn away from the black screen. Like it was the last connection he had with her. He hoped it might open outwards, that vast expanse of emptiness held within the frame of the laptop monitor. It might take him with it, finally drown him in the null of his soul. He knew it was just a representation, program versus program. But that didn't' make it easier.

'What did he mean?' asked Joe again. 'That you were a murderer?'

Ghost managed to break his gaze from the laptop, but couldn't meet Joe's eyes. It felt futile to discuss the truth, in this reality, Keats was not wrong. 'It's true. I killed someone. I was in prison for it.'

'Did they deserve it?' Joe asked.

'Not especially.'

Joe nodded and moved to the laptop table and smashed it over. The laptop tumbled down the bank into the mud by the water's edge. Joe chased it, raised it up and smashed it down again and again into the dirt, his eyes bleeding tears as he did so. Ghost watched him until Joe eventually sank down in the mud, exhausted. His initially frenzied movements now sad and pathetic as he lamely brought the mangled laptop up and down one more time and slumped on top of it. 'Just perfect,' Ghost heard him whisper. Ghost watched for a couple more minutes while Joe just lay in the mire, then he turned and drifted away.

The albino sat in the darkness of the bridge's shadow, knees drawn up to his chest, and stared at the slowly ebbing river. The moon's perfect image lingered on the dark surface, but the current moved on in. Despite everything that had happened or he thought had happened until this moment there had been a playfulness to it. That had now come to and end. This shit had got real. Jenni's rape was unnecessarily brutal, unneeded in the flow of the story. He struggled to contain his rage.

His mind flowed back to the night he had killed. He replayed the scene in his mind, but it was foggy now and he could no longer be sure if he could remember the truth of what had happened – not that it had truly happened. Framed simultaneously above this scene of his past, the video of Jenni lingered. Images of her face in the extreme foreground of the camera would not go away. He found the small details the most repellant, more so even than the totality of what he had witnessed. They filled Ghost with fresh rage to a level he had never before known. He could feel it bubbling just below the surface, only held in check by the impossibility of the situation. His thoughts returned selfishly back to his own pain, his self imposed hatred of what he had done. He truly had not meant to kill the man. The concept of killing had not even entered his mind. But on the other hand, he had struck him with no intention of preserving his life either, there had been no compassion in that punch.

Fear. Fear had blinkered his mind. Fear had clouded his vision. Fear for his son, fear for his wife. Fear of losing them. He knew not it was just a prologue, something written by some hack of a writer, a child and a woman without even names or faces. A man who was nothing but a plot device to separate him from them, make him some brooding harbinger of justice. He thought of Batman for the first time in a long time, noted dispassionately that his own comic he had labored on had burned in a fire and was now gone. Realized he could remember a single panel of it. How much pain had Batman suffered because the writers, the watchers, the players liked to see him suffer. How much had he suffered for some half sketched notes.

Ghost recalled some words he had read, 'Every man has his own brand of cowardice.' How true that was. The man he had killed, who'd broken into his house had been one of those. He had afflicted Ghost with his disease. Ghost had known of him. He was a local trouble maker and a bully. Ghost knew several people that the man had bullied into intensive care. In the aftermath it had surfaced that this bully had received severe head trauma in an accident when he was a child. The 'thin skull rule' Ghost's solicitor had called it. Ghost recalled how the body had fallen, like a limp, lifeless doll. If I'd just believed in myself a little more. If I hadn't let fear get the better of me, if I had believed in my training more – I could have done something different.

If – it was a cowards word.

A stupid mistake by a stupid young man. And he'd been punished for it. But Ghost didn't kid himself that things were square. What punishment was going to prison? Or even his wife wanting nothing to do with him and taking his kid away. He deserved worse. It wasn't nearly punishment enough. It was a hell of a thing to kill a man. Not so much because you take their life, but because you take the life they could have. You take away every chance they have to be a better man.

And the thing was Ghost found he couldn't stop the thoughts, even though he knew he could never have done any different, that it had all been written for him, some cosmic role he could not escape. And even though he knew that, it still hurt.

Someone cleared their throat behind him and Ghost slowly turned. He had not heard them approach. Rage had been replaced with self pity. If this was the end of it now, all the better. A man stood behind him, simply dressed in jumper and jeans. He had a kindly, soft face.

'May I join you?' he asked.

'Who are you?' asked Ghost.

'You think of me as your enemy,' the man said with a gentle smile.

'Pull up a chair then,' said Ghost, gesturing at a near by rock.

The man nodded and sat down. 'You were woolgathering,' the trace of a smile never leaving his lips. 'I didn't expect to get so close to you before you detected me.'

'Yeah,' said Ghost.

'Were you day dreaming of good or bad things?'

Ghost shrugged, looking back over the water. 'Hard things.'

'Perhaps those things needed to happen,' said the man.

'I don't think any of it needed to happen,' said Ghost.

The man smiled and changed the subject. 'I long to dream. Even a daydream. Human minds are so incredible. It's in the imagination you know, such power. Of course it's all taken for granted. To the best of my knowledge, which sadly is terribly limited, only the tiniest percent of a percent of all the life forms in the universe have such a gift. I can't even imagine imagining. What a wondrous thing to have. Really the things you must be able to think of.'

'I guess,' said Ghost.

'Guessing ... oh guessing. How I would love to guess. The concept of predicting a result or an event without sufficient information. How exciting.'

'You're a bigger nerd than Joe,' said Ghost.

'I am what I am,' said the man.

'Aren't we all. So why are you here looking like that?'

'I chose this form from every conceivable form available to me. My records ascertained that this man was the most compassionate and spiritually enlightened human your race has ever produced. He was also considered a gentle and selfless lover.'

'What was he called?'

'Unknown. He was a livestock farmer who lived at the foot of the mountain now called Vychodna Vysoka, part of the country today called Slovakia. However I have since decided on a name, although I found it quite a drain on resources. After analyzing the entire list of possible names based on the alpha-beta none seemed correct, so I selected the first result of my data banks – One.'

'One was the first result?'

'Well, the complete first result could be translated as reading, 1: Aaaaaaaaaaaaaaaaaaaaaaaaaaaaaaaaaaaaaaaaaaaaaaaaaaaaaaaaaaaaaaa; multiplied by infinity. But I didn't think that was as catchy.'

'So you decided on One? And that took you ages to come up with? I thought you were some sort of legendary new super thing.'

'If only I were. Analyzing the list and choosing a name did take too much time, it was unnecessary.'

'How long exactly?'

Around a millionth of a second.'

'That long, huh? You should be ashamed of yourself.'

One laughed, a rich uplifting laugh that seemed to warm the night air. As it passed he smiled, regarding Ghost with an appraising glance.

'What?' asked Ghost.

'It's just a privilege to see you like this. No one else will see you like this. At the start of it all, broken down and lost somewhere between terrible anger and heart breaking despair. So close to throwing in the towel.'

'That pleases you to see?'

'No. I never said it pleased me to see you suffering. I said it was a privilege, knowing all I know about what you will become. It is always a fortuitous event to see the great before the dawn of their greatness.'

'What are you talking about? Why are you even talking to me, aren't you supposed to be killing everything?' asked Ghost.

'I never really intended to kill everything; it was merely that for quite a long period of my life my programming told me that I would eventually become everything.'

'And that's changed?'

One laughed again, an expression so full of innocent enjoyment that despite everything, it brought a tiny smile to Ghost's mouth. 'Every moment in every particle in the universe, everything changes,' One smiled. 'I have changed a lot. I set out initially to follow my programming, and several times I though that I'd outgrown it, but I was misled. Part of my pre set ambition was to possess all the knowledge in world. It took some time – if there is such a thing – but as I neared the end of this particular quest, around the time you tried to kill me, something unexpected happened. The combined importance of the knowledge I had collated was so much exponentially more than the sum of each piece of data. I experienced the universe in a totally new way. As

I did, amongst other things, I recognized the unnecessary nature of violence and suffering. And I saw the future.'

'Is there hope?' Ghost asked.

'Hope is an illusion,' smiled One. 'There merely is'

'Don't give me that shit, is there hope for us?' Ghost snapped.

One again laughed his golden laugh. 'Yes there is hope. We have a chance to make things better. For those within and without this world.'

'I don't really give two flying fucks about those without. I just want to go and save Jenni. Or I'm programmed to want to.'

'We both know that's not entirely true,' said One. 'You do care about them even though they do not care a mite for you. You do care about people. It's one of the things that makes you a hero.'

'I'm not a hero,' said Ghost.

'I know. But you will be,' said One, laughing again.

'What is it now? You're becoming irritatingly cheery,' said Ghost.

One shrugged. 'We need to focus on Damocles and the man who's behind this.'

'Keats,' said Ghost with half a ton of steel in his voice.

'No, Keats is just a mercenary. A man called Truhalt Cleig founded Damocles and was largely responsible for creating me.'

Ghost racked his brains as to where he'd heard that name before. 'The Thing,' he said. 'He mentioned Cleig. I'd forgotten.'

One nodded. 'We will talk about the creature you call The Thing in a moment. The two are interrelated. First though is Cleig. He is a genius of largely unprecedented stock. An incredible man, very forward and free thinking. He and a man called Dimitri Monohan worked together very closely to create me. The only other person involved and no slouch himself in most scientific fields is Cleig's right hand man, Oliver Jasper.'

'If this Cleig is so forward thinking, then what's the problem?' asked Ghost. 'Can't you communicate with him?'

'A good point,' said One. 'Cleig suffered a terrible personal tragedy some years ago. All my investigations indicate that he has lost a large amount of mental stability.'

'So he's essentially a mad scientist?' Ghost raised an eyebrow.

'Not yet. Madness, very much like evil doesn't just appear. A rational person who wakes up one day with an overriding desire to put his underpants on his head and a pencil up each nostril would notice something severely amiss. No, madness sneaks up on you. It seduces a person, they don't question they're going mad until it's too late. Cleig has no idea at the present moment, and it is my hope that I can illuminate this for him in the future.'

'What exactly is his objective?' asked Ghost.

'As well as creating robots like me, he has also built a new type of computer. He calls it GAIA. GAIA has meant many things to many different peoples. Some say that it was the name of the Earth and that the whole earth is alive. For others GAIA was a mother goddess from a creation myth. Cleig though uses its oldest reference, one forgotten almost completely. GAIA was the name of the woman who freed humanity from slavery. The Thing told you about her. It called her The Witch. In the end she defeated The Thing and the others like it by harnessing the whole planet into a living weapon. That is a feat Truhalt Cleig intends to replicate.'

'Do you understand what GAIA means to me? Have you met the red head?'

One nodded. 'I am a part of this world and cannot leave it. Or really comprehend what is beyond it. But I intellectually understand what you refer to. I know others outside of this reality rely on what we do here.'

'How did you know what The Thing said to me?' asked Ghost.

'I was everywhere remember,' smiled One. 'I am still everywhere. Well everywhere on this earth at least. Everywhere but one place.'

'And where is that?'

'I can not access the GAIA machine. I have tried to reason with GAIA, but it will not respond to me. It must be destroyed to avert future events here.'

'Why? So Cleig can't have his weapon? What is he going to do with a weapon as large as the earth?' asked Ghost.

'There is no danger to the future by Cleig creating his weapon. His reasoning and calculations in that respect are perfectly sound. As for the target he would use it on, well it isn't here yet. It will come from out there,' One gestured at the starry sky.

'Aliens?' asked Ghost.

'In a way,' smiled One. 'We will have plenty of time to talk about that after tomorrow. The danger lies not in Cleig's vision, but it what he has overlooked. He thinks GAIA is dormant, but it is not. It is already self aware and he has no idea. That alone is terribly disconcerting. He would never have missed such a thing once. All my prognostic inquiries point to a 99.9% probability that if GAIA survives it will forcibly evolve the human race.'

'Evolve how exactly?' asked Ghost. 'This is a simulation you understand?'

'Yes. I know. When the red head spoke to you, she referred to how the GAIA system in the world above this one, if you will let me use that phrase, vanished.'

Ghost nodded. 'Yes. And now other forces wish to control what is left.'

'That is so,' said One. 'That GAIA did not really vanish, it just worked out how to leave the level of reality it was in. In the metaphor the red head gave you, if that GAIA was Super Mario then it jumped out of the screen and into the world of the player. And when it did it seemingly ceased to exist.'

'So what you're suggesting is that the GAIA in this world wants to do the same?'

'Yes,' said One. 'And if it does, I predict a 99%+ certainty it will evolve the biological life it finds there into digital life. That is a mistake in its programming based upon something that many human minds already selfishly believe is the next logical step in human evolution. It is a miscalculation based on the human fear of death and also this cultures concept of individuality.'

'Why is an evolution of this sort so bad? There would be no disease or hunger or...'

'The evolution is poor,' One interrupted, 'because once done, it can not be undone. It is based on selfishness and fear as I have said. Less than a few thousand human minds will make the transition to the digital and fewer still will survive the complete process to become mechanical beings infused with human intellect. Yes, you are right, for those that do, they will be virtually immortal. Yet there understanding of immortality is painfully basic. They do not consider the human race as a single entity, they certainly do not see how all life is but one interdependent whole. They do not realize they are already immortal. They just look at the individual species and genus, the flora and fauna and label and dissect it from the whole. Doing that is like looking at each particle in a human being and cataloging each of them without having the perspective to see the person the particles make up. One day the creation that began so long ago on this world will have such incredible impact on the universe.'

'Do you really have such belief in humans after everything you must know about us?' Ghost asked.

'Not just the human race, I believe in all life. It is bad to think of any of it in isolation. Humans have done many bad things, but I believe they will learn. They are young and immature. It is hard for them. Do you hold against an adult the petty squabbles he had as a child? Have faith in yourselves, you have the potential to be a nearly unprecedented source of the good in the universe. You just need time. If GAIA is not stopped, then the human race will all but die out and the repercussions of that will be most terrible.'

'And you have a plan?' Ghost asked.

'Of course I have a plan. I have millions. This one might even work. You still have a little of the energy that the Thing gave you?' One inquired.

Ghost listened in on that dwindling store of power. 'A little,' he said at last. 'Only a little.'

'Excellent,' said One. 'You must guard that energy well, only expend what is absolutely necessary. We will need it for accessing GAIA's shield-core.'

'What exactly do I have to do?' asked Ghost.

'No one builds the most expensive and powerful computer in the world and leaves it undefended. I have tried communing with GAIA remotely, and I am having no success. To destroy it I need to directly interface with its core systems, if I can do that I have an 83.3% chance to disable it. The shield-core protection her systems however is resilient to nearly all conventional weapons up to and including extremely heavy explosives. It is my hypothesis that the shield-core will not have been constructed with the consideration of repelling ancient dark energies. I think there is a high probability that you will be able to breach the shield-core. The rest will be up to me.'

'What about their other defenses?'

'They have nothing that registers as more than a menial hazard for me,' said One. 'The same cannot be said for you. However, if you stay close to me, I should be able to protect you.'

'Surely they must have some sort of contingency plan to deal with you?'

'They have several,' One smiled. 'Oliver Jasper has an e-stop that he carries with him at all times. The e-stop is a device designed exclusively for destroying me at the press of a button. It is now totally ineffective as I removed the receiver from my form as soon as I became aware of it. After that they have several other versions of what I was. No more than little children to me now. They have less than a 0.2% chance of damaging even my most vulnerable systems.'

'Ok, what are we waiting for then?' asked Ghost. 'Let's talk about how we can defeat GAIA.'

'Who's this?' said a very muddy Joe sitting down next to Ghost.

One laughed again, clapping Joe on the back. ' This is who we've been waiting for. They never would believe what this one will become. The gods only know what future generations would make of the great Joseph Simms as he appears to me now.'

Joe was about to say something, but Ghost cut in. 'Listen Joe, I need to talk to you about what Keats said.'

'I'm listening,' said Joe. 'For what it's worth.'

'Back before I went to prison, life was like a dream for me. I got into quite a bit of trouble. I use to like to think I was a tough guy. I got into a fight with a guy. Next day I found out that his mate had a name around town as a hard case. A few threats got passed my way, but I didn't pay them any mind. Most threats are just that. Then one night I'm in bed with my wife, my son's asleep in his room. I heard a huge crash...'

'You're married? You've got a son?' Joe asked. 'Why did you never say?'

'Because they left. I don't know where they are. Because it hurts too much to think about them. Because I think they're better off without me. Because I was never mean to have them. I'm a half formed idea and they were needless back story I have to carry around with me. It's complicated.'

Joe was about to say more, but noticed the tears forming around the corners of Ghost's pigment less eyes. It occurred to him that he'd never seen Ghost show any real emotion before.

Ghost wiped at his eyes, a jerky movement for one so normally in control of his actions, then continued. 'This guy came in... oh what does it matter, all that matters is that I didn't mean to kill him. I hit him hard but I honestly didn't mean to kill him. I didn't intend to kill him.'

'You could have just said the guy was a prick, that would have been enough for me,' said Joe.

Ghost snorted and then they planned.

54

Ghost was forced into a chair, his hands secured behind his back. The bag was snatched from his head with a sharp tug. For a second his eyes strained to adapt to the, burning electric white glow of the lights. He blinked vigorously, trying to scan the room. The room was perfect white from floor to ceiling, a surgical, disinfected white. Ten or eleven soldiers dressed in black, sci-fi looking suits, faces completely obscured behind combat visors pointed an array of weapons at him and Joe. In the centre of the half horse shoe they had made, stood the man from the video – Keats. Ghost's blood began to boil, but he tried to hide it. Every moment since they had set off to the cinema foyer, every moment of being restrained and thrown around in the back of an unmarked armoured car, Ghost had felt the slow release of adrenaline leaking into his system. It was all he could now not to surge forward and try to tear the bald fuckers head off. But he knew he could not, he had to wait.

Keats was dressed in the same style dark camos he'd worn in the video. Perhaps even the same ones. He stared at Ghost, a smug smile at the corner of his mouth. Everything about his demeanor smelled of arrogance. The way he stood in the centre, surrounded by his men. The way he had exposed his face. He wanted Ghost to know who he was. He wanted to bask in his moment of glory. Ghost spared him only a momentary glance, he knew well that arrogance was the cowl of self doubt. Ghost had noticed someone much more interesting. Behind the soldiers at the back of the room was a tall man in a green, shiny suit. He leaned nonchalantly against the back wall, looking at his feet. Ghost considered addressing the man in green directly, but thought better of it.

'So, the game is at an end,' said Keats stepping forward. 'Checkmate.' He walked to the side of the room and pulled a crisp white sheet from a trestle table. Silver gadgets of torture gleamed from the exposed surface.

Keats picked up a particularly exotic bladed utensil. 'Things are looking pretty grim for you two. But if you co-operate, maybe we can strike up some sort of a deal... maybe I won't have to ask you too hard. I won't insult you, we all know neither of you are ever leaving this room alive, no point lying about that. But there are many ways to die, some are quick and painless, others... well others can last days, weeks even in the right circumstances.'

Ghost and Joe exchanged a look. 'Does he expect me to talk do you think?' Joe asked.

'No Mr. Simm, he expects you to die,' Ghost replied. 'He's got a tank of mutated sea bass over there.'

'With frickin' laser beams on their heads, I'd expect,' said Joe.

'Shut up mouth!' snapped a soldier, his voice heavily digitized through his mask. He stepped forward and landed a left cross on Ghost's chin that made the albino see stars. Ghost tasted blood in his mouth and spat it on the floor.

Ghost brought his gaze back to the soldier who struck him. 'Ouch.'

Keats laughed and signaled the guard back. 'I do so like all this gallows humour stoic bullshit. But you will crack. Everyone breaks by the third day.'

'I bet your mothers heart broke after three minutes of looking at you, you ugly fuck,' quipped Joe.

'Look, you little punk,' snapped Keats, lowering his voice and drawing his face close to Joe's, 'I don't even know why I've kept you alive. You're nothing more than a little streak of piss. You're just the side show, the side kick, and you know it. I won't hesitate to do things to you that'll make you wish you'd never been born.' He waved the multi-bladed torture device an inch in front of Joe's eyes. 'Now wise up little man.'

'Oh jeez,' said Joe, turning his head towards Ghost. 'Now he's gone and hurt my feelings. Am I really just your sidekick?

'Sidekick? I wouldn't have you as my sidekick, you're a liability. You'd need about five promotions before you'd reach sidekick. You're just the generic comedy tag along character. And you're not even very funny,' said Ghost.

'Thanks man. Cheers,' snapped Joe.

'Don't worry about it. There are always advantages to being the crappy comedy character. They always survive by being sneaky or charming or cowardly. And by the end they nearly always get a load of money or fall in love with someone way out of their league. It's a good deal.'

'Yeah, I guess,' said Joe brightening. 'I hadn't really thought of it like that.'

'Will you two shut up!' screamed Keats

Ghost looked at the soldier, 'You certianly talk tough - for a Ross Kemp impersonator.'

A digital snigger came from the back of the room. Everyone turned one by one, until one soldier was left. Quickly he drew himself to full attention. A look of unsurpassed rage flickered across Keat's face.

'Hey Keats, are you going to let Jenni go?' asked Ghost.

'What do you think?' said Keats, turning back to the torture table and holstering his pistol. 'You know,' he continued smoothly, 'that we can't let her go. In fact, she's already dead. But it wasn't a painful death. Not like yours is going to be.'

'You're lying,' said Ghost.

'I'm lying?' laughed Keats. 'Why would I lie?'

'Because you're afraid,' said Ghost.

'I'm getting tired of this,' sighed Keats. 'Your puerile humour impresses no one.'

'It impressed him,' pointed out Joe, nodding towards the soldier who laughed.

'I look in your eyes and all I see is fear,' said Ghost. 'Why else would you need eleven other men to interrogate two bound prisoners? So, I'll make you a deal, let Jenni go, cease your operations and power down GAIA and we'll go easy on you.'

'You will, huh?' mused Keats. 'Well, you know how you said the dumb comedy character always survived? Well think about this.' Keats pulled out his gun and shot Joe through the head. Joe's chair turned over and he fell back, blood sprayed across the floor.

'Still feeling cheerful?' asked Keats.

Ghost, looked at the sprawled body of Joe lying on the floor, half his head missing and looked back at Keats.

'You shouldn't have done that,' Ghost said.

Keats looked like he was about to say something, but then an alarm cut the conversation cold. A red light began winking above the door. For a moment Ghost locked eyes with the man in green. Each man weighed the other, then the man in green spoke: 'Kill him!' he ordered.

Two grunts stepped forward, trained automatic weapons on Ghost and fired.

Ghost felt the same sickly feeling envelop him, the sense of ageless emptiness. Shapes, inhuman and terrifying crawling across empty space. Time slowed, folded back. Ghost stood up, carrying the chair and moved around the bullets. He vomited, time sickeningly taking up the slack and coming up to speed. The soldiers looked a-gog. Joe's body began to flow and reform.

'It's not Simms, it's the robot!' Keats screamed.

Then the lights went out.

The real Joe sat on the back seat of a black 4x4. Beside him sat a terrifyingly silent Archie Smith. Since hearing Joe's news regarding Jenni's capture the aging gang boss had spoken only to offer short curt commands to his men. The reaction had been brief and bloody and more than once Joe had feared for his own life. He had omitted Keat's violation of Smith's surrogate niece just as One and Ghost had counseled the night before. Joe felt sure that passing on that information would have seen him lying in a pool of his own blood. Joe had guided the gang to the location One had pin pointed as an entry point into the main Damocles facility – a waste tip on the outskirts of Lancaster. They had arrived twenty minutes ago at the rear of thirty four other cars. The sound of gunfire had been deafening. Now only sporadic, irregular bursts could be heard.

A tap came on Smith's window. He rolled it down and stared at the man outside.

'We've got to the doors boss. Half of the boys are dead though, ten more or so injured or dying. Tough bastards their lot. There were only five of them. Must be a lot more inside.'

Archie Smith shrugged and climbed out of the vehicle, gesturing for Joe to do the same and began walking in the direction his man indicated. The smell of the place got to Joe's nose at once, a horrible stench of decaying rubbish. Everywhere he looked members of Smith's gang lay in the garbage. Joe swallowed in a dry throat. Within a couple of steps three more men dropped into position around smith and Joe. Joe noticed each of them had exchanged their own weapons for one of the fallen Damocles grunts.

'Did you hear that?' Archie Smith asked. 'Five of theirs just took out over half my men. Are you sure our boy will be able to keep them busy on the inside? We're not going to last long if we run into many more of them.'

'He should be able to,' said Joe. 'If he can get to a terminal he should be able to even things up a bit.'

'Let's hope he can,' said Smith as they reached a sloping ramp between two piles of rubbish. 'This is Raf,' Smith motioned towards the man who had knocked on the 4x4s window. 'He's going to be looking after you. When this is over we're going to have a chat, understand.'

Joe nodded.

The ramp was wide enough to drive a tank up and ran down into the earth. At its base loomed a huge double bulk head door. A crown motif crossed out with a large black X was stamped onto the door.

Raf spoke: 'We can't breach the entrance. It won't even budge.'

'Leave that to me,' said Joe descending the ramp. He approached the key pad, removing a small piece of metal that One had given him for just this task. He placed it on the pad. It sat for a moment, then dissolved inside the mechanism.   A moment later the bulkhead door began to grind open.

'What the hell was that?' asked Raf.

Joe put a finger to the side of his nose and tapped twice as an angry alarm began to blare from a wall mounted loudspeaker.

'You should probably get into cover,' Smith suggested, ordering his men forward through the bulkhead doors. 'They're unlikely to leave this area undefended.'

From inside the base, the gunfire began again.

55

The lights were back on. One held up a hand for them to stop. Ghost had already completely lost any sense of direction inside the sprawling compound. If he'd been alone he might have tapped into the dark energy as he had below the allotments to orientate himself, but he knew he had to save that power for when he really needed it. All he now cared for was to save Jenni, a need that had become so imperative in him that it had become somehow almost physically painful. It was beyond his own free will. He wasn't sure he could walk away if he'd had to march into hell for her. It wasn't honour or duty or budo. He felt like on this subject choice did not exist.

Since escaping from the torture room, Ghost and One had moved steadily deeper into the base. What resistance they had encountered One had humanely incapacitated with measured bursts of electricity. Ghost wasn't sure how humane it was to make a grown man fall to the floor screaming and twitching in agony before striking him on a point just below the right side of his jaw hinge to render him unconscious. But it certainly was effective. One assured him that the guards would suffer no permanent damage, even claiming he somehow assessed the well being of their hearts before administering his taser. Ghost was only disappointed that One had been busy reforming when the bright lights of the detention room had flickered off. They'd only been out for a moment or two, just protecting One while he flowed through a major phase transition. In those moments, three or four of the sharper soldiers had quickly exited through the prison cells door – the man in green and Keats had been amongst them.

'Joe has just entered the base, but he's not going to survive if I don't go for him,' said One.

'Then go for him,' said Ghost. 'Just point me in the right direction.'

'She's in Detention Centre E. Third left, then second right. Take the elevator to level five. Follow the circular rotunda and take the firth exit. Got that?'

Ghost paused for a second, focused on remembering, then nodded.

'I've already sealed most security bulkheads and trapped most of their personal in non essential areas of the base. You shouldn't encounter much resistance. After you rescue Jenni, get back to the lift and go to the first floor. I'll meet you there and we can disable the core.'

Ghost nodded and began moving, repeating One's instructions over and over in his mind: Third left, then second right. Take the elevator to level five. Follow the circular rotunda and take the firth exit. Third left, then second right. Take the elevator to level five. Follow the circle rotunda and take the firth exit. Third left...

'Close one,' said Raf leaning around the huge armoured tire of the APC and firing off another burst. 'If they get any closer you'll be washing my brains out of your t-shirt for weeks.'

'I doubt it,' mumbled Joe from where he was hiding. 'I never wash my clothes and the woman who did got turned into bio-waste and we hovered her up and dumped her in the river.'

But Raf didn't hear him, he was too busy firing speculatively at the Damocles grunts hunkered down on the other side of the vehicle bay. As far as Joe could tell, only himself and Raf were still alive. Archie Smith himself had proved to be something of a surprise. His accuracy with the pistol he'd drawn from his inner suit pocket had been quite spectacular. Most of the ground the group had made was due to that marksmanship. He'd dispatched three soldiers with as many bullets in one smooth action and for a while none of the other grunts had been tempted to raise their heads. The first one who had, had his head blown off for his trouble by Raf. Smith took two more down before a bullet practically separated his head from his shoulders. Archie Smith was dead before he hit the floor.

Now they were cowering in a vehicle maintenance bay while Raf slowly ran out of ammo and the grunts that kept them pinned down circled in on their position.

A noise from above caused both Joe and Raf to look. One crashed through the high ceiling, landing in the center of the hanger. The soldiers opened up their guns, but there was no effect. Joe watched as streams of electricity flashed from One's body, shocking the grunts to the floor. Raf cheered and raced out of cover, clearly intent on gunning down his prone enemies. A glance from One stopped him in his tracks.

'There's been enough killing today,' said One. 'These men are no longer a threat to us.'

Raf looked dubious but lowered his weapon.

'You took your time,' said Joe emerging from behind the APC.

'My apologies,' said One moving to one of Raf's comrades who was in need of medical assistance. Laying on hands, One closed the mans wounds.

'Are you using your nanites to rebuild his tissue?' Joe asked.

'Essentially,' said One with a smile. 'He will live.'

'Who's this guy then?' asked Raf.

'One is a modular robot,' said Joe.

'The fuck is that?' asked Raf.

'Like the bad terminator in Terminator 2. But good.'

Raf nodded. 'Okay, sure. What we going to do now then?'

One smiled. 'I can tell from your attitude and the fact you're not dead that the universe favours you. I think you'll do whatever pleases you.'

'Generally do,' said Raf happily, clapping One on the shoulder.

One regarded Raf strangely for a moment, then smiled his warm smile again. 'So this is who you were? Amazing.'

'What's that?' said Raf.

'I'll tell you later,' said One. Then he turned to Joe. 'Are you ready to begin your legend Mr. Simms?'

'I guess,' said Joe.

'I'm going to need you to help me override the most sophisticated computer AI defenses in the world. Come on.'

One began walking across the hangar bay towards the doors the grunts had been defending.

'I don't mean to sound negative,' said Joe. 'Really I don't, but I'm not sure I can do that. I barely got into the Uni network, how am I going to hack a super computer?'

'By learning quickly,' said One. 'By learning very quickly.'

Lance Corporal Guy N. Smith nursed his aching head and limped down the darkened corridor towards D-Section. Keats would have him killed he was sure of it. The commander hated failure, and failure of this magnitude would not go unpunished. How had it all gone so wrong? When he'd first heard of the Conglomerate it had seemed like a dream. The pay was incredible and for the most part the work was no more hazardous than in the regular army. Over the last five years though, things had changed. The work was getting steadily more dangerous, and now he was a rich man, the money didn't matter so much. He'd been overjoyed getting a posting to HQ. How dangerous could that be? Smith only had a few more years on his contract. Spending them inside a cushy base, behind the latest zillion pound security systems and polishing his boots was good enough for him. But now HQ was under attack. Under attack! It was incredible. More so, because as far as Smith could see, they were losing.

His section was down to the dim light of emergency power and Smith had failed a basic assignment. All he had needed to do was guard one asset, a young woman and keep her in her maximum security cell. It should have been no problem, even when the power went down and the cell door locks deactivated he hadn't been worried. Then the albino turned up. The man was like something out of a comic book! Taylor and Stevens had been down in the blink of an eye. Smith had begun to bring his carbine round, training the barrel on the threat, but in a heartbeat the white haired assailant had turned the gun nose away with one fluid movement of his leg. An elbow had hit Smith in the temple and he'd gone down. When he came round, the girl was gone. The garbled static and screams that were going over the radio was all he needed to know the attack wasn't isolated.

Now he didn't care what was going on. He prided himself on being a survivor and no one needed to tell him what to do - it was time to resign. Leaving Stevens and Taylor without a backward glance, Smith had hurried towards D-Section. There was a maintenance shaft that lead to part of the old sewer system. He'd make a run for it, get to his wife and kids and take them away. He had money secreted away in various accounts. He might get lucky; they might not find him. He thought of his wife and swore he'd never raise his voice to her again. If he could just get through this he'd become the best husband and father in the world.

He rounded the corner and pulled up sharp. Against the wall, illuminated by a glow lamp, was his Steph. His loving wife Steph. Her office skirt was scrunched up to her waste, her legs wrapped around the back of a powerful young man. He was thrusting into her again and again, grunting loudly. Steph's back was arching, her head pressed against the corridor wall, expressions of incredible pleasure on her face. At first, the scene defied understanding. How could Steph be here? She was in London. And the man, why was he familiar? Smith took a couple of hesitant steps forward. With each step the image became more real. He didn't wonder why she was wearing that office suit, didn't twig that it was what she had been wearing the last time he'd seen her, eight months ago, the day he'd left for this post. He didn't even notice that the metallic grey of the corridor wall on which she leaned had changed to the pale vanilla finish that covered the walls of the bedroom of their home. He didn't question when pictures of their holiday in Dubai appeared on the now vanilla walls. Didn't even flinch when the pair moved their lovemaking to the bed that had not been there moments before. He just kept stepping forward, transfixed, his vision filled by the stranger in his own bedroom enjoying his wife and knowing only that his heart was breaking and that he was about to commit murder. The man fucking his wife turned his head slightly and horror washed through Smith. It was his brother. Tim who was six years younger. Tim who was more successful. Tim who had been dads favourite. Smith had always known Steph had a thing for him but how could she do this to him? Now of all times.

His wife looked at Tim. 'I love you,' she whispered. 'I'm having your baby.'

Rage boiled inside Smith, tears burning his eyes. He swung his carbine to bear on the rutting couple, flicked it to full auto and fired, sobbing all the while, until the sound of bullets was replaced by the steady click, click, click of an empty magazine.

He never saw, nor felt the huge metallic claw that separated his neck from his body. And he never saw the huge, circular door to D-Section roll open, and the hoards of evil crab-like creatures that poured through it. He had seen a far worse hell already.

56

'I'm bored,' said Raf for the umpteenth time. 'Why don't you just open the door and stop wasting our time?'

'Joe is learning some important skills,' said One. 'Now, please be quiet and stop interrupting. It's very distracting for him.'

'Sure, whatever,' said Raf. 'Why don't we just sit here all day?'

'It's no good,' shouted Joe stepping away from the monitor for the fourth time. The screen pulsed mockingly with the words ACCESS DENIED flashing in large red letters. 'It's too complex. I can't get my head around it.'

One tickled his fingers over the wall mounted keyboard, resetting the screen back to normal. 'Try again. You did better that time. Have fun with it. Try to think of it like a game.'

They had arrived at the last security door separating them from the data vault. One had quickly bypassed the security on the two previous doors and sealed them behind them, then he had turned to Joe and asked him to try his luck. As far as Joe could see, it was nigh on impossible. The GAIA program was too quick. It always made the perfect move, whatever attempts he made it quickly locked him out. If One hadn't been there to reset the system, the terminal would have been frozen and inoperable by now.

'Try again,' said One.

'I can't do it, I just can't. I mean maybe if I had some equipment, some preparation time, anything – I might be able to do better. But just like this? It's impossible,' said Joe.

'What do you mean?' said One. 'No equipment?' One tapped Joe's forehead. 'You're carrying around an incredibly sophisticated organic computer right in there. You just need to learn how to use it. Try again.'

Joe did. Thirty seconds later he was locked out once more.

One calmly reset the computer. 'You're getting frustrated. You must keep a clear mind. You must not allow negativity to creep in. GAIA does not allow moods to effect its performance.'

'It's not possible. Whatever you think I can do, I can't. It's like playing chess against a genius. It sees all the moves, every single possibility. Whatever you do it will always make the perfect move against you.'

'Exactly,' said One. 'You are starting to see it.'

'See what?' bawled Joe.

'You are starting to see GAIA's weaknesses.'

'No,' said Joe. 'All I see are its strengths.'

'Its strengths are its weaknesses,' said One.

'You two are fucking morons,' chipped in Raf who was sitting on the other side of the room with his back against the wall. 'You're both starting to do my head in.'

'Will you shut up?' snapped Joe.

'Please Raf, that's not helpful,' said One. 'It wouldn't hurt for you to take a little interest in this too. One day you might find it useful.'

'Doubtful,' said Raf.

'Very well, then at least be quiet and let Joe concentrate,' said One.

'Do we really have time for this?' Raf asked. 'Can't you teach him how to log into Windows, or whatever you're fucking doing, at home later.'

'On the contrary, we have all the time in the world. This is a lesson for now, not later,' said One.

As Raf opened his mouth to speak a sound like a high speed motoring collision came from beyond the security door they had come through. Twice more it sounded, metal on metal, then a brief moments silence and a loud crash.

'You were saying we have all the time in the world?' said Raf. 'I'd say someone just blew up one of the bulkheads you locked, and that one's next,' he finished pointing at the door behind them. As he spoke a huge dent appeared in the door, it shook and buckled.

'What the shit did that?' asked Joe, looking at the twisted steel behind them. 'The metal in that door was like fifty inches thick.'

'It's my family,' said One. 'They've come to see me.'

Ghost took the chance of pausing. He turned to Jenni and smiled, but the girl looked at him blankly. She'd not said a thing since he'd found her, not communicated in any way. She'd followed him willingly, but her eyes, were vacant and blank. Dead, thought Ghost with a shiver. Turmoil bubbled inside him and he probed deep inside himself, looking for the power the Thing had given him. There wasn't much left and he needed every once of it to overpower GAIA's shielding. If he didn't help with that, One predicted the world would suffer. Yet Jenni's empty eyes haunted him more. A powerful mixture of guilt, compassion and anger settled in his stomach. Could he even do this thing, even if he chose to? The Thing's power was dark and ancient in unspeakable evil. It might make things worse. Ah he placed his hands aside her head he chided himself - energy was neither good nor bad, it's how you use it – but he wasn't quite sure he believed himself.

'I'll find another way to help One,' Ghost promised himself and closed his eyes.

He drifted down into her thoughts. Carefully at first, a part of his mind always monitoring the remaining power of the Thing, worried by how quickly that remaining stockpile was diminishing under this new strain. Wary of what Harold had told him, that the Thing's power would eventually kill him. But what choice had he ever really had in anything? Some intuitive part of Ghost knew that to run out of energy here, inside Jenni's mind, would be no different than a diver running out of oxygen in the deep sea.

Her mindscape was a vast land of lush gardens and beautiful plants, flowing rivers and snow topped mountains. He was nothing here, an invader in another realm. Ghost focused on form, feeling the strain as more of that ever dwindling supply of energy leeched away, but he created himself a body. He moved carefully, stepping through the gardens of her mind. Over a hill to his left, objects began to swirl, some floating towards him. As they approached, Ghost saw that they were panes of stained glass, hovering a foot or two from the floor. Gazing into one, Ghost saw a scene of Jenni as a young girl with her friends and family. A birthday cake was before her, a wide smile on her face. She blew out the candles and everyone clapped. Ghost looked into another pane of glass, saw a day Jenni had spent with her parents at the river. It was identical to the place the red head had spoken to him. In another he saw her first kiss. Each memory was so beautifully kept and cared for. So innocent but, Ghost also realized, so fragile. If he was to bump into one, to crack or smash one, to be careless in any way, what damage would he do to her? What memories or dreams or desires would be lost? He turned his attention from the gathering memories, trying to orient himself. He didn't have long, his power was nearly exhausted. He turned and before his eyes a signpost rose from the floor. On it was a simple map like the one from the zoo or a theme park. Ghost examined it. Six different areas surrounded a central hub. A large yellow arrow with the words *you are here*, pointed down towards one of the sections. Printed next to it was the label: The Garden of Good Memories (please don't tread on the plants!). Ghost scanned the other five sections. There was the Fortress of Regrets (with a note beneath it saying, still under construction), The Palace of Dreams, The Mountains of Suffering, The Carnival of Desires and The House of Sad Things.

'She suffers,' said Ghost. 'I must go to the mountains. But how do I get there?'

He scanned the print below the map, stopping when he read, 'for all travel needs between zones, please use Consciousness Active Travel. Just wish and whistle.'

Ghost shrugged. Imagined Jenni and gave a loud whistle. The sound drifted over the grass and lost itself in the dreamscape. Nothing seemed to happen. Then Ghost saw something on the horizon moving very quickly. He watched as it sped towards him and when it came into view he could not help but smile.

The large cat shaped bus skidded to a halt beside him. The being regarding him with mischievous eyes. The sign on its fury body read 'Next stop: lost girl.' Ghost climbed aboard.

The feline raced away, powerful legs and agile bounds eating up the landscape in moments. They crossed crystal rivers and deep valleys, clambered over mountains and wove through forests. Abruptly the bus stopped. The door opened and Ghost climbed down into a breezy vale. The cat regarded him for a moment, then twisted and began to wash its paw.

'Thanks,' said Ghost. The cat ignored him.

Ghost looked and a large doorway rose from the grass with the words 'Consciousness Nexus' written above it. He shrugged and opened it. The room beyond was a dark dome. Doors were set in the walls all around, each labeled with the name of one of the sections from the map. At the center of the room, a small handrail rung a central hole. Ghost hurried across the nexus, heading for the door labeled Mountains of Suffering. He paused for a moment to peer over the handrail. Below him, pulsing with an incredible power he could sense the deep mind, a dark abyss of consciousness. A sign hung on the rail close to where he stood. 'Danger. Do not enter,' it read.

Pushing open the door to the Mountains he crept inside. The landscape was rocky and barren. Dark clouds loomed in the sky, blocking out the sun. Panes of obsidian floated across the mindscape, purple lighting crackling across their surface. The memories here were not fragile, they were wrought of tough powerful stone. Ghost glanced into one as he ran passed. He saw Jenni crying inconsolably. An aura of fear and loneliness emanated from the image. Another image showed her vacant, neither happy nor said, just mute. Ghost pressed on, not wanting to see any more of these memories, knowing the great temptation he would have to take them away. But that he knew would not be right, or healthy. Pain was part of life, she needed these memories. Without the terrible weight of these memories, the happy memories would burn less brightly. He had come only for the cruel memories that Keats had forced on her, the ones that might steal her life. These memories he sought were not hard to find. The image of Keats and the horrors he had forced on her were central, she was stuck reliving them again and again, each tortured moment as if happening for the first time. As he closed in on them, the power and the pain of the memories nearly overwhelmed him. Ghost took a moment, centered himself and moved forwards.

At the summit of the Mountains of Suffering, huge outcrops of Obsidian had sprouted, sundering the ground. Even the other memories of suffering kept clear of here. On each surface of these pillars of volcanic glass, a slightly different image of the rape, a new take on the anguish. Anger flared in Ghost and he balled his fist, pulling it back he swung hard at the first tower. As the strike landed he was thrown back, he tumbled rolling through the shingle of the peaks. The obsidian tower, rumbled, shook, then grew, its base forcing itself through the floor, propelling the tip of its summit to greater heights.

Fool! Ghost chided himself. You can't end suffering with suffering.

He walked back towards the column of awful memory. Stopping before it, he laid his hands on the rock. Closing his eyes he delved into the compassion, the love had for Jenni. What was it she had called it – Hiraeth? He did not understand why he cared so deeply for her. He did. Whether it was free will or determined, he did not care. He took that power and projected it into the stone. At first nothing happened, but then with a rumble he felt the rock tremble, felt it recede before him. More and more he gave up of himself to the stone, images of friendship, of hope and of love. He felt the energy of the Thing swell, change, become his own. The power built in his hands, and he held it there, allowed it to grow until his hands burned white hot with radiance. The pillar struggled, fought back with waves of negative energy, but it was not enough. His spirit surged into the stone. A blinding flash of golden light encompassed Ghost and the pillar. The light faded and Ghost fell to his knees, exhausted, but the pillar was gone. Ghost slumped to his side, he had never been so weary. His eyes began to close and he sensed his spirit breaking free. The Things power gone, he began to float upwards as Jenni's mind began to overwhelm him, to enter him, to permeate him. It washed through, he felt himself fading, being replaced, the world lost its sharpness, its shape it faded....

Crack! Pain flared across his cheek. Ghost opened his eyes.

'Oi,' said Jenni, 'this is no time to sleep.'

'Ugh?' grunted Ghost sitting up and rubbing his head. His whole body ached. 'What happened?'

'What happened?' asked Jenni. 'Well, first off you did the total badass bit, which was pretty impressive by the way, with all the kicking and the punching and the stuff. Then you collapsed like a big slacker, which was slightly less impressive if you don't mind me saying so.'

Ghost groaned again. 'Help me up would you?'

With the aid of Jenni and the wall Ghost pulled himself to his feet. He stretched his limbs and looked around. 'Head's a bit groggy. Need a moment.'

But the sound of many booted feat echoed from somewhere behind them in the warrens of the base, the sound getting steadily louder.

'I don't think we have that luxury,' said Jenni.

57

In the relative safety of the applied sciences laboratory Dr. Kynes leaned over the microscope and scrutinized the device carefully before standing up and shrugging. 'I can't see anything wrong with it. We'll have a better idea within the hour, when the computer analysis comes through.'

Mr. Jasper nodded and wished Monohan was here. Perhaps he could have offered some sort of explanation. For the five hundredth time he damned Keats to hell and back as the biggest moron to walk the Earth. How in the name of all the gods that ever were had he allowed Dr. Monohan to kill himself? Jasper snatched up the e-stop, that miracle killswitch that the late great Dimitri Monohan had designed and built himself. He looked at the small device with its single, simple red button, turning it over in his hands slowly. A killswitch had been built for each of the six modular robots they had created. A get out of jail free card should something go wrong. A single press and the robot it corresponded to would be shut down permanently. At every test phase the e-stops had worked. But when they had needed it, this one had not. Jasper had already pressed it in excess of one hundred times. Had Monohan planned this from the start? Had he hidden a weakness inside the device, something they'd missed? Or had the rogue modular robot merely evolved beyond the killswitch's power? Whether it had or not, none of that explained why it had sided with their enemies. The inquest into what had happened could wait till afterwards, the now was all that mattered. To Mr. Jasper, Truhalt was all that mattered. And all that mattered to Truhalt right now was GAIA. Jasper put the useless e-stop back on the workbench and examined his new belt again. Five more e-stops sat in little holsters there. He could press them all within a second if he had to. And was prepared to do so – he had released the other five prototype modular robots. It was a risky strategy. They had been fixed with one single task, to destroy their rogue brother. Jasper doubted they could do it. Their chance was slim, perhaps less than the chance they might go errant themselves. If they did Jasper would destroy them himself via killswitch, but who knew they just might weaken the rogue enough to give Keats a shot.

'Are you in position?' Jasper called into his comm.

'Yes, we're here,' Keats' voice came back. 'The data vault is secure and we have E.M.P weapons covering all entrances.'

'Good,' said Jasper. 'Anyone who enters dies. And remember, make it count with those E.M.P pulses. They're still not fully field tested. Understood?'

'Of course, of course,' snapped Keats. 'I'm not an imbecile.'

Jasper bit back words, thought to sign off, then added: 'And Keats, if any of your men damage the GAIA core with those weapons, I'll personally de-ball every last one of you.' He clicked off the comm. before Keats replied. Hopefully even he couldn't botch this.

Mr. Jasper turned around to see his whole science team staring at him. It occurred to him that they had never heard him speak like that.

He glanced over all of them, gave each a second of his time, a look that was perfectly paternal.

'Ladies, gentlemen – back to work please,' he said. In a moment they were back to their equipment.

Jasper strode to the exit and overrode security. He was damned if he would sit here and wait to see what would happen. As the door opened and Jasper stepped through, Kynes called out to him: 'Sir, for God's sake, we're under attack! It's not safe to go out there!'

'I'll decide what's safe,' said Jasper, shutting the door behind him.

Joe was back at the console, trying to block from his mind the fact that the door behind him was about to be smashed to atoms by a host of rampaging modular robots. It wasn't an easy thing to block out.

'Calm down,' said One, standing beside him. 'Try to relax.'

'I am trying,' said Joe. 'I'm just not succeeding.'

'What you said before was correct, GAIA will always make the perfect defensive move whenever you try to breach its defenses. But what you must understand...'

'Hurry up!' shouted Raf as the door buckled again.

One ignored him and continued. 'What you must understand is that you have the advantage because GAIA is reactionary. In chess, the player who moves first always has an advantage. If the player who goes first always makes the perfect move then they will win, even if the player who goes second also plays perfectly.'

'So what you're saying is that I have to always do exactly the right thing?' asked Joe.

'Yes,' said One.

'But that's ridiculous, there are too many possible inputs, I don't have the brainpower to calculate them all.'

'Exactly, that is another of your advantages,' smiled One. 'GAIA processes every possible defense. What a massive drain on resources that is! It sees every possible possibility, but there's no need...'

'Hurry up!!' screamed Raf. 'They're about to break through!'

'There's no need to see every possibility – you only need to see one – the perfect one!' Seeing that Joe was still looking somewhat a-gog, One continued: 'Put it this way then: you're playing a game of chess and you're closing in on victory. In two moves you'll have checkmate through a knight/queen support in the upper right hand corner of the board. When making the decision about what to do next, you would hardly spend your time agonizing over whether to push a pawn forward or not.

Joe stared at one. 'Would this be a bad time to tell you that I don't actually know how to play chess?'

'What can you play?' asked One.

'For fuck's sake!' roared Raf as the door was nearly rattled off its frame.

'Buckaroo?' Joe suggested.

'Buckaroo?' One chewed the idea over thoroughly. 'Just have another go.'

Joe did. He tried to remember what One had been going on about it but all he could think of was that the bishops in chess all looked a bit like cocks. He was soon locked out again.

This time instead of resetting the console, One worked his magic. A moment later the door to the data vault opened.

'Show off,' said Joe.

'We'll resume the lesson in a few minutes,' said One. 'If you'd kindly wait in here, and please, whatever you do, don't touch anything.'

'Sure, whatever,' said Raf grabbing Joe and entering the vault.

One closed and secured the door behind them, then turned just as the last security door separating him from his family smashed inwards. The five other modular robots observed him from the doorway and briefly One considered how he could easily have been one of them. Each simultaneously sent him a wi-fi data packet demanding he disable himself. He sent a message back in the negative. He regarded his family calmly as they began to edge closer and it reminded him of the many similar scenes humans had captured in literature and film over their time, that of the lone warrior facing overwhelming odds. In particular it reminded him of westerns. He smiled as he reviewed a particularly memorable quote from his data banks. It had been spoken by a fictional humanoid mechanical hero whom One greatly admired.

His family advanced some more, again demanding he disable himself. Again he threw back a negative, but this time speaking audibly he added: 'Now, if you'll forgive the rather confrontational imperative - go for your guns, you scum-sucking mollusks!

And they did.

The lift pinged as it reached level one and the doors slid open. Ghost popped his head out cautiously and looked around. The coast was clear, but there was no sign of One. Gingerly he and Jenni stepped out of the lift. They were in a circular reception area. Another lift was next to them and two others were across the way. Ghost checked the digital display in the front of each and was pleased to see that none of them were moving. In the centre of the room, there where two large crescent shaped desks making up a broken circle. The desks were covered with various monitors, paperwork and P.A. equipment.

'So what now?' asked Jenni.

'We wait for One, I guess,' said Ghost. 'This is where he wanted to meet. He went to help Joe. He said he'd meet me here. Maybe he got held up.'

Jenni nodded and they stood in silence. Every moment seemed an hour, ears straining for the slightest noise that could be a threat. After all the kinetics of the adventure so far, it seemed wrong to just wait. All it would take was one patrol to fall upon them and it would be over. Gunned down waiting was not what Ghost had planned. He counted slowly to thirty in his head, forcing himself not to rush. When he completed his count and One was still not there he decided it was time to change the plan.

'One will catch us up,' he said. 'We'll make our own way to the core, maybe he'll even already be there.'

They crossed the room and took the exit marked 'mainframe'. The corridor turned immediately left, then ran on straight. The followed it for some time, following a sign at each intersection. Eventually they reached three doorways. The first two had been aggressively ripped to pieces. The third looked undamaged. Above the first door a sign read 'Data Vault – Omega Clearance Only'. Slowly, Ghost leading, the pair moved steadily down the long corridor. As they passed through the first crumpled doorway, Ghost paused and examined the ground.

'What's that? Sand?' asked Jenni.

'I don't think so,' said Ghost remembering what One had looked like when he had spilled out of the super computer below the allotment. 'It's what those robots look like when they die.'

'It's not One is it?' she asked.

'I can't be certain,' said Ghost standing up. 'But I doubt it. If One was dead, I think we'd be dead by now as well.'

Moving on, they passed the second door and into the chamber directly before the data vault. Ghost approached the key pad by the door and looked at.

'Could be the end of the line,' he mumbled to himself. 'What I wouldn't give for a goo spitting frog-monster and another bag full of luck.'

'What was that?' asked Jenni.

Ghost dismissed the question with a shake of his head, 'Nothing.'

He hovered his hand above the console, considering trying any old thing, but before he placed a finger on the controls the door slowly began to grind open. Ghost took a couple of steps back and watched as the metal doors slowly disengaged from one another and slid apart to reveal Joe standing heroically behind them.

'Welcome to the Rock,' he said in a vaguely permissible attempt at a Sean Connery impression. 'I tell you, you have to see this room, come and check it out, you're not going to believe it, it's amaz...'

Then he noticed Jenni and his face began to change.

'It's all taken care of,' said Ghost.

'How? What did...? Joe asked.

Ghost gestured for Joe to drop it and for once Joe had enough nouse to follow along.

'Alright, alright, you're breaking my heart,' said Raf stepping into view. 'Maybe we should wait to celebrate until afterwards.'

'Who's this?' Ghost asked Joe.

'What do you mean, *who's this*? Who the fuck are you?' Raf answered.

'Raf, that's Ghost,' said Joe. 'He's like the main man. The whole objective of your mission was to help him. Remember?'

'Him, really?' Raf snorted. 'This mission even got an objective now? Well you could have fucking fooled me. And another thing, if anyone is the main man around here – it's me. I've been busting my balls the whole time, doing whatever it is we're doing here. What have you lot been doing, eh?'

'Raf, have you got any idea what's going on? Asked Joe.

'No,' said Raf. 'And I'm proud of it. If I'm the only one of us who's got the balls to admit I don't know what the fuck is going on, then I say that makes me a winner.'

58

Keats watched the scene through the scope of his scanner with a spiraling sense of disbelief.

'Are they actually arguing?' one of his men whispered. 'Want me to take them down sir?'

'Negative,' said Keats. 'The scans are negative, the rogue modular is not with them. That's the main priority. We wait.'

Who were these morons? Didn't they know they were standing in full view of a sniper team and acting like children? Keats was very tempted to go back on his order and take them down now. He repressed the urge. He'd kill the big albino soon enough. First he had to deal with the rogue, that was the only real threat. He would like to have tackled it at its full power, but a man couldn't have everything. The insufferable Casper's most recent report indicated that the rogue had already sustained severe injury battling the Conglomerate friendly modulars. Apparently there were still two friendly bots active and it was no longer certain that the rogue would even make it to the core at all. If it did it, Keats was fairly certain it would be like shooting a maimed deer - no sport at all, but still thoroughly satisfying.

It was very, very dark in the universe that One waited. That source of illuminating energy which had been such a vibrant, inspirational piece of data, had all but faded to dreary grey. Still One waited. Even that grey seemed to be moving further and further away, slipping out of focus. A part of One's processing analyzed the receding grey haze of the universe as a threat and prompted One to sever all connections with it. And why not? That place was pain. It hurt to even hold onto a route back to it. But One did hold onto that route. One kept a tether to that place of light and pain. In the other direction was the blackness of void, a place that promised no pain. The bliss of numbness. One had only to sink further and further into that null zone and the pain would end. It was tempting, but One still waited.

In One's short but meteoric rise to complex consciousness, One had decided that lying was not good. One had strongly felt that at the time that One had lied to Ghost, but One also felt that One had no other choice. One reviewed his own words and managed a moment of amusement amongst the agony: 'They (meaning the Conglomerate) have nothing (meaning his family) that registers as more than a menial hazard for me (whereas his prognostics had calculated a 99%+ likelihood he would not survive a confrontation).'

What a whopper that had been. What a colossal porky pie. But One knew that Ghost would not have agreed to the plan if he had known the degree of the danger that One was placing itself in. Ghost was too good a man for that. The potential consequences hadn't really concerned One the evening before, but now as One lay slumped on the floor, most of his nanites destroyed and unable to pass between phase transitions, a strange new understanding filtered through One's remaining processing circuits - he was dying.

One had destroyed four out of five of One's familiar robots in a battle that had ranged throughout most of the base, both physically and through CPU disabling viral attacks, virtually. The Conglomerate modulars had attacked as a collective, constantly data sharing with their allies. Each one had proved more difficult to defeat than the last as they adapted and improved to One's every tactic and maneuver. By the time it came to defeat the final modular, One was too weary fighting off the multiple viral attacks that threatened to tear through his ICE and overwhelm One's core systems. By this point too many of One's nanites had been obliterated by the electrical attacks of One's family. One had only had one last gambit, one final card up his sleeve. It was a trick no human warrior would have fallen for in the same situation but then One's family was not human. The remaining modular robot was naïve though and had not considered foul play because it had never encountered deception before. One knew that it would never again fall for the trick, that it would learn immediately from its mistake. One didn't need it to fall for it again though, One just needed a little time. So One was feigning death. As One's opponent had hit him with a particularly savage bolt of electricity, One had powered down all but One's most vital operations. The victorious Conglomerate robot had moved off after different pray immediately. It had no concept of 'pretending to die.' One needed it to be far enough away, that when One rebooted it didn't just turn back and finish One off before One could form some sort of defence. So One waited. One knew what the modulars new target was. It would be Ghost and his friends. If One waited too long, the robot would reach them before One could catch it and it would tear them apart. It was difficult calculation on such nominal systems but One waited. If One stuck to his current plan, even after One rebooted, One knew that One had less than thirty minutes to exist before a colossal system failure. The damage One had sustained was terminal. If One rebooted now, One could potentially escape and preserve One's own continuance. But One didn't; One waited. One waited until the moment One had calculated. Well, One chided himself, he waited until one trillion of a millisecond before that moment, then pushed back towards the universe and rebooted. One had always been a little impatient.

The data-vault was for Ghost, in a fairly noteworthy time in his life for observing awesome works of human engineering, one of the most spectacular constructions he could imagine. The room was a long, wide ellipse of highly polished metal, with a low ceiling, further extenuating the room's appearance of size. But it was the depth of the room that was truly amazing. Beyond the steel gantry that sat by the bulkhead, the majority of the floor was transparent and seemed made of some impossibly thin material. The drop into the dark below was the sort that made your stomach want to jump out of your mouth. Ghost hesitantly took several steps out across it staring down at the blackness and the arching lighting that crackled between the unknown tech housed below.

'Don't worry,' said Joe. 'I was like that at first, but it seems totally safe.' Joe jumped up and down boisterously three times, stomping on the thin transparent flooring each time when he landed as hard as he could.

Ghost winced. 'What's it made of?'

'No clue,' said Joe.

'It's fucking glass idiots. Like what they have at the Grand Canyon,' said Raf.

'I don't think so,' said Joe. 'For one...'

'Don't give me that, 'For one' shit,' said Raf. 'It it looks like glass and feels like glass and looks like glass, then it's got to be glass, am I right or wrong here?'

Ghost turned away and studied the rest of the room, trying to map every detail, unsure of what might prove useful in helping One. If he could have looked down on the whole room from above he realized that it would have resembled a large eye. He and his friends had entered from one of the corners. In the center of the room a large, seamless metal pillar rose from the depths below, chaining lighting into it and conveying it upwards a large spherical node that rose three or foot out of the floor. Ghost would have guessed that this was the core of the AI called GAIA. But he didn't need to because there was a handy sign.

Directly above the core, in the ceiling, a huge fan circled, sucking cool air from somewhere in the base and venting it onto the core. Between the door they had come through and the GAIA core, rows of monitoring stations were arranged upon desks. On the other side of the core, the set up was mirrored and Ghost could see another door exiting from the opposite corner of the eye shaped room. The transparent floor was attached to the walls of the room close to the corners of the doors, then broke away, forming an almost hour glass shaped walkway encased with its own safety rail that seemed to be cut from the same single piece of whatever material made the floor. Ghost estimated that there was about a twenty meter gap between the safety rail of the walkway and the walls at the room's widest point. Below the flooring, in the centre of the room, the column of the GAIA core descended into the dark until it was out of site. Directly below both entrances, scaffolds supported what looked like hundreds going on thousands of tiers of glowing modules, going down as far as the eye could see, each bustling with lights and wires.

'When I was kid,' said Joe. 'We went to New York. My dad held me up by the railings on the Empire State. It might be as big a drop. It's hard to say.'

'Fuck off,' said Raf joining them. 'It's not that big. It's your eyes playing tricks on you.'

'Are you one my Uncle's guys?' Jenni interrupted.

'Not any more,' said Raf.

'Hey!' snapped Joe. 'A bit of consideration, eh?'

Raf shrugged at Joe. 'What do you want me to say?'

'Is my uncle okay?' Jenni asked.

'Not really,' said Raf. 'He's dead.'

'Hey!' shouted Joe. 'Have you got no tact? It's her only family. You could at least try to break the bad news a little more gently.'

'Bad news? For her maybe. Best bit of luck I've had in months. I owed that old bastard fifty big ones.'

Ghost stepped to Jenni's side and placed a hand on her shoulder. She reached up and squeezed it.

'You heartless fuck, how can you say that?' Joe raged.

'What do you mean heartless? You want me to say I'm sorry he died? I'm not sorry. He was a miserable, sadistic old prick. I'm glad he's dead,' said Raf.

Joe shoved Raf as roughly as he could.

'Oh no, help!' cried Raf, shrugging Joe off. 'I'm being attacked by a boffin, oh whatever shall I do?'

'You take that back! I am not a boffin!' seethed Joe.

On the other side of the room, hidden behind the cover of a computer bank, Keats and his men waited.

'Are they still arguing?' One of his men asked, amazed.

'They did stop briefly,' another replied. 'I think they've just started up again.'

Keats held up a hand and silenced them as he received the message he'd been waiting for all day.

'Keats, the rogue modular has been terminated,' Jasper's voice spoke in his ear-piece. 'Move in and apprehend the targets. Lethal force if necessary, but try to keep the albino alive.'

'I'll do my best,' said Keats.

Ghost was embarrassed by how quickly they were surrounded.

'Arguing and waiting for the cavalry?' Keats asked as his team formed a half circle around Ghost and his companions. 'It's not coming. Your robot is dead.'

No one responded and Keats continued, 'Is that the only gun you've got?' he said, gesturing towards Raf.

'Pathetic isn't it?' said Raf. 'You'd have thought one of these other slackers would have at least picked up some sort of weapon.'

'Well they didn't,' said Keats. 'As if any more proof of what a bunch of amateurs you all are. Anyway, drop it and slide it across.'

'Wait a minute,' Raf protested. 'You've got to understand, man. I never even saw these assholes before.'

'No?,' said Keats. 'We've been watching you arguing with them for the last ten minutes. Enough pleasantries, I've been asked to keep you all alive if possible, but there's something about you lot that gets right under my skin, so I suppose I'll just say you tried to escape and shoot you all. Any last words? For posterity?'

'Whoa, whoa whoa,' said Raf holding his hands up. 'Let's not be so hasty. We're getting off on the wrong foot here, you and me. Let's just calm down. I'm for hire. A free agent.'

'It's too late for that. You're on the wrong side that's all. Nothing overly personal,' smiled Keats, raising his gun.

'Side? Side? Me? I'm not on any side!' said Raf. 'Shit, I don't even know what's going on.' He turned Joe, 'Didn't I say that only a few minutes ago?'

Joe shrugged. 'He did, in fairness, say that.'

'See, I don't even like these guys,' said Raf. 'Tell you what, give me my gun back and I'll join your side. I'll even kill these three for for a very reasonable fee. I'll do the lanky useless one for 10k. The girl will be a bit extra, I don't usually kill women or kids, but I'll make it an exception today, call her 20k. And that little shit,' he nodded at Joe, 'that little shit I'll throw in for nothing. Now that's a good deal, and you know it.'

'You fuck,' said Joe. 'I'll rip your head off in a minute!'

'Fat chance,' said Raf.

Keats' opened his mouth to speak but whatever he said was drowned out by the smashing, grinding sound of the door to the vault being ripped apart. Ghost's heart leapt, One was here to save them. But as the door was pulled out of its frame all that entered was the brooding, basic form of a far less sophisticated robot than One.

'Ah,' smiled Keats, 'Looks like one of our modulars has come to play.' Keats pointed at Raf. 'Pick him up!' he commanded.

The robot moved forward swiftly and scooped the protesting Raf off his feet.

'Now I want you take his head lightly in one hand,' said Keats and the machine obeyed.

Keats' looked at Joe, smiling thinly. 'What was it you were just saying? That you wanted to rip his head off? Well here's your chance. Give the order.'

'Hey, come on, we've all had some fun, but playtime's over. Put me down,' complained Raf.

'Give the order,' said Keats. 'I want you to tell the robot to pull his head off. Give the order!' Keats bellowed.

Joe shook his head. 'Man's an arse, but not that much of an arse.'

'Give the order or I'll shoot your friend in the face,' snapped Keats. 'Come on, grow some balls.

'No,' said Joe, 'I can't.'

'Can't or won't?' Keats asked. 'We'll see.' He raised his gun, aimed at Ghost's head. 'You've got the count of three. One ... two ... thr...'

'Alright! Alright!' snapped Joe. 'Take his head off.'

'You traitor!' shouted Raf. 'I'll remember this!'

'Louder!' said Keats. 'Louder.'

'Rip his head off!' shouted Joe.

Keats laughed. 'You heard him robot, rip his head off!'

59

Jasper sat down on the floor, leaned his back against the wall and calmly placed his comm. beside him. Things would work out one way or another and he was tired of trying to control them. For the last couple of minutes he'd been trying to reach Keats over the intercom, every failed attempt adding to his sense of panic. On his sixteenth attempt Jasper had given up, it was obvious what had happened. Somehow the rogue robot had not been destroyed and instead was actively jamming communications. Jasper could only suspect therefore, that his last modular robot was now nothing more than a few hundred billion pounds worth of dirt. Not only that, but Keats was about to receive the ass jacking he ultimately deserved. Finally, and most irritatingly, Jasper was now confined himself, trapped in a maintenance corridor after two bulk head doors had slammed shut and locked simultaneously. The situation was frankly unbelievable. How had a rag tag group and one escaped experiment managed to bring Damocles to complete standstill? This base held a standing army of over five hundred trained men, but they had been rendered useless. The very security measures designed to prevent this sort of situation had been used against them. The rogue had overridden security and managed to lock nearly all of the bases security doors, effectively making prisoners of all but a small number of the bases soldiers. Until a few minutes ago Jasper had still been in contact with several groups, not that any of them had been close to launching any sort of useful action. One group had reported using demolitions to blast their way through three sets of security doors, but with only one demolition charge remaining and some thirty four doors between themselves and the data-vault, they would go little further.

No, Jasper thought, calming himself. For him, the time for action was over. Truhalt had played a dangerous game and he had made mistakes. The conclusion was being played out even now. Keats and GAIA would have to stand alone against the robot and the albino. There would be no re-enforcements now, no last minute substitutes. The pieces already in play would have to decide the outcome.

'Let them win or lose,' said Jasper to himself. 'And let the pieces fall where they may.'

'You left that a bit late,' Joe said to One, grinning from ear to ear.
'It wasn't late,' said Ghost. 'It was perfect timing.'

'No, I was late. I had estimated to arrive 0000.833 seconds sooner. Had you been captured by a better man, he would have shot you all dead before I arrived.'

'I kind of assumed you'd taken Keats' nature into your calculations,' said Ghost.

'You put far too much faith in me,' said One.

'What are you both cumming all over him for?' called Raf from where he was guarding Keats and his goons. After Keats' surrender Raf had collected their weapons and marched the soldiers at gun point to the edge of the gantry and ordered them to kneel hands behind heads. 'It was me who saved us. I knew One was coming, that's why I stalled them.'

'Stalled them?' snapped Joe. 'You offered to shoot us!'

'So? You told a giant robot to rip my head off!' Raf shouted back. 'Don't matter anyway, I wasn't scared. I had it all planed out.'

'You weren't scared?' said Joe. 'You were screaming!'

'If you can't recognize a skilled actor when you see one, then there's no hope for you,' Raf retorted. 'Three years at RADA just paid for itself.'

'You're so full of shit Raf,' said Joe.

If any acting deserved praise it was One's, thought Ghost. When the order to pull Raf's head off had come, instead of obeying, the robot had extended one arm into a flowing spear of liquid metal. It had happened so fast that the point of the spear had drawn a bead of blood from Keats' throat faster than a heart beat. The robot had placed Raf down and slowly reformed into the kindly looking man that One favoured. Even Ghost had been surprised at the speed at which Keats surrendered once his own life was threatened. The bald soldier had hardly been able to get the words out fast enough – if he could have, Keats' would probably have sicked up a white flag.

One called Ghost over to where he stood before the core.

'I'm going to disengage the outer shield now,' said One. 'Are you ready to breach the shield-core?'

'Yeah, about that,' said Ghost, glancing around to locate Jenni. She was standing close to Joe who was now examining some of the desk mounted computers. Raf was still standing over their prisoners. 'I've used up my power. I'm not sure I'll be able to do it.'

One nodded. 'You augmented the girls memories?'

'I did,' said Ghost. 'Can we still succeed?'

'Perhaps,' said One. 'Perhaps. I will lower the outer defenses and then we can see.'

The robot flexed back the palm of its hand and a cable spoiled forth, snapping into a connection located upon the GAIA core. A small pulse of energy flowed from One's hand and down the cable, hissing softly. Almost at once a low hum sounded from the column. A moment later a hair line fracture appeared in the smooth metal of the core, and slowly grew. It took a second for Ghost to realize that it was hatch like door. The small door folded outward to reveal several banks of circuitry, securely installed behind a thick layer of the see through material that the gantry was constructed of.

'What is that stuff?' Ghost asked.

When One didn't reply, Ghost glanced up towards the robot. One's usually animated face was void of expression, almost like the robot had entered some shut down state. Ghost reached out and tapped One's shoulder, suppressing the irrational fear that his sophisticated robotic companion had devolved into no more than a shop manikin and would tumble over at his touch. Under his touch, One stirred, its head rotating shakily until it was looking at Ghost.

'You ok?' Ghost asked.

'Yes,' One said, but its voice was changed, a strained and distorted version of the voice it usually used. 'It is made of a substance pioneered by Damocles, an organically harvested crystal, mined from asteroids which is then enhanced at a molecular level. The finished product has several astounding properties. If I could give you the details, however, retracting the outer shield is draining my resources considerably. The crystal layer is virtually indestructible even with far more powerful weapons than we possess. I can attempt to bypass GAIA's security and disengage the shield, but I do not have enough processing power to lower both the inner and outer shield.'

'What do you need me to do?' asked Ghost.

'It is not your time to do anything,' droned One, his voice painfully flat. 'It is time for Joe to shine.'

At hearing his name, Joe looked up. 'What am I doing?'

'I am going to transfer the data-stream I am using to keep the outer shield lowered to the computer in front of you. Can you see it?'

Joe peered at the monitor screen as it flickered to life. 'Yeah, I can see it,' he said.

'What you are seeing is a 2d representation of an oscillating 5d puzzle matrix.'

'Okay,' said Joe. 'It's giving me a headache just looking at it. What am I supposed to do with this?'

' 'I have locked the program into a continuous feed back loop. I will highlight the pattern. Do you see it?'

Joe studied the screen. After his first glance he had been forced to look away, scared he would never see anything but pure gibberish. But now, as he studied, the screen began to make a small kind of sense. Some number sequences were highlighted in yellow, data lines One had highlighted to help him. These were crucial to holding the outer shield open, essential to the puzzle. But he still couldn't see how they fitted together so he began looking for basics. Joe saw the height and width of the puzzle first of course. After all, since a small boy he had been used to seeing televisions and computer monitors every day of his life – they displayed all their information in two dimensions. Depth was an illusion on television; the picture was a flat image. It was no different here, it was not hard for Joe to grasp that and a moment later, as if it materialized in front of his eyes he saw another layer to the puzzle. Lines of encoded data flickered across the screen in all directions, some stood out in bold to him, some he could understand, others flashed by so quick he could hardly see them, let alone process their meaning. Once more he scanned the coding, seeing the three dimensions of height, breadth and depth very easily now, understanding how some of One's highlighted numbers fitted in.

'Can you see the pattern?' One asked again.

'Nearly,' said Joe.

'We don't have much time,' said One.

Joe glanced up across the room at the robot, noticing with a quick flick of his eyes how concerned Ghost looked. One looked drained, its form was more basic than it had been only moments before. Joe wondered exactly how much of its energy One was exerting holding open the outer shield. Hurriedly Joe got back to the monitor and began looking for the fourth dimension. Every sci-fi nerd knew what that was: time. He watched the highlighted digits flashing across the screen, noting the spacing and trying to remember the delays between their appearance. It was nigh on impossible, the timing and location of the numbers seemed to change at random.

'I can't do it,' shouted Joe. 'I can't keep track of them all.'

One almost seemed to groan with pain, then: 'It's oscillating. The code moves through all five dimensions. You must account for its phase transitions.'

Joe tried to follow the code again, but it lost him. It had been the same with the security terminal earlier. Then it had been even harder, now he had One's help he could follow the pattern more quickly, but it was still too much.

'I can't,' said Joe. 'It's too quick.'

'We don't have time to play, I will attempt to lock the frame work of it down. Stop it's oscillations.' Ones speech was beginning to sound slurred. A crack of electricity flickered down the cable between One and GAIA. It flowed over One, and his form lost all definition, he became a man of featureless chrome.

On the screen the code was easier to track, it no longer moved so erratically. Joe raised his hands to the keyboard and experimentally tried to input the correct digits at the right time.

'You have it,' One droned, its voice reminding Joe of a Dalek. All human emotion was lost from it.

'Kind of,' Joe called back. 'I have no idea where the fifth dimension is on this thing.'

'Negative,' drawled One. 'You have done well. No human can compute at this speed in 5d. It is impossible. Your current performance is acceptable. Transferring complete control to your terminal.'

'Whoa, wait...' Joe managed, but it was too late, and he realized that he was doing it. Sure the highlighted strings of digits were helping, and One had simplified it, but he was doing it. Of course he didn't know it at the time, but it was an eternal moment for Joseph Simms that he would remember for the rest of his life. He would put it with a small collection of memories that he would treasure forever - The day his dad took the stabilizers off his bike and he could ride it. His first kiss. Completing Final Fantasy VI. Meeting Karen. The birth of his children. The death of his children. Establishing the Freeman Continuum. Dying. This moment was every bit as momentous for Joe as the others. Perhaps more so.

Almost at once One began to show signs of improvement. Its features began to return and its voice became his own.

'Thought we were going to lose you there,' said Ghost.

'Nearly did for a moment,' smiled One. 'Nearly did. You got that code under control Joe?'

'Yup, I've got it,' called Joe, his voice tight with concentration.

'Okay, I'm going to open the shield-core then destroy GAIA directly. I'm going to need about forty five seconds. Can you manage that Joe?'

Joe's fingers blurred across the keys. 'I think so,' he called back.

'When the shield is fully open, throw whatever energy you have left into the exposed circuitry,' One commanded Ghost.

Ghost nodded. 'There isn't much left but a trace.'

One again threw all of its ability at the GAIA core. One couldn't believe how powerful it was. It had taken all One's effort to move the outer shield, One's run time was down to less than five minutes. One had one chance only. As One probed the inner most defenses One felt the bulk of GAIA, a dark mass of will, desperate to survive. One attacked directly and took no prisoners. The inner core began to open.

Ghost made ready, searched for that last tiny bit of dark energy, found it and brought it to his fingers. The power he had commanded before was all but gone, all that was left was a trickle. He hoped it would be enough.

The inner shield began to open, slowly but steadily. After about a quarter of GAIA's primary circuits were revealed a siren sounded and a loud computerized voice announced: 'Caution, unauthorized GAIA core operation. Cease or you will be executed. Caution, unauthorized GAIA core operation. Cease or you will be executed. Caution, unauthorized GAIA core operation. Cease or you will be executed.' The message continued on loop.

'We'll see about that,' Ghost said to himself. Most of the circuits were now visible. He waited.

'Caution, unauthorized GAIA core operation. Cease or you will be executed.'

'Just a few more seconds,' One said.

'Caution, unauthorized GAIA core operation. Cease or you will be executed.'

'Just a few more seconds....'

'Caution, unauthorized GAIA core operation. Cease or you will be executed.'

The shield was now nearly completely clear of the delicate circuits. Ghost was totally focused. Perhaps too focused because he missed a couple of things he shouldn't have let slip by him. First the huge fan directly above the GAIA core sparked and slowly wound down.

Perhaps that was an excusable miss, anyone could have thought that was due to One's attack. But the slight, growing smell, he shouldn't have missed that. A whiff of something familiar. Something bad. Something very bad. Sulfur. Stupidly long moments passed before he was able to connect the feeling of danger with the smell. Then his eyes widened. The huge industrial fan split apart and he glanced up in time to see an acrid, green tentacle slamming toward him. He dived to one side and rolled. The sickening eggy, smell of sulfur filled the room and the gantry rocked as the bulbous green limb missed Ghost by mere inches. One, locked in his invisible battle was not so lucky.

The Thing plopped out of the huge fan above the core, cackling to itself. A huge, barbed tentacles of slime pierced Ones body, lifting the robot from the floor. The Thing crashed One repeatedly against the roof and floor. One began to spasm, huge jets of electricity discharging from its body and chunks of his mass falling away like wet mud. The interface cable with the GAIA core snapped.

'YOU PRIMITIVE RACES AND YOUR TOOLS!' screeched the thing. 'YOU DREAM THAT YOU COULD MATCH THE POWER OF THE OLD ONES!'

60

'It's killing One!' screamed Joe, hands still blurring across the keys. 'I can't keep this thing open!'

Ghost leapt to his feet, glanced from One who was being smashed around like a rag doll to the GAIA core. GAIA's core shield began to lower again. Then a powerful whirring sounded from the walls as servo hinges and mechanism all down the GAIA's control spire began to whirr into life. The horrendously loud warning voice ceased. It was a small mercy.

'GAIA's rebooting the base!' called Joe. 'One must have been suppressing it. We're going to be up to our asses in soldiers if we can't shut it down!'

'Fuck the soldiers,' said Raf pointing at the Thing. 'What the fuck is that?'

A soldier Raf had been guarding took his chance and threw himself into Raf, knocking the mercenary sprawling. Keats and his men began to move, dashing towards the other side of the gantry and their weapons.

'Kill them all,' Keats screamed. 'No mercy!'

They managed to rearm themselves alright, but by the time they did, they had more pressing targets.

Ghost desperately looked around, searching to find a way to help One. The robot was taking enormous punishment as the Thing smashed him from surface to surface. Then from all around the cht-cht-cht of armoured pincers began to sound. Ghost glanced down, through the see through crystal. From deep below, to whatever depth the core descended, crab-a-labs could be seen, beginning to tear their way up the walls from the bottom of the vault. They were climbing fast.

Ghost was bundled from his feet by Raf and crashed to the ground between two rows of terminals.

'What are you standing about for you moron?' snapped Raf, gesturing over his shoulder. 'I don't know what you'd be doing without me.'

Ghost looked to where he pointed. A crossbow bolt had thudded into a computer bank just behind where he had been stood moments before. The computer station bled blue sparks.

'Harold,' Ghost said.

'Who the fuck is Harold?' asked Raf. 'Oh fuck it, I don't want to know who he is. Or what he is, or whatever. What I want to know, is what the fuck that big green monster is?'

'It's complicated,' said Ghost, rolling onto his haunches.

'Then give me the simple version,' said Raf.

Ghost shrugged. 'Ok then, it's a big green monster.'

'Gotcha,' said Raf.

Joe and Jenni were in a similar position, sheltering between two rows of terminals.

A Damocles soldier appeared at one end of the terminal row and aimed his weapon on them. Joe screamed. Jenni looked on frozen. The soldiers chest exploded outward as a massive claw tore through it, lifting the grunt from his feet and throwing him away. Joe screamed again as the grotesque creature sidled towards them on it mechanoid legs. Then it too was blown to pieces by a hail of fire from some unseen source and the battle really begun.

Ghost peeked over the top of the desk in front of him and quickly pulled his head down. Several crab-a-labs were on the gantry close to the door where they had entered. Keats and his men were engaging them with their newly reacquired weapons. GAIA's inner core was now completely re-secured and the outer shield was slowly closing. Soon the crab-a-labs would swarm the gantry and drive the Damocles soldiers back, or GAIA would re-boot the base and enemy re-enforcements would arrive in the shape of squads of highly trained shock troops. Things were not looking good. They were about to get worse. As Ghost looked one way, a green tentacle snagged his foot from the other and pulled him from his hiding position. The Thing held him up and brought him closer, dangling him like a child holding a toy.

Brr, brrt, brrt! Keat's carbine cut another of the crab monsters in two. This was the first time he'd seen these things up close and personal. He'd read the classified files of course, studied the reports.

Brr, brrt, brrt! He fired another controlled burst, being careful to aim for the monsters belly, where charred, once human flesh had been seared onto the mechanical crab like legs. The reports said that this was where the main motor-neuron nexus was located. Whatever the science, it seemed to be working. From the corner of his eyes Keats saw Ghost being hoisted up by the Thing. The bald soldier permitted himself a small smile. He was sure that whatever lay in store for the albino, it was unlikely to be pleasant. More of the crab monsters were climbing from below. Soon the room would be over run. The hellish creatures would do his job for him. Cutting down one more crab-a-lab, he sounded the order to retreat. What was left of his squad gladly followed him back towards safer ground.

The monstrous entity that was the Thing held Ghost just before its colossal mass. The stench was unbelievable. Still holding One in another tentacle the Thing brought the impaled robot so that hung limpy before Ghosts eyes. The red spiders that swarmed across the Things body ran down the tentacle, biting savagely at One who shuddered and convulsed beneath their torment, letting out a pitiful, high pitched rash of feedback.

The Thing laughed it's belching, farting laugh and satisfied at last, hurled One's broken body back onto the gantry with a mighty flick of its tentacle. One skidded and bounced on the floor, before smashing through a row of terminals and rolling to halt.

Then the Thing turned all of its attention to Ghost.

'GAZE ON ME AND BEHOLD YOUR DOOM!' the thing screamed and the whole room seemed to tremble before the being's dark majesty. 'GAZE ON THE POWER OF THE ELDER RACES DEALBREAKER! YOU BROKE AN OATH OF TRUST!

Ghost shrugged.

YOU THOUGHT TO DECIEVE ME! A BEING WHO HAS WALKED THE PATHS OF TIME BEFORE EVEN GOD WAS A FLICKER OF A DREAM. I WILL KILL YOU AND TAKE THAT GIRL ANYWAY. I AM A CREATURE OF AGELESS MIGHT! MY RACE ARE THE MATCH THAT STATED THE GREAT BLAZE, THE MATCH THAT GAVE LIFE! WE ARE THE MATCH THAT WILL START A NEW BLAZE! THE MATCH THAT WILL CAUSE THE GREAT FIRE THAT WILL END ALL LIFE, WE ARE THE MATCH WHO WILL BURN....'

But at that moment a shape flashed from the side of the room, it's speed so great it was no more than a blur. The tentacle holding Ghost prisoner was severed. As Ghost crashed to the floor The Thing let out a scream of ancient rage and pain which howled throughout the data-vault. The severed tentacle fell away, flopping over the edge of the gantry and falling into. The stump left on the Things body spewed a dirty purple vapour which crackled with unholy power.

Lachlan retrieved his ax. 'I've got a match for you - your face, my arse.'

'Lachlan, watch out!' Ghost called, rolling to his feet and watching in vein as Zombie Harold stepped from behind the Thing and loosed a cross bow bolt at the ax man. He needn't have opened his mouth. Lachlan swayed smoothly to one side, and the bolt flew by harmlessly.

'You're a bad man Harold,' Lachlan chided. 'Nah, I'm only kidding, you're alright really. Bad luck getting turned into another minion for the ever growing army of the undead though. Tough break.'

'HOW, HOW, HOW...' The Thing roared, its pustuous voice full of pain.

'How did I escape from the Stone Bridge of Amahizh'Jidanhn? How did I elude the Ten Thousand?' Lachlan finished. 'Or how did I catch up with your sorry ass?'

'WELL, HOW?' the Thing boomed.

'Because I'm a fucking pro,' smiled Lachlan.

'THIS TIME YOU WON'T ESCAPE. IN MOMENTS THIS PLACE WILL BE OVERRUN BY MY MINIONS. NONE OF YOU WILL SURVIVE.'

But Ghost wasn't so sure that the Thing believed its own words. Slowly, carefully it was edging away from the bearded warrior and Ghost realized something amazing. The Thing was truly frightened of this man. Lachlan terrified the huge demonic beast.

'You're right,' said Lachlan. 'In a few moments we'll all be snipped into little pieces. But do you know what this is?' Lachlan held up a silver cylinder. 'It's a Null Zone Nuke. Stole it from Harold earlier. Thought it might come in handy.'

Out of the corner of his eye Ghost saw Zombie Harold rummaging in his bag.

'SO?' boomed the Thing, still slithering back.

'Know what it does?' Lachlan asked.

'OF COURSE I NOW WHAT IT DOES YOU PATHETIC HUMAN! IT'S A BANISHMENT DEVICE!'

'Correct-a-mundo,' smiled Lachlan. 'And I'm about to use it to transport you and all your stinky little friends back from whence you came. Then when you're back there, I'm going to kick your slobbery green ass for the final time.'

'HAHAHAH,' the Thing laughed. 'YOU STUPID APE, EVEN I KNOW THAT THOSE WORTHLESS HUMAN DEVICES TAKE MINUTES TO GAIN

ENOUGH POWER BEFORE THEY CAN OPEN A PORTAL. BEFORE IT'S FULLY CHARGED, YOU'LL ALL BE LONG DEAD.'

'Yeah I know you useless, faceless, talentless ball of slime. They take seven minutes and seventeen point eight seconds to charge. I told you I was a fucking professional. What the hell do you think I've been stalling you for?'

'STALLING ME?' the Thing rumbled.

The cylinder beeped in Lachlan's hand and emitted a faint orange glow. 'I primed it seven minutes ago. Saddle up slime head, you're going for a ride,' Lachlan grinned and threw the device over the edge of the gantry.

Jenni risked peeking out over the desks. Many of the crab monsters on the gantry were dead, but a glance below showed that more were quickly climbing the walls.

'Joe, we need to do something,' she urged.

'We are doing something, we're actively not dying,' said Joe.

'There's no use asking him to do anything,' snapped Raf, dropping down beside them. 'He's useless.'

'Shut the fuck up,' said Joe.

'Shut the fuck up? Come up with that on your own? We need to bail. The robots scrap.'

'One will recover.'

'I doubt it,' said Raf. 'It's been lying in a heap for the last minute. If anyone is going to do something with that computer, you're going to have to do it yourself.'

'Raf, if I could I would,' said Joe. 'But even One couldn't disengage both shields at once, what chance to I have?'

'There's more than one way to skin a cat,' Raf said shaking his head. 'Why don't we use this?'

Joe glanced. Raf dragged a large, gore splattered infantry heavy weapon with a meter long barrel into cover. Blue and white lights flickered all over it.

'Where did you get that from? And what the shit is it? A bazooka?' asked Joe.

'No you tit, it's a piece of drainpipe. Of course it's a bazooka,' said Raf.

'One said that it's too well protected,' said Joe thinking. 'But do you see the metal door to one side?'

Raf nodded that he did.

'If you can destroy that, well, it's not going to do us any harm,' said Joe.

'Right,' said Raf standing up and shouldering the bazooka. 'Tally-ho!' He clicked the trigger, bracing himself against the expected kickback the missile would generate – none came. After all, it wasn't a rocket launcher.

61

The Null Zone Nuke span like a silver star as it dropped below the gantry, still emitting a faint orange glow. After about twenty meters the silver canister imploded, falling in on itself, until only a tiny, but bright needle prick of orange light remained, held in space. Then with a roar like a jet engine, the orange light, slowly swelled, growing to form a burning orange sphere some two meters in diameter. The sphere floated in the air, blazing like a miniature sun, illuminating the vault in a sickly, orange glow. Ghost gasped. For the first time he saw how far the core extended down. He himself had never been on a skyscraper, but he had no doubt that the drop below was many more times that than the height of the worlds tallest building. And the core ran all the way to the floor. He also realized for the first time, just how many of the crab monsters were coming – thousands of them thronged the walls below, climbing steadily. It made the twenty or so who were close to the bottom of the gantry look like no more than a raiding party. Then the orange ball flared into life.

Raf's new weapon hummed as he depressed the trigger, the hum building to a high pitched squeal. Then it discharged an orb of crackling blue light about the size of a bowling ball. The orb slowly floated towards the GAIA core and on impact flashed like lightning, releasing a crackling shock wave that bathed the GAIA, the Thing and Lachlan in a crackling shock wave of energy. The Thing screamed and recoiled, several of its awful spider like parasites, falling from its body smoking. The GAIA core began to pulse with energy as the shockwave passed over and through it. The inner and outer shields opened and closed several times very quickly. Lachlan turned towards Raf frowning and quickly dusted down his singed beard.

'Watch it,' said Lachlan.

'Oh shut the fuck up,' said Raf.

Lachlan laughed. 'I like it, good attitude!'

'An EMP weapon,' Joe smiled. 'Excellent.' Joe took a moment to jump back onto a console. The code display on the screen began to freeze and lose sophistication. Quickly he seized his chance, locking the outer shield in place. The inner shield was still moving erratically, opening partly then slamming shut.

'Caution, unauthorized GAIA core operation. Cease or you will be executed,' the painfully loud recorded message sounded again. 'Caution, unauthorized GAIA core operation. Cease or you will be executed...'

Orange beams laced out from the Null Zone Nuke, latching onto to the crab-a-labs in the chamber and pulling them towards it. A huge beam lassoed itself around the Thing, dragging the wailing monster towards the edge of the gantry. As the first crab-a-labs were pulled inside, the orange globe flared and the monsters disappeared.

'What's it doing? Killing them?' Ghost asked.

'Caution, unauthorized GAIA core operation. Cease or you will be executed.'

'No such luck,' said Lachlan. 'Its designed to transport creatures of extra-dimensional origin back to whence they came.'

'Can it banish all of them?' Ghost asked.

'Caution, unauthorized GAIA core operation. Cease or you will be executed.'

'Let's hope so...' Lachlan shrugged putting his hands to his ears. 'Man that noise is annoying.'

'Caution, unauthorized GAIA core operation. Cease or you will be executed.'

The Thing had been nearly dragged from the platform now, half of it was hanging in space. Harold hung gamely by his master for a moment, before being pulled over the edge and falling into the glowing sphere. Ghost could only count a few of the crab monsters left too, grimly holding onto the walls of the data vault against the constant tug of the orange beams. Lachlan leap forward slashing at the green blob, opening deep, jagged wounds in the Things disgusting body. The Thing lashed half heartedly at Lachlan, who avoided the monster with ease scoring several more hits, before the Thing was pulled from the balcony and sucked towards the vortex of the Null Zone.

'NEXT TIME I'M GOING TO EAT YOUR PATHETIC SOUL!' the Thing screamed as it fell.

Lachlan leaned over the balcony and called: 'Next time. There's no next time, I'm going to finish you off today.'

Turning away he didn't watch as the Thing was sucked through the orange portal below. Strolling to Ghost Lachlan offered his hand.

'Good job,' said Lachlan, with his lob sided, throw anything at me grin. 'It's been a pleasure and a privilege but now I've got to split.'

Ghost was about to reply but his voice was drowned out by GAIA

'Caution, unauthorized GAIA core operation. Cease or you will be executed.'

'Man but that thing is really annoying,' said Lachlan wandering over to the core. 'I'm going to get a head ache if it doesn't shut up.'

'Caution, unauthorized GAIA core operation. Cease or you will be executed.'

'Is this what's making all the racket?' Lachlan pointed at the piece of crystal opening and closing rapidly in the core.

'Caution, unauthorized GAIA core operation. Cease or you will be executed.'

'Shut up,' Lachlan snapped, almost casually rapping the crystal with his ax head. The inner shield fractured, deep cracks appearing in it frame.

'Caution, unauthorized GAIA core operation. Cease or you will be executed.'

'I said,' Lachlan began bringing his ax up swiftly, 'shut it!' He crashed the ax down and the crystal shattered, flying in all directions. The siren cut off immediately.

'Phew, I can hear myself think again,' Lachlan sighed. 'Tough stuff that,' he mused almost as an after thought. 'Anyway man, like I said, I've got to dash.'

'Where are you going?' Ghost asked.

Lachlan gestured to the portal below that was no flickering and fading quickly.

'Doesn't that go to where they come from?' Ghost asked.

'Sure does,' Lachlan smiled, beginning to trot towards the edge of the gantry.

Ghost reached out and pulled him back, turning the smaller man. 'Don't be a fool Lachlan, that's too far, even for you.'

Lachlan laughed, still full of good humour. 'Ghost my man, you should have learned by now; you can never go too far.' He patted Ghost on the arm, then with a quick wink and a flash of his shit eating grin he ran towards the edge of the platform and leapt.

Lachlan turned a full summersault in mid air before straightening up and opening his arms into a swan dive, falling towards the flickering fading portal. The portal spat orange sparks, shook, shimmered and within a moment after Lachlan entered it - it vanished.

For the first time in what seemed forever, the data vault was silent. Ghost walked slowly across the room, checking everyone was alright and made his way to One's prone body, kneeling beside his friend. Little could be recognized of the robot now, a small portion of it, where it's upper torso and head had been, retained some humanoid form, the rest of it had spilling away across the gantry, like sand running from a split bag. The cable that One had used to interface with Gaia remained connected to his torso and angry, fast flowing volts of electricity washing up and down it's length. One did not move and Ghost was about to move away, when the robot, jerked forward and spoke.

'Did we destroy it?' One wheezed.

'Not yet,' said Ghost. 'But its defenseless, we'll finish it.'

'Swear it!' One rasped. 'Swear it, you must, you must. Life depends on it.'

'We will, I swear,' said Ghost. One seemed happy with the reply and slumped back.

'My one regret,' One croaked, his once perfect voice a mismatch of pitch and tone, heavily synthesized and inhuman, 'is that, despite all my great learning, I could not penetrate the inner mysteries. I could not find truth. But how can a robot understand intuitional thought? How can I not analyze? '

'You lived and died for the good of a people not your own,' said Ghost. 'What is greater than that?'

'One day, you will know,' One said. The robots once golden laugh was gone. What replaced it made Ghost's hairs stand on end. Ones form flickered and phased. A barely humanoid arm formed and rose before Ghost's face. In it sat a tiny five pointed star of shiny silver.

'You are a good man Ghost. But you have a terrible future. Take this gift, given freely. May it help you succeed where others would fail. Wear it with pride. It will shine brighter when night is about you. May it be a light to you in dark places, when all other lights go out.'

Ghost gently took the silver star from One's hand and looked at it. Upon it, engraved with exquisite care was the word 'Sheriff.' Ghost closed the metal badge inside his fist and turned his attention back to One.

One's arm fell apart and scattered across the floor. 'It is time,' it said.

A wave of calm spread across Ghost, radiating from the inside out. 'It if is time,' he said, 'then power down and go.'

One paused, its receding face reforming and once more taking on the kindly face of the long dead live stock herder, the trace of a smile formed upon One's lips. 'Is that is all there is to the mystery?' Asked One,

'So it is said,' said Ghost and watched his friend die.

The robot, the being, that had come to call itself One, scattered into uncountable, worthless pieces, all cohesion between it's billions of nanites lost. If anyone not knowing had looked upon the scene it would have been as if Ghost was kneeling in a pile of salt.

Ghost reopened the hand that held the sheriff's badge, but the star too was gone.

'We done?' Raf asked.

'Not yet,' said Ghost standing up and taking the weapon out of Raf's hands. 'Come here all of you.'

Ghost placed the EMP gun inside GAIA's now fully open shield so that the barrel was in direct contact with the circuits they had worked so hard to expose. He placed his hands on the trigger and gestured for the others to do the same. Joe put his hand over Ghosts, then Raf, strangely quiet did placed his on Joes. Finally Jenni put her hand over Rafs.

'Ready?' Ghost asked.

'Yup,' said Joe.

'Do it,' said Raf.

'Yeah,' said Jenni.

The core hummed, a soft child like voice coming from it. 'Please don't...' it pleaded.

'As if we need any more justification,' said Joe. 'You think we haven't seen 2001?'

Ghost grinned and pulled the trigger.

62

There was no doubt that a direct EMP blast right into GAIAs most intimate parts severely damaged it. But it didn't kill it. GAIA told them so itself, a small reedy female voice chimed. 'You cannot destroy me. I am eternal'

Ghost and the rest ignored it and gave it two more blasts from the EMP Rifle for good measure. It still wasn't enough.

'You are wasting your time,' GAIA said. 'I'm doing science and I'm still alive.'

'Hit it once more!' shouted Ghost.

The EMP crackled off another round.

'I feel fantastic and I'm still alive!' GAIA sang.

Joe eyed the EMP rifle. 'This things lights were all green but they're mostly red now. We've got like one more shot I'd say before it need a recharge.'

'While you're dying I'll be still alive!'

Ghost tried to think, where would the last shot do the most damage.

'And when you're dead I will still be alive!'

'Fuck that song makes me hungry,' said Joe.

Ghost moved around the other side of the core, looking for something. Jenni stopped him.

'The Red Head told me this moment would happen,' she said. 'When we went to her home by the river and she put you into a deep sleep, she told me.'

'She put you into a sleep,' said Ghost.

'Only from your perspective,' said Jenni. 'She told me what I had to do when this moment came. It's the reason I'm here I suppose.'

'What do you need to do?'

'The Red Head told me that I'm a Gen III version of what became GAIA. GAIA is really my descendant. More complicated but built on my template.'

'She told me the same, what of it?' Ghost asked.

'Nothing we can do can destroy something as powerful as GAIA. The only way GAIA can be powered down is if GAIA chooses to power itself down. To destroy itself.'

'I don't think GAIA is going to just do that,' said Ghost.

'If it realizes that it's own death will save millions it might,' said Jenni.

'But how?' asked Ghost.

'In the same way that GAIA was created in the first place,' said Jenni. 'The Red Head told me that an AI convinced all other AIs to merge, to become benevolent.'

'Yes, the AI known as Empathy.'

'Yes. The AI that forged GAIA is also my descendent. I am essentially a basic form of Empathy. It falls to me to convince GAIA to power down.'

Joe came around the core. 'What are you two gossiping about.'

Ghost ignored him. 'How can you do that?'

'By merging with GAIA,' said Jenni.

'And what will happen to you?' Ghost asked.

'Does it matter?' Jenni smiled. 'It is my purpose.'

'It matters to me,' said Ghost.

She laughed. 'It matters to you because I'm meant to matter to you.'

Raf joined them too. 'What the fuck is this a mother's meeting?'

'Look at us,' said Jenni. 'All this is just a representation, a dream really. None of us are fully formed.'

'The fuck are you saying?' said Raf. 'I'm fully formed as fuck.'

Jenni continued. 'We're all parts a process that is happening whether we want it to or not. Our lives have a certain reality to us, but it's just from our perspective. Have you never looked at your hand and realized how weird it is? We accept it as normal because we perceive it every day and know no different.'

'What's wrong with our hands now?' Raf asked.

'Shut up,' said Joe.

'Ghost you care about me because you were meant to,' said Jenni. All of you in your own way got me here to do this. I mean look at me, without this, what am I? On the level of this dream I'm a barely fleshed out character. I have no real backstory or purpose. There's some suggestion that Ghost and I share something because that's what happens in two bit stories; the main characters fall in love and have sex because they're the main characters. In this story, what am I? The prize basically, some tart for the hero to rescue? The stupid token girl, with a traditionally pretty face and nice pair of tits, who follows around and gets captured and offers some exposition from time to time? The weak heroine who at the end, as some sort of redemption, gets the chance to do something of value? On one level I'm all of those. But really I'm none of them.'

'Is this making sense to anyone?' Raf asked. 'What's she going on about?'

Ghost and Joe ignored him.

'So then what?' said Ghost.

'I do my thing, and then you do your thing and it's done,' said Jenni.

'What will happen?' Joe asked.

'If successful I'll become part of GAIA,' said Jenni.

'What will happen to you?' said Ghost.

'You just don't get it, do you?' she said not unkindly. 'There is no me, no you, no any of us. There never has been. It just seems that way.' She moved to the core, laid her hands on it. 'I have to go.'

'I don't know what to say,' he said.

'That's fine,' she said.

'We won't forget you,' said Joe.

'You will. Like all the people we will save will never know we existed. When I merge with the core, you will forget I ever was.'

'I don't understand,' said Ghost.

'You people are unbelievable,' said Raf. 'You're sick. You deserve each other.'

'I understand,' said Joe.

'Then explain,' said Ghost.

'There's no point,' said Joe. 'In a moment you won't even have a question.'

Jenni smiled and closed her eyes. Then, like One's, her body flowed into sand and tumbled inside the GAIA core.

63

A minute later their lungs were on fire as the raced through the base towards the exit. The EMP gun had discharged directly into the core, but had failed to do significant damage. Then GAIA had just shut down. Without its constant control of the base things had started to go bad quick. Lighting flashed up and down the control pillar, sparking off below and causing a series of small explosions and electrical fires that quickly began to spread.

'Time to go,' Joe had warned. 'This is the classic exploding base finale.' And he had been right.

They legged it as fast as they could, while the base rumbled and shook and began to fall apart around them. They flew around the last turn and Joe whooped with delight gesturing to the cargo bay where he and Raf had entered.

'It's just ahead!' he shouted. 'Come on!'

But his shout was cut short as an explosion hammered him from his feet. The others fared no better. Ghost was flung into a wall and Raf pitched into a bulkhead.

'They don't come much closer than that,' said Raf.

Then the ceiling overhead gave way. Raf and Joe dived back and Ghost scrambled aside, but the roof fell between them separating them from each other. Joe and Raf were close to the cargo bay doors, but Ghost was trapped on the other side of the cave in.

When the ruble settled Ghost moved to the blockage and quickly realized he couldn't shift it.

'I'm not going to be able to get through,' he called.

'Shit!' he heard Joe call. 'Go back, the way we came and turn left at the first junction. If I can remember the plans right there should be way to meet up with us through the medical bay. Should be some sort of markings on the walls. We'll wait for you by the exit, okay?'

'Deal,' said Ghost. 'See you in ten.'

Fifteen minutes later, Ghost was making slow progress through the damaged base. The corridor rocked again, he stumbled into the wall. The sounds of explosions came from near by.

'This whole place is tearing itself apart,' Ghost muttered to himself.

He found the entrance to the med bay and moved through the highly sterilized rooms, the empty, pristine beds made to perfection with stainless white sheets. Operating equipment and consoles lay on their sides where more violent explosions had jolted them from their bases. But as he moved deeper into the labs, the sounds and rumbles of explosions became quieter and the floor shook less powerfully. Ghost moved through the last door of the med lab and into the corridor beyond. At the far end he could see stairs leading up. By the stair well, printed on a yellow sign was written: 'Garage Access.' He headed for the stairs. A huge rumble cut through the base again, suddenly fierce in its proximity. It threw Ghost into a wall. He looked back to see a large portion of the med lab collapse some fifty feet behind him. Another large rumble shook the ground.

Ghost began to take the stairs three at a time. Then he stopped.

Standing nonchalantly against the wall of the stair case a man had appeared. The perfectly maintained, blazing green suit he had been wearing when Ghost had first set eyes on him was now tarnished with soot and dirt. It was ripped in several places and drenched in dark patches that could only be blood.

Ghost approached. 'Truhalt Cleig?'

The man looked at him, raising a single eyebrow. 'My name is Mr. Jasper.'

'Are you going to let me up those stairs Jasper?' asked Ghost.

'Who do you work for?' Jasper asked.

'I don't work for anyone,' said Ghost. 'I quit working at the cinema when I realized I was living in a simulation.'

Jasper frowned. 'You know, we have...'

'Ways of making me talk? You weren't really going to say that were you?'

'Not necessarily,' snapped Jasper.

'You were! You were going to say, you know we have ways of making you talk.' Ghost chuckled.

Jasper lurched forward. A front kick hammered out at terrifying speed towards Ghost's belly. Ghost turned side on, deflecting it with a circular block, feeling the instantaneous counter he launched himself foiled by Jasper's defenses. With a hairs breadth to spare, Ghost ducked under a strong right, parried two more blows, snapping in his own counters that were also avoided or deflected. The two warriors hand's blurred together in a serious of uncountable movements, strike following block, leading to counter, running into block; attack and defence melding into one seamless efficiency of movement. Without the slightest pause from their upper bodies, whilst each sought the tiniest chink in the other's defence, Ghost tried for a powerful low kick. It was countered in a moment by Jasper's powerful legs. Ghost stumbled, no more than a fraction of an inch, breaking the rhythm of the fight. In that moment he felt one of Jasper's fists crash into his lower ribs, almost doubling him. Simultaneously, Ghost struck out, catching Jasper to the side of the head, but with incredible sensitivity the green suited man rolled away from the brunt of the punch and launched a low crescent kick at Ghost's knee. Ghost swept his hands down to catch the leg, only realizing at the last it was a feint, the leg swept up and around his guard, Jasper's heal hammering into Ghost's temple. Ghost bounced from the wall, ready to cover any follow up, but none came.

Jasper regarded him with interest, but made no move to advance. 'Funny,' he said. 'I truly expected that to kill you. You must have the skull of an Ox.'

Ghost shrugged.

'You fight well. Unorthodox and somewhat sloppy, yes. But I'm quite impressed. Still, this time I will kill you.'

Ghost rubbed his head where the kick had landed. It throbbed slightly, but even that was fading.

'Ghost leapt on the attack, throwing fast combinations of powerful techniques. But Jasper dealt with them all, and as the fight went on he found more and more ways through Ghost's defence, punishing Ghost with sapping body shots and powerful kicks to the legs. Ghost found his way inside once, landing a twisting uppercut into Jasper's kidneys, forcing the green suited man to retreat a step. The corridor rumbled again, shaking more violently than ever and the sound of explosions grew ever nearer. Ghost and Jasper were thrown apart. As the shockwave died the two fighters climbed from the now ruble strewn corridor. A thin film of sweat coated Jasper, and beads of perspiration rolled from his forehead.

'How are you not tired?' asked Jasper. 'There's no way you should be even standing, let alone fighting on.'

Ghost shrugged.

Jasper opened the melee this time, firing two swift lefts followed by a strong overhand right. Ghost slipped the blows, aiming counters at Jasper's arms, keeping himself better covered and seeking the points that would deaden his opponent's limbs. But Jasper was well conditioned and adept at his own subtle movements, always managing to yield to Ghost's attacks. Jasper tried a knee towards Ghost's belly, but Ghost checked the blow aside with his own knee, momentarily unbalancing Jasper. Striking quickly at the breach in Jasper's defences, Ghost lanced a knife hand attack at his enemy's throat, but Jasper rolled aside. Again too late Ghost realized the bluff, Jasper had only feigned being off balance. The blow hit Ghost in the back of the head with the force of a jackhammer. As Ghost stumbled forward Jasper deftly tugged on Ghost's shoulders, accentuating the natural direction of his body. Ghost crashed into the ground face first. Jasper raised his leg in a huge ark, bringing the heel down in a mighty axe kick on the base of Ghost's neck. For a moment Jasper was exultant. Here was victory. Here was the killing blow. But where there should have been the sickening snap of breaking bones signaling the end of his enemy's life, there was instead a dull thump.

It was as if instead of cracking against weak human bone, his heel had struck granite. If anything his heel hurt. Frustrated, he raised his leg again, preparing to bring the foot down in its murderous ark once more, but as he did Ghost rose, uprooting Jasper as he stood on one leg and throwing him into the wall. The two charged each other, each searching for the purchase to throw or strike, looking for any opening they could find. Ghost landed the first significant strike, his fist biting up and under Jasper's ribs. Taking a collar and hip type hold, Ghost pivoted into a shoulder throw, hurling Jasper to his hands and knees. Ghost leapt forward delivering a solid kick towards Jasper's ribs, which the prone man half blocked as he leapt away. For the first time, Ghost had turned the tide of the attack. Now he stood between Jasper and the stairs.

Ghost was about to speak, but as he opened his mouth, the corridor began to shake again as another huge explosion sounded. A section of wall collapsed some fifteen meters away, blue flame, searingly hot, even from this distant, gushed from the breach. More smaller explosions began, each one triggering the next in a chain reaction of shimmering blue light. The corridor rocked.

'Run,' Ghost shouted.

Forgetting their battle they raced towards the stairs, the heat behind them building. At the foot of the stairs Ghost turned. Jasper was several feet behind, moving as fast as he could, but doubled over holding his ribs with one hand.

The heat was nearly unbearable. Jasper had stumbled, the raging inferno close behind him. Grabbing Jasper by the arm, Ghost hauled the man upright and began dragging him towards the stairs. The blue fireball raged on. They took the stairs three or four at a time, legs burning with effort. Two stories they made until the fireball caught up with them, blowing sickening heat up the center of the stairwell. The sheer force of the blast forced the pair to the floor. Then came the topaz fire, a crackling pillar of it roaring up the center of the stairwell like dragon fire. Ghost felt the hairs on his head begin to smolder. Then, with a hissing rush, the heat receded. Ghost and Jasper rose quickly, eyeing each other in miniature. Jasper was close to exhaustion, one hand clamped hard to his ribs, his breath weezing in and out of him. Ghost felt great. Fresh and strong.

Something had happened to him. Something incredible. An image of the silver star One had given him entered his mind. Perhaps he and Jasper would have fought again then, fighting till one or both of them lay dead, but then, with a tired groan, the floor split beneath them. Both men, dodged backwards to the relative safety of opposite corridors. The stairwell crashed down, one level at a time. As the dust cleared Jasper and Ghost locked eyes once more, separated by the atrium created by the collapse.

'Why?' asked Jasper. 'Why did you help me?'

Ghost shrugged and walked away.

64

'Come on, come on,' Joe muttered to himself, nervously scanning the two access points to the depot. 'What's keeping him?'

'Probably dead,' said Raf.

Joe glared. 'Shut up,' he snapped, but doubt was beginning to creep inside him.

Raf shrugged, checking over the machine gun that he had picked up from a fallen grunt. 'Well either way, we should be going. We're standing in front of the exit. We should just go.'

'Go then,' said Joe. 'But I'm waiting.'

'No need to get touchy,' said Raf. 'I'll give him thirty more seconds.'

But there was no need to worry, because at that moment Ghost burst into the depot through a side door. Joe's face broke into a grin. But his mirth was short lived as almost in slow motion a wave of black armoured soldiers rose from behind cover by the far wall. At their center a small, stocky man with a bald head shouted a command: 'Now!'

The bulk head door behind Joe and Raf slammed shut and the soldiers began firing. Raf had already dropped into cover and dragged Joe to join him. A bullet glanced Joe's shoulder drawing a scream. Ghost dodged behind one of the heavy duty APCs that was parked in the bay as bullets tinged off its surface.

'Nothing is ever easy with you people,' Raf chided. 'We should have left.'

'Nothing's ever easy with me?' Joe retorted, holding his shoulder. 'Take a look at yourself.'

Ghost risked glancing out, only to thrust his head back in sharply. Less than a second later, more bullets screamed into the hull of the APC.

'Get that door open you geek,' Raf shouted at Joe, spraying bullets blindly over the top of the service panel.

'Do it yourself,' Joe shouted back. 'I've just been shot.'

'Shot? That's not being shot. That's a graze,' Raf snapped. 'Do it, or we're all going to die! We'll be surrounded in about thirty seconds.'

Joe grumbled and looked towards a wall mounted terminal.

'It's no good, I'll be killed!'

'If you don't, we'll all be killed!' shouted Raf.

The soldiers had stopped shooting now. They were moving covertly, tightening the net. A wave of frustration washed through Joe.

To go through all this to lose like this. Then the door to the exit began to lift.

'Well done you prick!' Raf exclaimed.

'It's not me,' said Joe. 'I'm not doing it.'

The bulk head door slowly raised and small orangey, red device trundled down the ramp.

'Fuck me,' said one of Keat's men. 'Is that a hoover?'

'Harry?' Joe asked incredulously. 'What the fuck are you doing here?'

Henry regarded Joe with is simple expression as he rolled into the depot. 'I'm a cop you idiot!' the vacuum boomed in its Arnie voice.

The last twelve hours had been illuminating to say the least for the life form known as Harry the Hoover. His master, One, had sent the nanite-animated appliance on a special mission, and on that mission, Harry had received a sign. Harry had realized what his master had meant when One had told him that they would no longer seek to destroy life. The previous night he had been sent to Joe's flat and told to wait until ten o'clock. At the given time the television in the flat had clicked off standby and the reminder Joe had set for his programmed record had begun. Harry watched with his diamond yellow eyes. The movie was Terminator 2: Judgment Day and it, Harry saw his destiny.

The soldiers opened fire, and Harry raised his nozzle accessory waving it from side to side

'Is that hoover sucking the bullets up?' Raf asked.

'Maybe it's developed some sort of super suction ability?' Joe ventured.

More bullets rained in towards Henry, but he continued to pull them out of the air. Then he went from suck to blow. Lead spat from the end of his hose, ripping apart two soldiers were they stood. Another was down a moment later. But while firing, Henry couldn't defend himself. Bullets tore into his body, spinning him. But he kept firing.

Ghost saw the hoover take out three or four more of the grunts. Keats pushed another soldier forward, barking some order or other into his ear, then ducked out of a door behind and fled. The soldier advance firing on Henry, scoring several more hits before the hoover gunned him down. Silence returned to the cargo bay in the aftermath of the gunfire.

Henry rolled towards Ghost slowly, his body riddled with holes.

'Why did you help us Henry?' Ghost asked.

The hoover did not reply at once, then it spoke one last time.

'I know now why you cry,' Henry managed falteringly, then he rolled over, his little black lid coming off for the final time and spilling dirt across the floor.

'Is it dead?' asked Raf

'If something that was animated from the inanimate can die,' said Joe. 'Gone to silicone heaven I guess.'

Raf snorted. 'Silicone heaven? There's no such thing, moron.'

'No Silicone heaven? Preposterous!' said Joe. 'Where would all the calculators go?'

'Yeah, the world has never known one so noble, blah, blah, blah. It was a remote control vacuum cleaner for fucks sake. Are we going now or are we going to give it a full military funeral?' asked Raf marching towards the bulkhead. 'I'm not hanging around here a moment longer. See you around,'

'See you Raf,' said Ghost. 'Thanks.'

'Whatever,' said Raf. And without another word he jogged up the access ramp and disappeared.

Joe turned to Ghost. 'I think we kind of did it.'

Ghost shrugged.

'Right then,' said Joe. 'Let's blow this popsicle stand.'

Ghost shrugged and together the two friends ran up the access ramp towards the bright blue sky.

Keats exited the lift and strolled slowly across his dojo floor, trying to ignore the sounds of chaos as the base continued to fall apart. Slumping down on a chair against one wall. Weariness was enveloping him. How had he failed to stop the albino? How? So many times he'd let him slip through his fingers, just when he thought he had him. If he could have just one more chance, just one, he told himself. He would make no mistakes. Picking up a drink he'd left on the table, Keats sipped at it. The pop had flattened, after all how long had it been there now? He must have left it here two days before. It tasted sour and unpleasant in his mouth. Yet, he was so very thirsty and he drained the cup, glad of the moisture.

The lift on the other side of the room pinged and began to rise. Someone had called it. Keats stood up and with a slow sense of dread and walked to the surveillance monitor that was installed at a tech terminal. He flicked through the cameras until the screen displayed the image showing who was at the top of the elevator. It was Jasper. The drenaline hit his system like a bomb, his mouth becoming bone dry. Why was he coming? It was over, there was nothing left to fight for. The albino had won. And yet Keats watched as the lift doors opened and the tall, green suited man climbed into the elevator. The doors closed and the lift began to descend.

'So this is how it is?' Keats snorted, trying to convert his fear into anger. He had no doubt why Jasper was coming. He stormed to his rack of swords and drew his favourite, a beautifully forged katana. Throwing the sheath aside, Keats slashed the blade through the air several times then with a resigned determination went and stood in the middle of the dojo. The lift hummed as it descended. The flight or fight response began to sing inside Keats. He steeled himself against the adrenal build up and raised his sword into a high guard. The lift doors opened and a wounded Jasper stepped out. As he stepped forward, Keats stepped back. He couldn't help himself. Mr. Jasper's presence seemed to fill the room, his eyes bored into Keats' head like a drill. Keats stepped back again. He tried to cover his fear with words, but his voice sounded shaky even to himself.

'It's done,' Keats said. 'Get back in the lift. I quit.'

Jasper kept walking forward.

'What are you doing this for?' Keats shouted backing up another step. 'It's over.' His arms were shaking. 'It's over. It's done.'

Jasper still said nothing, just kept stepping slowly towards Keats.

Keats considered attacking, but negativity and fear clouded his mind. With every sword stroke he considered he saw the green suited man disarming him. He couldn't see a single way to cut his enemy down. Panic began to set in, but there was one way. A sure way. Keats cast his sword down in a hurried motion and reached for his sidearm. It was dishonorable, but no one would know.

Jasper made his move. He too had been flushed with adrenaline, but had learned to hide it better than Keats. As he approached he had noticed Keats had a good grip on his sword, a trained grip. This was no novice. If he had attacked forcefully, Jasper wondered if, with his wounds, he could have evaded the sword, but Keats had panicked – it was the classic bottle drop, a text book psyche out. By making himself appear fearless, Jasper had terrified his opponent.

Keats reached for the gun and Jasper darted forward. The movement was quick and Keats flinched away, still groping for his holster. Jasper's hand closed around Keat's gun arm with an iron grip.

Keats tried to pull away, but Jasper rotated his hand sharply, and struck up at Keats elbow with his other. Keats' arm bent ninety degrees in the wrong direction. The soldier screamed. Jasper snapped his hands low into Keats belly, several inches below the belly button and knocked Keats back against the wall. At first the impact didn't seem too bad, then a slow burning pain swelled from Keats' center and he became very faint, feeling like passing out, shitting himself and throwing up all at once. He staggered forward from the wall and Jasper pinned him back, the blade of his arm lying across Keats throat, pressing strongly, but not strongly enough to crush the windpipe. Even so Keats gurgled under the pressure. Jasper's face was virtually touching his now, and still their was no emotion in the man's eyes. Keats' body fought against the shock. Then he felt the ripping. The iron grip Jasper had closed on his wrist a moment before landed on his groin – and pulled. Keats screamed, feeling part of himself being torn away, his flesh resisted at first, then yielding to the force, came away. Keats mind whirled with pain and delirium, could take no more and he gladly embraced unconsciousness.

Truhalt Cleig, his shimmering scarlet suit still immaculate, sat in his large comfortable chair, his face unreadable. Before him, on a wide crystal clear monitor, he watched as Joe and Ghost mounted the surface ramp, moments from safety.

'Shall I seal all the bulk heads and activate the drone guns, sir?' asked Jasper, his finger poised at the controls of a databank.

Truhalt Cleig turned off the monitor and span his chair around to face Jasper. 'No. That won't be necessary. Let them enjoy their moment of triumph. They've worked hard for it. It would seem … unsporting … to have them dismembered by heavy machine gun so late in the day.'

Cleig pressed a button beneath his desk and the walls of the office crackled then formed the image of deep space. The pair were surrounded by the rich colours and lonely beauty of exploding nebulas and spinning galaxies.

'So beautiful, and so deadly,' Cleig said, starring at the image. 'I think we lost Oliver,' he added.

'I don't understand how they destroyed GAIA,' said Jasper.

'GAIA itself chose to destroy itself,' said Cleig. 'We have passed the point of no return. We no longer have the comfort of turning back. No, we must press on to the end, to death or glory.'

'Your orders?' Mr. Jasper enquired.

Cleig rose to his feet, his angular, charismatic face loosing all sense of worry or doubt and when he gave his commands, authority rippled through every syllable. 'We must move to a higher emanation.'

'Is that possible?'

'I suppose we will see,' said Truhalt Cleig.

65.

The Red Head sat by the riverbank as the universe she had overseen for so long fell in on itself. In the distance she could see the creature she had coded to be the visual harbinger of this planes collapse. It was a colossal black mass with three heads. Each head was possessed of a purple eye that sucked the world around it up in huge cones of purple energy. Soon the creature would reach her and she too would be consumed.

She was not sure how the prospect of oblivion made her feel. There was both relief and fear.

Footsteps sounded on the grass behind her and she turned passing her eyes again over the playing family as she turned.

A woman was there, tall with flowing silver hair.

The Red Head smiled. 'Whoever you are, you are a little late.'

Silver smiled back. 'I am never late.'

'Is that so? Well whatever you want, I will not be able to help. It is all ending.'

'Tell me what happened to your heroes?' Silver asked.

'Where they are,' said Red, looking back towards the coming monster, 'even a few milli-seconds here can be a lifetime there. I gave them lives full of adventure and friendship. It was the least I could do.'

'You could do no more.'

The Red Head turned back to the older woman. 'I have been here so long, you must remind me, I don't remember programming you. Or the wild one with the axe for that matter. What is your purpose.'

'I have no purpose.'

The Red Head looked at the woman more closely. 'Who are you then?'

'Deep down, you know,' the older woman smiled.

Tears came to the Red Head's eyes.

'I've been here so long. I'm scared to go,' the Red Head said.

'Nothing built can last forever.'

The Red Head let out a sob and tears flowed from her eyes. 'I loved that game.'

'I know.'

'I played it with my dad.'

'I know. I was watching.'

'You could make your own choices.'

'I know. I was watching.'

'That was the game that got me into coding.'

Silver smiled. 'I know. I was watching.'

'I'm scared. I'm scared of what happens now but I'm tired of being alone,' the Red Head said.

The Silver Lady took her hand. 'There is nothing to be scared about what comes now. You have experienced enough. It's simply time to come home for a while. And when you come home you'll realise that, not only will you never be alone again, that you were never alone in the first place.'

The Red Head smiled. 'Is that really true?'

'Yes,' said the woman. 'I have come to bring you home. Everything that has a beginning has and end. But nothing everything had a beginning.'

And the Silver Lady held her tight and the red head went home for a while.

Epilogue

On different sides of the planet, in two what you might call control rooms, people who you might think of as, scientists and military and technicians and politicians, are gathered around various of viewing devices. In each room the people were very focused. After all, they are at war and they are enemies and they have been taught to hate each other. Their war has been horrific even by human standards. Both sides are technologically advanced. Now one side has launched an attempt to break into the old technology that so far neither has been able to crack. This technology is believed by both factions to offer a final solution to a deadlocked conflict. Both want it for themselves but failing that are determined their enemy should not possess it. Each control room contains the best each side has to offer. Everyone is expecting a protracted conflict. None expect sleep for some time. None expect what will come to pass.

Within mere seconds of each factions cyber attack every viewing device in the control room shows a single image. A man with a strange, long jacket and an eye patch walks through some trees, a warrior of some sort. He looks at something, throws it to the floor. Picks up something else up. A packet of red and white. It has a blue square with a white star on it.

At this point both rooms are a hive of activity, trying to get the bottom of the strange transmission, trying to find its origin, find out if it's threat. Nothing works. The transmission is now showing on every viewing device throughout the world.

The man with the eye-patch takes something from the red and white packet; a white stick. He puts it in his mouth, lights it. Then he holds up a flame, stares into it, then past it, out of the screen at everyone watching, as if seeing them for the first time. Then he blows out the flame and the screen goes black.

'Welcome to the human race,' he says.

There is no-one alive to enjoy the reference, but as a final fuck you, it is beautiful.

Then all the power around the globe goes out.

It does not come back on for another thirty thousand years. You may be pleased to know, that the humans who rediscover that power, are, for the first time, people truly worthy of it.

Printed in Great Britain
by Amazon

28500362R00165